MURDER IN VEGAS

MURDER IN VEGAS

NEW CRIME TALES
OF GAMBLING AND DESPERATION

EDITED BY

MICHAEL CONNELLY

A TOM DOHERTY ASSOCIATES BOOK
NEW YORK

This is a work of fiction. All the characters and events portrayed in this book are either products of the author's imagination or are used fictitiously.

MURDER IN VEGAS: NEW CRIME TALES OF GAMBLING AND DESPERATION

Copyright © 2005 by the International Association of Crime Writers

A Forge Book
Published by Tom Doherty Associates, LLC
175 Fifth Avenue
New York, NY 10010

www.tor.com

Forge® is a registered trademark of Tom Doherty Associates, LLC.

ISBN 0-765-35365-2
EAN 978-0-765-35365-8

First edition: March 2005
First mass market edition: April 2006

Printed in the United States of America

0 9 8 7 6 5 4 3 2 1

COPYRIGHT ACKNOWLEDGMENTS

"The house doesn't beat the player.
It just gives him the opportunity to beat himself."

—*Nicholas (Nick the Greek) Dandalos*

"A Smith & Wesson beats four aces."

—*American proverb*

CONTENTS

INTRODUCTION:
10,000 EYES IN THE SKY

There is a saying in Las Vegas that is as crude as it is accurate. What they say is that in this town there is a paddle for everybody's ass. What they mean by that is that you can't know everything about Las Vegas. Just when you are foolish enough to think you do, just when you are dumb enough to think you have it figured out, a new paddle comes along and you get knocked down again. There is no sure thing in Las Vegas. There is no sure bet.

Las Vegas is a destination city. Whether you come here to live or to just play, it is one of the few places on the planet where most people come from somewhere else. They come with their hopes and desires on their sleeves. Their greed, too. But the city carries a big paddle in return. The city pays out in the smallest margin of returns. Not just at the tables, but in everything. Everybody who comes here with his or her dreams of a new life and a new existence faces a limited return. And that's what makes it attractive to writers of mystery fiction. This town represents the ultimate long shot. For everyone who makes it, who hits the jackpot in life or at the blue felt tables, there are ninety-nine who don't. And the line between those that do and those that don't is where the grist of high stakes character and drama arises.

That's what this book is about. Those ninety-nine people who walk away empty-handed. Vegas is the unifying vision, of course, but beneath all the neon and glitz is the unifying desire to win, to start over, to begin again. That is the true character of this place. Each one of these stories is in some way the story of a dreamer and a schemer. Someone looking for a small redemption. These are stories of characters at the raw edge of humanity. Why not place them in the city that represents the raw edge of our society?

Las Vegas may be the most monitored city in the world. On the strip alone there are more than ten thousand eyes in the sky.

Those are the cameras that track you from the moment you step into a casino to try to take away their money until the moment you leave—with or without it. And that ten thousand doesn't even count the cameras in the garages and elevators and hallways. Over the intersections and above the people movers. In the restaurants and showrooms and focused on the pools. When you come to Las Vegas you are never alone for long. Yet here is the place that draws the schemers. Here is the place where people transform themselves, where they become alter egos and the kind of people they are assuredly not when they are back home. Despite the unblinking eye of the camera, there is a dark freedom afforded by the neon city. It is its greatest draw.

The characters in these stories have been drawn by that darkness. Ride with them to and through this place. You'll be met at the Nevada border by a seventy-five-cent grifter and from there it is onward to the city of sin. You'll learn what it's like to play craps when you have to win. I mean *have to win* because you're just one step ahead of the kind of debt collector who takes late payments in blood. You'll meet schemers who are out-schemed by other schemers or even their own marks. You'll meet a class of clientele to which violence is a given. (I mean, when the first line of a story is "Is he dead?" and is delivered by a character named Snake, then you know you are riding in dark territory.) And then, when perhaps you think there is no hope left for humanity, you'll come across a woman who just wants to preserve something good and natural in the desert from which the mirage of Las Vegas rises. So press on and you will find moments of human grace in these stories as well.

I guess what I am trying to say is that there is a paddle for everybody's ass in this collection. Don't think you know anything about Las Vegas until you ride with this group. But be warned. Don't think you know everything there is to know about Las Vegas. Not ever.

Michael Connelly

THE SUNSHINE TAX

JAMES SWAIN

"Welcome to Nevada," the convenience store manager said.

The manager's name was Huey Dollop. He was fifty, and he had tobacco-stained teeth and a head shaped like a honeydew. His store was the first thing motorists driving from California to Las Vegas saw when they crossed the state border on I-15. A concrete pillbox sitting off the highway with a neon Budweiser sign in the window.

The couple who came into Huey's store looked beat. Two tired kids driving a Volvo they'd stopped making fifteen years ago. The girl had red hair, and eyes that said she'd seen a lot. The guy, maybe the same age, wore a Dodgers cap and was built like a stump. He made a bee-line for the cold beverages, leaving the girl at the counter.

"Good afternoon," Huey said. "What can I do for you today?"

Huey said his lines with a smile on his face. It was the way he addressed every customer that came into his store. It always put them at ease.

"This is our first time visiting Las Vegas," she said, nodding at her boyfriend in the back of the store. "Troy won a chunk of change on the lottery, and figured maybe it was time to give lady luck a spin."

Huey nodded. He'd been running his store twenty years, and had heard a lot of stories. Most were hard luck. This one wasn't, only the girl seemed afraid, like she sensed that they were about to get taken. A pair of virgins in Sin City.

"Ever gambled before?" Huey asked.

She nodded. Then said, "We taught ourselves on the Internet. It was fun. But . . ." Her voice trailed off, and she lowered her eyes and stared at the faded counter top.

Huey picked up an open can of Dr. Pepper, and took a sip.

They made it with prune juice, gave it a unique flavor. He said, "But?"

"We weren't playing with real money." She lowered her voice. "Troy's afraid of getting cheated in a real casino. You know, like once he starts to win."

"Casinos don't have to cheat," Huey said.

"Hey, Amy, what you want to drink?"

"Yoo-Hoo," the girl replied. To Huey she said, "What do you mean?"

"The house has an edge in every game. That's how they pay their bills."

"An edge? Like a percentage?"

"That's right. Locals call it the sunshine tax."

"But do people *ever* win?"

"Sure," Huey said. "People win all the time."

Amy leaned her thin frame against the counter. "People like Troy?"

"People just like Troy. Last week, a man came in who'd won a million dollars on a slot machine at the Bellagio, looked just like Troy."

"The what?"

"The Bellagio. It's a casino on the Strip. It's got the fountains in the front."

"Did he tell you which machine?"

Huey smiled, and took another sip of his soda. Troy came to the front. He placed two drinks and some food on the counter. He wore a faded tee shirt with the words I'M BLIND, I'M DEAF, I WANT TO BE A REF!

Amy said, "This man says the games aren't rigged."

"I told you that last night," Troy said, taking his wallet out. Throwing a twenty down, he said, "We just need to know which casinos to play. They all don't have the same rules. Guys at the shop told me that."

Amy looked at Huey. "That true? Are some places better?"

Huey rang up the items. "Several casinos have liberal rules for blackjack, and looser slot machines. They're definitely better places to gamble."

"Which ones?" Troy asked.

Huey lifted his eyes and met the big man's gaze. "The Riviera, the Sahara, the Stardust, and all the casinos in old down-town, like the Nugget and the Horseshoe."

"What are loose slot machines?" the girl asked.

Huey tore the receipt from the register's printer, and handed it to Troy along with his change. "The management sets them to pay out better. Sometimes they have signs outside that say ninety-eight percent payoff on slots. Go to those places."

"What's the payout like at the other casinos?" Amy said.

"About ninety-four to ninety-five percent," Huey said.

"That much less? That's cheating."

Huey said, "That's the sunshine tax."

Troy put his change into his pocket, and handed Amy the re-ceipt. Then he scooped his things off the counter. Huey saw the girl's eyes wander, and said, "I'll tell you one other little secret about the slot machines."

She looked up at him expectantly.

"The looser machines are usually near the doors, or places where people congregate inside the casino," Huey said. "The management does that to create excitement, and entice other people to play. Play those machines."

"Near the doors," the girl said.

"That's right."

"Thanks," she said under her breath.

The couple started to leave. Huey said, "One more thing," and they came back to the counter. "This is really important," he said. "Always bet the maximum number of coins the ma-chine will take. That's the only way you can win the jackpot."

Troy looked at the girl. "You remembering all this?"

Amy recited the names of the casinos, and the pearls about the slots, saying it like it was the most important thing she'd ever been told.

"Much obliged," Troy said.

"Good luck," Huey replied.

Through the curly-cues of the Budweiser sign, Huey watched the couple get into their old Volvo. The car started up, and went about twenty feet. Then it stopped, and the girl got out, and marched into the store.

"Forget something?" Huey asked as she approached the counter.

She was holding the receipt, and pointing at it.

"What's this?" she asked.

Huey stared at a charge for $.75. He scratched his chin. His eyes drifted to the Three Musketeers bar on the counter, next to the cigarette lighters. Picking it up, he said, "Your boyfriend didn't take his candy bar."

She shook her head. "Troy don't eat no candy."

"My mistake."

Huey put the candy bar on the shelf behind him. Then he hit the NO SALE button on the register. The cash drawer popped open, and he fished out three quarters, and laid them onto her palm. She left the store without saying a word.

The Volvo left a cloud of dirt in the parking lot. When it settled, another car had taken its place. Four young women piled out. In the back of the car, Huey saw pillows, and guessed the women were planning to share a room.

He took the candy bar off the shelf, and placed it back on the counter on the spot it had occupied since he'd opened his store. The women came in, and he smiled at them.

"Welcome to Nevada," he said.

PASSLINE

S. J. ROZAN

Oh yes, he'd always hated Vegas.

The gambler's Mecca. In the old days bad enough, fading shabby casinos forcing smiles. Putting out like weary whores: free drinks, cheap rooms. As though he gave a damn. He never gave a damn.

The first time, when he was young (he was very young), it was pulse-pounding thrilling. Staring out the window the minute anything below looked like desert (he'd never left the East before, Pittsburgh—Jesus Christ, Pittsburgh!—as far as he'd been). Leaned that way an hour, waiting. (Catch him doing that now. Forget it, now he took the aisle.) Practically first off the plane (but he'd never been first), laughed like a kid to see slots at the airport. Had to stop and play them. Lost forty bucks. That was funny, too.

Then the rented car. (Red Thunderbird. Oh, he was one impressive stud, all right.) Then the ten-minute drive. (Too long for him, drumming on the wheel, bopping to the radio.) Then the truth.

The room small, too cold, the sun too hot, burning, relentless. Sand on the wind, stinging. The music too loud, the drinks watered, the girls smiling like their feet hurt.

He wondered if Muslims hated Mecca when they finally got there. Same-same, anyway: hideous buildings, sun and sand.

And Vegas just got uglier. Each time he came, he marveled. (Did pilgrims do that in Mecca, too?) Pirate ships and dancing water (in the desert!) and the Brooklyn Bridge. And hey, you want to talk who knew what and when they knew it, tell me why they never built the Twin Towers into the skyline of New York, New York.

He'd said that to Bennie a few months ago, like Bennie would know, like he'd give a damn.

"You're an asshole, Taylor." That's what Bennie said. That's what Bennie always said, unless you were placing a bet or paying one off. Or he was paying out, paying you. That did happen. Not often and God knows not to Taylor lately, but it did. Then Bennie handed you your cash and said, "Fuck you, Taylor."

"Pleasure doing business with a gentleman," he'd smile at Bennie. He'd always smile.

Bennie'd say, "Fuck you, Taylor."

———

"Ladies and gentlemen," said the stewardess, which was sort of the same as, "Fuck you." He buckled his seatbelt. The plane banked, dove, bounced, stopped. He sat and waited. People in pastels yanked luggage from overhead. Taylor bet himself how many would get clonked with carry-ons before the door opened. He'd have bet the guy beside him but he was one of the yankers. Taylor's number was four. By the time the line in the aisle charged forward—a slow-motion charge, like the OJ low-speed chase—he'd only seen three. Losing already, Jeez, that was great.

He stood in the empty aisle, took his case down, brought up the rear. Exited the jetway and the slots still stood, blinking and dinging. Nothing funny about them.

Nothing much funny at all, except that he'd gotten this far.

Could be Bennie was asleep at the switch. But Taylor thought not. Bennie knew where he was. Knew what he was doing and was letting him try, because this was his last time. Win or lose, Bennie was through with him, oh yes. Taylor could almost see him, washing his pudgy hands. (That was metaphorical: Bennie didn't wash much.) Taylor figured, twenty-four hours. All Bennie'd give him. All he'd need.

And shit, in this loud-mouthed, self-important, soulless town, all he could take. (Could Vegas see itself in a mirror? No, uh-uh. He was sure.)

He did know, though, after all these years he knew why the glaring neon, the fiberglass, the dancing water. The swollen buildings, the music aimed like a pile driver at the base of your skull. He knew why each casino was huger and stupider than the last one, what all the over-the-top shrillness, bigness, brightness was about.

It was the desert.

The heat, the distance and the hard flat sand would suck the life right out of you. The second it got a chance it would dry you and desiccate you until (weightless, colorless, crisp as a snakeskin) you'd scrape and tumble along. Finally, roped by a hot gust, you'd whirl over the hills and disappear.

At first they'd named the casinos The Sands and The Dunes. That was a mistake and they'd figured it out. Now it was Bellagio, Treasure Island, Luxor, and Grand. You needed bracing here. Shoring up. You had to think of the desert as a vicious, insidious sea. It would take you if it could. And it didn't have to rise up, throw itself around, pound things and howl like the ocean. It just had to wait.

Taylor knew. He thought, really, everyone knew. He thought, really, that was part of it for every hustler and high roller who came here. The rush, the adrenaline high when your heart thumps and your skin sizzles and you hold your face like marble and keep your body quiet while the lightning rages inside you: the rush speeds fastest when the stakes are highest. Inside the Bellagio and the Luxor (looming windowless liners sailing nowhere) people watched the wheel spin and the cards fall, fed endless chump change into ravenous electronic mouths, and knew. Knew what waited outside, if they lost.

And the people who built this place (not the first time, not the old days, but now), they knew, too. They built everything huge and so obviously fake because of it. No one talked about it (that was part of it, the shared secret) but they didn't want you to forget it. They knew the rush was better because of the desert. They knew the illusion only worked because of the truth.

And the truth was, if he didn't come home with $400,000 for Bennie, Taylor was a dead man.

Bennie had people here. Or Bennie's people had people, someone had people and they'd be watching him. They already were. On the plane, maybe the bored guy with the crossword puzzle book, maybe the middle-aged lady who actually ate the lunch. Maybe the eight-year-old who kicked his seatback all the way across the country. That would be like Bennie, to send someone to kick his ass. Make sure he didn't turn and run. Slip out as soon as he checked in, fly off to L.A., Honolulu, Sulawesi, Pago Pago. He didn't really care because he wasn't going anywhere. No. He'd taken every cent he had with him and he was going to play it all. Dead man playing. Maybe they'd make a movie.

Did it matter where he played? He couldn't decide. That was funny. Couldn't decide whether to flip a coin, or to decide. Time was, Taylor my man, when you were decisive. A man with a plan. He heard himself say that as he cruised the rented car (this time a tan Cavalier, and what more was there to say?) down the new strip that wasn't the Strip. He heard himself say it but had he said it out loud? He couldn't decide.

Time was. A plan, a wife, a split-level ranch. A job, a future, and a gambling habit. Now, stripped down, cleaned away, trimmed and cut back. Nothing left but the habit. That was the wrong word but Taylor let it slide. Did other men have eating habits? Breathing habits? But okay. Why argue? Time was (that same time, and overall it was a good time, he'd never say it wasn't) when he'd argued with Lily. At first sometimes, later often, by the end always. Even arguing, he loved her. But she didn't love him. She loved some other man, some man who was Taylor but didn't care how the dice rolled, or the cards fell, or what horse crossed the line. Finally she'd left to go find him. That man.

After that the job seemed extraneous (it was boring anyway, cross-eyed boring, long dull days and no rush at all). The house was a millstone and the future was a deck of cards. Nothing wrong with any of it. Taylor had enjoyed it, yes, that was the truth. And he'd been into Bennie before, made the strike, gotten out. Hell, Bennie wouldn't have let him get in this deep this time, if he hadn't been over his head lots of other times.

"Fuck you, Taylor," he'd heard Bennie say, more than once, as Taylor paid off a loan in full, the vig, everything. "I was looking forward to breaking your legs."

Well, since Bennie got his rush from that (Bennie never gambled, except on people like Taylor, and his odds were always good because he was the one who set them, take it or leave it and everyone took it), he was probably bubbling over right now. Quivering at the thought of his people, his people out here, sauntering up to Taylor. Late tonight, early tomorrow, whenever it was he played his last few bucks. One standing in front, one standing behind. The short drive to the airport, the long flight home. Or would Bennie come out here, while the people waited with Taylor in some too-cold hotel room? Would they all play cards while they waited? That was funny. No, it wasn't. Yes. It was.

The Trop, Taylor suddenly decided, cutting the wheel, sliding left through the intersection in a screaming of horns. Oh, come on, he said (out loud, this time he was sure), aren't your hearts beating faster? You stomped on the brakes, got that charge up your spine, come on, it was good. You know it was.

He flipped his keys to the valet parking kid, lifted his overnight bag out of the trunk. Like he was going to sleep. Like he'd even take a room. But they don't let you on planes anymore without luggage. Not like the old days when you could come out here with nothing but your wallet. He had, once or twice: come out and played all weekend. (Yes, he hated it here. But when your luck was bad, say at Atlantic City, you had to change something.) Coke to keep him up and sharp, scotch to keep him steady, played all weekend and flew home on the Sunday redeye, off the plane, do another line and straight to the office. That was when he still had the job. When he still thought it was his fault he and Vegas didn't get along, thought he should keep trying. Yes, the Tropicana: makeover after makeover, but still the old Vegas. Like an old girl getting her cheeks tightened, her lips plumped, her wrinkles Botoxed until she looked like a horror movie version of her same old self. Taylor had a soft spot for girls like that, and one for the Trop.

Inside. Instantly, lights blinking, bells ringing, turquoise and neon, and goddamn, *goddamn* if his heart wasn't racing. His cheeks were flushed, he could feel it, the backs of his hands tingled. Like high school, like walking the endless but too-short corridor to where the clump of giggling girls pretended to ignore your approach, all of them wondering what you were wondering: Did you have the balls to ask Amy Gold if she wanted to go to the dance on Saturday night? Nobody knowing whether you'd do it until you stopped in front of her, gave her that hey-by-the-way-and-I-really-don't-give-a-shit smile and out came the words and everyone heard them.

Yeah, okay, so he didn't like Vegas but it made his heart race. Amy Gold turned out to be not such a prize, either. Nothing like Lily, nothing like her slow smile that could slow his heart to match it, make him feel like he'd suddenly dropped anchor in a cove on a fog-bound coast. Like everything else was gone, everything, only silence to hear and gray velvet to see and a soft long rocking the only thing to feel. Like it was all decided, no outcomes, decisions, scores, high hands, rolls of the dice or spins of the wheel left, nothing to choose, hope, hedge, yell, cheer, pray to Jesus or curse the devil for. Lily the only thing ever able to make him hate the rush, because it burned off the fog, shattered the silence and churned up the sea.

And Lily was gone and he was in Vegas and Bennie was back in New York, with people out here, counting the hours.

He found the cashier's cage, took the whole $50,000, everything he had, and changed it all. Saved two twenties in case he wanted a sandwich, a steak. Drinks were still free, and he wasn't going to be here long enough to want anything else.

Quarter slots by the door, fifty cents and five dollars as you went deeper. He went deeper. Past all that. Found the craps tables. It's what he'd decided.

He'd thought about poker. There had to be a high-stakes game; he could find it. But hell. What were you saying when you did that? That you could control it. Not the desire, the need, the adrenaline jones: no one thought that. (Well, yes they did, if they still knew how to lie to themselves. But not Taylor.) But control the outcome. If you were smart and cagey, concentrated and focused, you could win Bennie's money back; if you did, it was because you were *good,* if you didn't you'd screwed up. But you know? That was bull.

Or maybe it wasn't bull. But it wasn't the point. Not now.

Control.

Oh, sure.

Taylor had been out of control since junior high, when he started taking the other kids' action on the football team, on the girls' track team, on whether Mr. Grady would wear the pink tie the third day running. He didn't remember what it was like to be in control. He knew what it was like to think you were, but he was past that now.

But maybe not quite. Really past that, ready to throw it all in the laps of the gods, you played roulette. Roulette had no odds. On an honest wheel (the Trop's was straight) any number, either color was as likely to come up. People played this and they hedged that but really, it was silly.

Dice, though, dice had odds. Some numbers came up more than others. He liked that. It was the right game right now.

Because, if his number didn't come up, his number was up.

Walking toward the table, Taylor laughed.

They made room for him. People always made room for Taylor at the tables, at the wheel, at the big-money window. They were lovers, amateurs, vacationers. They could tell he was different: an initiate, a priest. Dedicated from a young age to the faith. They got a thrill playing beside him, went home and told the story: "There was this guy . . ."

Sometimes, especially lately, smack on the peak of the rush, a dark smothering thickness would descend on Taylor. Like an ocean tide covering the glittering beach, and suddenly nothing was clear, nothing was shiny, it was hard to hear and hard to breathe. That tide was partly this, knowing how he was seen and discussed, part of other people's entertainment, one of the fascinating phenomena of their days, marveled at and soon forgotten. It was other things, too, and partly this. He'd enjoyed it, once. He'd enjoyed all this, once.

Taylor settled his chips, settled himself. A hand was in progress, a stony Chinese grandma throwing with thick, arthritic fingers. The point was eight, lucky for the Chinese. Taylor held off, soaking in the flurry of chips and calls, felt his heart speed up more, his skin start to sizzle. He liked this part, the part just before: it was like swimming, he was always a guy to walk in slowly, not plunging underwater until he was up to his chest, until his long deep breaths disturbed the surface as his chest rose and fell. Then, suddenly, he'd dive through. Then the cold shock and the sudden silent, swirling green world where you wanted to stay forever. But you couldn't breathe. (And when you came up, took a breath and went back down, it was good but it wasn't the same, it was never the same.)

She was hot, the Chinese grandma, and when she finally hit the point the table erupted in hooting and laughing. Lots of people had made lots of money: a friendly-faced bald guy, an intense black woman, a young sweaty guy with glasses (which of them was Bennie's?). The grandma too, but her face didn't change. She just dumped her chips in a bucket and carried them off.

The dice moved to the player two to Taylor's right. As she reached her hand to choose her dice from the stickman's six, Taylor looked at her (up to now it had been the table, always the table, the numbers, the chips). A woman, his age, black hair, black dress, bare arms. Small silver earrings, red lipstick, and otherwise as God had made her. She caught Taylor watching her, met his eyes, didn't smile, but knew him, as he knew her, as members of a tribe or a cult or a team know each other. As though they'd given the secret handshake and the password, flashed the signet ring. The crowd, he noticed, made way for her too.

Taylor bet the pass line, five thousand, starting small, wading in. She rolled, the black-haired woman, his teammate, the other one like him. Supple, small wrist, nails shaped and polished but no color, no distraction. Her focus on the tumbling cubes as burning as his (but how burning was his, he wondered in the endless second before they came to rest, if he noticed hers?). And it was seven.

Okay, good beginning, Taylor thought, piling the chips and letting them ride. She threw again, turned up six. The dealer marked the point, called it out, the little ritual. Everyone had his own, the players, the amateurs, even the casino, the rituals what it's about, the rush and the rituals. Taylor stayed with the pass line, doubled behind it, placed the eight, the nine. The woman threw and she was hot. She kept throwing, Taylor kept winning. He let his chips ride, he watched them pile up. What the hell: He bet the horn, and damn, she hit for him. Then back to basics (he thought about a hard eight, but that was stupid, and it was too early to get stupid). He stayed with his placed bets, racked his chips.

Taylor was making money.

Bennie's money. Okay, Bennie's money.

Taylor kept with the pass line, stacking the chips the dealer passed him (never one of those players too superstitious to sort his chips, and now no superstition for him at all, because that was just another way to pretend to control) and nodded to the woman, his benefactress. She flashed a look around as people took care of business. Taylor let his winnings ride until he reached the table limit, then racked what was beyond it. A few more throws and she hit her six and her streak was over.

And Taylor was way up.

The dice moved to the sweaty guy with glasses. Lucky as the woman had been for Taylor, she'd been bad for him. He was way down, and reached for the dice grimly, if you want something done right do it yourself. Oh, Taylor thought, oh; and he bet the don't-come. The come out roll was ten. Lay odds, Taylor told himself. Behind the don't-come? This was something Taylor never did. Just one of his rituals, bad luck, not for everyone but for him. He did it. Two throws later the guy turned up seven. Groans everywhere, except from Taylor. He'd made ninety thousand dollars.

As he racked it he spotted them. Bennie's people. Two men he didn't know, polo shirts and khakis. Feeding coins into the slots, not enough to hoodwink the Trop's security people but enough to signal their intention: we're just watching, we won't make trouble. Inside.

Okay, Taylor thought, you're here to watch? Watch.

The sweaty guy sent Taylor an envious, burning glare, as though the money Taylor had just made was his. Sorry, Charlie, thought Taylor, It's Bennie's, Taylor feeling that tug as the adrenaline tried to push a grin through the marble mask. The guy slunk away, shoulders hunched.

The dice were Taylor's now. Well all right! From the six he took the two closest to him, never did it that way before, always looked for the lucky ones but he did it that way now. He felt them, shook them, their sharp little edges meeting his skin, leaned over the rail and threw them. His point came up four. Oh shit, that was hard, but so what? Throw, and throw, and throw, taking the odds, up at the limit, and throw again. Oh yes, now it was happening. Prickles rose on the back of his neck, he felt like his skin was tightening. Oh yes. Sounds grew sharper, lights got brighter. The bald guy whispered to the woman beside him while they placed their tiny bets, their fifty bucks, what they'd budgeted themselves, what they could afford to lose (Taylor could afford to lose nothing, absolutely nothing) and they watched Taylor.

Another throw, another, and then he said, "Hard eight," in a calm, stone voice, a voice of ice, as though the fifty thousand he was putting on it was nothing to him, was not the sum total of what he'd come out here with, the sum total of who he'd been when he'd come to this table (though he was someone else now, because fifty thousand wasn't much of a dent in his pile). He shook and threw and came up two fours, his hard eight, his high odds, his score.

He almost laughed, almost cracked his marble mask. The woman beside him smiled a tiny smile. At his right shoulder he felt a presence, a man in a suit, a floor boss, summoned by a dealer with a button or a nod or whatever they used at the Trop. The dealer gave the stickman six new dice. The stickman rolled them out, pushed them to Taylor to make his choice. This time he took the ones farthest away.

Three more throws and he hit his point, raked in his chips. People laughed, thanked him; he'd done well for some. And for himself, oh yes, oh yes.

Hours, many more hours it went on like that. Sometimes it was other people, sometimes it was the woman like him or it was him, sprinkling the dice like confetti over the green felt, bouncing them off the rails, everyone drawing breaths, holding them, puffing them out. The dealers passed chips out and repossessed them, piles of red chips and black ones, green and purple, orange and gray, rising and falling around the table like some lunatic living bar chart. The boxman, the stickman and the dealers rotated out, replaced by others. The floor boss stayed. And the whole thing was in slow motion and fast-forward simultaneously, around Taylor everything whirling and dinging, in front of him everything sweeping and clicking, and also everything crystal clear and completely under control.

Control. No such fucking thing, Taylor thought, his stomach knotting, his heart pounding, his face the familiar thrilling struggle between the mask and the mile-wide grin. No such fucking thing, and pass those dice to me, baby, send them over here. He held them in his hand, shook them, felt the edges, put a big pile on the pass line (oh, he was up, he hadn't counted lately but he was way up, and so was the woman beside him, they'd been lucky for each other, it sometimes worked that way) and as he threw he was clobbered by it, that smothering gray wave.

It broke over him, a tsunami, the kind caused by trouble on the ocean floor, no storm, no atmospheric disturbance, something deeper, more fundamental. He'd seen a film once, a wave like this, not even tall, a few feet but totally unstoppable, covering a Japanese island, one shore to the other, slowly, on a clear fine day. He thought of that film whenever this happened, all those people on the sand, people who'd been warned but hadn't left because they didn't believe it could happen like this. Taylor believed. Here, now, it wasn't day and it wasn't fine—it was night and Christ, it was the Trop—but this wave covered Taylor just the same. The lights were still blinking, but through sludgy water, the bells dinged but far away, as if over the sea. Taylor, weighed down, couldn't move, struggled to breathe.

He closed his eyes.

And heard a whoop, and opened them.

The dice had settled. He'd thrown a seven. He'd hit again.

The tsunami drained away and was gone. Lights and sounds were clear again, but not with the microscopic clarity of the rush. He could breathe, but his heart wasn't pounding, his skin had no tingle. His face was neither marble nor fireworks, just his face, stubble, weary eyes, the sour-sweet taste of scotch.

And though he hadn't counted for a long time now, he gave the pile in front of him a practiced glance and knew he'd made Bennie's money back.

Taylor was tired, tired.

If the dice weren't his he'd have walked away right then, racked and cashed out and left the neon and the goddamn blinking lights behind, oh yes, he was ready, but you can't do that, you can't do that. He bet the pass line, but not high, didn't lay odds. The come out roll made five the point, and he hit it in four throws. That was it. He was done.

Taylor had colored up by now, long since really, his early multi-colored pile of chips mostly gray, sprinkled with orange. He racked them. The woman beside him racked hers, too, and they headed together to the cashier's cage. The floor boss walked with them. People made way for them.

"Jack Taylor," he said to the woman as they walked. Not, You're lucky for me, or, you're my lucky charm, not a pick-up line, just his name, he felt she deserved that.

"Angel Dale."

"Angel?"

She gave him a dark look, daring him. You're my angel, you look like an angel, you throw like an angel, he was sure she'd heard it all, all so idiotic, and not so long ago he might have said it himself, he hoped he wouldn't have but he wasn't sure.

"Just," he said, "you look more like Jane. Ann. Mary."

She smiled. "Tell my folks."

"You up?" Taylor asked. He and Angel walked between rows of fifty-cent slots, like passing through an Alice-in-Wonderland honor guard of people's backs.

"Enough."

Enough, Taylor thought. How right you are.

He cashed out, Angel too. $402,500, a nice win at the Trop but not earthshaking. The floor boss walked away with a solemn congratulatory nod.

"Where are you staying?" Angel asked.

"I'm not."

Angel nodded. Just came to play, she knew about that. "I'm at the Luxor."

They walked outside, Taylor braced for a blast of hot desert wind but getting just exhaust, spray from the Tropicana fountain, recorded birdsong, and disappointment. His own, or what was in the air? He wasn't sure. Angel tipped her head toward the footbridge that would take them over the highway to the Luxor, letting him know.

"Wait," he said. "Another minute." It wasn't even a minute. The men in polo shirts and khakis materialized and approached.

"That's Bennie's," one said, pointing to Taylor's bag.

Taylor handed it to him.

The men looked surprised; Angel looked surprised.

"Tell Bennie, 'Fuck you,' " Taylor said.

The man with the bag opened it, checked for the money. This easy, it had to be a trick, Taylor knew he was thinking that. "No trick," said Taylor. The man closed the bag, nodded, walked away. The other man glared at Taylor another little while, brow furrowed. Surprised, and angry, also, that one, lost his chance to break some bones. Too bad, thought Taylor, but that's Vegas for you: a mile-high pile of lost chances.

Actually, Taylor was surprised, too. Not surprised that he'd given over the bag so easily, no argument, no tightening of his grip, no pang at such a huge stake slipping from his fingers. Surprised, though, that he'd been able to use it in the way he'd hoped, and not told himself he'd hoped, to fill it with his debt to Bennie and send it on its way, with Bennie's people, without him.

The people climbed into a cab. Taylor watched the doors slam and then he turned away. Maybe they drove off, red taillights dwindling as they headed for the airport. Maybe they sat in the driveway all night, and maybe they beamed back to the mothership.

He didn't give a damn.

"Jack?" It was Angel, a few paces away, her eyes wary. Maybe he wasn't what she thought he was. What she was. Oh, but I am, he said, silently, this time he knew that, Oh, but I am.

He told her. "From Bennie. My bookie. I'm into him."

"For all that?"

"Just about."

"You know them?"

"No."

"How do you know, then? Where they're going? They could skip."

"Doesn't matter."

"You'll be on the hook."

"God," Taylor said, "it's hot out here." This because a blast of dry desert wind had broken over them, the grit riding on it scouring the fountain mist and the car exhaust out of the air, blowing away everything fake, the birdsong and the forced smiles and Bennie's goddamn money, his goddamn money.

Taylor turned, faced into the wind. Daybreak, the sun just cracking the sky above the low hill behind the airport (the sun heading to Vegas from New York, just like he had! He wondered, did it hate it when it got here, too?) and already too hot to breathe.

Angel smiled at him. "The Luxor's cool. A little too cold, even."

The sun found her, outlined her for him, a fierce glow edging her black hair, her curved hip, her supple wrist. Ah yes, the sun was doing its job here, just like he had, but it was angry. Didn't want to be here. Angel raised a hand to shadow her eyes, and he looked into them, so like his.

He might have answered, he might have turned with her, taken her arm, walked over the bridge and into the glass and neon palace across the way; might have, but he saw it coming, saw the smothering gray wave rolling toward him—he'd never seen it before, always been taken by surprise when it smashed him down—and so he stood and looked at her and then he shook his head. "Something I have to do," he said.

She nodded. "Later?"

He didn't have an answer to that. "Thanks," he said.

"For what?"

"Luck."

He turned, walked east.

The airport was close; half an hour of walking as the sun stalked higher into the sky, he was almost there. A plane was landing. Shirt-sleeved men, women in shorts would soon be grabbing their bags, jostling each other in their rush to get to the illusion, the lies. Some, so desperately eager to believe, would stop in the terminal to play the slots.

Another ten minutes and he was past it (it was so small, really, when you thought of airports and not of magic gates to fabulous kingdoms). He kept walking, following the road.

After another hour he was alone; everything had stayed behind. Or maybe the gray wave had come and swept it all away. Or maybe—this, he thought, coughing in the heat, the dryness, this was what was true—maybe everything was nothing, it had faded away, it was never here at all. This was here: the sand, the wind. In the shimmer at the corner of his eye he saw Angel. He turned. She was not there. In the other direction, Lily, and she also was not there. He smiled: looking into the swaying waves of heat above the asphalt, he did not see Bennie, so fuck you, Bennie.

Another hour, or maybe less, or more, and the road began to curve north, into the hills. It didn't face into the sun now, so Taylor left it, stepped from it onto the hard flat sand to keep heading east, as though that were home. The sun blinded him, pushed against him like walking into wind. Or water. He was having trouble breathing, he was choking in the heat. Like the wave! The desert, the sun; the thick gray wave—no difference! The smothering heat, the enveloping fog—the same thing!

Taylor laughed, cracking the marble mask, laughed to finally know this.

East, heading east, he walked out over the sand. Grit scraped his face, clung to his skin like salt spray.

He walked.

Sweat poured down him.

He walked.

Like wading into the ocean, deeper, deeper, before the dive, the last, ecstatic plunge.

Oh, yes. Oh, yes.

The same thing.

DUST UP

WENDY HORNSBY

10:00 a.m., April 20
Red Rock Canyon, Nevada

Pansy Reynard lay on her belly inside a camouflaged bird blind, high-power Zeiss binoculars to her eyes, a digital sound amplifier hooked over her right ear, charting every movement and sound made by her observation target, an Aplomado falcon hatchling. As Pansy watched, the hatchling stretched his wings to their full thirty-inch span and gave them a few tentative flaps as if gathering courage to make his first foray out of the nest. He would need some courage to venture out, she thought. The ragged, abandoned nest his mother had appropriated for her use sat on a narrow rock ledge 450 vertical feet above the desert floor.

"Go, baby," Pansy whispered when the chick craned back his neck and flapped his wings again. This was hour fourteen of her assigned nest watch. She felt stiff and cramped, and excited all at once. There had been no reported Aplomado falcon sightings in Nevada since 1910. For a mated Aplomado falcon pair to appear in the Red Rock Canyon area less than twenty miles west of the tawdry glitz and endless noise of Las Vegas, was singular, newsworthy even. But for the pair to claim a nest and successfully hatch an egg was an event so unexpected as to be considered a miracle by any committed raptor watcher, as Pansy Reynard considered herself to be.

The hatchling watch was uncomfortable, perhaps dangerous, because of the ruggedness of the desert canyons, the precariousness of Pansy's rocky perch in a narrow cliff-top saddle opposite the nest, and the wild extremes of the weather. But the watch was very likely essential to the survival of this wonder child. It had been an honor, Pansy felt, to be assigned a shift to watch the nest. And then to have the great good fortune to be on site when the hatchling first emerged over the top of the nest was, well, nearly overwhelming.

Pansy lowered her binocs to wipe moisture from her eyes, but quickly raised them again so as not to miss one single moment in the life of this sleek-winged avian infant. She had been wakened inside her camouflage shelter at dawn by the insistent chittering of the hatchling as he demanded to be fed. From seemingly nowhere, as Pansy watched, the mother had soared down to tend him, the forty-inch span of her black and white wings as artful and graceful as a beautiful Japanese silk-print kite. The sight of the mother made Pansy almost forgive Lyle for standing her up the night before.

Almost forgive Lyle: This was supposed to be a two-man shift. Lyle, a pathologist with the Department of Fish and Game, was a fine bird-watcher and seemed to be in darned good physical shape. But he was new to the Las Vegas office and unsure about his readiness to face the desert overnight. And he was busy. Or so he said.

Pansy had done her best to assure Lyle that he would be safe in her hands. As preparation, she had packed two entire survival kits, one for herself and one for him, and had tucked in a very good bottle of red wine to make the long chilly night pass more gently. But he hadn't come. Hadn't even called.

Pansy sighed, curious to know which he had shunned, an evening in her company or the potential perils of the place. She had to admit there were actual, natural challenges to be addressed. It was only mid-April, but already the desert temperatures reached the century mark before noon. When the sun was overhead, the sheer vertical faces of the red sandstone bluffs reflected and intensified the heat until everything glowed like— and felt like—the inside of an oven. There was no shade other than the feathery shadows of spindly yucca and folds in the rock formations.

To make conditions yet more uncomfortable, it was sandstorm season. Winds typically began to pick up around noon, and could drive an impenetrable cloud of sand at speeds surpassing eighty miles an hour until sunset. When the winds blew, there was nearly no way to escape both the heat and the pervasive, intrusive blast of sand. Even cars were useless as shelter.

With windows rolled up and without the AC turned on you'd fry in a hurry. With the AC turned on, both you and the car's engine would be breathing grit. If you could somehow navigate blind and drive like hell, you might drive clear of the storm before sand fouled the engine. But only if you could navigate blind.

People like Pansy who knew the area well might find shelter in random hollows among the rocks, such as the niche where the hatchling sat in his nest. Or the well prepared, for instance Pansy, might hunker down inside a zip-up shelter made to military specs for desert troops, like the one that was tucked inside her survival pack. Or navigate using digital GPS via satellite—Global Positioning System.

Not an environment for neophytes, Pansy conceded, but she'd had high hopes for Lyle, and had looked forward to an evening alone with him and the falcons under the vast blackness of the desert sky, getting acquainted.

Pansy knew she could be a bit off-putting at first meeting. But in that place, during that season, Pansy was in her métier and at her best. Her preparations for the nest watch, she believed, were elegant in their simplicity, completeness, and flexibility: a pair of lightweight one-man camouflage all-weather shelters, plenty of water, a basic all-purpose tool, meals-ready-to-eat, a bodacious slingshot in case snakes or vultures came to visit the nest, good binocs, a two-channel sound amplifier to eavesdrop on the nest, a handheld GPS locator, and a digital palm-sized video recorder. Except for the water, each kit weighed a meager twenty-seven pounds and fit into compact, waterproof, dust proof saddlebags she carried on her all-terrain motorcycle. The bottle of wine and two nice glasses were tucked into a quick-release pocket attached to the cycle frame. She had everything: shelter, food, water, tools, the falcon, a little wine. But no Lyle.

Indeed, Lyle's entire kit was still attached to the motorcycle she had stashed in a niche in the abandoned sandstone quarry below her perch.

A disturbing possibility occurred to Pansy as she watched the hatchling: Maybe Lyle was a little bit afraid of her. A champion triathlete and two-time Ironman medalist, Lieutenant Pansy Reynard, desert survival instructor with the Army's SFOD-D, Special Forces Operational Detachment—Delta Force, out of the Barstow military training center, admitted that she could be just a little bit intimidating.

10:00 a.m., April 20
Downtown Las Vegas

Mickey Togs felt like a million bucks because he knew he looked like a million bucks. New custom-made, silver-gray suit with enough silk in the fabric to give it a little sheen. Not flashy-shiny, but sharp—expensively sharp, Vegas player sharp. His shirt and tie were of the same silver-gray color, as were the butter-soft handmade shoes on his size eight, EEE feet. Checking his reflection in the shiny surface of the black Lincoln Navigator he had acquired for the day's job, Mickey shot his cuffs, adjusted the fat Windsor knot in his silver-gray necktie, dusted some sand kicked up from yesterday's storm off his shoes, and grinned.

Yep, he decided as he climbed up into the driver's seat of the massive SUV, he looked every penny like a million bucks, exactly the sort of guy who had the *cojones* to carry off a million-dollar job. Sure, he had to split the paycheck a few ways because he couldn't do this particular job alone, but the splits wouldn't be equal, meaning he would be well paid. One hundred K to Big Mango the triggerman, one hundred to Otto the Bump for driving, another hundred to bribe a cooperative Federal squint, and then various payments for various spotters and informants. Altogether, after the split, Mickey personally would take home six hundred large; damn good jack for a morning's work.

Mickey Togs felt deservedly cocky. Do a little morning job for the Big Guys, be back on the Vegas Strip before lunch, get a nice bite to eat, then hit the baccarat salon at the Mirage with a fat stake in his pocket. Mickey took out a silk handkerchief and dabbed some sweat from his forehead; Mickey had trained half his life for jobs like this one. Nothing to it, he said to himself, confident that all necessary preparations had been made and all contingencies covered. A simple, elegant plan.

Mickey pulled the big Navigator into the lot of the Flower of the Desert Wedding Chapel on South Las Vegas Boulevard, parked, and slid over into the front passenger seat, the shotgun position. The chapel was in a neighborhood of cheap old motels and auto shops, not the sort of place where Mickey and his hired help would be noticed. In a town where one can choose to be married by Captain Kirk, Elvis Presley, or Marilyn Monroe, where brides and grooms might dress accordingly, wedding chapels are good places not to be noticed. Even Big Mango, an almost seven-foot-tall Samoan wearing a turquoise Hawaiian shirt and flip flops, drew hardly a glance as he crossed the lot and climbed into the backseat of the Navigator.

Otto the Bump, a one-time welterweight boxer with cauliflower ears and a nose as gnarled as a bag full of marbles, ordinarily might draw a glance or two, except that he wore Vegas-style camouflage: black suit, starched white shirt, black tie, spit-shined black brogans, a clean shave and a stiff combover. He could be taken for a maitre d', a pit boss, a father of the bride, a conventioneer, or the invisible man just by choosing where and how he stood. As he hoisted himself up into the driver's seat of the Navigator, Otto looked every inch like a liveried chauffeur.

"What's the job?" Otto asked as he turned out of the lot and into traffic.

"The feds flipped Harry Coelho," Mickey said. "He's gonna spill everything to the grand jury this morning, and then he's going into witness protection. We got one shot to stop him. Job is to grab him before he gets to the courthouse, then take him for a drive and lose him as deep as Jimmy Hoffa."

"A snitch is the worst kind of rat there is," Otto groused. "Sonovabitch deserves whatever he gets."

"Absolutely," Mickey agreed. Big Mango, as usual, said nothing, but Mickey could hear him assembling the tools for his part of the job.

"How's it going down?" Otto asked.

"Federal marshals are gonna drive Harry from the jail over to the courthouse in a plain Crown Victoria with one follow car."

"Feds." Otto shook his head. "I don't like dealing with the feds."

"Don't worry, the fix is in," Mickey said, sounding smug. "I'll get a call when the cars leave the jail. The route is down Main to Bonneville, where the courthouse is. You get us to the intersection, park us on Bonneville at the corner. We'll get a call when the cars are approaching the intersection. When they make the turn, you get us between the two cars and that's when we grab Harry."

"Whatever you say." Otto checked the rearview mirror. "But what's the fix?"

Mickey chuckled. "You know how federal squints are, doughnut-eating civil servants with an itch to use their guns; they get off playing cops and robbers. A simple, good follow plan just doesn't do it for them, so they gotta throw in some complication. This is it: Harry leaves the jail in the front car. Somewhere on the route, the cars are going to switch their order so when they get to the courthouse Harry will be in the second car."

"How do you know they'll make the switch?"

"I know my business," Mickey said, straightening his tie to show he had no worries. "I got spotters out there. If the switch doesn't happen or the Feds decide to take a different route or slip in a decoy, I'll know it." He snapped his manicured fingers. "Like that."

Otto's face was full of doubt. "How will you know?"

"The phone calls?" Mickey said. "They're coming from inside the perp car. I bought us a marshal."

"Yeah?" Otto grinned, obviously impressed. "You got it covered, inside and outside."

"Like I say, I know my business," Mickey said, shrugging. "Here's the plan: Otto, you get us into position on Bonneville, and we wait for the call saying they're approaching. When the first car makes the turn off Main, you pull in tight behind it and stop fast. From then till we leave, you need to cover the first car; don't let anyone get out. Mango, you take care of the marshals in the second car any way you want to, but if you gack the marshal riding shotgun, you can have the rest of the bribe payment I owe him."

"Appreciate it," Mango said. "You want me to take out Harry, too?"

"Not there. I'll go in myself and get him. Otto, you stay ready to beat us the hell out when I say. We're taking Harry for a little drive and getting him lost. Are we clear?"

"Candy from a little baby," Otto said. Mango, in the backseat, grunted. Could be gas, could be agreement, Mickey thought. Didn't much matter. Mango got paid to do what he did and not for conversation. With a grace that belied his huge size, Mango rolled into the back deck of the vast SUV and began to set up his firing position at the back window. Quiet and efficient, Mickey thought, a true pro.

The first call came. Harry Coelho left the Clark County jail riding in the backseat of a midnight blue Crown Victoria. The follow car was the same make, model, color. After two blocks, as planned, the cars switched positions, so that the follow car became the lead, and Harry Coelho's ass was hanging out in the wind with no rear cover.

When the second call came, the Navigator was in position on Bonneville, a half-block from the courthouse, waiting.

The snatch went smooth, by the book exactly the way Mickey Togs wrote it, the three of them moving with synchronicity as honed as a line of chorus girls all high-kicking at the same time. The first Crown Vic made the turn. Otto slipped the massive Navigator in behind it and stopped so fast that the second Crown Vic rear-ended him; the Crown Vic's hood pleated up under the Navigator's rear bumper like so much paper, didn't leave a mark on the SUV. Before the Crown Vic came to a final stop, Mango, positioned in the back deck, flipped up the rear hatch window and popped the two marshals in the front seat—fwoof, fwoof, that breezy sound the silencer makes—just as Mickey snapped open the back door and yanked out Harry Coelho, grabbing him by the oh-so-convenient handcuffs. They were back in the Navigator and speeding away before the first carload of Feds figured out that they had a problem on their hands.

No question, Otto was the best driver money could buy. A smooth turn onto Martin Luther King, then a hop up onto the 95 freeway going west into the posh new suburbs where a behemoth of an SUV like the Navigator became as anonymous and invisible as a dark-haired nanny pushing a blond-haired baby in a stroller.

After some maneuvers to make sure there was no tail, Otto exited the Interstate and headed up into Red Rock Canyon.

10:50 a.m.
Red Rock Canyon

The hatchling was calling out for a feeding again when Pansy Reynard heard the rumble of a powerful engine approaching. Annoyed that the racket might frighten her falcons, she peered over the edge of her perch.

The sheer walls of the abandoned sandstone quarry below her were a natural amplifier that made the vehicle sound larger than it actually was, but it was still huge, the biggest, blackest pile of personal civilian transport ever manufactured. Lost, she thought when she saw the Navigator, and all of its computer-driven gadgets couldn't help it get back to the freeway where it belonged.

For a moment, Pansy considered climbing out of her camouflaged blind and offering some help. But she sensed there was something just a little hinky about the situation. Trained to listen to that quiet inner warning system, Pansy held back, focused her binoculars on the SUV, and waited.

The front, middle, and back hatch doors opened at once and four men spilled out: two soft old guys wearing suits and dress shoes, a Pacific Islander dressed for a beach party, and a skinny little man with a hood over his head and his hands cuffed behind his back. The hood muffled the little man's voice so that Pansy couldn't understand his words, but she certainly understood his body language. Nothing good was happening down there. She set the lens of her palm-sized digital video recorder to zoom, and started taping the scene as it unfolded below.

The hooded man was marched to the rim over a deep quarried pit. His handlers stood him facing forward, then stepped aside. With a cool and steady hand, Beach Boy let off two silenced shots. A sudden burst of red opened out of the center of the hood, but before the man had time to crumple to the sandstone under him, a second blast hit him squarely in the chest and lifted him enough to push him straight over the precipice and out of sight.

"Kek, kek, kek." The mother Aplomado falcon, alarmed perhaps by the eerie sound of the silencer or maybe by the burst of energy it released, screeched as she swooped down between the canyon walls as if to dive bomb the intruders and distract them away from her nest. The two suits, who peered down into the abyss whence their victim had fallen, snapped to attention. Beach Boy, in a clean, fluid motion, pivoted the extended gun arm, spotted the mother and—fwoof, fwoof—she plunged into a mortal dive.

The hatchling, as if he saw and understood what had happened, set up his chittering again. Pansy saw that gun arm pivot again, this time toward the nest.

"No!" Pansy screamed as she rose, revealing herself to draw fire away from the precious, now orphaned hatchling. Binoculars and camera held aloft where they could be seen she called down, "I have it all on tape, you assholes. Come and get it."

Pansy kept up her screaming rant as she climbed out of the blind and rappelled down the backside of the cliff, out of view of the miscreants, but certainly within earshot. She needed them to come after her, needed to draw them away from the nest.

When she reached the canyon floor, Pansy pulled her all-terrain motorcycle out of its shelter among the rocks, gunned its powerful motor and raced toward the access road where the men could see her. The survival kit she had packed for Lyle—damn him, anyway—was still attached to the cycle's frame.

Otto the Bump scrambled back into the Navigator while Mickey and Mango pushed and pulled each other in their haste to climb inside lest they get left behind.

"Feds," Otto growled between clenched teeth as he started the big V-8 engine. "I told you, I don't like messing with Feds."

"She ain't the freaking Feds," Mickey snapped. His face red with anger, he turned on Mango. "You want to shoot off that piece of yours, you freaking idiot, shoot that damn girl. Otto, go get her."

The old quarry made a box canyon. Its dead-end access road was too narrow for the Navigator to turn around, so it had to back out the way it came in. Pansy was impressed by the driver's skill as he made a fast exit, but she still beat the Navigator to the mouth of quarry. For a moment, she stopped her bike crosswise to the road, blocking them. There was no way, she knew, that she could hold them until the authorities might arrive. Her entire purpose in stopping was to announce herself and to lure them after her, away from the nest. She hoped that they would think that size and firepower were enough to take her out.

Pansy'd had enough time to get a good look at her opponents, to make some assessments. The two little guys were casino rats with a whole lot of starched cuff showing, fusspot city shoes, jackets buttoned up when it was a hundred freaking degrees out there. Beach Boy would be fine in a cabana, but dressed as he was and without provisions . . . Vegas rats, she thought; the desert would turn them into carrion.

Rule one when outmanned and outgunned is to let the enemy defeat himself. Pansy figured that there was enough macho inside the car that once a little-bitty girl on a little-bitty bike challenged them to a chase, they wouldn't have the courage to quit until she was down or they were dead. Pansy sniffed as she lowered her helmet's face guard; overconfidence and geographic naivete had brought down empires. Ask Napoleon.

Pansy didn't hear the burst of gunfire, but twice she felt the air wiffle past her head in that particular way that makes the hair of an experienced soldier stand up on end. As she bobbed and wove, creating an erratic target, she also kept herself just outside the range of the big handgun she had seen. Still, she knew all about random luck, and reminded herself not be too cocky herself, or too reliant on the law of averages.

Because she was in the lead, Pansy set the course. Her program involved stages of commitment: draw them in, give them a little reward as encouragement, then draw them in further until their training and equipment were overmatched by the environment and her experience. Play them.

The contest began on the decently paved road that headed out of Lee Canyon. Before the road met the freeway, Pansy veered onto a gravel by-road that took them due north, bisecting the canyons. When the road became a dry creek bed, Pansy disregarded the dead-end marker and continued to speed along; the Navigator followed. The canyons had been cut by eons of desert water runoff. The bottoms, except during the rainy season, were as hard-packed as fired clay and generally as wide as a two-lane road, though there were irregular patches of bone-jarring imbedded rocks and small boulders and some narrows.

The bike could go around obstacles; the four-wheel-drive Navigator barreled over them.

Pansy picked up a bit of pavement in a flood control culvert where the creek passed under the freeway, and slowed slightly to give the Navigator some hope of overtaking her. But before they could quite catch her, she turned sharply again, this time onto an abandoned service road, pulling the Navigator behind as she continued north.

At any time, Pansy knew she could dash up into any of the narrow canyons that opened on either side of the road, and that the big car couldn't follow her. She held on to that possibility as an emergency contingency as she did her best to keep her pursuers intrigued.

The canyons became smaller and broader, the terrain flatter and Pansy more exposed. Sun bore down on her back and she cursed the wusses behind her in their air-conditioned beast. At eleven o'clock, right on schedule, the winds began to pick up. Whorls of sand quickly escalated to flurries and then to blinding bursts. Pansy pulled down the sand screen that was attached to her face guard, but she still choked on grit, felt fine sand grind in her teeth. None of this, as miserable as it made her feel, was unfamiliar or anything she could not handle.

Always, Pansy was impressed by the skill of the driver following her, and by his determination. He pushed the big vehicle through places where she thought he ought to bog down. And then there were times that, if he had taken more risk, he could have overcome her. That he had refrained, clued Pansy to the strategy: The men in the car thought they were driving her to ground. They were waiting for her to fall or falter in some way. She used this assumption, feigning, teasing, pretending now and then to weaken, always picking up her speed or maneuvering out of range just before they could get her, to keep them engaged. Some birds used a similar ploy, pretending to be wounded or vulnerable as a feint to lure predators away from their nests.

The canyons ended abruptly and the terrain became flat, barren desert bottom. There was no shelter, no respite, only endless heat and great blasts of wind-whipped sand. Pansy could no longer see potholes or boulders, nor could any of them see roadside markers. Though Pansy could not see the road, and regularly hit bone jarring dips and bumps, she was not navigating blind. Three times a year she ran a survival course through the very same area. She had drawn her pursuers into the hollow between Little Skull and Skull Mountains, headed toward Jackass Flats, a no-man's land square in the middle of the Nellis Air Force Base gunnery range.

———

"Get her," Mickey growled. The silk handkerchief he held against his nose muffled his words. "I have things to do in town. Take her out. Now."

Mango's only response was to reload.

Otto swore as he switched off the AC and shut down the vents. Sand so fine he could not see it ground under his eyelids, filled his nose and throat, choked him. Within minutes the air inside the car was so hot that sweat ran in his eyes, made his shirt stick to his chest and his back, riffled down his shins. There was no water, of course, because this was supposed to be a quick job, out of Vegas and back in an hour. He had plenty besides heat and thirst to make him feel miserable. First, he thought he could hear the effects of grit on the car's engine, a heaviness in its response. Next, he had a pretty good idea what Mickey would do to him if he let the girl get away.

How could they have gotten so far into this particular hell? Otto wondered. In the beginning, it had seemed real simple. Follow the girl until they were out of the range of any potential witnesses, then run over the girl and her pissant bike like so much road kill. But every time he started to make his move, she'd pull some damn maneuver and get away: she'd side slip him or head down a wash so narrow that he had to give the road—such as it was—his undivided attention. The SUV was powerful, but it had its limitations, the first of which was maneuverability: it had none.

And then there was Mickey and his constant nudging, like he could do any better. By the time they came out of the canyons and onto the flats, Otto was so sick and tired of listening to Mickey, contending with the heat, the sand, and the damn girl and her stunts that he didn't care much how things ended, only that they ended immediately. He knew desperation and danger could be found on the same page in the dictionary, but he was so desperate to be out of that place that he was ready to take some risks; take out the girl and get back up on the freeway and out of the sand, immediately.

Between gusts Otto caught glimpses of the girl, so he knew more or less where she was. Fed up, he put a heavy foot on the accelerator and waited for the crunch of girl and bike under his thirty-two-inch wheels.

———

Pansy heard the SUV's motor rev, heard also the big engine begin to miss as it became befouled by sand. With the Navigator accelerating toward her, Pansy snapped the bottle of wine out of its break-away pouch, grasped it by the neck, gave it a wind up swing as she spun her bike in a tight one-eighty, and let the bottle fly in a trajectory calculated to collide dead center with the rapidly approaching windshield.

As she headed off across the desert at a right angle to the road, she heard the bottle hit target and pop, heard the windshield give way, heard the men swear, smelled the brakes. The massive SUV decelerated from about fifty MPH to a dead, mired stop in the space of a mere sixty feet. Its huge, heavy-tread tires sliced through the hard desert crust and found beneath it sand as fine as talcum powder and as deep as an ocean. Forget four-wheel drive; every spin of the wheels merely kicked up a shower of sand and dug them in deeper. The behemoth SUV was going nowhere without a tow.

When she heard the rear deck hatch pop open, Pansy careened to a stop and dove behind a waist-high boulder for cover. As Beach Boy, leaning out the back hatch, unloaded a clip in her general direction, Pansy, lying on her belly, pulled out her slingshot, strapped it to her wrist, reached into the pouch of three-eighths-inch steel balls hanging from her belt, and, aiming at the dull red flashes coming from the end of Beach Boy's automatic, fired back. She heard random pings as her shot hit the side of the Navigator.

"She's packing heat," Otto yelled. Pansy continued to ping the side of the car with shot; sounded enough like bullet strikes.

Mango finally spoke. More exactly, Mango let out an ugly liquid-filled scream when Pansy's steel balls pierced his throat and his cheek. Mortally hit, he grabbed his neck as he fell forward, tumbling out of the SUV. With the big back window hanging open, the SUV quickly filled with fire hot, swirling yellow sand.

"She got Mango!" Otto yelled in Mickey's direction. "We try to run for it, she'll get us, too."

Mickey Togs, feeling faint from the heat, barely able to breathe, pulled his beautiful silver-gray suit coat over his head, being careful not to wrinkle it or get sweat on it, and tried, in vain, to get a signal on his cell phone. He didn't know who to call for help in this particularly humiliating situation, or, if he should be able to get a call out—and he could not—just where he happened to be for purposes of directing some sort of rescue.

Otto the Bump heard Mickey swear at his dead phone, and nearly got hit with it when Mickey, in a rage, threw the thing toward the cracked and leaking windshield. Not knowing what else to do, Otto reached for the little piece strapped to his left ankle.

"I'm making a run for it," Otto said.

"Idiot, what are your chances?" Mickey asked. "You got thirty, forty miles of desert, no water, can't see through that damn sand, and a lunatic out there trying to kill you."

"If I stay in this damn car or I make a run for it, I figure it's eighty-twenty against me either way," Otto said. "I prefer to take it on the run than sitting here waiting."

"Ninety-five to five." Mickey straightened the knot in his tie. "You do what you think you gotta do. I'm staying put."

"Your choice, but you still owe me a hundred K," Otto said. He chambered a round as he opened the car door, brought his arm against his nose, and dropped three feet down to the desert floor.

5:00 p.m., April 20
Downtown Las Vegas, Nevada

Without pausing for so much as a perfunctory hello to the clerk on duty, Pansy Reynard strode past the reception desk of the regional office of the Department of Fish and Game and straight back to the pathology lab. Pansy had showered and changed from her dirty desert camouflage BDUs—battle-dress utilities—into sandals, a short khaki skirt, and a crisp, sleeveless linen blouse; adaptability, she knew well, is the key to survival.

She opened the lab door and walked in. When Lyle, the so recently absent Lyle, looked up, she placed a large bundle wrapped in a camouflage tarp onto his desk, right on top of the second half of a tuna sandwich he happened to be eating, and then she flipped her sleek fall of hair over her shoulder for effect.

Eyes wide, thoroughly nonplused, Lyle managed to swallow his mouthful of sandwich and to speak. "What's this?"

"I went back to the nest this afternoon after the sandstorm blew out." Pansy unfastened the bundle and two long, graceful wings opened out of the tarp chrysalis. "I found her in the canyon."

"Oh, damn." Lyle stood, ashen-faced now, tenderly lifted the mother Aplomado falcon and carried her to a lab bench. He examined her, discovered the deep crimson wound in her black chest. Through gritted teeth he said, "Poachers?"

"Looks like it," Pansy said.

"What about the hatchling?"

"He's okay but he has to be hungry." With reverent sadness, Pansy stroked the mother falcon's smooth head. "Another week or two and the baby will be ready to fend for himself. But in the meantime, someone needs to get food to him. Or he needs to be brought in to a shelter."

Lyle sighed heavily. He was obviously deeply moved by this tragedy, a quality that Pansy found to be highly attractive.

"What are you going to do, Lyle?"

"I'll ask for a wildlife team to come out," he said. "Someone will get up there tomorrow to rescue the hatchling. Too bad, though. We've lost a chance to reestablish a nesting pattern."

"Tomorrow?" There was a flash of indignation in her tone.

"He'll be okay overnight."

"What if the poachers come back tonight?"

Again he sighed, looked around at the cluttered lab and the stacks of unfinished paperwork. Then he turned and looked directly into Pansy's big brown eyes.

"Pansy, I need help," he said. "Will you watch the nest tonight?"

"Me?" She touched her breastbone demurely, her freshly scrubbed hand small and delicate looking. "Alone? Lyle, there are people with guns out there."

"You're right," he said, chagrined. "Sorry. Of course you

shouldn't be alone. You shouldn't have been alone last night and this morning, either. It's just, I got jammed up here in the office with a possible plague case in a ground squirrel, Chamber of Commerce all in a lather that word would get out. I couldn't break away."

"Ground squirrels aren't in danger of extinction," she said.

"I am sorry, very sorry," Lyle said, truly sounding sorry. "Look, Pansy, I really need you. If I join you, will you be willing to go back to the nest tonight?"

She took a long breath before responding, not wanting to sound eager. After a full ten count, during which he watched her with apparent interest, she nodded.

"The two of us should be able to handle just about anything that comes up," she said. "I'll meet you out front in five minutes."

"In five," he said as he peeled off his lab coat. "In five."

THE KIDNAPPING OF XIANG FEI

MICHAEL COLLINS

As we walked along the strip hunched in jackets to keep warm—Vegas can be damned cold in November—Kay said, "There's a dark blue Lincoln following us."

We were on our way back to the Mirage from one of those cheap all-you-can-eat dinners where gimlet-eyes watch for people who try to stash extra prime rib or cheesecake under their shirts or bras.

"I know." I didn't look back. "Don't worry, but listen. That car's going to pass us and stop at the curb up ahead. A man is going to tell me to get in. I'll get in. If I haven't called by midnight—"

"I'll call the police. Dan, what—"

"Not the police. Call a lawyer named John Jeffries in L.A. His number's in my Rolodex." I slipped one of my business cards into her hand. "Tell him to call the numbers I've written on the card."

I squeezed her hand, and we walked briskly on toward the hotel, but my mind was racing. It had taken me the better part of three days to smoke them out. Now they were here.

———

The call had come into my office in the back of the old hacienda where Kay and I live at 4:53 p.m. the previous Monday.

"Dan? Marty Gebhard. I need a favor." Professor Martin Gebhard was once the pride of the UCSB political science department, and one of my Tuesday night poker game regulars. A year ago he'd taken the Tardash Chair of International Political Studies at the University of Nevada Las Vegas. I don't know if UCSB misses him, but the poker regulars sure do.

"There's a grad student here, Donald Lewis, who wants to hire a private detective." I heard the hesitation. "It's sort of a difficult and, ah, delicate matter."

"You want me to drive to Vegas?"

"He'd prefer a flying carpet, but do it your way. He'll pay whatever you ask."

I was alone in the office, but I think I cocked an eyebrow. "Whatever I ask?"

"Money isn't his problem."

"Will he pay for Kay too?"

"He'll pay for the cat. Just come as soon as possible."

"Tomorrow afternoon."

Marty always smiled when he lost big at poker, which was most of the time, and "difficult and delicate" always gets my interest. Besides, he hadn't laughed when I pushed Kay into the deal, and he sounded worried.

I went into the kitchen. "Vegas tomorrow? Free, with expense account?"

"I can visit all my stores." Her business is what pays for Santa Barbara.

———

After Barstow, the high desert stretches all the way to Vegas, and I-15 is so straight it lulls drivers into a trance. Sin-Mecca beckons, feet get heavy on the gas, and people die.

Then there were the billboards.

As I drove in the cool late November sunlight, Kay chatting about the buyers she would call on, the billboards came to meet us long before the city or even Nevada was in sight, scars on the austere beauty of the arid land with its tough bushes, thorny cactus, and tougher, thornier animals.

The early Spaniards, the hungry prospectors, the settlers heading west to California found in a barren desert valley a tiny oasis of springs and green meadows. The Spaniards named it Las Vegas, "the meadows," and the Yankee drifters and land seekers welcomed the brief respite. But the billboards do the welcoming now, proclaim a different kind of oasis, and the meadows have long since vanished with the cactus and the thorny lizards.

The first trumpet call of glitter appears at the border with a clutch of casino hotels one inch into Nevada, and soon the whole rhinestone symphony rises up on that distant horizon. Sprawled across the desert like a skin condition, the Strip looms first. Bugsy and the boys did not want the marks from L.A. to drive one extra mile, time was money.

I dropped Kay at the Mirage where she would shower, change into her own line of high fashion clothes, and call on her buyers, and drove on to the university that is tucked conveniently close behind the Strip on Maryland Avenue, between Flamingo and Tropicana. A large but relatively compact campus of ultramodern buildings, rectangular, round and domed, basically in pale sand colors, but with a lot of bright primaries. Mondrian in sand and stone.

I parked as near to the political science building as I could, and walked.

Marty Gebhard is a pleasant man of forty-odd who wears jeans and a sweatshirt, sports a scraggly black mustache, and, today, three-day's stubble. He knew I had only one arm. Donald Lewis didn't, and most people have some reaction when they first see me. Lewis had none.

Tall, pale, bone thin, and so agitated he all but lunged at me. "You've got to find Xiang Fei and arrest those men who kidnapped her!"

"Okay," I said, and sat down in the only extra chair. "Now tell me who Xiang Fei is, and when she was kidnapped."

Lewis wasn't sitting, and was so intense and distracted he couldn't seem to comprehend I didn't know Xiang Fei, or when she had been kidnapped.

Gebhard rescued him. "She's a Chinese graduate student on scholarship from her government, Dan. Donald insists she was kidnapped from the shopping mall on Tropicana a week ago." Marty sounded more than a shade dubious.

"What do the FBI and the metros think?"

Donald paced and raged, "The police don't believe there was a kidnapping! They don't believe me or the witness. They refuse to even notify the FBI!"

This time I did arch an eyebrow. "Witness?"

Marty Gebhard said, "Donald found a man who was drinking coffee in the mall Starbucks."

I looked from one of them to the other. "This man says he saw her kidnapped?"

Donald nodded eagerly. "He saw her talking to two men, and no one's seen her since."

Talking isn't kidnapping. I could see from Gebhard's carefully neutral expression that he knew it if Donald Lewis didn't. "Why don't the police believe the witness?"

"I don't know," Lewis was nearly wringing his hands.

"I take it no ransom notes, no contacts, no demands?"

Lewis said darkly, "Those aren't the only reasons for kidnapping a woman."

"No," I said, "they're not. All right, exactly what's your relationship to Ms. Xiang, Mr. Lewis?"

"We're going to be married." A stubborn tone of defiance joined the distress in his voice.

That told me Xiang Fei might have a different slant on their relationship, and Gebhard knew it, hence the difficult and delicate part. He'd probably told Donald, as gently as he could, that Xiang Fei had simply gone off somewhere as college girls will, and the police had told him there was no evidence of a kidnapping. Donald refused to be convinced, and Gebhard hoped if a bonafide private detective backed him and the cops, Donald might finally believe and give up the idea.

I obliged. "I'll be honest, Donald. The police take even a whiff of kidnapping seriously. They're obviously not taking this kidnapping at all seriously. It looks to me like your girlfriend has simply gone on a trip, and she'll call when she's ready. Marriage jitters, second thoughts, last fling, research, who knows? I get five hundred a day plus expenses and extras. This is going to cost you a large nut, and I don't think you'll get your money's worth."

Donald Lewis's eyes flashed anger. "You're wrong! I want her found! I want whoever kidnapped her caught! Money doesn't matter."

From the way he said it, there was a lot of money behind Donald. A privileged rich boy. It was there in the quick anger, the stubborn refusal to believe Xiang Fei could possibly have gone anywhere without him, the requests that were more like commands. The Metro cops must have loved him.

"She's never been gone for a week before?"

"Not without telling me when and where and how long. We had a dinner and movie date for the day after she vanished. She'd never break it without letting me know why."

Even if their relationship were nothing more than a college romance for a girl heady with the discovery of a different world, most college girls would have at least told him before they vanished for a week.

I asked Gebhard. "Is she missing classes?"

"She isn't taking classes this quarter. She's finishing her dissertation."

"Does she need to do more research?"

"No, not really," Gebhard admitted grudgingly.

So she should be at her computer. "You have a photo, Mr. Lewis?"

He dug into his wallet and handed me a small snapshot of the two of them in front of some building. Donald was easily six-three, and the top of the girl's long, thick black hair came inches above his shoulder. Xiang Fei was tall by Chinese standards, probably five-ten. The oriental fold that gives Asian eyes the appearance of being slanted was barely there. She was lean, but not thin. Sturdy. Donald grinned in the picture like a school-boy with a prized possession. Xiang Fei looked at the camera with a half-mocking smile.

That smile, and the photo, told me a great deal. Xiang Fei wasn't a beautiful girl, she was a handsome woman. A woman who didn't look the type to break a date or walk out on a man without explaining. It wasn't much, but factor in the witness, and Donald Lewis's anguish, and it rated a look.

I've learned to pay attention to emotions.

"Write a check for two days in advance. The bill comes later."

Donald quickly wrote out a check for two thousand, more than I'd asked, gave me Xiang Fei's address, and had to leave for a class. Marty Gebhard watched the closed door to his office as if he thought Lewis might still be standing outside with his ear pressed against it.

I asked, "How old is Xiang Fei?"

He nodded. He'd been waiting for the question. "She's twenty-nine, has a master's from Cambridge, and knows who she is. Donald's twenty-four, has too much money, and no idea what he is or wants to be. She's a strong woman. That's powerfully attractive to some men, and Donald's one of them. I don't think—"

"Would you," I interrupted, "be another, Marty?"

He thought about it. "I find her fascinating. The determined way she goes about everything. But I'm your standard quiet professor. A very nice wife, peace, and a routine low-stakes poker game suits me fine."

"But not Donald?"

"Donald's father is a self-made billionaire, and a powerful personality. His mother's a gentle woman. I think Xiang Fei is the surrogate mother Donald always wanted to stand up against his dad for him." He shrugged. "Sorry. Pop psychology. A simplified guess at a far more complex situation."

"But you think their 'marriage' is mostly in Donald's mind?"

"Oh, Xiang Fei seems to like him a lot. Why, I have no idea. But I don't think he's anywhere in her intended future, Dan."

"You know what she intends her future to be?"

"I know it won't include marriage to a spoiled American boy."

"Not even for money?"

"That would be the last reason for Xiang Fei to do anything."

"You've thought a lot about her," I said.

He nodded. "She has that effect on people. She either fascinates them, or they're afraid of her."

I'd only seen a photo of Xiang Fei, but she was intriguing the hell out of me.

"Okay, she's Chinese, smart, strong, and twenty-nine. What else? What did she do in China? Who are her parents?"

"She doesn't talk about herself or her past. Or China, for that matter. Her records give only her parent's names and occupations, and her academic transcript. Her father is Zhao Zhongwu, a minor civil servant, and her mother is Zhao Sooling. Xiang did her secondary school in Chongqing, her undergraduate in Beijing, and her M.Phil. at Cambridge."

"Why isn't her family name the same as her father's?"

"I have no idea."

After agreeing to get together with him and Carol at least for drinks, I left Marty staring into space as if seeing Xiang Fei, wherever she was.

———

Xiang Fei lived in a low-rise apartment building on a shaded back street near the university. The apartment she shared with two other girls was on the second floor facing the street. Her roommates were home, drinking beer and watching television. The police had talked to them. They weren't too worried about Xiang Fei, but they were a little worried.

Sally Fanelli said, "Like, she still had laundry in the dryer. I mean, she was doing her laundry, and needed a coffee fix, you know?"

Nancy Devlin added. "We were out of coffee, so she went to the mall Starbucks. She was supposed to bring us back double lattes."

"She didn't?"

"She never came back."

"What about Donald? Did she have a date with him the next day?"

Sally nodded. "He took her expensive places. She liked that, but, there was, like, you know, no spark."

"It's 'cause she's older," Devlin explained with the wisdom of nineteen.

"Can I see her bedroom?"

"Sure," Devlin said.

"You won't find much," Sally said. "The cops took most of her things."

"Really?" If the Metro police didn't believe in the kidnapping, why take her possessions?

———————

Las Vegas Metropolitan Police have various geographical commands, sort of like super New York precincts. I drove to the downtown command where I knew one detective lieutenant. I'd only been to Vegas on the job twice before, both missing girls cases. (Girls tend to run to Vegas or Hollywood. Boys head for Mexico or Malibu. Both escape to New York. They're the biggest dreamers.) I'd found one girl, and had worked with Chris Yost both times.

He grinned when I walked in, and waved me to a chair in his cluttered cubicle. "What's her name this time, Fortune?"

"Xiang Fei. She's a Chinese student—"

The grinned vanished abruptly. "I know who the hell she is. What's your interest in her?"

"Hired by her fiancé."

"Lewis?" Yost leaned back in his chair, shook his head. "Hell, I don't believe for a damned second he's anyone's fiancé except in his dreams."

"You also don't believe the woman's been kidnapped."

He gave me a pitying look. "Don't tell me you believe his fairy tale? No ransom note, no political demands, no damn contact at all? Come on, Fortune. The kid's been dumped and doesn't want to believe it."

"The witness?"

Yost snorted in derision. "Some guy having a cappuccino inside Starbucks sees a woman who might have been Xiang Fei talking to a couple of guys. Talking, that's all. No grabbing and shoving into a car, no struggle, not even an argument. He turns his attention to something else, and when he looks back all three are gone. How long he looked away, who knows? Damn it, Fortune, he didn't know if the woman was Chinese, Japanese, Vietnamese, or Russian! He can't even say what the two guys looked like except they were both white."

"Then why pick up all her stuff?"

"You know damn well we have to act on any report of kidnapping. We talked to the Lewis kid, her roommates, and her professors. We hauled in her things looking for a motive. We talked to the alleged witness. We canvassed the scene. We came up empty. It never happened. She's off somewhere on her own."

I shook my head. "I don't know, Lieutenant. She's twenty-nine, a woman, not a girl. Everyone says she's steady, responsible, serious. She stands up a guy she's at least dating regularly. She leaves laundry she's doing in the dryer. She's supposed to bring coffee back to her roommates, and doesn't. She's been gone a week without telling anyone where or why. She talks to two guys, and hasn't been seen since. I have questions."

"We don't. The so-called witness didn't see anything that looked remotely like a kidnapping. Everything else suggests a spur-of-the-moment decision to go somewhere. Plus there's no motive."

"Except the reason more women are grabbed than money or politics."

Yost sighed. "Come on. In a shopping mall, with people all around, rapists grab and run. The victim fights, screams. No one saw anything like that. And any other motive means ransom or hostage, and there would be phone calls."

He was right, but I owed Marty at least my best shot. "You have the witness's name and address?"

Yost was interested in the ceiling of his cubicle. He hesitated far longer than I thought normal. "Sure. Frank Goss." He wrote down the address.

It turned out to be a house buried in vegetation less than half a mile from the mall. When I got there I found an empty garage, and a recessed door with tall plants on both sides that no one opened. I waited in my car, but when Goss still hadn't come home by 6:00 p.m., I climbed back out and gave the front doorbell one last push. Nothing.

It was growing dark, and I decided to pack it in for the day. It looked more and more like Xiang Fei was off somewhere having fun, and the bad news for Donald could wait until tomorrow.

Still, why had Lieutenant Yost hesitated so long before giving me the name and address of a witness he said had been useless?

In Kay's new dark blue S-type Jag I'd reached the corner of Frank Goss's house when a red Mercedes 560SL pulled away from the curb across the street. It had not been there when I arrived, or while I waited, so had to have parked while I was giving the bell that one last ring. Coincidence or a tail?

I placed my SIG-Sauer 9mm on the seat beside me, and led the 560 on a chase along the rapidly darkening back streets, not too fast and not too slow. I found the mall where Xiang Fei had gone for coffee, parked in front of the Starbucks, and went in. I ordered a decaf latte, and sat at a table near the window.

The 560SL was parked three cars up from Kay's Jag. I carried my latte out to the Jag without looking at the car, and opened the passenger side door. I bent in low out of sight of the Mercedes as if placing the latte into a coffee holder on the floor. Leaving the coffee on the floor and door open, I stayed low and circled to the 560.

Donald Lewis sat in the driver's seat. When he saw me, he rolled down the window. "Have you found her?"

"What do you think you're doing?"

"I expected a call by now."

"Did you?" I went around, opened the passenger door, and sat beside him.

For the first time he noticed my missing arm. "Does that make it harder to do your work?"

"It makes everything harder."

"How—?"

"A crocodile bit it off," I told him. "Now listen closely. I'll do your job. From what I've learned so far you're not going to like the result, but you let me handle it, or I quit. No hovering, no tailing, no calling every ten minutes."

He heard nothing except that he wouldn't like the result. "You're the same as all the rest. You don't believe me."

"I believe you think she's been kidnapped, and I believe you're worried. The police don't, and so far neither do I. But I'll work on it until I'm sure. Now go home. When I have something, I'll call."

He glared at me as I climbed back out, but when I reached my car I heard the Mercedes start and screech off. An impatient young man who liked his own way.

I drove to the Mirage, and went up to our room. Kay was propped on the bed, shoes off, legs stretched out, a Newcastle Brown in her hand, looking tired.

"How'd the calls go?" I said, sitting in the armchair facing her.

"Sold five gowns, six suits—skirts and pants—and accessories."

"Good," I said. "You can play the rest of the time we're here."

"What did you have in mind?"

"Dinner, a good one on the first night. A show. Back to the room. Not necessarily in that order. Or are you too tired?"

She drained her Newcastle, and smiled. "Not that tired."

———————

Next morning at 8:00 a.m. I stood on Frank Goss's doorstep.

"I told the police what I saw. They said it was meaningless."

"I'm not the police. Tell me."

"Why the hell should I?"

"Because I'm working for the woman."

He stared hard at me, then stepped back. We went into a large living room with a cathedral ceiling and good modern furniture. He pointed to a chrome and fabric couch, sat in a matching arm chair. "I'll tell you exactly what I told them. I saw this tall woman in a long brown skirt, brown boots, and tan jacket. When she got out of her car, these two guys walked up and talked to her."

So they either knew she was going to Starbucks and were waiting, or they had tailed her. "What kind of car? What did the two guys look like?"

"An old, light blue Dodge Aries. I didn't get a good look at them. Two white guys like everyone else you see in a mall."

"Tall or short? Light or dark hair. Formal clothes or casual?"

"Sort of tall, maybe six-feet even. Both of them. One dark-haired. The other wore a baseball cap. Mall clothes. You know, windbreakers, chino slacks, jeans."

"They didn't touch the woman? Or argue? She wasn't alarmed?"

"Not when I saw them. My attention was caught by something else, and when I looked back they'd all left."

"Her car was gone too?"

"No. It was still there. I remember wondering where she'd gone."

That caught my attention. "She didn't come into Starbucks?"

"Starbucks? No, of course not. I'd have known if she was Chinese, or Japanese, or possibly Vietnamese if she had."

Supposedly, Xiang Fei had gone to the mall for coffee and nothing more. So where had she gone?

"You told the police all that?"

"Damn sure did."

"Was the Aries gone when you left the mall?"

"Almost. After Starbucks, I had to buy some books and CDs at Border's, and when I came out they were towing it."

"Towing it?" No one had mentioned towing. "The police were towing it?"

"I don't think it was the police. Just a regular tow truck. I suppose the car had broken down or wouldn't start."

"The woman was with it?"

He shook his head. "I didn't see her."

To say Goss had painted a vastly different picture wouldn't be true. But the picture was different. More detailed, with a woman who did not do what she had gone to the mall to do, and a towed car. I remembered Yost's hesitation before he gave me Goss's name. The police were lying. Why?

———

In my car I dialed the number of the roommates.

"Mr. Fortune? Hi, it's Nancy."

"What car does Xiang Fei drive, and what was she wearing?"

"An '87 Dodge Aries, pale blue. She had on her nice calf-length brown cord skirt, cordovan boots, dark brown man-tailored blouse, and her beige jacket."

"Thanks," I said. "Are any of her clothes missing besides those?"

"Gosh, we wouldn't know. The cops took everything."

I sat in the car for a time. All right, the police were lying, probably about more than I knew, and I didn't think they were going to fill me in any time soon. Where did I go next? If Xiang Fei had been kidnapped, why did they have it under wraps?

What was special about Xiang Fei? I could only think of one place to ask that.

I drove to Las Vegas International, and bought a round trip to San Francisco. First class.

———

Relations with China had changed dramatically since 1983. What had been a Chinese mission in San Francisco then, was a consulate now, and the man who talked to me was the consul. He wore an impeccably tailored business suit complete with white shirt and conservative tie.

"What is your interest in Xiang Fei," he glanced at my card, "Mr. Fortune?"

"Her fiancé hired me to investigate what happened to her."

He didn't ask who her fiancé was. "What has happened to her?"

Some things never change. He was as inscrutable as his counterpart in 1983. It had nothing to do with being Oriental, only with being a bureaucrat in a foreign country. I enlightened him with what Frank Goss told me, especially the towed car.

He never changed expression. "It is essentially what I have been informed by your authorities. What seems to be your problem?"

"If her car was towed, how could she have gone away in it?"

"Most probably the car was repaired, and she then went on her trip. She could even have taken a bus. Or flown."

"She could have levitated," I said.

He smiled a thin smile. "Amusing. But I'm told the police have found no motive, and I can think of none. I don't understand your concern, Mr. Fortune."

Someone had filled him in thoroughly about Xiang Fei.

"I don't understand your lack of concern. In my experience, Chinese officials raise holy hell when there's even a hint of danger to one of your citizens abroad."

This produced a faint narrowing of his eyes. "I am confident Xiang Fei is in no danger. I have full trust in your fine police."

"Even though they've lied to me?"

"Possibly the police do not feel obliged to tell you everything. Do your job for you, as it were."

"You're taking our State Department's word for all of it?"

A furrow appeared between his narrowed eyes. "Since their word fits all the facts, I am. Might I suggest you do the same, Mr. Fortune?"

"Is that what you'd advise if we were in China?"

"In China your profession does not exist."

I stood. "Now that you're going capitalist, it will."

"China is not going capitalist. That is a mistake many in the West make. We are a socialist nation adapting to the free market world beyond our borders, which, at the moment, we cannot change." He almost smiled. "Have a good day, Mr. Fortune."

I drove south back to San Francisco International, thinking hard. A Chinese consul should be howling his head off to have Xiang Fei located, wherever she was. The police were lying. Or, at least, not telling me everything they knew. Something was wrong. A piece was missing. I mulled it over all the way to the airport, and by the time I arrived by the bay a possible explanation had dawned in my mind.

I looked hard at her photo again.

Then I switched flights to Santa Barbara. It was Donald's money.

Jan Brouwer came out of his darkroom with the enlarged negative of the snapshot Donald Lewis had given me. Or part of the snapshot. The part I hoped would confirm the bells ringing in my mind.

"The guy used a damned expensive 35mm SLR. A Leica M6 TTL or better. It took a hell of a blowup before it grained out. Now let's print the sucker."

Minutes later he dropped an eight by ten glossy on his desk in front of me. A head shot of Xiang Fei and her sardonic smile. I studied it. The thick black hair was coarse. The aquiline nose, prominent cheekbones, and pale brown skin color of the long face leaped out at me. A lean face already slightly weathered at twenty-nine. Her large dark eyes were round, and had the squint creases of a land of strong sun and stronger winds. It was a face that dropped into place like the final move in a chess match.

I called Donald Lewis on my cell phone. "How much will your father back you with money to get Xiang Fei back?"

He could barely speak with excitement. "They've asked for a ransom? Who are they?"

"Answer my question."

"As much as I ask him to when he knows what it's for. Who—"

"I'll get back to you." I rang off. Fortunately, he didn't have my cell phone number, or our room number in Vegas.

The next call went to Los Angeles and the law offices of John Jeffries.

"Dan Fortune," I told the receptionist. "I need to speak to him."

It wasn't long before the voice that made prosecutors and judges grind their teeth came on the line. "Dan, my boy. It's been a long time."

I explained the bare facts of what I suspected. "How's your time frame?"

"How's your money frame?"

"Promising."

"Then I have time. Details?"

"For now, this is a heads up."

My final call was to *The Los Angeles Times*. Larry Norris was a Pulitzer-winning investigative journalist. I told him more of what I suspected than I had Jeffries.

Then I headed for the airport again.

———

At the reception desk of the Metro police when I asked for Lieutenant Yost, I got Captain Bruccoli. His office had two windows and a real door. "Don't sit down, Fortune. What I have to say won't take that long."

"What I have to say might."

"You don't get to talk. You listen. You're interfering with an ongoing police investigation. You're meddling in matters that don't concern you, and that could land you in serious trouble. I'm telling you stop whatever you think you're doing. Now."

I smiled. That annoys petty tyrants more than anything else. "You finished?"

"Yes, and so are you. Get out of here."

I opened my manila envelope, and dropped the enlarged face

of Xiang Fei on his desk in front of him. "I suggest you look at this because it tells the whole story. Maybe you don't know enough, but believe me, this photo at the top of an *L.A. Times* feature story is going to make a lot of people unhappy."

He pulled the photo to him. As I expected, it meant nothing. But I had his attention. "What feature story?"

"The one that will explain who those two men who talked to Xiang Fei were, and who towed Xiang Fei's car. Or whatever her other name is."

"Other name? What the hell are you talking about?"

"Just tell the sheriff I want to meet with those guys before I put the story in motion and hire the best lawyer Donald Lewis's father's money can buy."

Bruccoli wasn't exactly sputtering when I left, but I hadn't made a friend.

If I were right, I didn't give a damn.

Now, as Kay and I walked home along cold and windy Las Vegas Boulevard, the midnight blue sedan pulled to the side of the road in front of us. The rear door opened. "He'll talk to you. Get in."

I gave Kay a kiss, and climbed into the sedan. The man closed the door, the driver squealed away.

The John Lawrence Bailey Federal Building in Las Vegas is at 700 East Charleston Boulevard. The man I faced this time across his desk was tall and wore the mandatory dark suit. Except his suit was a custom-made charcoal gray, and his office was a large corner one. He pushed my business card around his desk with one finger as if playing with a small animal.

"What do you think you want, Mr. Fortune?"

"I want to talk to her."

"Why?"

"To hear what she has to say before I go to a lawyer and the *L.A. Times*."

"You can't see her, and neither can your lawyer or the *L.A. Times*."

I sat watching his finger toy with my card. "Exactly who is she terrorizing?"

"That's classified." The *Mister* was gone. He gave me a cold stare Captain Bruccoli couldn't begin to match.

"You like what you're doing?"

"What am I doing?"

"Throwing a woman into a cell alone and incommunicado, when she's done nothing in this country, or against this country. No lawyer, no judge, no visitors, no charges, no telephone call, no civil or human rights. No admission you're even holding her. She disappears. Exactly like Chile or Argentina."

"Chile and Argentina were political civil wars. Our war against terrorism is international. We've been attacked. We're defending ourselves."

I took an interest in the darkness outside his windows. We were high enough, and facing in the right direction, to see the dark even in Las Vegas. "Don't you get a sense of déjà vu? That we've all been here before?"

"If you're talking about the McCarthy era, there's no resemblance."

"Actually, I was thinking of the Alien and Sedition Acts passed by Congress and President John Adams in 1798."

"Never heard of them, but I expect Adams knew what he was doing."

No one knows history anymore, not even our own.

"Ben Franklin didn't think so: 'They that can give up essential liberty to obtain a little temporary safety deserve neither liberty nor safety.' Tom Jefferson rescinded those laws as soon as he became president."

"Ben Franklin and Tom Jefferson lived in different times, without terrorists who target civilians and strike without warning, nuclear bombs in satchels, and biological weapons that can be carried in a pocket."

"They lived in times of Indians who targeted civilians and struck without warning on a thousand mile frontier. A time of two superpowers who encouraged and armed the Indians against us, and were ready to attack us at any time. And a far more dangerous and vulnerable homeland."

"Then President Adams knew what he was doing after all." It was his turn to look out at the dark. "You're wasting your time and mine. The woman isn't a citizen. She's Chinese."

"I don't think she is."

His eyes were suddenly cautious. "You don't think she's what?"

"Chinese. And legal resident aliens who have done nothing are supposed to have rights here. That's what America is about."

He sat there staring down at my card as if trying to understand something. He either gave up, or decided he didn't care. "We're in a war against terrorism. She belongs to a terrorist organization on our list. It's national security. Period."

I said, "Whose national security? Ours or China's?"

This time he only stared at me. "Go home, let us do our job."

I shook my head. "For twenty years we've been pressuring Beijing to improve their human and civil rights record. Three years ago we would have been loudly demanding Xiang Fei's rights and freedoms. Shouting for democracy. Now, she's done nothing against us, but we arrest her without charge and throw her into a cell without trial."

"Things have changed."

"Not for her, not for China, and not for me," I told him. "I'm going to John Jeffries, I expect you know who he is. I'm going to report to my client. His father is very rich, and that means connections as well as the money to pay Jeffries. I've already talked to Larry Norris at the *Times*. He loves the Chinese spin on this story."

"The *Times* won't print it."

"Norris will write it, and someone will print it. It's too good a story. That's America too. At the very least it'll embarrass your bosses. Everything is spin these days, and a lot of their supporters won't like this spin."

He thought about that. "I could stop you."

"Not with lawyers and feature writers already knowing exactly what I'm doing. Too big a kettle of fish. Very bad PR. I'll make the same deal I came to make. I'll talk to her before I do anything else. It could change my mind."

He hesitated longer than Lieutenant Yost had three days ago. Then shook his head. "It's not going to happen."

I stood. "You'll hear from Jeffries. Do I get a ride home?"

He reached for his phone. "Drive Fortune back to his hotel."

I didn't look back as I left. I didn't have to. By the time I was in the midnight blue sedan down in the garage he'd be on the phone to the director in D.C. The director would call the attorney general. In the car, I watched the lights of Vegas, bright and busy at any hour. Traffic was still heavy. We're a busy people, too busy most of the time to think about yesterday or tomorrow.

I heard the car phone ring. The conversation in the front seat was muted.

Then the agent in the passenger seat turned and said, "We're going back."

I took out my cell, called Kay. I knew she wouldn't be asleep. "It's okay. Go to bed. I'll be in the hotel by morning if not earlier."

They had Xiang Fei in an isolation cell. She lay on the bottom bunk reading a book, still wearing the clothes she'd disappeared in.

"I'm Dan Fortune, a private investigator hired by Donald Lewis to find you." I held out my card. "He thinks he's your fiancé."

She lowered her book. "He's a nice boy."

"What's your non-Chinese name, and which Central Asian ethnic group are you? Kazakh? Kirghiz? Uighur? Uzbek? Maybe Tajik?"

She closed the book. "Why have they let you talk to me?"

"Let's say you're a special case, I have connections, and Donald has money."

She stood, and walked to the window. Taller than I'd thought from the snapshot, leaner and sturdier. A woman who could ride a horse all day with a baby on her back and a rifle over her shoulder. None of which would help her here. She looked out at the shining glitz of Las Vegas. "My name is Aimur Imin. I'm a Uighur from Kashgar."

"Yet the Chinese sent you abroad for an education. Isn't that unusual?"

She turned. "What do you know about the Uighurs?"

"You're a Turkic people of Central Asia, mostly in China, and you're Muslims."

"An ancient Turkic people long before we were Muslims. We rode with Ghengis Khan and Timur, perhaps with the Huns.

Nomadic warriors and sheepherders who have mostly settled down and become farmers. The Han Chinese want to destroy our ethnic identity and our culture. The Han don't recognize anyone else on earth as people, and they want to assimilate us."

"Like the Borg in the *Star Trek* television show?"

She smiled. "There is a similarity. One of China's ways is to offer a Han and Western education to special Uighurs who will then teach Han and Western culture to Uighur children. I am half Han, so I was the perfect candidate."

"But to yourself you're all Uighur, have no intention of helping the Han, and somehow they found out."

"It would seem so."

"What's the name of your 'terrorist' organization?"

"Uighurstan Liberation Organization."

"Which is now on our attorney general's list of terrorist groups."

She shrugged. "We have never acted against anyone but the Han, never attacked civilians, never acted outside Central Asia, but your government wants China as an ally in your war on terrorism, so we are now terrorists."

I said, "I look at you, and I see a highly educated, sophisticated, independent woman. Someone ethnicity should sit lightly on, if it sits at all, and who knows as well as anyone that Uighurstan is a remote dream in today's world."

She sat down again on the edge of her bunk. "Do you know Kashgar?" She caressed the word, Kashgar, as if it were the name of a lover.

"I know it's a city on the Silk Road."

"We call the ancient trade route the Golden Road. The Golden Road to Kashgar, to Samarkand, to India, to ancient Rome, to the entire world. Kashgar lies between the deserts to the east, and twenty-thousand foot mountains to the west. The Chinese arrived to claim us in your first century A.D. Kashgar had already been a trading center of the known world for over a thousand years. Marco Polo came and rediscovered Kashgar for Europe in 1274, when it was over two thousand years old." Her intense eyes could see the deserts and the mountains and the two thousand years. "We've been governed by Ghengis Khan's Mongols, Timur himself, many Turkic empires, and, from time to time, by the Chinese who never controlled us for long. The last Turkic kingdom was that of the great Yakub Beg, who was not Turkic but a Tajik general who made Kashgar the center of a kingdom in 1865, and remained there, opening ties with Britain, until 1876 when the Chinese came again. In 1930 my grandfather and a Chinese Muslim general declared a Republic of East Turkestan, but the Chinese came once more. The Chinese always come."

She could see the Chinese. "I will tell you two stories. In Kashgar, the tomb of Abakh Hoja, an Islamic prophet who died in 1639, is a great hall with a dome of brilliant green tiles. Also in the hall is the tomb of his granddaughter, Iparhan. She was captured by one more Chinese army in the mid-eighteenth century, and taken to the Forbidden City to be concubine to the Qing emperor. But she cried every day for her desert home, and rejected all his advances. Some legends say she refused him for twenty-five years, others that she survived less than a year, but in the end she killed herself. The devastated emperor sent her in death on the three-year return journey to Kashgar. She is known in Chinese history as Xiang Fei, the Fragrant Concubine. When I disowned my Han father, I changed my Han name to Xiang Fei."

She began to pace the tiny cell. "The second is modern. In 1953 the Chinese sent a thousand soldiers into the desert of our remote Xinjiang, and told them to build a city. There were wolves, heat, little water, and they lived in holes in the ground, as many of your own early pioneers did. They used cannon as plows, machine guns to mark furrows, and they built Shihezi that is now a city of six hundred thousand. It has movie theaters, visiting music and dance groups from eastern China, a Mandarin radio and TV station that broadcasts only within Shihezi, and the population is ninety percent Han. There are no minorities in Shihezi, and nearby villagers are not allowed to enter."

She let the silence in the cell stretch for a full minute. "In their eyes, the Han are your westward pioneers in a thousand Hollywood movies. We are the Indians."

By noon the next day I was in L.A. in Jeffries's office. I told him everything I knew, and everything Aimur Imin had said.

Jeffries radiated outrage. "She's no threat to the U.S.! For God's sake, she's one of the people for whom we demand democracy. You get Norris to write the story, and I'll get her into court."

I wasn't as optimistic. In anxious times of fear, crisis and hysteria—real, imagined, or invented—standing up against the tide is not the way to get ahead. "Norris will write the story, but the bureau chief is right. There's a good chance the *Times* won't publish it, and judges aren't in a human rights mood these days."

"You find out all you can about these Uighurs and the Chinese, and I'll find a federal judge who doesn't believe in suspending the constitution for any reason."

I said, "Maybe you won't want to, John. When I reported to my client, he wasn't all that pleased to have been right. He's suddenly not certain his father's going to foot your bill, and he's not so sure he wants him to. He doesn't seem as enamored of Aimur Imin as he was of Xiang Fei. Maybe because taking an unpopular position won't help his father sell a lot of widgets."

"Yeah," Jeffries said with disgust. "So this one I do pro bono. I never really wanted to be rich. She'll be back in class in a month, trust me."

I wanted to believe him, but Aimur Imin and her Uighurs *were* the Indians, and it's not only in revolutions that eggs are broken. Deserts and oases vanish, small animals become extinct, societies are destroyed, and people disappear and die in the march of progress, the building of empires.

KILLER HEELS KILL TWICE AS DEAD

T. P. KEATING

The great thing about revenge is that, once decided upon, there's not a great deal else to consider. Like a topless show, innovation isn't necessary.

For stranding me in the Red Rock Mountains, for making me

miss the TV audition in Los Angeles today, there'd be a huge price to pay. On the drive back to the city, I stopped my beat-up sedan to stretch my long legs and take the late morning desert air. A nearby burro regarded me, standing next to one of the evenly spaced creosote bushes that gave the valley floor a curiously gardenlike, arranged appearance. My pink spandex bikini, fishnet hose, and eight-inch heels no doubt drew its attention. For showgirl Lilah Starr, morning, even late morning, is a rarely sighted beast.

I'd determined to become Vegas personified. A place that feeds off the intoxicating rush of blood to the head, a red liquid that keeps the predator alive in the midst of arid desolation. That liquid now fueled the engine of my hate. I slipped into a less attention-grabbing outfit of gold hotpants and halter top before driving on. The donkeylike creature twitched its furry ears and maintained the cool stare at my departure. I decided to add the stubbornness of the burro to my approach.

My immediate quarry lived in a quiet street towards the southern city limits. Leaving my heels at the open back door, my dancing skills allowed me to skip nimbly over the white carpet and knock out the occupant. Georgia, a fellow showgirl from my revue, had been seeing huckster Jonn Brooks all spring. There are no easy rides when you sleep with the enemy.

I slipped on a pair of elbow-length pink cotton gloves and began my search. Then again, her collection of kitsch figurines could be considered as sufficient punishment, or simply a cry for help. I located her handbag and removed the address book. Sure enough, Jonn was listed in her childish scrawl. Hmmm, I could drive my vindictive heart to his house in three minutes.

Given the way he treated his employees, no wonder he kept his address private. Because today's episode represented only part of a long list of his attacks on my dignity. The watertight contract that I'd signed when he got me drunk had been the start. Then came my enforced silicone implants. Didn't the moron understand that skin is out and family-oriented offerings are in?

That's when I began to organize my departure. Or escape, if you will. When I'd discussed the idea with Georgia, I didn't realize I'd been talking directly to him. When he next visited my silicone valley, his head would literally be buried there.

Gee, that Jonn's such a gentleman. Why, he'd thoughtfully abandoned me with my sedan. That more than compensated for being ambushed by his henchmen in my dressing room. A shame that the chloroform needed to wear off before I could slip behind the wheel. I'd cleared my head by putting on my false eyelashes one by one, while the time drifted by. Now my gun would make both Jonn and my contract null and void. The sight of the weapon in the glove compartment reassured me, along with the same phial of chloroform and ball of cotton wool that he'd used on me. A further deliberate sign of his swaggering arrogance. I winked a soft brown eye back at my luxurious lashes in the rear-view mirror, pausing briefly to consider the satisfying sight of applying several thick lashes to his own rear view.

The instant I saw his black SUV, spotless and gleaming, he swanked in and eased away from me. I let three cars overtake mine, and I stayed at that respectable distance. We turned left. Left again. The fourth left told me that, once more, I'd fallen short of respectable. He braked suddenly, clambered out and waddled his dumpy frame towards me. I stopped. If I shot him there and then, I'd have too many witnesses to an act of such selfless compassion. So I lowered the window, hoping that I could kidnap him if he stuck his ugly mug inside. No such luck, he kept to the sidewalk.

"Hi Lilah. Okay?"

"No-kay, you sewer rat."

"Surely, there's no hard feelings over that little joke?" His chest strained against the dull cream-colored shirt, while a red and green check tie dangled over his beer belly. A light grey suit and ever-present cigar completed the ensemble.

"I want out, Jonn. Out of my contract and out of Nevada."

"Honey, we've discussed it, remember? I'm very attached to my performers. Didn't your trip to the mountains help clear your head?" I'd launched myself out of the car and pressed my gun into his gut in the flash of a downtown neon sign. "Hey, I'm meeting Senator Smythe later on. If I don't show, questions will be asked."

"What say you join me for a spin?" I roughly maneuvered him into the passenger seat and hit the gas. Unless his senator turned up right now with more firepower, he'd have to take his turn. That's democracy.

"Lilah, be careful. Steering with one hand isn't very sensible." Funny, how he could be so confident when surrounded by his heavies at the venue.

"Yeah, and I've only got one eye on the road. Heck, wouldn't want to be in the dead man's seat right now."

"Okay, I'll revoke your contract. Only, I'll need to speak with my lawyers first . . ." We screeched to a halt outside Georgia's.

"No, Jonn. We go inside and you write out the change immediately. Capice?"

"Capicing you loud and clear."

Carrying a handgun, Georgia let us in. When she saw my own gun trained on our Caesar's back, she frowned deeply.

"Put the weapon down please, Georgia," Jonn insisted. "She must've hit her head during a recent performance." With a quizzical look my way she complied. As two tall, perfectly poised showgirls, we eyeballed each other at least a foot over Jonn's balding head. I admired her surgeon. You'd need to be an expert to spot her nasal beautification and various other collagen injections. Though her bust was all natural, allegedly. I admired her front.

"Jonn wants a pen and some paper," I explained. "He's got a legal nicety to produce." I shoved him onto a white settee, while I lounged against the white wall and kept my gun trained on him. The pen and paper duly arrived. He glanced my way, recoiled a bit at the lilac paper with the border of red hearts, took a deep breath and started to write.

Georgia, in her white catsuit and heels, leaned over his shoulder. "That's all you've asked for, Lilah?" She looked genuinely astonished.

"Now now, honeybuns, it's really no big deal," Jonn soothed, too damn lightly for my tastes.

I pointed my loaded truth seeker straight at his head. "Care to elaborate on that pillow talk?"

"I've got a little bit stashed away in the desert for a rainy day, that's all."

"You're telling me," said Georgia. "Hey, Lilah, ever wondered why our glitzy venue took twice as long to build than the estimate? This here is the king of skimming. He probably owns the desert too."

"You so-called ladies won't be returning from your next visit to the mountains, and I'll go to my grave before I show you where to find my money." The petulant look came so naturally to him.

"Lilah, I'll go with you. I've had enough of Vegas. Too much glamour can be fatal. This city ain't what it used to be. For all the private security guards this guy maintains, I got attacked in my own home not half an hour ago. In this very room. I want out, and I made a duplicate of Jonn's secret treasure map as insurance. See, Jonn, you're not the only one with private security arrangements." My, but his crest fell at that news like a wave hitting a stony beach.

We left him tied up and chloroformed in the brightly lit, whitewashed basement. By my estimate, we'd be in California with the booty when he surfaced, ready to appreciate the army of figurines that occupied the many display cases. I filled the tank with gas before leaving our twenty-four-hour neon city behind.

"Which way, Georgia?"

"Take the highway to the Red Rock Mountains."

While jazz played on the radio and the air conditioning cranked it out at the max, I considered how I'd been wrong about my fellow showgirl. The Strip is packed full of hidden security cameras, which for legal reasons aren't allowed to record audio. But that wouldn't stop a feral gambler like Jonn. I shuddered at the intrusive nature of his surveillance. Best to consider the future, which lay thirty minutes or so in front of us.

The miles vanished under the wheels. Creosote bushes gave way to blackbush as we climbed, then Mojave yucca and Joshua trees. A shame I didn't pursue botany in college. Instead of pursuing the boys in the clubs. Pretty soon I'd realized that I went for the clubs, not boys.

"We're here," Georgia announced.

"Here appears to be nowhere."

"The next stage is on foot." I changed into gold platform trainers (hers were white, of course) and we climbed a steep slope. More steep slope. Still with the slope. Ahead of me, she ducked behind a big boulder. I got a woozy feeling, and it wasn't all because of the prickly heat. Had my plan for revenge, simple straight and true, been led astray by unnecessary, cluttered action?

The boulder hid the mouth of a cave. When I joined her, some ten yards inside, she was peering intently at a section of jagged wall. New doubts arose. I'd stranded myself with a less than stable showgirl and no means of defense. At least the air this far in was marginally cooler, and I appreciated the shade.

"Georgia?" My voice echoed slightly.

"I also brought along the key." If she removed a key-shaped piece of rock from a pocket, I'd know she was insane and I'd have to act accordingly. My thoughts strayed to the chloroform in the glove compartment.

She removed a key-shaped piece of rock from a pocket and I slugged her out cold from behind. Again. Poor Georgia. For sure, Jonn must take responsibility for tipping her over the edge. Interesting key, though. I picked it up and wiped the dust off. On closer inspection, it was made of red metal, with a black button at the round end. The rock look was only a textured finish. What the heck. I pointed it at the wall and pressed. Then I wondered about my own sanity.

With a low reverberating rumble, a section of wall slowly rose to the ceiling, stirring a small cloud of debris as it did so. I closed my eyes, not solely to keep the debris out. If I opened them to see glitter balls and a casino, staffed by dwarves, I'd book myself into the nearest helpful medical institution. Hi Ho.

"What the . . ." asked an out-of-focus Georgia.

"A boulder fell from the ceiling. You'll be okay." She shook her short blonde curls. She accepted my hand and I helped to haul her back to her feet. Thankfully, her concussion concealed the total absence of boulders on the floor.

"Wow, thanks, Lilah. You're the only true friend I ever made in Vegas. Is that the treasure?"

Glad for the distraction, I turned back to the breach in the rock wall. A whole bunch of silver and gold coins filled a dozen metal shelves, all in transparent plastic bags. Only in Vegas, my friend, only in Vegas. Once more, visionary human endeavor had created and sustained outrageous architecture in a harsh environment.

Together, each softly whistling her own tune, we carried the desert loot back to the car. After closing the rock door and sweeping our footprints, to leave no trace of our visit, we drove on through the mountains. For several minutes, the jazz and the air conditioning took the place of conversation. If detectives ever interviewed us separately, there's no way that any cover story would stand the strain.

I slammed on the breaks and shouted, "It's not enough!"

"Lilah, those coins will go a long way."

"Not that. Jonn. This isn't the revenge I wanted, damn it. He's probably got secret hoards all the way between here and the Valley of Fire." I curled a lock of my long blonde hair around my fingers and continued to fume.

Georgia drew her mouth into a thin line. "You have a plan?"

"Which means, he won't be expecting us. And these coins should buy a way through his armor. What do you say?"

"A friend of mine is a coin dealer, no questions asked. Gary's Numanistics on Sixth Street."

"Don't you mean Numismatics?"

"Whatever."

"Yeah, I'm familiar with it."

"Tell you what," she suggested, "I could call in a favor with Senator Smythe, find out where he's dining tonight." It sounded like a plan to me. On our way back to Vegas, I added a few more illegal miles per hour to our speed. Truth be told, the thought of crossing the desert on a summer's day didn't exactly thrill me. What with the risk of the car overheating, the tires blowing out from the heat and getting stuck without water, even seeing Jonn again was more appealing. Well, marginally so. The image of Georgia using her recent wealth to buy yet more china and porcelain nightmares entered my head, and I shook it out immediately.

Back at Chateau Georgia, we found that Jonn had already escaped. No doubt his innate sliminess allowed him to slip through his bonds. She made the call, often dropping her voice low, probably to whisper sweet nothings.

ShowTime turned out to be in the Top of the World Restaurant, perched at the summit of the Stratosphere Tower. Stopping very briefly to retouch our makeup and fix a low-cal snack, we set off anew. With the curtain due to rise about ten minutes before we arrived, after dealing with the coins, it meant that we wouldn't be cooling our high heels backstage for too long.

We turned off the Main Street and drove directly into a garage, where we parked. Three other cars were being worked on. Background electrodisco spilled into the foreground. A man in his early forties, no taller than Jonn but trim and fit, left a small office, wiping his hands on a clean towel. We stepped out to greet him.

"Hiya Lilah, hiya Georgia. I gotta say, you two don't need any bodywork."

"Gary, darling, this isn't a social call," Georgia trilled.

"Yeah, sorta figured you weren't hankering to become car mechanics."

"We're here about your hobby." At my comment his demeanor changed to full-on serious.

"You've got the spare change with you?" We nodded. "Hey boys, coffee break," he shouted across the garage. Half a dozen employees trooped out in a well-rehearsed fashion and closed the garage door. I wondered if failed deals had led to their thralldom. "I love garage sales. What have you got for me?"

I opened the trunk. He picked up one of the bags, looked closely and gave an appreciative grunt. He delved deep and repeated the process. A third bag sealed the deal. "A check for each of you?"

"Gary, we love you," I said.

"Say, did they take an interest in your topless *War and Peace* idea?" He didn't smile, but the twinkle in his eyes betrayed him.

"Nope. They wouldn't agree to my topless *Crime and Punishment* either," I shot back.

"But they did say yes to my idea, a fully nude tribute to America's cheerleaders," Georgia enthused. We loved her too.

The Stratosphere drew closer. It marks the unofficial divide between Old Vegas and the new ritzy casinos of the strip. The town gets its bearings from the Strato-sphere, so it made an ideal place for me to establish my bearings with Jonn, after way too long. The needle of my vengeance pointed due north.

"Georgia, you gotta tell me, what the hell is it with you and those figurines?" We'd stopped at a red light.

"Sweet, aren't they?"

"Sickly you mean."

"Well, perhaps my collection of commemorative plates will be more to your liking?" I eased us away from the junction.

"No, not commemorative plates. Anything but commemorative plates. You're going to waste your half of the bounty, aren't you?"

"Lilah Starr, it ain't none of your business what I spend Jonn's money on." She frowned, crossed her hands over her chest and found the cityscape engrossing to watch. "It's not like your tiresome fixation on old show posters is worth a fig."

"Actually, it's worth quite a . . ."

"Shut up, Lilah."

Shortly after 5 p.m., our ears popped as we rode the elevator from ground level. Sure, reservations are required to dine, but no one has reservations about showgirls on the Strip. When it comes to paying by plastic, 36FFs lead the way.

I slid mine into the space next to Jonn at their panoramic window seat. Georgia followed suit with hers next to Senator Smythe, a ruddy-faced, portly man in his sixties with a shock of suspiciously black hair. Suddenly, the panoramic view lost its appeal. A map of new territories to conquer occupied their greedy eyes.

"Evening boys," I cooed, straightening Jonn's boring tie.

"Evening ladies, care for some wine?" asked the senator, his bonhomie fully engaged. "If white's not to your liking, just say."

"Yes please, Senator, white's fine," Georgia replied. I nodded and he poured for us.

"Hey, you're Georgia de la Rose, aren't you?" The senator smiled at the happy memory who sat beside him.

"Aw shucks, Senator, it's so nice for a girl to be recognized." I saw his arm curl around her waist, and noticed that she didn't object.

"Lilah, what's this about?" Jonn asked. "I thought you two had left for the coast hours ago?"

"You wish, you mean," I countered. "Senator, are you aware that Jonn is the only person ever caught cheating in the International Burro Biscuit Toss in Oatman?" The senator looked suitably disgusted. "Go on, Jonn, tell us about the steroid injections in your throwing arm."

"Geez almighty, Jonn, is that true?" Smythe was grilling a slippery witness at a hearing on Capitol Hill. Georgia covered her mouth with her hand in mock horror.

Jonn put down the fork in his well-developed hand, the seafood no longer so appealing. "I'll ask you again, Lilah, what's the point of this visit?"

"Hey Jonn, no need for the hostility." The senator didn't want to antagonize the voters. "Lilah, Georgia, is it a matter that your ever-approachable representative could help with?"

Georgia held his gaze. "Can't we go someplace quieter to discuss this? It's a very personal issue, which needs a delicate touch." Wow, Georgia, don't be too subtle. But Senator Smythe had already melted over his seat. It suited me fine to be left alone with Jonn.

"We'd like that too," Jonn piped up, rather nervously. So, he'd understood my train of thought. He'd become a worried man. Good. Even if a bodyguard could be called, they were obviously too far away to be of any use to him. For once, I felt grateful for his overbearing arrogance. He lit another foul cigar and inhaled deeply.

Four glasses of wine hastily finished, the senator ushered us to his suite of rooms in the hotel below. Whether he owned them or they came with the job didn't matter to me. At that moment, they simply represented an ideal opportunity. On our way, he regaled us with his plans to extend the monorail, which didn't exactly make for thrilling listening. The line, no, make that lines, would apparently stretch to infinity. Though I'm sure he mentioned the Hoover Dam. Or maybe I simply wished that's where I could retreat to, not to hear his masterful voice projection.

"I've been considering collecting boring old movie posters," Georgia trilled as we exited the elevator. "You'd be surprised how much money they can cost, and the dullest ones are the most expensive. In fact, it's the dull ones I look out for."

"Actually, I've just come to appreciate the value of figurines," I airily confessed. "There's no such expression as too mawkish for me, and no amount of money I'm not willing to pay. Heck, I'll even take out a loan to get a particularly sickly looking specimen."

"A loan, girlfriend? Why stop at a loan? Let's be honest, if you want the item, why not sell your house?" She smiled.

"Girlfriend, no need to be all cautious. Sell your house and sell your soul in a contract with the devil too, that's my motto." I smiled harder.

Smythe and Brooks clearly struggled for a suitable reply to our outbursts, while we strode along the plushly carpeted corridor. I noted that my final comment had seriously turned the heat back up on Jonn's discomfort, so well done, Georgia. My, didn't he just run a finger inside his collar, to let out some steam? We came to a halt outside an unnumbered door. The senator tapped out a code on a keypad and we entered his inner sanctum.

The theme of Smythe's many rooms was a Roman villa, with frescoes of topless Roman lovelies on every wall, mosaics of topless Roman lovelies on the floor, and topless Roman art all over the place. The large entrance contained a fountain, which depicted nymphs badly in need of a decent toga shop. Several shut doors to left and right whispered of secrets that lay beyond. A veritable Hideawayus Maximus, as the Ancients would've surely called it. Although I'd definitely call it a mock-Roman orgy of bad taste.

"We can party as loud as we want, these rooms are sound-proof. Yeah, thought you'd enjoy the decor, Lilah. Care to see my bust?" Smythe asked Georgia, tugging her towards an inner door.

"Hey, that's my line, Senator," she giggled.

"You'll find out why they call me a big shot."

"I'm a bit of a collector myself," Jonn announced, "can we see the bust too?"

The senator looked taken-aback. "Easy, pardner, this is strictly a private senatorial audience." A consummate politician, he maintained his facade until the moment for action came. He produced a gun and made to aim at Jonn's back.

"No!" I cried, managing to grab and deflect the arm before the blow could be struck. He shot into the air. I prized his chubby fingers from the handle, then pushed him away. He stumbled, whacked his head against a plinth and fell unconscious. Above him, a toga-clad statue of Senator Smythe struck a heroic pose. Though minus a nose, which he'd just blown away.

"But Lilah, didn't you want revenge? Weren't the coins supposed to find a way through to Jonn?"

"This is my revenge, my show, my choreography."

"I knew you were up to no good." Jonn's eyes darted between

Georgia and me as he backed towards the door. He reached inside his light grey jacket. In front of me, Georgia fired a warning shot. The hand stopped.

"Stand over in the corner," she insisted, carelessly pointing with the barrel in what I considered a rather dangerous, frankly unprofessional manner. He complied, enabling me to press the cotton wool, drenched in chloroform, over her mouth. Once more, I'd turned her lights out. Sorry babe. My own gun in hand, I faced Jonn.

"Now what, Lilah? You gonna waste me, that's it? A little cheap psychiatric help from a bullet? What did I ever do to you?" Bad mistake. He made me remember all the stuff he'd done to me. Which in turn tensed my trigger finger and made me fire. That must've been his plan, as next second he hurled himself behind the plinth and through a door. King of skimming be damned, this here was the king of rats. I chased his tail.

In a faux forest clearing I had him pinned, crouching behind a marble discus thrower. Though I couldn't recall reading of any female discus throwers in Ancient Rome, I strongly doubted that they'd go topless. Wouldn't it hinder the throwing action? Panpipes softly played from hidden speakers, in amongst the plastic trees and shrubs.

"Look, Lilah, you don't really want me dead, do you?"

"If you must plead for your pathetic life, get on with it." My response surprised me. Could I be softening?

"The real loot is in Calico ghost town."

"Keep going."

"I've got the key right here. Just point it at the correct spot inside Maggie's Mine and it's all yours. The map is inside the key."

"The key. Now." Another metallic key tumbled through the air to land by my heels. "Step out from behind the statue."

"A deal's a deal, Lilah, okay? You leave and I promise not to follow you, okay? You trust me?" When he appeared, the gunshot I gave to his right knee meant that I trusted him. Wow, was I really going all caring and sharing in my dotage? Well, until he loosened off a round at my retreating back, grazing my left thigh and ruining my new gold hotpants, I was. I turned and fired as an automatic defense mode. He slumped, face down, in a growing pool of blood on the artificial turf. Pan, unfazed, played on regardless amongst the green foliage. This sacrifice hadn't been in his honor.

Georgia and Smythe tottered in, their eyes glazed, leaning on each other for mutual support. At the sight of the body, Smythe let out a piercing scream and turned away, though he still remained propped up on Georgia's shoulder.

"Is he . . ." Georgia began.

"Yep, show's over. The fat lady sang, and she wasn't even topless."

"That'll never do for the Strip."

"What the hell are you two girls going on about?" He spoke with a tremor and stayed facing the door.

"With the soundproofing, no one heard the gunfire." I began to stroll around the glade.

"But we can't leave him here."

"That thought had crossed my mind, Georgia. By the way, Senator, if you're so squeamish, how come you were willing to shoot the late Chuckles?"

He looked sheepish. "Go on," Georgia prompted, "no point trying to keep it a secret any longer."

Shifty replaced sheepish. "I kinda owe my election victory to Jonn. And lately, well, he'd been asking me to do some, that is to cover up some, very, very bad things."

"What, worse than vote rigging, you mean?" He let that remark go without a rebuttal. "Yeah, now you mention it, I did wonder about your late surge at the ballot box. You strike me as an early surger." He swiveled to give me an annoyed look. Good, his grip was returning.

"I suggest that Jonn keeps watch on his mini-vault from the inside." Georgia and Smythe concurred with my proposal. They would smuggle the body out of the hotel in a laundry basket. But not before Georgia had agreed to star in my next venture, a brand new show, and the senator had consented to support my planning application for a stunning new venue on the Strip. Naturally, I'd be the artistic director. I could almost hear the ecstatic applause of the audience, see the stacks of cash that rolled in at the box office. Lilah Starr proudly presents . . .

Damn, don't henchmen announce their arrival by kicking down doors anymore? These two had probably disabled the electrics, in order to creep with fox-like stealth into the faux forest clearing. So Jonn had managed to get a signal out after all. I suspected that his pockets would yield a hi-tech signaling contraption.

"Put your hands on your head," one of them barked. As they were dressed from head to toe in black and brandished mean automatic rifles, we all sensibly complied. While one of them dropped down to one knee in the entrance, the other took a cautious route to Jonn past us startled deer. He glanced at the blood-soaked body then turned round to face us, peering intently at each of us in turn. In my opinion, he rather lingered over the exquisitely toned and shapely view of Lilah Starr that this posture afforded. All natural, unlike some.

"That's Jonn Brooks. My employer, you know?" He spoke softly, with a faint Irish brogue. We all mumbled nothing in particular. "Hold on, you're Senator Smythe, aren't you?" he added.

"That's right, son."

"You, the one with the gun. You mentioned something about a new show?"

"Er, yeah." Who says my mind freezes up in a crisis?

"I can sing. Very well too, though I say so myself. Name's Craig Anthony."

We all kinda mumbled hello.

"Over by the door, that's James Quinn Marshall. He's one killer dancer. You may have heard of him, he moonlights in several chorus lines. Goes by the name of El Gato."

We turned about for further mumbled greetings and a serious case of the nodding heads. El Gato? A bell of recognition jangled slightly.

"We're not sorry he's dead," James/El Gato declared, in an accent that could've hailed a New York taxi at half a mile. "In fact, if you hadn't killed him, our own plan was well on the way to fruition. And I don't believe that ours was the only plot."

"I'm Lilah," I announced. "This here is Georgia. Before we get roles in the new production assigned to each of you, Georgia and the senator could use a little help with disposing of the body." They mucked in like true backstage troopers.

On my way to Calico, I vowed to never force the showgirls in my revue to get implants. With pecs like theirs, Craig and El

Gato certainly didn't need them. Hmmm, I considered stretching Georgia's cheerleader idea to include a tribute to Jocks.

So, my gamble had paid off. In Vegas, the gamble always does, when you have the guts to make your own luck.

IGGY'S STUFF

J. MADISON DAVIS

A true connoisseur of weed—and Herbert "Exemel" Knapsdale certainly qualified in all respects—knows that a new batch takes some adjusting to. Normally he bought his weed from Chuckster, but Chuckster was lying low in Tijuana, so he bought an ounce of Iggy's stuff. Soil, light, acid rain, age, mold from a bad drying: all these things can tweak the chemistry of a natural substance. Your brain's, like, test-driving a used car. The brakes are a little spongy; the steering's tighter or looser.

That's why Exemel didn't immediately react to what he saw through the patio doors. Listing to the left because of the fifty-pound bucket of chlorine tablets and loops of vacuum hose on his right shoulder, he squinted behind his sunglasses. The wind was gusting, lifting dust off the desert. The light glinting from the pool slashed at his image in the glass.

But, yes, there, hovering above the reflection of the desert behind him, through himself, within his image, he could see the creamy white of a woman's buttocks, their perfection narrowing pear-like to her broad shoulders, black hair, and her arms stretched over her head. She was dancing for him. She was stripping off a tee shirt. Her hands stretched above her. And she held—No, she didn't hold. It was a rope, looped over an iron hook on the pine beam, wound around her wrists six or seven times. She was hanging there like a side of meat, swaying slightly.

Exemel blinked. He tore off his sunglasses leaned forward into the bright light, bending sideways to see better.

"Holy—!"

Exemel dropped the bucket and the hose and charged the door. He clawed at the latch, but it was locked on the inside. He put his face flat against the glass and was certain she was dead, but he banged on the glass. "Lady! Lady!"

She pushed the marble floor with her toes and twisted slightly. She only got halfway around before her foot slipped and she twisted back. He saw a blood-red rubber ball gagging her. There was frenzied terror in her eyes.

He clawed at the door again, then reached for the bucket of pool tablets. He swung it twice to build up power, then hurled it. The tempered glass exploded into a million rough diamonds. He skidded and slipped on the pebbly fragments as he rushed to her across the granite tiles.

"Are you okay, lady? Watch the glass. Who did this—?" He put his arms around her naked waist to hoist her up and get the rope off the hook. The scent of a strawberry oil came down to him from her bare breasts rubbing against his forehead, and the loop wasn't slipping over the edge. The woman's body tensed against him, and he looked up. She whined panicky noises out her nose against the gag. He turned and followed her line of sight.

A bulldog of a man had come out of the corridor wearing a leather mask, a spiked leather dog collar, and leather pants he hadn't finished lacing down the side. He was bare from the waist up, wooly gray hair covering him like the unruly fleece of a neglected ram.

He looked at the glass on the granite tiles, then at Exemel.

"What the—?"

"You don't move, dude," said Exemel. "Who are you anyway?"

"Why, you son of a bitch!" he growled and started for Exemel with his huge fists raised.

"Hey! Hey!" said Exemel, backing away. "Stop it! I mean it! Don't make me—! Stop—!"

Exemel didn't even see the first punch, as it whizzed by, just clipping his nose. He stumbled backwards down two steps into the pit area around the fireplace, landing hard next to a campaign trunk used as a coffee table. The woman was twitching and swinging, screaming against her gag, trying to get off the hook. "Shut up!" said the man. He grinned with crooked teeth, snatched up the poker.

Still on his back, Exemel grabbed a tall bronze statue of Shiva off the trunk and held it across his torso to block the blows. The man raised the poker and savored the pleasure of what he was about to do. "You need a lesson, you son of a bitch!"

Exemel, however, kicked out, somehow tangled his shoe in the loose laces of the man's leather pants, and with the down-swing of the poker, it caused him to lose his balance and fall on Exemel. His bleary eyes stared into Exemel's, and his whiskey breath beat on Exemel's lips.

Exemel turned his face away but was pinned under the man, who hardly moved, as if he'd got the wind knocked out of him. The puffs of his breath, hot and wet, came out at long intervals, and Exemel began to squirm, pushing at him, desperately trying to get out from under him.

The man howled then, raised himself on all fours, then rolled onto his back. Shiva hung on his chest. The arm of Shiva had gone into him up to the bronze god's shoulder.

"Man," whispered Exemel. "Man." He crawled toward him and gingerly reached out to pull the statuette out of him, but hesitated, not sure how to grip it or even if he should.

The woman flexed her body and whined a muffled plea against her gag. Exemel left the man where he lay, arms spread by the fireplace, and went to get a chair from the ultramodern dinette table. Pink and blue and black sex toys of many sizes and odd configurations, as well as three bottles of bright lubricants, had been lined up on the table with the cold precision of instruments in an operating room. He dragged a chair across the floors and stood on it to lift her off the hook. She gasped for air, bending at the waist, as he unfastened the strap holding the ball gag. She was Asian, either Filipino or Vietnamese, he thought. Beautiful.

"Are you okay?" He tried to avoid looking at her nakedness as he picked at the tight knots on her wrist.

"What the hell took you so long?" she said. "You were sup-posed to be here an hour ago."

He blinked. "Uhh, there was an accident out on 215, traffic was stopped both ways. A big truck—"

"I didn't want to go through his crap again. Ever." She turned toward the man by the fireplace, pulling her bound wrists from Exemel, and spit. "Sick bastard!"

"It's a good thing I came along when I did," said Exemel.

"Get something to cut these damned ropes!"

"Uh, yes, ma'am." He spun toward the kitchen. On the other side of the dinette counter he saw a chef's knife in a wooden holder. By the time he got back, the woman was standing over the man.

"He's still breathing," she said.

Exemel looked at him. "I don't think so."

"I tell you he's still breathing. Garbage doesn't die."

"Maybe we should call the cops or something."

"Oh, like *right*," she said drooping her jaw. "Why don't we just call the *Sun*? Or how about Fox News?" Her face twisted with anger. She lifted her foot and stomped the man's lower belly with her heel. The man's arm flew up, then dropped limp.

"Whoa!" said Exemel. "He moved."

"I told you!" the woman shrieked. She grabbed the arm of Shiva that wasn't embedded in the man. Her wrists still tied together, she rocked Shiva back and forth like a video game joystick, then tugged the statuette. It made a sucking sound. She raised it high and, with a grunt and an *aiee!*, threw it down. It bounced off the man's head and clanked against the hearth. Shiva's bloody arm was now bent in half.

"Whoa!" said Exemel, reaching to her, forgetting the twelve-inch knife was still in his hand.

"Watch it!" she barked. "You could cut me with that thing!"

"You shouldn'ta done that!"

"Will you *please* shut up and cut these damned ropes off!"

"Okay. I'm sorry." He concentrated and carefully sawed the thick rope in the space between her wrists. "You're gonna be okay now."

"Just don't cut me. How did you get in this business anyhow?"

Exemel shrugged. "I didn't have any other possibilities. I hate not having possibilities. I was a games programmer. The business tanked. You ever play Galaxy B72?"

She laughed. "That's what people used to ask me. How I got in the business."

Exemel had sawed through the first strand, but the rest of them did not fall away. She struggled with them, staring at the dead man. "Then I *thought* I got out of the business. The American dream! Right. Marriage is the same thing, only worse. Worse *and* boring. The time never runs out."

Finally the ropes fell away. She rubbed the raw, red bands on her skin.

Her nakedness had distracted him and what she had said slipped through his grasp like a handful of sand. "I'll get you something to cover up," he said.

"Never mind that," she said. "What are you going to do with him?"

"With him?"

"You're supposed to clean it up."

The pool?

"Well, what do you do? Bury him in the desert?"

What?

Her eyes narrowed and she took the chef's knife out of his hand. "Do you need to cut him up? I want to help. I know exactly where I'll start. You think he could still feel that? Maybe he's looking down on us from somewhere. I'll cut it off and leave it somewhere the coyotes could eat it." She laughed. "It might make them sick."

He grabbed her upper arm as she turned toward the body. "Whoa, Jesus, lady. We're not going to chop him up. Man! Look, I understand you don't like the dude. He hurt you. I'm with you on that, but he's dead now. What if, like, coyotes dig him up and somebody finds him? How are you gonna explain that? They can find teeny-weeny drops of blood and hair and DNA and, uh, stuff." He could see she was thinking. "You get me. You're just going to, like, tell the truth, see?"

She suddenly tossed her head and laughed. "You're right."

"You've got to tell it like it happened. Exactly."

"Then everything matches the clues. Ha! I love it."

"There'll be publicity, you can't help that. It'll be embarrassing, but people forget stuff and you'll get over it."

She smiled. "Sure. Perfect. You don't look like you know what you're doing, but you do."

"Uh, thanks." Exemel stuck his thumbs in his belt loops.

She rubbed her hands across her hard stomach, smearing two drops of blood towards her navel. She pursed her lips. "I ought to give you a bonus. I'd like that. How about it?"

This kind of thing had happened to Exemel before in the boredom of the upper class suburbs like Red Rock and Spanish Trail. Old man's out golfing, the wife is sunning by the pool getting ideas from reading *Cosmo* or some book about men in riding boots. But the woman was usually so old or so fat or so ugly that turning them down *wasn't easy*. They'd get offended after he left and call for a different pool boy. He said he was gay a couple of times, thought that would work, but one woman offered to cure him and another offered her husband, provided she could watch. He said he had an infection one time. She freaked and wouldn't let him clean the pool. So sometimes, if he could stand it, it was easier to go ahead with it until she kept calling up over tiny spots of algae and he couldn't stand it anymore and decided that cleaning that particular pool was more work than, well, really cleaning a pool. This time the woman looked a lot more like pleasure than work, but there was a guy who was, like, dead, ten feet in front of the huge leather sofa that she was lying back on.

"It would be, ahh, unprofessional," he said. He waited for her anger, but she merely wiggled her hips.

"Oooh, a professional!," she purred. "Now I know I would *really* enjoy it."

"We got a code. Well, it's not a code, but it's sort of a code."

She sat up and shrugged. "That's amazing! Even more studly."

"Don't, like, be offended or nothing."

"I'm not. I'm impressed. I didn't think you handled it well at all, being late and everything—"

"There was a big pile-up on 215—"

"—but the proof's right there. My life's about to get a whole lot better." She flipped a finger at the dead man. "Sick bastard!"

"You want me to dial the cops for you?"

"I can handle it," she said. "I'll just concentrate on those five million reasons to say the right thing. Cha-ching. It's my jackpot. The jackpot every tourist dreams about."

He nodded.

"I'll get your money," she said, walking along the far wall and avoiding the glass.

"But I haven't—" she was already in the corridor to the back "—done the pool yet."

Exemel stared at the dead man. He knew he was missing something. This was like one of those games where you have to travel through some cyberspace world gathering objects like keys and talismans and sometimes you know where the last door is, but you can't figure out what opens it. Of course you can always cheat and go to the chat board at Gamester.com and somebody will tell you, but only junior high kids who don't appreciate the tao of gaming would ask or answer a question like that, though he'd have to admit that once or twice when he was really stuck. . . .

He didn't notice her return until she said, "Catch!" A sealed envelope hit his chest and before he could disengage his thumbs from his belt loop, it had fallen to the floor. He picked it up. It was almost an inch thick. Most people wrote a check, he thought. What was this? All ones?

"You want to count it?" she asked.

"Uh, if you're trusting me, I'm trusting you. That's what I say." With a roll of his head, he smiled and stuffed the envelope in his back pocket. "I'd better get to work."

"On what?"

"The pool," he said.

"Very funny," she said. "You get out of here, a long way out of here. I don't know you and you don't know me. Have a good life. I've got things to do. You'll read it in the papers. The guy who broke in was black, about six feet, with a shaved head, a Mexican accent, and an earring."

He squinted, still unable to decipher the lock on that last door, but nodded and picked up the bucket of chlorine tablets that still lay in the lake of broken glass. The handle was hot from lying in the open doorway and seemed a lot heavier than usual. The vacuum hose had unrolled all over the patio. As he wound it, he barely noticed the telephone ringing inside.

"Marty?" she said. "It's just great! Just perfect! I'm going to call the cops and—"

Exemel straightened up and squinted into the house. Just great? Just perfect?

"You had to slip out to a pay phone? Why? No records, I understand, but—?" Suddenly she looked up at Exemel. "What?" she said. "That can't be. He's right here. Talk to him yourself. He's about six foot two." She listened carefully. "No," she said slowly. "This guy could fall down a drinking straw." Her eyes widened. She walked toward Exemel. "Marty sent you, right?"

"Marty? No, it was Lester. Marty don't work there no more."

She shuddered her head trying to clear it. "Where? Where does Marty work—? Used to work?"

"Desert City Pool Services. My real name's Herbert, but everybody calls me Exemel. Like in XML, you know, 'Extensible Mark-up Language.' It was kind of a joke."

Her mouth fell open and she did not move. The phone was squawking in her hand. "Shut up, Marty," she finally said. "Just a minute, damn it!" She blinked, thought, then smiled like a mother holding a newborn. "Uh, umm, Hexa-bel, or whatever, could you come back inside for a minute?"

"Exemel. But really, ma'am, I'm flattered and all, but the code, you know . . . I got three more pools this afternoon and we don't get overtime."

"Just—" she said, barely controlling herself, "just come in for a minute. Please. My nerves are shot. Just a few seconds."

Exemel crunched in across the glass. "You don't look so good. I mean, you look *good,* but, you know, you don't look good. I can wait for the cops with you. I got no problem with that." He glanced back over his shoulder. "Maybe a toke or two would help. I'll just step out to the truck. It's new stuff so it shouldn't smell too much like chlorine yet."

"Just—damnit—stay there. Don't move. I—I want to get a robe. Promise?"

"Sure."

Exemel gazed at the dead man sprawled in front of the fireplace. With the leather pants and mask, his skin pale and unreal, he looked like a really big action figure. An X-Man or something. Deathmaster. Sado-Man. Sick Bastard Dude.

He heard the padding of the woman's feet on the granite floor. She was still naked, but she was holding an enormous nickel-plated pistol in front of her.

"Whoa," said Exemel.

She stiffened her arms. The heavy gun wobbled in front of her. "Look, I'm really grateful for all you've done, but Marty knows about things like this and he says you've got to die."

"Me?"

"You heard Marty's name. It's tough luck for you. What can I tell you? I mean, I didn't know you weren't the guy."

"But I *am* the pool guy. Exemel Knapsdale. That's me!"

"Not for the damned pool! The guy who was supposed to off Ted. He was killed on 215. All burned up. He was in Marty's car."

"This is the Marty who used to work with me?"

"No! The guy with the car! Will you pay attention?! Marty owns the Pleasure Garden! I used to work there. He hooked me up with Ted. I pretended to be just off the boat and the sick bastard married me. Marty said he'd arrange it. He knows people."

"Okay," said Exemel. "Okay. But what's this got to do with the pool?"

She ground her teeth in frustration and closed her eyes. "Never mind! It wasn't a black guy. You broke in, looking for drugs or something. Ted tried to defend me. I ran for the gun. You killed Ted. I killed you." She licked her lips. "That will work. Yeah."

"Well, I did kill that dude," said Exemel. "That dude is Ted, right? It was an accident, but it's still, like, killing. So it's like karma coming back on me or something. I started work on a game called Karma once, but they pulled the plug on it because like Hindus or somebody might get the wrong impression—"

"Will you shut up?!" The gun wobbled, but she gritted her teeth and squeezed. Nothing happened. She looked at the gun in astonishment and tried again. Nothing happened. "What the—?"

"Some joke," said Exemel, taking one step toward her. "That wasn't funny! You really had me going there!"

The woman's face twisted in fury. It seemed to morph and massage itself, and Exemel hesitated at the sight, waiting for her to turn into an American Werewolf or just explode like in *Scanners*. Before he could react, she snatched the chef's knife off the dinette table, raised it, and charged him.

This was no joke, dude. His sneaker went out from under him as the glass pellets skidded. He stumbled over the patio door sill and dropped to one knee. He covered his face with his hands and braced to feel the knife in his back. He stared into the darkness of his hands to see what Death or God or Shiva or whatever it was really looked like.

But there was only the pain in his knee and a strange noise: *whee! whee!*, like the sound of a tiny, distant bird. He spread his fingers and saw the woman sitting in the glass pellets. She had slipped on them as well. The noise was her breathing, growing weaker and weaker. The knife was buried deep under her rib cage.

"Lady!" said Exemel. "I'll get a doctor."

Her eyes rolled up to look at him. Her mouth gaped. She seemed to want to say something to him, and shook her head. "The jackpot," she said and her pupils rolled up like cherries on a slot machine. She fell back white-eyed.

"Lady?" he asked. "Lady?" He looked at her and wondered what she would have looked like with clothes on. He'd never see that now. She was seriously dead. He crossed the room. Ted was even deader than he'd been a while ago. He thought about the envelope of money in his back pocket, and about Marty, and about the dude who was burned up on 215 and blocked the traffic going both ways. If he could write a will for Ted, he'd be rich! Dude, would that be stupid. Greed is *not* good, no matter what the evangelists say. He thought about DNA, and blood spatter stuff, and he was glad he hadn't taken her up on the offer, which he'd really wanted to, but not with the dead guy watching.

He concentrated. It wasn't easy because he wasn't in, like, that stoned way that makes you understand everything real clear. After thinking for what seemed a very long time, wandering through several mental detours about whether Shiva could materialize and be a witness, he picked up the woman's phone.

"Man," he told the woman who answered, "something's happened at the house down here! Dude, it's like Sharon Tate or something!"

A short while later, under the pergola by the pool house, the detective lifted his stetson and set it on the chaise lounge next to him. "Okay, Mr. Knapsdale—"

"My friends call me Exemel." He had brought a bucket of granular chlorine from the truck and was using it as a stool.

"I'm not your friend, Mr. Knapsdale."

"I thought—" He was going to say that the police were supposed to be our friends, at least that's what they taught him in elementary school. "You can call me Exemel, anyway. If you like. My real name is Herbert."

"So you're sure she said 'Marty'?"

"I think so. Sir."

"She didn't say a last name?"

Exemel narrowed his eyes and thought.

"Well?"

"No. Just 'Marty.' " He nodded.

"And you don't know who this Marty is?"

"There used to be a Marty who was my boss, but he moved to the coast a year ago."

"And do you know *his* last name?"

Again, Exemel narrowed his eyes and thought. "No. Just 'Marty.' "

The detective scribbled on his note pad.

"You think Marty knew these people?"

Exemel shrugged. "If we did their pool back then."

"They moved in here seven months ago."

"Marty was already gone. The good life in L.A., you know. I used to live in the Silicon, you know. Ever play Galaxy B72?"

The detective adjusted his underwear at the crotch and stood. Another detective, much younger, approached. "Mr. Knapsdale, when you went inside, what did you touch?"

Exemel thought. "I don't know, man. I was, like, freaked out. I came around the corner with this bucket of chlorine—" he touched the container he sat on "—and the hose and saw the glass was smashed in and then I saw her on the floor and I ran inside and I saw the dead dude and, I don't know, I was checking her out and him out and—"

"Yeah, yeah, so you said. Did you move anything? It's all pretty much as you found it?"

"I might have moved something when I was checking them out, but I didn't take nothing."

The detective nodded. He spoke to his older partner. "It's her, all right."

"I knew it was her," said the older man. "I busted her and Marty Grego bailed her. I figure he rolled her john, too, but the vic wouldn't come back from Pennsylvania to testify. I made sure his wife found out about it, though."

"You think Grego did this?"

"He or one of his goons."

"The killer comes around back, maybe by the desert. There are some four-wheeler tracks out there, but the wind has been blowing. He grabs a bucket of chlorine tablets by the filter over there and smashes the patio door, surprising the couple, who are in the bedroom cleaning up after their afternoon recreation: untying, taking off the perv outfits. Out comes Ted Bigelow. They struggle, the killer smashes him in the head, then stabs him with something."

"I think he used the statue for that, too."

"That's pretty weird," said the younger detective. "The wound could be a bullet hole or some kind of knife."

"The lab will figure it out. Either way, then out comes the missus with the gun."

"She wasn't able to fire it. It was loaded and the safety was off, but she didn't jack a bullet into the chamber. Goon knocks it away, stabs her with her own knife. Or maybe he had a gun and forced her to put hers down."

The older detective pulled at his lip. "Marty Grego would normally use Paul Champion, but he was killed in a car accident today."

"There was an untraceable .22 in the car and the car was Grego's, but it was coming this way."

"Maybe Champion left here, went somewhere south, then turned back north. Make sure about the time of death. Of course, I'd rather pin it on Grego. A dead Champion is a little less likely to squeal on Grego than a live one, but only a little less."

The younger detective suddenly cocked his head. They had forgotten about Exemel. The older detective turned to him. "You got big ears, Knapsdale? You been listening?"

"Huh?" said Exemel.

"You know a man named Marty Grego?"

Exemel narrowed his eyebrows. "I don't think so. He the guy who moved to the coast?"

The detective shook his head. "Look, Knapsdale, you don't breathe a word about what you've seen here. Anything about this crime scene gets out and you're looking at obstruction of justice. You got me?"

"Yes, sir."

"I'll bet if we had a reason to get even with you, we wouldn't have any trouble finding an illegal substance or two," said the younger detective.

"You'll get no trouble from me, sir." Exemel stood up and hefted the bucket of chlorine. "If you need me for anything, you can just call Desert—"

"Goodbye, Mr. Knapsdale," said the detective, picking up his stetson.

Exemel was relieved the questioning had ended. He didn't know how long it might take the money in the envelope, buried in the granular chlorine, to get all burned up or bleached out. He felt like some *fine* weed had kicked in. Dude! He now had possibilities. Sweet possibilities! Maybe start up his own game company, and finish Karma. Maybe he could go to India and work the deal there. It would take some thinking how he could spend that ten thou, but you can't spend it if it's all eaten up or bleached white. He was also thinking he wouldn't buy any more of Iggy's stuff. Back to Chuckster and the tried and true. Iggy's stuff was way too weird.

"Loser," whispered the younger detective.

"To the problem at hand," said the older. "Let's find out how Grego spent his day."

"He'd better have an explanation for every minute," said the younger.

"Every minute," repeated the older. "If Marty Grego even stepped out for a phone call—"

"Toast," said the younger.

A Temporary Crown

Sue Pike

Dolores shuffled into the Solarium looking for the paper cups the nurses used to distribute the meds. It was a hobby of hers, collecting the tiny, fluted cups. She liked to put treasures in them and line them up on the windowsill of her hospital room.

Leonard was slouched on the sofa watching TV and scratching his head. Leonard was always scratching his head. It was sort of a hobby of his, Dolores thought. She spotted four abandoned cups on the card table, but just as she was gathering them up her attention was caught by an image on the TV. She sucked in her breath as Bryce and a young woman drove onto the screen riding a huge black motorcycle, the pink sand of the Nevada desert glowing behind them in the evening sun. They skidded to a stop, pulled off their helmets and waved at the camera. The woman shook her head, catching Bryce full across the face with a sheet of long blond hair. Bryce brushed the hair away, threw his arm around the blond girl's shoulder and laughed. Then Leonard started laughing and Dolores had to flap her hands to shush him so she could hear the commentary.

"Bryce Campion, best known for his role in *Worlds Apart*, and Marie-France Lapin, of Jazz Hot, the all-girl band from Paris that's been making waves all over the country, announced their upcoming nuptials today in Las Vegas. Bryce is currently headlining a brand new show at the Three Crowns. . . ."

Her knees wobbled and she dropped into a chair, sending the paper cups skittering to the floor. That made Leonard laugh some more, but when she started to shush him again she caught herself. His eyes had that glittery look that meant something crazy was going on in his head and she'd better watch out.

She leaned closer to the screen. "The wedding will take place next week in the Little White Wedding Chapel, a Las Vegas landmark."

Dolores began to hum two notes over and over. It was something she did when she could feel her heart beating too fast. She was going to have to decide what to do but she couldn't think in here with the TV and Leonard scratching his head and laughing too loud in all the wrong places. She grunted as she leaned over and picked up the cups from the floor and then she pulled herself to her feet and shuffled away as fast as her swollen legs would carry her.

Back in her room, she tore a sheet from the steno pad Dr. Bradford gave her at their first session. She was supposed to be using it for a journal, writing about all the times she felt angry and all the times she felt sad. But the pages were mostly empty and every time he asked her about it she just hummed a bit and stared at the floor while he gripped the desk so hard his fingers went white.

She reached between the mattress and the box spring and fished out a silver pen she'd found on Dr. Bradford's desk one day when he was looking at something in her file. After scribbling a few words on the paper, she reached into the crevice under the radiator where she'd hidden the blank stamped envelope she'd found a few weeks ago at the nursing station when the matron had gone to the bathroom. She addressed it to Bryce Campion, Three Crowns Hotel, Las Vegas, Nevada, and then tucked it into the zippered compartment of her bag. They were releasing her to the group home tomorrow and she'd be able to slip out and mail it once the social worker was through talking to her. She sat on the edge of the bed for a minute or two and then reached behind the radiator again to check the money hidden in there. She liked to think of it as her nest egg. That's what her grandmother had called the money in the cookie tin she kept high up on the shelf over the icebox. Dolores had stood on a chair and reached for the tin one day when she thought her grandmother was lying down in the next room. It slipped out of her fingers, and the coins had clattered to the floor. Her grandmother had shot into the room and yanked the chair right out from under Dolores making her crack her head on the table as she fell. The social worker had asked how she'd hurt herself, but she never said. Not that time. Not ever.

———

Dolores stepped out of the cool of the Greyhound Bus Terminal onto South Main and caught her breath. The noise and heat and brilliant sunshine jumbled together inside her head and made it hard to think clearly. She shuffled a few blocks before she dropped her pack onto the sidewalk and leaned against the wall of an office building. She put both hands behind her and pushed hard against the wall, feeling the stucco bite into her fingers, trying to read the bumps as if they were Braille. She took a deep breath and tried to think about the mantra Dr. Bradford had taught her, but sounds and images were jittering around in her mind so fast she couldn't remember how it began. After a while she rummaged in her bag for a jam jar of water and with a few sips she felt strong enough to push away from the wall and pick up her pack again. She stood for a moment and tried to get her bearings. In her letter she'd described the donut shop where he should meet her. It was one she'd discovered last year when she'd come here to be with him. But she didn't want to think about that time and had to hum very loud to keep it out of her head only the trouble with that was it kept the location of the donut shop out of her head as well. But it was on the Strip, that much she could remember, so she set off again humming even louder to take her mind off her heartbeat and her sore ankles.

When she'd gone to the group home the social worker had watched her unpack her bag and fold things into the dresser drawer. Dolores smiled, remembering how easy it had been to push everything back in the bag and drop it from the window the next day. When she walked out the front door she'd called to Stella, who was in the kitchen making lunch, and told her she was just going for a walk and then she'd gone around back, picked up her pack and walked to the bus terminal. It took most of her nest egg to buy the one-way ticket.

Dolores walked on, stumbling a bit every once in a while, holding onto the walls of buildings when she was afraid she might fall. She thought about Dr. Bradford and how he made everything he said sound like he was talking to a child. "Doris," he'd said, always calling her Doris even though she'd corrected him so many times. "Doris, sometimes people think they have a connection to people they've never met. Especially celebrities. Some even believe they're married to well-known men like Bryce Campion." He'd looked sad when he said it, like it was one of the big tragedies of the world. "You understand you're not married to him, don't you?" He'd twisted his pencil between his lips, making it squeak and then he'd pulled it out with a wet popping sound and leaned forward, trying to catch her eye. "You can get rid of this obsession, Doris. You have the power to make yourself better." She'd had to hum hard into her pillow that night, remembering the little frown between his eyebrows that made an upside-down V like the pitched roof on her grandmother's hen house. But she didn't really blame Dr. Bradford. He didn't know any better. He hadn't seen the look Bryce had given her that night in the movie theatre. He hadn't been there the night Bryce had asked her to marry him. She could still remember it as clear as day. She was sitting in the second row and he was looking down at her from the shiny, pebbly screen. There was a hurt look on his face, as though afraid she'd refuse. "Dolores," he'd said, "Marry me, Dolores. Please." She'd said yes right there, out loud. Some people in the audience laughed, but she didn't care. He'd said the words she'd been waiting to hear all her adult life. After that she'd watched every movie he ever made. And she'd gone to the library and looked through all the movie and entertainment magazines in hopes of finding a photo of him. When they stopped making musical films he'd taken a job in Las Vegas, singing in one of the smaller hotels. And she'd gone along last year to be with him. But it hurt to think about that right now.

She'd managed to make her way to the area known as the Strip with its confusing jumble of moving lights and jangly music that hurt her head. The pack was scraping against her so she put it down on the sidewalk and slumped onto it, splaying out her legs.

"Hey, watch it." A young girl veered around her, her roller blades screeching on the sidewalk just inches from Dolores's worn plastic thongs. The girl flipped her hair and a barrette dropped to the sidewalk.

"Watch it yourself," she shouted back, scooping up the barrette and running her fingers along its surface. It was just the right size to fit into one of the fluted paper cups she had stacked in her bag. She shoved it into a side pocket and struggled to her feet again. She had to find the donut shop fast in case Bryce was waiting for her. She stared along the Strip, humming to keep her heart from pounding. It was packed with people looking in shops and restaurants, but they weren't looking at her so that was okay. She walked on, stumbling a bit with fatigue and confusion and then she spotted it, just a little way down a little side street, nestled between an adult video store and a newspaper shop.

It was wonderfully cool inside. She dropped her bag into a booth and peeled a couple of dollars from what was left of the nest egg in her pocket. A young man with acne and a tattoo of an alligator on his left arm took her order for three chocolate glazed and a large coffee and then, balancing her meal in both hands, she squeezed between the moulded chair and table and began the serious business of eating. Dr. Bradford would have a fit if he saw her. He'd handed her some diet sheets at one of their last sessions and made her promise to read them. Easy for him to eat all those fruits and vegetables, half of which she'd never even heard of. He didn't have to live on the little bit of money she got from welfare.

"Mind if I share your table?" A young woman with black hair swept back into a wide red ribbon made Dolores jump. She looked around the restaurant but almost all the other tables were empty.

She shrugged and chocolate crumbs cascaded to the white plastic table.

"Man," the woman giggled. "Is it ever hot today." She tossed a couple of parcels onto the bench beside Dolores's pack and threw her cotton jacket on top.

"Looks like you could use another coffee." The woman was still standing, the smell of perfume wafting about her, "can I get you anything else?"

Dolores shrugged again without looking up and the woman strode away leaving her jacket and parcels behind. Dolores sneaked a peek at the top one. Neiman Marcus, it said. Well, well. All right for some, she thought, resentment pinching her lips together.

"Here you go. I picked up a couple more donuts as well." She giggled again. "I'm Jennifer, by the way. What's your name?"

Dolores pulled the new bag of chocolate glazed toward her and counted four. They would have cost a fortune, she thought toting up the total in her head. "Dolores."

"Well, *bon appetit*, Dolores!" Jennifer smiled brightly while she dusted the bench and perched gingerly on the edge. She stacked a pile of napkins onto the table and placed a carrot raisin muffin in the exact center. She turned the napkin pile around a couple of times before breaking off a tiny portion from the top and popping it into her mouth. A couple of miniscule crumbs dropped onto the table. "Mm mm," she said, and giggled again while she touched the corners of her mouth with the longest, pinkest, nails Dolores had ever seen. She pushed her own hands with their gnawed nails into her lap while she examined the woman across from her. Jennifer had one of those smiles that made her nose scrunch up, the kind the girls in high school used to try on in front of the restroom mirror until they caught her watching and made her leave. It was definitely the kind of smile for girls who giggled a lot.

"So," Jennifer studied her largely undamaged muffin and then looked up. "Where are you from?"

Dolores hesitated wondering if this was a trap. "Why? What makes you think I'm not from here?"

"Oh I don't know. Nobody you meet around here is actually from Las Vegas. Most people are tourists." Jennifer leaned toward her conspiratorially. "I'll bet you flew here, right?"

Oh sure. On her budget. "Huh uh. Bus from Chicago."

Jennifer flapped her hand with its pink nails in front of her mouth indicating it was full, but the muffin sitting on the tidy pile of napkins appeared almost whole. "Chicago?" she said after she swallowed. "I love Chicago!"

"Um . . ." Dolores looked into the donut bag and selected another chocolate glazed. She didn't want to talk about Chicago. It made her think of Dr. Bradford and the little roof-shaped frown.

"What did your mother call you, Doris?" he'd asked at their last session.

"I told you, I don't have a mother."

"Grandmother, then. What did she call you?"

"You know," she'd mumbled. She wished she'd never told him about the Doris Doolittle rhyme.

"Huh?" she looked up at Jennifer, realizing she'd missed a question.

"I asked if you had a place to stay."

Dolores shrugged.

"I could help you find a nice motel room and give you a lift, if you'd like."

Dolores scanned the seats in the donut shop again. "No, thanks. I'm meeting someone."

"Oh!" Jennifer beamed at her. "A boyfriend, I'll bet." She looked around herself at the mostly empty tables. "Is it a boyfriend, Doris?"

"My name's Dolores." The familiar anger bubbled up, pricking her eyes with tears.

"Oops. Sorry." Jennifer grinned. "I'll bet he's gorgeous. Is he gorgeous?"

Dolores shrugged. "He's not all that young any more."

"A sophisticated older man. They're the best kind. I'll bet he's nice. Is he nice?"

Dolores thought about the last time she saw him. She remembered the restraining orders and the policeman who'd yanked her arms behind her back and bent her over the hood of the squad car. "I dunno. Not nice exactly."

"Men, huh?" Her frown looked a lot like Dr. Bradford's. "Well, he should be here to meet you. That's for sure." She rummaged in her purse and produced a cell phone. "Why don't we call him and tell him to get on over here." The long pink nails hovered over the keypad like butterflies waiting to land. "What's the number?"

"I . . . I don't know the number. It's probably unlisted." Dolores could feel her breathing getting fast again. She wanted to hum but thought she'd better not. "Anyway, he's probably just busy." She wanted to tell Jennifer about Bryce's act at the Three Crowns and that he couldn't just drop everything at a moment's notice but she was afraid, afraid she'd get that look on her face like Dr. Bradford's. She was afraid Jennifer would talk about obsessions and stalking and all those things people said when they didn't understand about Bryce and her.

But Jennifer wasn't even looking at her. She seemed to be looking at something inside her own head and her eyes had gone all glittery, like Leonard's did when he had his scary thoughts. "Men need to be taken down a peg, don't you agree? Think they can walk all over us." Her laugh was a little bit like Leonard's too. "My own so-called boyfriend tells me the other day he's going to marry someone else. Didn't want me to see it first on TV, can you believe it?" The pink fingernails were drumming the table so hard the tip of the middle one snapped off, but Jennifer didn't seem to notice. "I've been his secretary, his lover, even his laundress." She made a disgusted snort. "I've answered thousands of letters from his retarded fans. And now he tells me he's knocked up some blond bimbo and he's going to marry her. Can you believe it?"

"Um . . ." Dolores wanted to tell her about the fingernail but Jennifer suddenly sniffed and then giggled again. "Well enough about me. I'm just a teensy bit angry." She crumbled a corner off her muffin, popped it into her mouth and bit down hard on it. Suddenly her eyes widened and she grabbed her jaw. "Oh shit." She fished around inside her mouth with the thumb and forefinger of her left hand, withdrawing something white.

Dolores was alarmed. It looked like a tooth. She'd had enough teeth yanked out of her head to know how painful it was, but when she looked at Jennifer's face the woman seemed more furious than wounded. She sucked the thing once and then dropped it into the ashtray and got to her feet. Dolores stared at it.

"Is that your tooth?"

"That piece of shit is a temporary crown. I'm not getting the real thing installed until tomorrow." She rolled her tongue around inside her mouth and then turned away. "I'm going to the washroom to rinse out my mouth."

Dolores stared at the thing, tipping it this way and that in the ashtray, amazed at the contours, trying to imagine where it had come from and if this one was temporary what the real crown would look like.

Jennifer reappeared and gathered up her parcels from the bench. The muffin lay abandoned on the table. "Okay. I think we need to take you to your boyfriend's place."

"Um. That's okay. I'll wait here a while."

"He's never going to come." The giggle and the scrunched-up smile had vanished but the eyes were still glittering. "You need to have it out with him, Doris. Once and for all." She grabbed her parcels and the duffle bag and headed for the door. Dolores sat for a moment, humming softly and when she looked over and saw the woman and her bag disappearing out the door she scooped the temporary crown into a napkin and shoved it in her pants pocket. The tip of the pink nail was harder to find. It had slipped under the pile of napkins holding the scarcely touched muffin. Dolores gathered the whole thing together and put it in the pocket of her shirt.

She pushed through to the heat and confusion of the street and found Jennifer standing beside a black convertible, holding the passenger door open. Dolores sank with difficulty into the seat and then had to pull her swollen legs in after her.

She peered at the console once they were moving. "What is this thing?"

"You're kidding, right?" Jennifer frowned at her. "You've never seen a Jaguar before?"

"Um . . ." Dolores found she could hum under her breath and the sound of the motor masked it.

Within minutes they were pulling up to the shipping entrance to Three Crowns. The woman reached across Dolores's stomach and pushed the passenger door open. "Out you get. I'll go and park this thing and then I'll get the key for you from the front desk." She checked over her shoulder watching for an opportunity to pull out, but then she appeared to change her mind and reached across again, this time to open the glove compartment. Dolores was stunned. Inside was the biggest pile of quarters she'd ever seen. Jennifer scooped up two handfuls and thrust them into her lap.

"You can play the slot machines while you wait." She gave Dolores a little shove. "Off you go. But stay in the lobby, okay? That way I can find you again."

Dolores stumbled out of the car, shoving coins into her pant's pockets. Several quarters dropped to the sidewalk and she had to stoop down to retrieve them. When she looked up again the car and the woman and all Dolores's possessions had disappeared.

She stood still for a full minute, trying to make sense of what had happened, feeling the pockets of her yellow knit pants stretch under the weight of the coins. She wanted to sag against the wall and close her eyes but she hadn't liked that glittery look in Jennifer's eyes so she pulled herself together and shuffled around to the front entrance of the hotel.

She gasped. A big poster advertising Bryce's show took up most of the front of the building. He seemed to be looking right into her eyes and she ran her fingers through her hair trying to tidy it. She didn't want him to see her looking like she'd just stepped off the bus. There were little trees in cement boxes lining the drive and she stood behind one for a moment watching the doorman in his red and black uniform. A limousine pulled up to the curved driveway and the man tugged at his tunic and ran over to open the driver's door. Dolores could hardly believe it. Jonathan Finn from *Las Vegas Nights* stepped from the car and handed the doorman the keys. He took the stairs to the entrance two at a time and just before he pushed through he turned and smiled at Dolores. She thought she saw his lips move, saying, "I love you, Dolores." She had to hang onto one of the little trees for a minute and take a deep breath. What would Leonard say about this? It was his favorite TV show. She waited another minute until the doorman got into the limousine and began to drive it off, and then she sidled through the revolving doors and into the lobby of the Three Crowns. Jonathan Finn was nowhere in sight, but she knew what she'd seen. He loved her. She hummed to herself, hugging this new knowledge to her heart.

She wanted to stop and stare at the colors in the carpet and the impossibly soft sofas and chairs but she knew from last year that if the management noticed her they'd ask her to leave. She spotted banks and banks of slot machines lining the walls and found an unoccupied one tucked away behind a huge potted plant. She watched a man put his quarters into the machine next to hers and listened to the jangly sounds. She was astounded. They sounded a lot like the notes she hummed when she tried to get calm.

Dolores had no idea how long she'd been standing there sometimes shoving quarters into the machine and sometimes staring at the flashing lights. Once she was surprised by a shower of coins but was afraid of the noise the machine made when she won, fearing people would be drawn to it and ask her what she thought she was doing in such a fancy place. Hunger pangs and worry about Jennifer and her duffle bag made her eat the muffin in her pocket and now she was hungry again.

Suddenly Jennifer was there, standing beside her, just as she had been in the donut shop. Only this time she was wearing a scarf, dark glasses and black leather gloves and she was holding out a plastic card with a strip on one side.

"Here's the key to your boyfriend's suite." She pushed her sunglasses onto her head for a moment and her eyes glittering even more than Leonard's when he was about to do something crazy. "I think you'd better get right up there. Tell him how you feel about things."

Dolores took the card and ran her finger over the surface. It wouldn't fit in the little paper cups but she'd keep it anyway. "My bag . . . ?"

"It's still in the car. I'll go and get it while you're going to the room."

"Where do I go?" Dolores was confused about so many things; all she really wanted to do was lean against the wall and close her eyes.

"He's on the top floor where the big suites are. The elevators are over here." She put the sunglasses on and took Dolores's elbow, pushing her across the thick carpet, past the gorgeous sofas and into a marble foyer with elevators along both walls. "It's straight ahead when you get out of the elevator." She seemed to remember something. "You know how to use this key?"

Dolores stared at the floor.

"Okay, you shove it into the slot above the handle with the strip away from you. Bring it out again and when the little light turns green, you can open the door."

"But my bag? Where'd you say my bag was?"

"I'll be waiting right here with your bag." Jennifer was talking very softly now, almost whispering. "When you've told him . . . well, whatever you want to tell him, come back here and I'll give you your bag." She pushed something with her gloved finger and the elevator door slid open.

Dolores hesitated but Jennifer pushed her in and reached behind her to push a button inside the elevator.

When the elevator stopped, Dolores peered out, making sure there was no one in the hall. She held the card that Jennifer had called a key but the door across from the elevator was already ajar. She pushed it farther open and stuck her head in, humming the two notes as loud as she could. When no one stopped her she stepped into a light green vestibule with a huge painting of cactus and desert sand on the right wall. She hesitated and then called out softly, "Bryce?" She wished she'd rehearsed what she'd say to him but there was no answer. She walked into a living room, with another of the scrumptious sofas on a pale beige carpet. Two glasses half full of some kind of liquid and melting ice cubes sat on the coffee table. She glanced at the kitchen but it was empty. There was another half-open door leading off the living room. She walked over and pushed it fully open.

At first she thought they were sleeping, Bryce on his back, his naked torso partly covered by a sheet and the girl with her long blond hair spread out on the pillowcase. But then she saw the blood and the hole in Bryce's forehead where no one should have a hole. And when she leaned over to get a better look, she noticed the girl's hair was covering a section of her cheek that was red and pulpy and leaking blood.

A gun lay on the counter. She thought for a second about picking it up, but it was much too big for her treasure collection so she left it where it was. She felt sad about Bryce and about the pretty girl too. But she knew in her heart that what Dr. Bradford had said was true. She and Bryce weren't really engaged. It was just a kind of dream of hers.

She heard a siren and then another and when she looked out the window she saw several police cars pulling up to the hotel's entrance. The doorman was tugging on his tunic and flapping his arms around.

Dolores decided to take the stairs down. She could stop at each floor and see if there was any sign of Jonathan Finn. He might be wondering where she'd got to and she didn't like to keep him waiting.

Before she left she looked again at the couple on the bed. She'd like to leave a gift for them, some sort of memorial like people left her when her grandmother died, but all of her treasures were in Jennifer's car. Then she remembered the temporary crown in its little bed of napkins in her shirt pocket. She pulled it out and dropped it near Bryce's hand. She noticed the little pink fingernail was caught in the folds, but it looked so pretty against the white sheet she decided to leave that as well.

THE GAMBLING MASTER OF SHANGHAI

JOAN RICHTER

The three of us were hanging out in the kitchen that Saturday afternoon, when we heard the mail truck pull up at the end of our driveway. I'd come back from basketball practice a half-hour ago and was having a Coke. My mother was at the counter slicing vegetables for a stir-fry for supper that night. Dad was at the table with the newspaper spread out in front of him. "I'll go," he said.

He was gone a while. Mom and I figured he'd probably run into the man next door, who liked to talk baseball, but as soon as Dad came back inside, I could tell something was up. His face had that tight look it gets when things aren't quite right.

My mother heard him come in and stopped her chopping and turned around.

"It's a letter from Shanghai," he said, nodding at the light blue envelope in his hand. We could see he had opened it.

Mom stared at him. "From Shanghai? We don't know anyone there."

Both my parents had been born in China, but came to the states when they were little kids. They met one another in their last year at Northwestern and were married a couple of years after that. I was born in Chicago.

"It's from Uncle Ho," my father said.

My mother put down her knife and wiped her hands on a kitchen towel. "I thought Uncle Ho died in the Cultural Revolution."

My father nodded. "That's what I thought. That's what everyone thought."

By everyone, my father meant our relatives, who were scattered all over the U.S. In typical Chinese fashion we got together every few years for big reunions. The elders liked to exchange memories and tell Uncle Ho stories, which always led to talk of gambling. It seems, at a very early age, Uncle Ho had been a Gambling Master, which in Chinese lingo makes Michael Jordan a Basketball Master.

Everyone liked telling Uncle Ho stories. The relatives tried topping one another with a new piece to an old story, or an entirely new one. And since they all thought Uncle Ho was dead, it didn't matter if the truth got bent a bit.

"Uncle Ho is coming here," my father said.

My mother frowned. "What do you mean he's coming here?"

"I mean here. Las Vegas."

My mother had the next toss, but her sudden stony silence said she was deferring to my father.

The way he cleared his throat told me she wasn't going to like what he had to say.

"He's coming to Vegas on one of those casino-sponsored deals there's been so much talk about."

"You mean Uncle Ho is one of those 'whales'?"

My mother sent me a look that would freeze Salt Lake.

I should have known better, but it just popped out. I dipped my head in apology and tried to look contrite. I did a retake on the "whales" story.

It hit the news a couple of months ago. American casino interests had decided to take advantage of the big economic boom in China and the Chinese centuries-old love of gambling. They were sending agents over there to scout for rich guys who liked high-stakes games. They called them whales. Once a whale was sighted, the only thing he had to do was offer some proof of his wealth, then the agents took care of the rest. They helped with visas, air travel, and hotels. It was only at the gaming tables in Vegas that the high rollers were on their own. And guess what? The casinos were counting on them losing big.

The media loved the story and ran all over the place with it. Reporters speculated about where the whales' money came from, with edgy suggestions that it was hot, embezzled, or siphoned off from companies and corrupt government agencies. Another flyer was that the money came from smuggling— drugs, arms, trafficking in women.

A few reporters got to the practical question of how these rich guys managed to get their money out of China, since the country had rigid restrictions on currency going offshore. The conclusion was that a lot of people were getting paid to look the other way.

"The whole thing is going to start all over again," my mother said.

She was a little off the point, but I knew what she meant. So did my father. He nodded.

Three years ago the relatives had come to Vegas. It was the off-season, rates were good, and we took over one of the small hotels on the outskirts of town. There was a swimming pool for the kids and a room large enough to have a real Chinese banquet on our first and final nights. The Strip offered plenty of entertainment of all kinds. The relatives weren't opposed to gambling, in fact they loved it.

My parents never went near the casinos. They skirted the

slots, which were everywhere, as if they sprayed the plague. The relatives didn't quite believe it. Some came close enough to suggesting my parents were secret gamblers. It was in our blood, after all. It could be traced to Uncle Ho, which is what my mother meant when she said it was going to start all over again.

In all fairness, when someone moves here it's sort of taken for granted that gambling is a big draw. I was only five when my parents made the move, so I don't remember a lot, but I've heard their story enough times so it feels like it's my own. We had been living in Chicago, where my father had a good job as an accountant, when out of the blue, through one of his clients, he was offered a partnership in a big firm in downtown Las Vegas. Mom freaked out. Sin City!

The two words became a drumbeat in her head, until she was driving home from work one day and heard a long-range weather forecast for the Midwest. The coming winter was supposed to be the coldest in fifty years. Record snowfalls, ice storms, and power outages. She started thinking about the bitter winds off Lake Michigan and soon she was on the phone checking out housing, schools for me and job opportunities for herself. She was a physical therapist. When she discovered she could line up a job before we even left Illinois, the deal was done. Vegas it was.

According to my mother, when the relatives got wind of our Nevada move, the phone lines crackled with so much gossip they could have caused a power failure all their own. It went on, not just for months, but years. It's sort of quieted down, but it's not a dead issue. And now Uncle Ho was coming to *our* town.

The relatives would have to be told. First, of course, that he was alive and then that he was coming here to gamble, at the invitation of the casinos. It was easy to see why Mom was upset.

She looked at my father and reached for the letter. He handed it to her and pulled a chair away from the table and sat down.

"It's in English," she said.

Dad laughed. "Did you think I'd suddenly learned to read Chinese?"

Neither of them had ever learned to read the language.

"How is it that *your* Uncle Ho knows English?"

I was careful not to laugh. Actually, Uncle Ho *was* my father's relative. It's a bit complicated. He was the youngest son of my father's grandfather's youngest uncle. It's easier to say in Chinese.

My father shook his head. "I don't know any more about Uncle Ho than you do. I never met him. All I know are the stories. You've heard the same ones I have."

"Maybe he had someone write the letter for him," I said.

This time my mother eyed me with approval. "That's a possibility. You were right about something else, James. It looks as though *your* Uncle Ho *is* one of those whales. He's going to be put up at one of those fantasyland hotels on the Strip."

Now he was *my* uncle.

She looked at my father. "At least that means he doesn't expect to stay with us."

This didn't sound like my mother at all. It seemed a little inhospitable for the legendary Uncle Ho to come all the way from Shanghai and not stay with us, if only for an overnight. We had a guestroom with its own bath, so it isn't as though we didn't have the space. But I kept my mouth shut.

My mother handed the letter back to my father. "He's arriving tomorrow. You didn't tell me that."

The level of electricity between them had just shot up. I decided to make myself scarce. I put my Coke can in the recycling bin, mumbled that I'd be back later and went out the side door, grabbing my basketball out of habit. It was hot, but I was used to it. The court was about three blocks away. Some of the guys were bound to be there. A few shots and another pickup game wouldn't be bad. Then I'd run home and get cleaned up again in the outside shower. I didn't remember much about Chicago, but in terms of climate the change had been a great trade.

At supper that night we sat down to the stir-fry and steamed rice and Dad gave me the news. "We've decided to meet Uncle Ho's plane. His flight from Los Angeles gets in at four tomorrow afternoon. We'll let him decide if he wants to spend time with us."

Somehow I didn't think Uncle Ho would be satisfied with a quick hello at the airport, otherwise he wouldn't have sent us the letter. But my parents were feeling their way, and there was no point in my adding to their confusion.

"How will we recognize him?"

"Your mother thought of that. We'll take along a sign with his name on it, put it on a stick and hold it up. That way *he* will be able to find *us*. Maybe you could take care of the sign, James."

"Sure. What should it say? Uncle Ho?"

My mother was quick to answer. "No. Mr. Ho."

"Got it."

The other thing they decided was not to call the relatives just yet. "It's better if we wait until Uncle Ho gets here. There will be more to tell them after that."

It's hard to remember exactly what happened that next day, except that there were more surprises. We left for the airport with lots of time to spare. My parents were nervous. I was curious. When we got there, parked the car and started for the terminal, I was carrying the sign. There weren't a lot of people around. Sunday can be a sleepy day. A lot of people go to church, although it was a little late in the day for that.

I was the first to see him, seated on a bench off to the side of the terminal entrance, in the shade of some eucalyptus trees. He was holding a sign with his name on it. He saw mine. We waved our signs at each other. His baggage was alongside him, not very much—a small suitcase and two square boxes, tied with heavy cord. A bamboo pole was threaded through a loop at the top of each box. They were identical, cube-shaped, the size that could hold a basketball.

My father apologized for being late, even though we were early. He explained we thought the plane wasn't due for another half-hour.

It turned out Uncle Ho hadn't come by plane. Someone had driven him from Los Angeles.

"Where are all the others?" my mother asked.

Uncle Ho looked puzzled. "Others?" he repeated.

"Your traveling companions. Your letter said you were coming with a group."

He nodded. "They will come later. They are taking a trip to the Grand Canyon."

Through the years, without really knowing it, I'd formed my own image of Uncle Ho—someone sort of ancient, drawn in charcoal, stepping out of the pages of an old storybook. Since yesterday, I had been trying to recast him as a high roller, wooed to Las Vegas by big gambling interests. I couldn't get it to work. And now, here he was, in the flesh. What I saw didn't match anything I had imagined.

It was hard for me to get a fix on his age. His hair was thick like mine, but streaked with a lot of silver. He wasn't real old, but he sure wasn't young. He would have been ordinary looking if it weren't for the scar that ran from the center of his forehead down to his left eyebrow. I couldn't help but wonder how he'd got that. It must have been some gash. Blood must have poured into his eyes.

The pajamalike pants and gray quilted jacket he was wearing sure made him look more like a peasant than a millionaire. But a lot of Chinese dress that way. Besides, during the Cultural Revolution, Uncle Ho *had* been a peasant. He'd been sent to the countryside to work in the rice fields. According to all the stories I'd heard, he had died there, drowned in a ditch. It wasn't an accident.

I was a bit surprised by what my father said then, but Mom wasn't having any trouble with it, so I guessed they must have worked it out.

"Uncle Ho, we would be glad to take you to your hotel, but if you would like to come to our house, you are welcome."

Uncle Ho stared ahead for a minute and then responded with a nod. "I would be glad to go to your house."

My father motioned to Uncle Ho's suitcase. I picked it up. Uncle Ho reached for the bamboo pole and brought it to his right shoulder, balancing one box in front of him and the other behind. Another charcoal drawing slid across my mind.

My parents led the way. Uncle Ho followed and I took up the rear. We were an odd little procession.

At the car my mother suggested Uncle Ho sit up front with my father. I helped him with the seat belt. We didn't usually drive along the Strip, unless we had to, but Dad thought it was a good idea to show Uncle Ho where he would be spending his time when he hooked up with the rest of his group.

As we approached the skyline of hotels, archways and towers, brightly lit even in broad daylight, Uncle Ho leaned forward. He nodded. "I have seen many pictures in travel brochures. But it is different, when it is real. It reminds me of when I went to Beijing for the first time and saw the Forbidden City. It can be described, but it cannot be imagined."

———

Our house was in one of those residential communities that have a tidy look about them, uniformly landscaped plots, planted with cactus and shrubs indigenous to the desert, and groundcover that doesn't need much water. Ours was a two-story with a two-car garage. On the first floor there was a large family room, kitchen and dining area, and my parents' bedroom. The second floor had three bedrooms.

My parents left it to me to take Uncle Ho upstairs. I carried his suitcase up first and then came down to help him with the two boxes. He took one and I reached for the other. I'd been expecting it to have some weight, but it was so light, it almost flew out of my hand.

Uncle Ho chuckled. "It flies like a bird, even when the bird is not there."

I'd already spoken more Chinese that day than I had in a year, but even so I thought I'd misunderstood him. I replayed what I thought he'd said, and it came out the same way. I didn't get it.

I led the way into the guestroom and showed him where the light switch was and how to work the blinds. I opened the empty bureau drawers, the closet and the door to the bathroom. I demonstrated how the shower worked and decided I didn't need to show him how to flush the toilet. If he had traveled this far, he knew what that was all about.

"I don't know your name," he said to me.

"It's James."

"That is short, like my name. Ho."

There were a lot of questions I would have liked to ask him, but it didn't feel right just yet. I said he probably wanted to unpack and take a rest. He should come down when he felt like it, or I would knock on his door when my mother had supper ready.

Back downstairs I saw that my parents' bedroom door was closed. I could imagine the questions they were asking each other.

—————

When we were seated at the dinner table that night my father explained to Uncle Ho that he and my mother had to leave for work early the next morning. "James is on vacation from school this week, so he will be here to take care of you."

Uncle Ho nodded. "My needs are simple. I will try not to be too much trouble."

An awkward silence began. It didn't look like Uncle Ho was about to initiate anything and my parents had the idea that it was impolite to ask questions. We'd heard so many stories *about* Uncle Ho, I thought it would be great to hear his side of things.

I began slowly, wary of my parents' reaction and a little uncertain of my language skills. I apologized in advance for mistakes I would make.

"You are doing very well," Uncle Ho said. "You have a question to ask me, I will try to answer it."

That put me on the spot. If I clammed up now, it would be a great loss of face. The relatives talked a lot about that.

What I really wanted to know was how he had gotten to be a Gambling Master, but I sure couldn't start off with that.

"I was wondering where you lived when you were my age. And what sort of things did you do?"

"And you are how old?"

"I'm sixteen."

Uncle Ho nodded. "We lived in Shanghai then. I also went to school. I was studying mathematics, but my family was poor and I needed to earn money. I raised crickets. Fighting crickets. I learned how to be a cricket handler and then to manage cricket fights. Many people came. They paid admission and they placed bets. The profits were good." He stopped there, and I could see he was waiting for my next question.

I wasn't sure just what to ask. I sure didn't know anything about crickets, so I went with the obvious. "How did you get interested in crickets?"

He chuckled. "Many children in China have crickets as pets. They are good companions. You can keep them close to you at night and listen to them sing. They are small and fit in a box you can put in your pocket. There are many different kinds of cricket boxes. Some are made from dried gourds, others from bamboo, clay, and fine woods. It is said that the last emperor kept his cricket in a box inlaid with ivory and gold. Antique cricket boxes are collector's items now."

We heard a lot more about crickets that night, with Uncle describing a cricket fight. "Fighting crickets are very aggressive," he said. "When two rivals enter an arena, they will jump at each other's heads, biting sharply, until one is vanquished."

———

I heard my parents leave for work the next morning and rolled over, looking forward to sleeping in. It was spring break. Then I remembered Uncle Ho. I set my alarm to sleep another hour.

When I got up I saw that my mother had slipped a note under my door. "Try to find out when the rest of Uncle Ho's group is supposed to arrive, and what hotel he will be staying at. I'll try to get home early, but it won't be before five. Dad and I are driving in together, so you can use my car. You might want to take Uncle Ho on a little sight-seeing tour."

Uncle Ho's door was closed when I headed downstairs, but he heard me and opened the door.

"Hi, Uncle Ho. How about some breakfast?"

"I would like to show you something first." He motioned me into the room.

He had slept in the twin bed close to the window. The quilt was neatly folded back. But it was the other bed that got my attention. Two birdcages sat on top of the bedspread.

I *had* understood him. "It flies like a bird even when the bird is not there."

"I will need your help," he said. "I must find a shop that sells birds."

Okay. What's a birdcage without a bird?

"The name of the shop is Fragrant Hills," Uncle Ho said.

It just so happened I knew the shop. It was in a strip mall next to a computer store where I'd had a summer job last year. A Chinese woman owned it.

"Fragrant Hills. I know where it is. But you just got here. How come you know about it?"

He smiled. "I will tell you when we get there."

Okay. He wanted to be mysterious.

My mother had set two places at the breakfast table and left English muffins out on the counter, along with a bowl of fruit and a canister of tea. I turned on the kettle and reached into the fridge for milk and a carton of eggs. I thought I'd scramble some and toast the muffins. I told Uncle Ho what I had in mind.

"I will have whatever you have, but only a small portion," he said.

He walked to the window then and looked outside, squinting. "The sun is very bright. It makes the sky look very big."

I hadn't thought of it that way, but he was right. Nevada has big skies.

Over breakfast I tried the same thing I did the night before, only this time I asked him about birds, not crickets.

"When I was a small boy in Shanghai, I liked to go to the bird market with my grandfather. He kept his birds in the bamboo houses you saw upstairs. He was very old and I often went with him when he took them for a walk."

"What do you mean, *took them for a walk?*"

Uncle Ho chuckled. "I will show you when we go outside."

Breakfast didn't take long and we left the house by the side door. Uncle Ho had a birdcage in each hand, held by the rings at the top of their domes. He grinned at me and set out past the garage door for a stroll down the driveway and back, swinging the cages at his sides. "Birds like the air. It makes them think they are free."

We got into the Toyota then and I set out for the store named Fragrant Hills. I'd looked it up in the yellow pages to be sure it was still there. Small businesses in Vegas come and go.

There were no customers in the shop when we arrived, but with all the twitters and birdcalls it was a lively place. All kinds of birds were flitting about in large and small cages, and in mini-aviaries suspended from the ceiling. Along one side there were shelves stacked with boxes of birdseed and whatever else people might want to buy for their birds.

At the far end of the shop a woman was seated behind a counter. She reminded me of one of my older aunts, who had been a dancer, and wore her hair the same way, pulled back from her face into a knot high on the top of her head.

The woman was bent over a ledger, a pen in her hand, but looked up when we entered. She stared at Uncle Ho uncertainly and then a look of disbelief moved like a wave across her face. Her hand flew to her mouth, suppressing a cry.

Uncle Ho placed the birdcages on the counter and leaned toward her. She was transfixed as he began to speak. His voice was soft and tentative at first and then gathered speed in a waterfall of words. Her hands rose to her throat and a whisper of wonder passed her lips. "Ho," I heard her say, again and again throughout their exchange, but I understood nothing else of what they said to each other. They spoke in a dialect that was strange to me.

Uncle Ho moved one of the birdcages close to her and she reached for it, clasping it with both hands. Beginning at its dome, she ran her fingers over its intricate webbing, feeling her way, until she reached the base. There she paused and began to explore in detail. She seemed to find what she was looking for, and I saw her ease one small finger between two narrow bamboo struts. She looked up at Uncle Ho. He nodded. She pressed down hard. A drawer sprang open.

A shallow cry escaped her and she bent her head to stare at the contents of the drawer. When she looked up, there was a mixture of wonder and fear in her eyes. Frantically, she pressed her finger down again. The drawer closed, hiding what was there. What I had seen looked like a collection of dried-up brown peas.

I stepped aside to let her by as she ran from behind the counter, headed for the front door. She bolted it and pulled down the shade.

I looked questioningly at Uncle Ho. A smile was playing at the corners of his eyes. "Madam Jia has put up a sign saying the shop is closed. Her home is behind that curtain. She has invited us to go there."

I followed them down a short corridor, lined with more shelves of bird supplies, to a door the woman unlocked with a key hidden in a jar. It opened onto a sitting room, bright with the light from a window that looked out onto a small garden. She motioned for us to sit down, and then looked toward Uncle Ho.

"I have told Madam Jia that you are a member of my family and that I stayed at your home last night. Jia and I are friends from a long time ago. Our grandfathers knew each other. As children we played in the alleys of the bird market in Shanghai. We made plans to have a bird stall of our own some day. Although they did not have names then, Jia said we would call ours Fragrant Hills."

He smiled at the woman. "Our lives have taken different paths. I am glad you chose that name for your shop here in the United States, or I might not have found you."

Their glances held for a moment and then Madam Jia turned to me. "Forgive us for having spoken in the language of our childhood. We will not do that from now on. Ho has many things he wants us both to know."

"Actually there are not so many, it is just that they are complicated. You already know how I gained entry into the United States. I was invited by one of the big casinos. I am sure you are both wondering how that came about." He smiled at each of us in turn.

"Even after so many years there are those who still speak of my days as a Gambling Master. Time and repetition of the story have magnified the truth, but that is what is believed. When the casino agent approached me, he referred to that reputation and assumed I was a wealthy man. At first I thought I should tell him that had been a long time ago, but as I listened to him I realized that my old standing would enable me to get to this country, and so I said nothing to contradict him."

"So, it is true that you have come here to gamble?" Madam Jia was leaning forward, staring at Uncle Ho.

"Life is a gamble," Uncle Ho said with a soft laugh, and then nodded. "It is true, now that I am here, I am expected to gamble. I know very little about the kind of gambling that goes on inside the glittering palaces on the wide boulevard you call the Strip. The only gambling I know is the betting that takes place in cricket fights. I will not find a cricket fight here, I am sure. Casinos do not like winners, so they are hoping I will lose. That might not be very difficult."

I thought of the "whales" story again, and the big bucks the casinos expected their high rollers to play. It didn't sound like Uncle Ho had that kind of money. It was scary to think what might happen if he reneged on his part of the bargain. The days of backstreet murders were gone, but there was still a lot of talk about those times, when a cheat could be found in an alley with his throat cut.

Something else was bothering me. It was those brown peas. I've seen enough old movies set in Macao and Hong Kong and Shanghai, to know something about opium dens. If those little brown pellets had anything to do with the poppy, I was in big trouble.

I set the opium thought aside for a minute and went back to my other worry. "Uncle Ho, do you have any money to gamble with?"

"If by money, you mean American currency, I do not have that. All my wealth is there." He nodded toward the birdcages.

Madam Jia's impatient voice startled me. "Ho! I cannot wait any longer. How did you manage to hide them all these years? You were in prison for so long, and then you were sent to the countryside. I thought you had died there." Tears sprang into her eyes.

"You must not be sad," Uncle Ho said. "Those times are in the past. I am here. Did you ever think that would happen?"

"Years ago I used to dream. . . ." Hastily she shook her head, chasing the memory away. "But enough of that. I am not the little girl you chased in the market alleyways. I have lived many years. You must tell me, now. Where did you hide them?"

"I am surprised that you have not guessed." A look of mischief sparkled in his eyes. It was clear Uncle Ho wasn't about to be hurried. "Do you remember the caves?"

"Of course, I remember the caves! How could I forget?"

Uncle Ho turned to me. "In Shanghai there was a small mountain range near where I lived as a boy. I climbed there often with my friends. The paths were steep, with giant boulders and tall pine trees that gave off a fine fragrance when the wind blew. We were always looking for treasure. We found pine-cones. It was a child's game.

"We wouldn't let Jia come with us. She was too small, and she was a girl. But she was curious."

Madam Jia leaned back into her chair, a quiet smile lighting her face.

"I should have known when I told Jia that we had found some caves, she would not be content to be left behind. Without our knowing, she trailed after us one day, but once she entered the caves she lost her way.

"Jia did not come home to her family that night. No one knew where she was. The next morning her grandfather came to my house and spoke to my grandfather."

"Ho found me," Madam Jia said, her eyes sparkling with the delight of memory. "He guessed what I had done, and he came for me. I was in a cave that had many niches carved into its sides. Before the light was gone, I counted them, from right to left and back again until I reached the top. There was one large niche all by itself. It seemed it was as high as the sky. I called it the moon niche. When Ho found me I told him that if we ever had any treasure to hide, that would be a good place."

Uncle Ho nodded, and their glances held for a moment, sharing an old memory. "It was many years later, when the country was under Mao's grip, that I thought of those caves. The government had been watching me and I knew one day they would come to my door and I would be thrown in prison. It had happened to many of my friends.

"I might die or I might live, but if I were to live I was determined to save my treasure for that day. I chose a dark night and made my way back to the hillside of my childhood and hid my winnings in the niche Jia had given the name of the moon.

"It would be a long time before I would return to that place and to Shanghai. I hardly recognized the city of those early years. New and towering buildings were everywhere, old ones had been torn down, streets and alleyways I had known were gone. At the foot of the hillside that led to the caves, bulldozers and cranes were in place, waiting to level the land and collapse the caves.

"I was dressed as a peasant, with a bamboo pole across my

shoulder, the day that I climbed the steep hills for the last time. I found the cave I was looking for and came out on the other side, so that if someone were watching they would simply see an old man taking his birds for a walk, and not guess what treasure he had."

Madam Jia brought her hands together at the end of Uncle Ho's story and rose from her chair.

"The time has come for us to see your treasure. I will bring the water and the bowls you asked for." She nodded toward a long table in front of the window. Sunlight splashed on its light blue cloth cover. "We will do our work there."

She asked me to come with her into the kitchen. She put a large basin in the sink and began filling it with hot water and gave me a stack of dishtowels and some soup bowls to take to the table. When the basin was full I carried it there. She followed with a large sieve.

I thought about asking a few questions then, but it looked as though I'd have some answers soon. And besides, they were both having such a good time.

I stood to the side as Uncle Ho sprang open the drawers in each of the birdcages. In small handfuls he dropped the brown pellets into the sieve which Madam Jia lowered into the water. It gradually turned muddy.

"They must soak for a while," she said.

We changed the water several times, until it finally became clear and the pellets were no longer brown. Uncle Ho counted and separated them, and Madam Jia carefully spread them on the dishtowels to dry in the sun streaming in through the window.

There were twenty-nine star sapphires, thirty-six rubies, and forty-seven emeralds, sparkling in the sun's bright light.

Uncle Ho was a rich man.

"There were many men who did not have the money to pay their gambling debts," Uncle Ho explained. "They paid me in gems. That gave me the idea to convert some of my other earnings into what you see here. I wrapped them in bird droppings so no one would know what they were."

He turned to Madam Jia then. "I think it is best to wrap them now, in soft cloth, and put them back in the birdcages. It has been a safe place for many years. I will take them with me to

James's house and think about what I should do next. But I must decide before tomorrow afternoon."

"Why tomorrow afternoon?" I asked.

"I must be at the airport then to rejoin the group."

"Were you supposed to go with them to the Grand Canyon?"

"Yes, but after we arrived in Los Angeles and passed through immigration, I slipped away. Since there were only six of us, it is certain that I was missed. When I join them, I will just say that I lost my way in the airport in Los Angeles. It is a confusing place."

Maybe they'd believe him, and maybe they wouldn't, but what I wanted to know was what happened after that. "And just like that, you found someone to drive you here? How did you manage that?"

Uncle Ho smiled. "I will tell you that at another time. We must go now."

I got up and said goodbye to Madam Jia and told Uncle Ho I'd wait in the car for him. Madam Jia let me out through the garden.

It wasn't long before the front door of the shop opened and Uncle Ho appeared with a birdcage in each hand. Madam Jia held the door for him. To anyone who might be watching she was just saying goodbye to a customer, not someone she had known a lifetime ago.

———

It was well past lunchtime when we got home. Uncle Ho said he wasn't hungry and wanted to rest for a while and think about what he should do next. I helped him upstairs with the birdcages, aware of how much wealth I held in one hand.

I made myself a sandwich and thought about all that had happened since my parents had left for work that morning. I grabbed a Coke from the fridge and went into the family room and turned on the TV. It was set to the local news channel. A bulletin came on, obviously a follow-up to a story they'd been monitoring all morning. One of the local anchors was reading an announcement.

Two helicopters collided and crashed in the Grand Canyon

*shortly after dawn this morning in a surprise lightning storm.
There are no survivors. The bodies of both pilots have been
identified. The passengers were Chinese tourists, traveling in a
group. Their final destination in the U.S. was Las Vegas. There
is some question as to whether there were five or six passengers
on board the flights. Only five bodies have been found.*

I sat there, staring at the screen, thinking I should probably
call my parents, but I couldn't imagine telling them all of this
over the phone. I thought of Uncle Ho. I wasn't ready for that
either.

Another bulletin came on.

*The families of the pilots have been notified of their deaths.
Authorities have released the names of the six Chinese tourists
who were scheduled to be aboard the two helicopters. As a special service to our viewers in the Chinese community, their
names can be found on our Web site.*

I went up to my room and sat down at my computer. The Web
site listed the names in Chinese with English transliterations
beside them. There were six names. Ho was one of them. I went
back downstairs and flipped on the TV.

I must have fallen asleep, because the next thing I knew my
mother's hand was on my shoulder, shaking me awake. Dad
was standing beside her. The TV was still on.

I sat up and stared at them. For a minute I thought the whole
thing had been a dream.

"We heard the news as we were driving home," my mother
said. "It's dreadful. I wonder if it's the group Uncle Ho was
traveling with."

"Where's Uncle Ho?" I asked.

"We just got home. I guess he's in his room."

"I'll go check."

I started up the stairs. All sorts of questions were chasing
around in my head. One thing was sure. The next time the relatives got together, I'd have an Uncle Ho story to top them all.

HOUSE RULES

LIBBY FISCHER HELLMANN

If Marge Farley had known what was in store during her vacation to Las Vegas, she might have gone to the Wisconsin Dells instead. At the very least, she might not have taken the side trip into the desert. But she'd been craving something new and different, which was why they'd come to Vegas in the first place. And she'd surprised her husband Larry with a trip to Red Rock Canyon to cheer him up.

But Larry ignored the petrified sand dunes, the waterfalls cascading into the canyons, and the red-tailed hawks soaring high above the Mojave. Polishing off both bottles of water, he stomped back to the car. He swiped beads of sweat off his forehead. Wet bands ringed the back of his shirt. "This isn't fun. It's too hot. And dusty. Let's go back."

Marge tried to focus on the craggy rock formations in the distance. The desk clerk at the hotel concierge said this was the place to visit. And Dr. Phil said there were times you had to decide what was important in a relationship. Lord knows, she was trying. But Larry'd had what you might call a setback last night. A fifteen thousand–dollar setback.

"It's not fair." He moaned when they'd stumbled out of the casino. "Why couldn't we have Benny Morrison's luck?"

She'd heard the story a thousand times. How their friend Benny took his wife to Vegas and won fifty grand at the tables before they even unpacked. How he flew up to their room, grabbed their bags, and told Frances they were going home—that very minute—to build a swimming pool in their back yard. Larry still did a slow burn every time the Morrisons invited them over.

But Larry had never had much luck. Marge pulled the visor of her cap down and contemplated a pink cactus flower not far away. So they'd skip the next vacation. Postpone the bathroom remodeling. Life wasn't about money, anyway. It was a spiritual journey. Like they said on "Oxygen." In fact, hadn't some woman said something about mantras last week? How they made for peace and tranquility? She should share that with Larry. As she tried to remember exactly what the woman had said, something near the flowers glinted in the sun and broke her concentration. "Look at that!"

Larry grudgingly turned around. "What is it now?"

Marge took off her sunglasses. "Something's over there. By the flowers. It's glittering."

"It's probably a frigging gum wrapper."

She headed over. "Then we should definitely pick it up. How could someone even think of littering in a place like this?"

"Marge . . ." Larry followed her over, bumping into her when she came to a sudden stop. "What the—?"

"Look!" Marge pointed. Behind the flowers a piece of metal was sticking out of the sand.

"Lemme see." Larry squinted and crept closer. "Looks like some kind of box." He peered at it, then felt around it with his shoe. They heard a metallic thump. Larry's eyebrows shot up. He bent over the box.

"Wait!" Marge cut in. "Don't touch it." She hugged her arms and looked around. "You have no idea what's in there."

Larry looked up. "For Christ's sake, Marge, it's just a box." He squatted down beside it.

"Hold on. Stop. Isn't—isn't this where they dump all the radiation stuff?"

"Huh?"

"You know, spent fuel rods, the waste from reactors? Like they talk about on TV? They transport it into the desert and dump it in places where nobody lives."

"Marge, that's in Wyoming. And you're talking about huge containers. The size of railroad cars. Not little boxes."

"Still . . ." She pleaded. "You never know."

Larry shot her one of his looks, the kind where the lower part of his jaw pulsed, the way it did when he disagreed with her. An uneasy feeling fluttered her stomach. "You were right, Larry. This isn't fun. Let's go back to the car. We'll get a nice, cold drink at the hotel."

Instead, he knelt down and started scooping up chunks of dry, hard-packed sand.

"Honey, didn't you hear what I said?"

But he kept scrabbling through the sand. Then he stopped digging and sat back on his haunches. Jiggling it to pry it loose, he lifted up a gray tackle box about a foot square and five inches deep. Its surface, at least the part not covered with sand, was dingy and battered.

Marge was just about ready to go back to the hotel without him. Let *him* get poisoned by some weird biological toxin. "Larry, you just leave that thing right there."

His response was to shake the box from side to side. A swishing noise could be heard.

"Larry." Marge started to feel anxious. "It doesn't belong to you."

He looked around, a strange light in his eyes. The sun was casting long shadows across the desert, suffusing everything with a rosy, warm light. No one else was in sight. "It does now." Cradling the box under his arm, he started back toward the car. "Let's go. And for the love of God, don't say a word to anyone."

Marge pursed her lips. She knew better than to argue. She'd spent her whole life following the rules. School rules. Secretary rules. Wife in the suburb rules. She pasted "Hints from Heloise" into a scrapbook. She knew ten ways to get out stains, how to keep potatoes from budding, how to keep her husband happy. And anything she didn't know, she learned on Oprah. Rules were there for a reason. You play by the rules, you find what you're looking for. So what if she'd been a little restless recently? That didn't mean she was looking for trouble. She stole a worried look at her husband. She never understood rebels.

As they hurried back to the parking lot, a man in a car at the edge of the lot flicked a half-smoked cigarette out his window. He seemed to be watching them, Marge thought. She shook her head. She must be imagining things.

Mirrored bronze panels reflected a series of chandeliers that drenched the hotel lobby in a giddy display of light. The casino was off to one side. Larry gave it a wide berth and headed for the elevators, but Marge peeked in as she passed.

A room as big as a football field, the perimeter was rimmed with slot machines for the little old ladies and pigeons. Circular pits for poker, roulette, and blackjack took up the center, with rectangular crap tables around them. It was barely six o'clock, but coins were already clinking, cards were being dealt, roulette wheels clacked. Loud electronic music made it impossible to think. But then, that was the point, wasn't it? Hundreds of greedy souls flocked to the place every night, each thinking they were the exception to the rule. They would beat the house. Larry had been one of them, Marge thought.

As she crossed to the elevator, she wondered how long it would be before someone noticed the bald, pudgy man with a dingy box under his arm. He did look suspicious. She slipped in front to shield him. She knew this wasn't a good idea.

"But I had it when I checked in." A brassy redhead in tiger-striped pants complained loudly at the front desk.

"Ma'am, I'm doing everything I can." The desk clerk's tuxedo was wrinkled, and stringy hair grazed his shoulders. He fingered one of several earrings in his ear. Marge wasn't partial to men with earrings, but she knew she was supposed to be tolerant.

"I talked to housekeeping," he was saying. "Put up a notice in the employee lounge. I even put a reward out for the bracelet."

"Sure you did." The woman glared. "You got some nerve, you know? Our money's not good enough for you. You gotta steal everything that's not nailed down."

The desk clerk broke eye contact with the woman and—impolitely, Marge thought—looked around. His eyes swept past them but then came back and focused, Marge realized with a start, on Larry and his package. She stepped closer to her husband, but it was too late. The lady in tiger pants was still carping, but the desk clerk couldn't take his eyes off Larry. As the elevator doors opened and they stepped inside, he picked up the phone.

Back in their room, Larry took the box into the bathroom. He wiped it down with a damp towel, then felt around the seam.

Marge stood at the door. "Please, Larry. It's not too late. Don't open it. What if it's anthrax?"

"Marge." He growled. "If you aren't gonna help, at least get out of the way."

Her mouth tightened. "At least let me try to find you some gloves."

"Huh?"

"Rubber gloves. I saw a drugstore around the corner."

Larry shook his head. He didn't care about germs. Something was inside that box. It was a sign. And it couldn't have come at a better time. What with the lousy economy, he hadn't made his quota last quarter. Then there was last night. He needed a break. And God was finally sending him one.

"Let me wipe it with a little bottle of bleach," Marge persisted. "It destroys viruses."

He caught his wife's reflection in the mirror. She'd always been a little loony, but now it had become big time. Quoting all those bimbos on TV. Yakking away about the environment. Refusing to let him eat fries or Cap'n Crunch. Too many carcinogens. He didn't know what she wanted anymore. It wasn't like he hadn't been trying. He'd agreed to come here, hadn't he, even though he liked the Dells just fine. But Marge wanted something new. Exotic. Well, he scowled, she sure got that in spades. He picked up the box and looked underneath.

"I'm going to put some alcohol on it." Marge pulled out a bottle of alcohol from her travel kit. Saturating a cotton ball, she dabbed it on the box. A sharp, antiseptic smell filled the room.

"For cryin' out loud, Marge."

He snatched the box out of her hands. She was acting like Donna Reed on steroids. He wanted to pry open the box, but the lock seemed to be warped, bent at an odd angle. Even with the right tools, it would be tough to open. But he didn't even have a screwdriver. He wondered if he should call a repairman. An "engineer," they probably called them here. A fancy place like this probably had a slew of them, ready to pocket a huge tip just for changing a frigging light bulb.

He grabbed the faucet and splashed cold water on his face. In the mirror he saw Marge paw through her bag again. Frigging thing was big enough to hold an entire Wal-Mart. She pulled out a small, chunky red plastic object. With a white cross on it. A Swiss Army knife! He spun around. How the—

She smiled as if she was reading his mind. "I was reading this survey of female travel writers—you know, in *New Woman* magazine? It said if you don't have a travel alarm or a Swiss Army knife, you're not properly packed." She handed it over. "Most women like the scissors and the small blade, but I kind of like the bottle opener."

Larry swallowed his astonishment—every once in a while, his wife still amazed him. Snapping it open, he started levering the blade in and out of the box.

"One woman actually fixed the engine of her rental car with it," Marge went on. "Another fixed her hair dryer. Of course, you have to check it in your luggage these days. But it's worth it."

Larry ignored her. Jimmying the blade, and then the screwdriver, he slowly widened the space between the lid and the base. Finally, a sharp upward tug of the screwdriver sprang the lock, and the box flew open. Larry took a breath, said a prayer, and looked in.

"My god!"

"What is it?" Marge crowded in behind him.

He lifted out a large plastic bag. Inside were at least a dozen smaller baggies, all filled with a white, powdery substance. He gingerly opened one of the bags, stuck in his pinkie, and brought it to his tongue. It tasted bitter and tingly. Maybe a slight numbing sensation.

He gazed up at the ceiling and smiled.

———

The knock on the door made Marge jump. She and Larry exchanged looks.

"I'll take care of it." Larry started toward the door, closing her in the bathroom. "You stay in here. And keep the door shut."

"But what if—"

"Just do what I say."

Marge obediently sat on the toilet. Shivering, she draped a towel over her shoulders. They always kept these rooms too cold. Through the door she heard muffled voices. Larry's and someone else. A woman's.

"No thank you," he was saying. But the heavily accented voice—Spanish, Marge thought—drifted closer.

"I turn down beds. And put towels in bathroom." Marge pictured a Hispanic woman with dark hair and a gold cross at her neck.

"No!" Larry yelped like a wounded dog. "I'm sorry," he added. "I mean—my—my wife's in there. She's not feeling well."

"I give towels. She feel better."

Something jingled as she swished across the carpet. Keys. Maids carried those big silver rings, didn't they? The jingling was followed by a smacking sound. Marge knew that sound. Whenever Larry was upset, he slapped the palms of his hands against his thighs.

Larry's hands smacked back and forth. The jingling edged closer. Marge's heart thumped. If she didn't do something, the maid would burst through the door. Jumping up from the toilet, she locked the bathroom door and slid open the door to the shower. She carefully stowed the box in the bathtub as far away from the shower head as she could, then turned on the water. As a cold spray gushed down, she slid the door shut and plopped back on the toilet.

The jingling stopped.

"See, I told you," Larry said weakly. "She's not feeling well."

Silence. Then, "Ees okay. I help."

Good Lord, Marge thought. What would it take? She quickly grabbed the towel and bunched it in front of her face, hoping her voice would sound like she was inside the shower stall. "Just leave them outside."

"You sure, meesus? I get medicine."

She was about to issue a sharp retort when it occurred to her the woman was just doing her job. Following the rules. Marge was annoyed with herself—she should be more tolerant. "Thank you. I'll manage. Just leave the towels on the floor."

Eventually, the jingling retreated, and the door to their room slammed. Marge waited a full minute before coming out of the bathroom. Larry was looking through the peephole, still slapping his thighs. The scent of cheap perfume hung in the air.

"That was close," he whispered.

"Is she gone?"

He nodded and headed back toward the bathroom. Marge grabbed his arm. "Larry, we can't do this. It's wrong. We've got to hand it over to the police."

"Are you crazy?"

"It's not worth it. If we get caught . . ."

A nervous laugh cut her off. "It's a little late to worry about that."

"It's never too late to do the right thing. We all do things we wish we hadn't."

"This isn't one of them. Anyway, what cop in his right mind'll believe we found this in the desert?"

"But we did."

"Sure. And while you're at it, don't forget to tell 'em it was your Swiss Army knife that got it open."

"What's that supposed to mean?"

"It means you're in this up to your neck, too. You're an accomplice, Marge."

Marge stiffened. All she'd done was pack her toiletry bag according to *New Woman*'s rules: a little detergent, cotton balls, and, of course, the knife. Did that make her a criminal? Larry had to be wrong. Maybe this was some kind of test. Of their values. Their relationship. She lifted her chin. "I'm going to the police."

His eyes narrowed. "You can't."

"We have to follow the rules." She started for the door, but Larry caught her by the arm.

"Marge, don't. Please. The box—it's a sign. I know it."

"A sign?" She searched his face hopefully. Hadn't she just been thinking the same thing?

"We can make a killing if we're careful. Do you know how much that stash is worth?"

Her spirits sank. "I don't care."

"Maybe millions!"

Money. She looked away. They weren't even on the same planet. Dr. Phil said there was a point you had to rescue a relationship or it died. They'd discussed it at her women's workshop: Marge, a newly pronounced lesbian, and two others so bitter over their divorces they couldn't possibly launch, much less rescue, a relationship.

"Our luck is about to change. All we have to do is find someone to sell it to."

"But that would make us . . ." she whispered. ". . . dealers."

"N . . . no. Not really," he said. "It wasn't ours to begin with."

"Exactly. That's why we can't do this, Larry. We've got to play by the rules."

Before he could stop her, she wriggled out of his grasp and bolted through the door.

———

Marge crossed the lobby, aware that the desk clerk with the stringy hair was watching her. She picked up her pace.

Outside, darkness was falling, but it was a false, noisy darkness. Gaudy neon displays sputtered. Fountains gurgled. Horns blared. Electronic dings spilled out from the casinos. As she pushed through the crowds on the Strip, she grew uneasy. She didn't like this city where night was day and dark was light. An air of abandon, a go-for-broke chaos, permeated everything, all of it sizzling in the desert heat. Marge fanned herself with the flaps of her sweater.

Finally, she caught sight of a black and white cruiser on the next block. Two cops lounged against its side. She was hurrying to flag them down when she felt a presence beside her. She quickened her pace, but the figure loomed closer. When she tried to break into a run, he clamped a hand on her arm. She started to scream, but her attacker grabbed her around the waist and buried his mouth on hers in a hard kiss. With the other hand, he jabbed something hard and cold in her side. She knew without seeing that it was a gun.

———

Alone in the room, Larry paced and slapped his thighs. The stash would more than make up for his losses. All he had to do was unload it. But he was a salesman from the Midwest. Where could he find a drug dealer in Vegas?

He pulled out the shirt Marge bought him before they came. You can't wear a golf shirt and chinos in Vegas, she'd said. Even if everyone else does. He slipped it over his head and checked himself in the mirror. Some slinky yellow material. He looked like a frigging Italian.

Italian. Everyone knew the casinos were fronts for the Mafia. The Mafia ran drugs. If he went down to the casino, maybe he could find someone—a card dealer maybe—who knew somebody. But what would he say? "Hey, you want to score—it's upstairs in my room?"

He pulled on the new pair of pants that matched the shirt. A tan weave. At least they weren't white. Damn. He sounded like Marge with all her frigging rules. He opened the box, took out one of the baggies, and stuffed it into his pocket. She hadn't always been this way. She'd been quite a number when he spotted her in the secretarial pool years ago. When had she changed? They were in their forties. The kids were living their own lives. You'd think she would have loosened up.

He closed the box and looked for a place to stash it. The safe? No. That was the first place someone would look. Under the bed? No. That was for amateurs. He looked around, his gaze settling on the mini bar. Twisting the key, he opened the tiny refrigerator, took out the nuts, candy, sodas, and tiny bottles of booze, and slid the box in. It fit perfectly. He threw the food into a laundry bag and shoved it under the bed.

He opened the door to the room. He half-expected to see the maid standing there, her arms full of towels, but the hall was empty. He rode the elevator down and crossed the lobby, nodding to the desk clerk as he passed. His luck was about to change. He knew it.

———

The moment she was accosted Marge wondered why she ever thought a trip to Vegas would be fun. She should have gone to the Dells. Larry and she could have stopped at the water park, like they always did, then shopped for cheese. They might even have taken a boat ride.

Now the man snarled in her ear. "You've got something that belongs to me."

Funny how your mind works, she thought. Here she was on the Vegas Strip, a gun poking her ribs, and she was thinking about the Dells.

The man jabbed the gun in her side. "You hear me?"

"The box?"

"I want it back." His voice was raspy, as if he'd smoked too many cigarettes.

"You can have it."

He positioned himself behind her so she couldn't see his face, but she thought the pressure on her ribs might have eased. "Smart move, lady. So where do I find it?"

"In our room."

"Good." The voice croaked in her ear. "You just keep nice and quiet, see, and no one'll get hurt."

As he hustled her down the strip, the greasy smell of fries and burgers from a fast food joint made her stomach grumble. She realized she hadn't eaten since lunch.

"And tell your husband to stop takin' things that don't belong to him."

She nodded, swallowing her hunger. This could still work out. If she could somehow flag down the policemen at the cruiser, she'd say the box belonged to this goon. Which, according to him, it did. So let him take the rap. She and Larry would be in the clear. Then they could start over. Together. She nodded again. Dr. Phil would approve.

───────

Larry tried to look nonchalant as he strolled down the Strip, but his armpits were damp and sticky, and sweat crawled on his neck. He checked out each passer-by, but most of their faces said they had more important things to do than notice a man in a yellow shirt.

He bought a beer at a dimly lit place off the strip. Two customers were hunched over the bar: a black man with a "THEY DO IT BETTER IN VEGAS" T-shirt and a woman with frizzy gray hair. Larry considered approaching the guy and tried to remember some rap. Home guys? Homies? He changed his mind when the man glared at him in the mirror.

Back on the Strip, the crowd was thick and boisterous. Larry elbowed his way into a resort with cobblestone streets and quaint cafes. Supposed to be a mock-up of Paris, he remembered. Wandering past a "French" bakery whose warm scented bread set his mouth watering, he spotted a scruffy-looking man on a bench. The guy's knee jerked up and down, but he didn't make eye contact with anyone. He shook out a cigarette from a crumpled pack. Touching a match to it, he sucked down a drag. Took his time waving out the match.

Larry walked over. The man threw him a surly glance and scuttled farther down the bench. His movement waved the scent of patchouli oil through the air. Larry remembered patchouli oil. A three-day fling in college with a hippie who never said much more than "far out" and "dig it." She'd had a perpetual buzz, and she reeked of the stuff.

He took a swig of his beer. Maybe this guy was the one. Then again, if he was wrong, it could all go south. He remembered how much he'd lost at the casino. He thought about the box and how much it was worth. He wiped a hand across his mouth and sat down.

"I have some stuff I need to move." He muttered. "Think you could help?"

The guy didn't move. Or even look over. Larry wondered whether he'd made a mistake. Two cops were leaning against their cruiser half a block away. Too close for comfort. He resisted the urge to slap his thighs. He stole a look at the guy. No response. Rows of slats pressed against his shoulder blades. He was about to bolt, melt into the crowd, when the guy gave him a tiny, almost imperceptible nod.

Larry's pulse started to race. It was working! "You—you want in?"

"What's the deal?" the man said.

Larry threw his arm over the back of the bench. The guy's lips were pencil thin, and his upper lip didn't move when he spoke. In fact, Larry wasn't sure he'd spoken at all until he repeated it.

"What's the deal?"

Larry told him.

"Where is it?"

"In my hotel room."

"Hotel? What the hell is it doing in a—"

Larry cut him off, surprised at how brazen he felt. "It's a long story. And I don't have all day. Yes or no?"

Silence. Both of them stared at a trashcan, one of those fancy, shiny ones that reflected lights from the hotel marquee. The man on the bench ran a hand over his head. Twice. "You're on."

———

The elevator doors opened, and Marge and her assailant made their way down the hall, the barrel of the gun still prodding her ribs. As they skirted a housekeeping cart outside her door, Marge remembered the maid with the towels. Was she in the room now? If she was, maybe there was some signal Marge could send her, something that would tell the woman to get help. Thinking furiously, Marge swiped her card key and pushed through the door.

To her surprise, the lights in the room were on, and a reedy voice called out from the bathroom. "So what are you waiting for? Check the cabinets."

Seconds later, the maid stomped out of the bathroom. When she caught sight of the man with the gun, she threw her hands in the air.

"Santa Madre de Dios!"

A noise came from the bathroom. "Estella . . . what the—"

Fear knifed through Marge. "Who's there?" She shouted anxiously. "Get out of my bathroom!"

Silence.

Marge glanced at her attacker, seeing him for the first time. He had thick dark hair, matted and bushy, jeans, denim shirt, and skin so bad it made bubble wrap look smooth. Why didn't he do something? But he just stood there, confusion stamped on his face. She'd have to save herself. But how? She frowned and arched her back, hoping to slip through his hold, but his grip was too strong. Then the bathroom door slowly opened, and the desk clerk with stringy hair and too many earrings emerged.

"You!" Marge planted her hands on her hips, her fear turning to anger. "Why are you here? Where is my husband?"

The maid unleashed a stream of rapid-fire Spanish, followed by a flood of tears.

The concierge fingered an earring, not at all perturbed. "The guest in the room below complained of a leak in their bathroom ceiling," he said over the maid's wails. "We were just checking it out." Flashing a look at the man with the gun, he added, "See? Nothing to worry about. So now, if you'll—"

The man with the gun suddenly seemed to snap out of a trance and pointed the gun at the desk clerk. "Stay where you are," he barked. "Not another step."

The desk clerk shot him a strange look. Almost as if they knew each other, Marge thought. She crossed her arms. "Where's my husband?"

"No one was here when we came in."

Marge fixed him with an icy stare. He looked defiant, but he could be telling the truth. At least about Larry. But then, where was her husband? And where was the box?

Her assailant waved the gun at the maid. "Stop bawling, woman. And get out of here." He turned to the desk clerk. "You too. And you ain't seen nothing. Or no one. If you know what's good for you. Got it?"

"Wait!" Marge yelled. "You can't do—"

Her attacker waved the gun at her. "You . . . up against the wall."

"But what about—"

"Shut up." He turned back to the desk clerk. "You got a problem with your hearing?"

Marge saw the look they exchanged. "Do you know each other?"

The two men didn't answer. She frowned. The sobbing maid was her last hope. She turned to her, trying to telegraph an SOS, but the desk clerk grabbed the maid's arm and shoved her out into the hall. As the door slammed, Marge heard him ream her out in Spanish.

"You got exactly thirty seconds to find that box," her assailant said.

Marge sagged against the wall. She knew it was a waste of time. The box wasn't here. But she searched anyway, sliding open the shower stall, the closet door, drawers.

Nothing.

Until she found the bag of snack food under the bed. Who did Larry think he was fooling? Maybe it would all work out. She hauled the bag from under the bed and stood up. "Try the mini bar."

"Open it." The man pointed to the cabinet.

"I don't have the key."

The man shot her a look and kicked the cabinet. It flew open, revealing the box.

Marge opened the refrigerator and pulled it out.

The man grabbed it and slid it under his arm. Then he cocked the gun. "Tough break. Now I have to shoot you. You know too much."

Marge blew out a breath. He was right. It was over. She resigned herself to her fate and squeezed her eyes shut, waiting for the bullet to end her life. She couldn't help thinking how humiliating it was to die in Las Vegas. And how none of this would have happened if Larry had played by the rules.

———

They both heard the click of the key card. Her attacker shoved her into the bathroom with the box. Jabbing the gun in her ribs—it almost felt familiar by now—he raised a finger to his lips.

Marge pasted her ear against the wall. Larry was talking. To a man. Drawers slid open and closed. The closet door slammed.

"I can't believe this. It's gone." Larry's voice took on a high-pitched, nasal whine.

"What do you mean, it's gone?" The man's voice was deep. And angry.

"I—I was only out for a few minutes," Larry stammered.

Then, "OK, Pal. Game's over. Get your hands in the air."

"What—what are you talking about?"

"I'm Officer Dale Gordon, Las Vegas police. And you're under arrest. You have the right to remain silent . . ."

"A cop!" Larry yelped. "You're an undercover cop!"

"That's right, pal. And you're in serious trouble."

Marge gasped. Police. It was a sign. She lunged for the door. As she did, she elbowed her attacker by accident, and something metal dropped into the toilet. The gun. She must have knocked it out of his hand. Out of the corner of her eye, she saw the thug trying to retrieve it from the bowl. He was cursing under his breath.

Banging her fists on the door, she yelled, "Help! Help me please!"

Footsteps raced over. The door was flung open. A scruffy-looking man who didn't look much like a policeman to Marge crouched in a shooter's stance, his gun pointed straight at her.

Her hands shot up in the air. "Don't shoot!"

She heard a click from his gun. "Who the hell are you?"

———

Marge was about to tell him when she heard a rattle out in the hall. The door opened, revealing the maid with a gun in her hands. She seemed to size up the situation right away and pointed her gun at the undercover cop. "Drop the gun. Now." Her English was suddenly unaccented.

The cop complied. The maid pointed at Marge with her head. "Get me the box."

Marge scurried into the bathroom, picked it up, and handed it over. The maid nodded and folded it under one arm. "Nobody moves for the count of ten."

She let the door close with a thud.

There was an instant of shocked silence, and then pandemonium broke loose. Everyone yelled at once. The cop whipped out a cell phone. So did Marge's attacker. Larry accused everyone of ripping him off. The chaos stopped only when they heard more shouts in the hall. The undercover cop ran to the door and flung it open. The two uniformed cops Marge had seen lounging against the cruiser stormed into the room.

"Took you long enough!" the undercover cop snarled. "Did you see her?"

The back-up cops exchanged looks. "Who?"

"The maid, dammit! She took it! Not even a minute ago!"

One of the cops cried out, "The door to the stairwell! It was just closing!" He bolted down the hall to the exit. The other cop followed.

———

They caught her before she hit the ground floor, but she didn't have the box, and she refused to say where it was. In fact, she clammed up and didn't say a word—in English or Spanish. After listening to Marge's story—several times—the cops searched the room, then took everyone into custody, including the desk clerk. Everyone except Marge.

They'd been trying to crack this narcotics ring for months, the cops said. They knew the drops were made at Red Rock Canyon late at night. They'd even busted one of the mules, but the others got away. Apparently, they'd buried the stash under the sand, figuring they'd come back for it when they could. The cops assured everyone they'd turn the hotel upside down to find the box, but even if they didn't have it, they had enough to make everyone's life unpleasant.

Marge promised the cops she'd call if she found the stash and told Larry she'd get bail money wired tomorrow. She watched them shuffle down the hall, all of them in cuffs. She was about to back in her room when she noticed the maid's housekeeping cart wasn't there anymore. But it had been—when she and her attacker had come up. For a fancy hotel, they sure didn't keep track of their equipment very well. Shaking her head, she closed the door.

A moment later, she opened it again. Scanning the hallway, she saw that the door to the hotel room door closest to the stairwell was seeping light around its edges. Marge crept toward it. The door was unlatched. She pushed it open. There was the cart, draped in skirting to hide all the cleaning supplies. Marge bent over, raised the skirt, and smiled.

She picked up the box. A grimy smell clung to it. No matter. She had a bottle of *Jean Naté* in her bag. *New Woman* said it was just the thing after a day in the hot sun. She stole back to her room.

She was in the bathroom dousing the box with perfume, the TV chattering, when an author started to talk about her book, *Your North Star: Claiming the Life You Were Meant to Live.* Marge straightened up. A few hours ago, she wasn't sure she'd have a life to reclaim. Was this a sign?

Slowly she examined herself in the mirror. Then she turned sideways. Fluffed up her hair. When you really got down to it, there wasn't anything that a beauty shop, new clothes, and a few aerobics classes couldn't fix. Her gaze returned to the box. Maybe she'd pay a visit to the maid tomorrow. Make her a small proposition. After all, the woman had almost outsmarted them all. Marge was sure she'd know what to do.

She nodded to herself in the mirror. Yes, that was a good plan. She'd go see the maid. Maybe even bail her out of jail. Then she'd buy that book, read it from cover to cover, and reclaim her own life. After all, she always played by the rules.

ROLLING THE BONES

TOM SAVAGE

"**I**s he dead?"

"I don't know. I think so, but I'm not sure."

"Well, maybe we should shoot him again."

"Nah. He'll be dead soon enough. Trust me on this."

"Oh. Okay."

"'Sides, whaddaya mean 'we,' Snake? *I'm* the one shot him."

"Yeah, Artie, I know. It's just a figure of speech. Like when the Queen of England says 'we,' you know? Like, 'We are not amused.' Like that."

"What the hell *you* know about the Queen of England? You been hangin' out with her lately? Huh, Snake? She your new best friend, or somethin'?"

"Uh, no, Artie."

"Then shut the hell up."

"Okay."

"Here, help me roll him over. Yeah. Now take his feet. His *feet*, Snake! That's it, that's the ticket. Now let's get him in the trunk. Count of three, okay? One—two—"

"Um, Artie?"

"Yeah?"

"Could you maybe not call me that?"

"Call you what?"

"You know. 'Snake.' I hate that, I really do."

"Oh, for chrissakes—"

"No, *really*. One lousy roll, what, two years ago? And now

everybody calls me that. I don't like it, okay? That's all I'm saying."

"Sure thing, Snake."

"Knock it off, Artie. My name is Irwin."

"Sure thing, *Irwin*. Anything you say. Now, could you maybe help me with the stiff, *Irwin?* We haven't got all night here. Count of three. You ready?"

"Um, yeah."

"One—two—*Ouch!*"

"Sorry. His shoe came off."

"Well, put it back on! I nearly threw my back out! I swear to God, Snake, you're so bright your mother called you 'sun'!"

"Um, actually, she called me Irwin."

"Oh, Sweet Mother of Pearl! Count of three, *Irwin! Okay?*"

"Okay."

"Have we all got our *shoes* on now?!"

"Yeah."

"Terrific. Okay, here we go. One—two—*three.*"

"Ouch."

"Yeah, he's a heavy son of a bitch. Now, get him in the trunk . . . that's it . . . good . . . good . . . Okay, Snake, you can let go of him now."

"Okay."

"Now, get your hand out of the way. I'm closin' the trunk."

"Okay."

"There. We're ready to rock and roll. What time is it, Sna— um, *Irwin?*"

"Let me see. I have to get under the lamppost. Looks like it's . . . ummmm . . . four forty-seven. Yeah, four forty-seven. Forty-*eight*. The minute hand just went past the—"

"Okay, okay! Sheesh! Let's move. No, *you* get in the passenger side. *I'm* driving."

"Oh, yeah. Right."

"Right."

"You got the directions?"

"Um, yeah, Artie."

"Okay, which way?"

"Um, stay on this till we pass the Sands, then turn, and straight out of town into the desert."

"Ha! That's where *he* shoulda gone, eh, Snake?"

"Who?"

"*Him!* The *stiff*. Straight out of town. He shoulda done that before he ran up such a tab with Mr. Rios. Straight out of town and kept goin'. That's what *I* woulda done. Course, I never woulda been in this situation. Gamblers! I swear! They don't have the brains God gave a slug."

"Gee, Artie, I don't know. There's dumber things."

"Yeah, like what? Like what, Snake-pardon-me-*Irwin*?!"

"Like messing around with Mrs. Rios. Hey, *watch* it, Artie! You almost swerved off the road!"

"What the hell you talkin' about?"

"Huh?"

"What the hell you talkin' about, messin' around with Mrs. Rios?"

"You know, Artie. Molly Rios."

"Yeah? Who's messin' around with her?"

"Um, I thought *you* were, Artie."

"Where did you hear that? Come on, Snake, who the hell told you that? Who's been runnin' off their mouth about my business?"

"No one, Artie. Honest! I just thought—"

"Yeah? Well, do me a favor, Snake. *Don't think!* Okay? Thinkin' can get a dim bulb like you in a lot of trouble, know what I'm sayin'? A *lot* of trouble. Trouble like our pal in the trunk's got trouble. *Capisce?!*"

"Yeah, Artie. I understand."

"Good. 'Sides, Molly Rios is a nice lady. A beautiful lady. You shouldn't oughtta talk about a nice lady like that."

"A nice lady? Who're you kidding, Artie? When Mr. Rios met her, she was working the second string clubs at the other end of the Strip. You know what she used to call herself? Molly Tamalé, the Mexicali Gal. That was her stage name, Artie. Molly Tamalé, the Mexicali Gal. She was a stripper."

"Okay, okay. . . ."

"Yup. Molly Tamalé—"

"*Okay*, Snake."

"—the Mexicali Gal. . . ."

"*Snake! Enough*, dammit! You want I should make you *walk* the rest of the way?"

"Uh, no, Artie."

"Then shut up about Mrs. Rios, you hear me?"

"Yeah. I hear you."

"That's our employer's *wife* you're talkin' about."

"Yeah."

"So *don't*."

"Okay."

"Okay. So. Hey, this could take a while. You wanna stop for coffee 'fore we go out there?"

"No, Artie. Let's just get this over with, then we can stop at Dunkin' Donuts on the way back. We've got some digging to do, work up an appetite. Then we can have breakfast."

"Hmmm. Okay. I swear, I haven't slept in two days."

"Well, you've been busy, right? You were following Mr. Big Spender all over the place."

"Yeah. He sure did run up a tab, didn't he?"

"Yeah, that's what Mr. Rios said."

"A *big* tab, that's what I heard."

"Yeah."

"Don't ever gamble, Snake."

"No, I'm not a gambler, Artie. I never had much luck with the dice."

"Yeah, I know. You're the one rolled them snake eyes. That's where ya got the nickname."

"I hate that name. I like Irwin. I wish people would just call me Irwin."

"Well, *Irwin*, I don't cut the deck or spin the wheel or roll the bones. Uh-uh, not me, nosiree Bob! I stay away from all that. Gamblin' only leads to one thing—a ride outta town with two characters like *us*, know what I'm sayin'?"

"Yeah, Artie, I hear you."

"Nosiree Bob! None of that for me! I'm too smart for that. I'm on top of things, see?"

"Um, Artie?"

"I'm on top of things. . . ."

"Um, *Artie?*"

"Yeah?"

"You missed the turn."

"I *what?*"

"You missed the turn, Artie. That was the Sands back there. You missed it."

"Oh. Oh, so I did. Okay, hang on."

"*Yikes! Jeez Louise!* Take it easy, Artie! You almost hit that truck!"

"Relax, Snake. If there's one thing I know how to do, it's drive. Chill out. Here we go, *now* we're on the right track. *Now* we're cookin' with gas!"

"Jeez, Artie, you nearly gave me a heart attack! We almost got a face full of Mack truck!"

"Well, we didn't, did we? That's your trouble, Snake, always worryin'. Don't be such a momser."

"I am *not* a momser."

"Yes, you are!"

"Am not!"

"Are so!"

"Am not!"

"Momser, momser, momser!"

"Cut it out, Artie!"

"Heh-heh."

"Jeez. . . ."

"Heh-heh."

———————

"How far?"

"Huh?"

"How far outta town we supposed to take him, Snake? Did Mr. Rios say?"

"No, Artie. He just said the desert. He said use our judgment, look for a good spot. Then I'm supposed to call him when it's finished."

"Okay. I know a good spot, another twenty, twenty-five miles or so. Big pile of rocks and a clumpa trees near the foothills, 'bout fifty yards off this little dirt side road. We can pull in there, get the job done. Sound good?"

"I guess. How do you know about that, Artie? How do you know about that clump of trees off the side road? Have you done this before?"

"*Course* not! I only done four jobs for Mr. Rios before. Well, five. Yeah, five—but one didn't count, 'cause he didn't stay down."

"Oh. When was that?"

"'Bout two, twoanahalf years ago."

"Oh. How long have you been with Mr. Rios?"

"Three years next June. Yeah, 'fore that I was just a good-for-nothin' small-timer."

"Who did you work for?"

"No one in particular. Odd jobs. Did one for the Families once, but they like to use their own."

"Yeah."

"They're a *close* bunch, the Families."

"Yeah."

"How 'bout you, Snake? Who'd you work for?"

"Um, nobody, really. I guess I've been a free agent, like you."

"Ever do a job like this before?"

"Uh, yeah."

"Yeah? Who?"

"I don't like to talk about it."

"Come on! Tell, tell!"

"No, I don't like to talk about it."

"You ever been inside?"

"No."

"Well, that's good to know. I'd hate to think I was workin' with somebody whose bad luck went beyond a bad roll."

"No, I guess I've been pretty lucky."

"'Cept for that snake eyes!"

"Yeah."

"How much you lose on that snake eyes?"

"Uh, twenty."

"Wow! On one lousy roll? *Wow!*"

"Yeah, but Mr. Rios bailed me out."

"That how you hooked up with him?"

"Yeah."

"Gee, Snake, I just realized. You and me been workin' for the same guy—what?—two years now, and this is the first time he's put us together on a job. I usually work with Face."

"Yeah."

"You ever work with Face?"

"No. He's—he's an odd one."

"*Tell* me! Imagine havin' a face like that."

"What was it, a fire?"

"Acid. His former employers."

"Oh."

"Don't do to get on their wrong side."

"Uh, no, I guess not. You should, um, you should think about that, Artie."

"Think about what? What?! Come on, Snake, what're you talkin' about? You know something you ain't tellin' me? *What?!*"

"I'm just saying—"

"Oh, boy, what the hell is that? *Cops!* Just what we need, I swear! What the hell're they doin'? Turn around and look, Snake. What're they up to?"

"I don't know, Artie. Looks like they're just driving, you know, patrolling, or whatever. Doesn't look like they're particularly interested in us."

"They're followin' us."

"No, I don't think so, Artie. They're just driving."

"They're up to somethin'. I can feel it! Those guys are *always* up to somethin'.

"I don't—"

"You're packin', right?"

"Uh, yeah."

"Well, get ready. You might need it. They're gettin' closer. *God*, I hate cops, I really do! I'm gonna slow down a little, we'll see what they—"

"No, they're pulling out into the other lane, Artie. They're not—"

"Oh, boy! Get your piece out, Snake. Get ready to—"

"They're passing us, Artie, see? They're going right past us. They're not even looking over here. Look!"

"Oh. Oh, yeah. There they go. Whaddaya know? Boy-oh-boy, that was a close one!"

"Not really, Artie. Close would be if they pulled us over, asked to see your driver's license and registration. Asked us what's in the trunk. *That* would've been close. 'What have you got in the trunk, guys?' *That* would have been something to get all worked up about. They didn't even—"

"Snake?"

"Yeah, Artie?"

"Shut up."

"Okay."

———————

"It's kinda nice, isn't it?"

"What's nice, Artie?"

"That. Look. The desert at five o'clock in the morning. The sky still dark but just gettin' light, and the sand and the hills all blue. Deep blue, like the ocean. I knew a girl with eyes that color, once. Asked her to marry me."

"Did she marry you?"

"Nah. I ain't never been married. No family, no friends, no ties of any kind. That's the way I like it, Snake. Free as a bird on the ocean. Or the desert. Yeah, it's practically the same color as the ocean out there. . . ."

"No family? What happened to them, Artie?"

"Never had one. I was 'found,' that's what Sister Mary Margaret always used to say. She ran the place where they found me. On the freakin' *doorstep*, in a basket. They said I was just a coupla days old. A note pinned to the blanket. '*His name is Arturo. Please take care of him becuz I can't. God bless you.*' Whoever she was, she spelled *because* wrong. She spelled it B-E-C-U-Z. Ain't that a bitch?"

"I guess so."

"The freakin' *doorstep*!"

"Yeah."

"I kept that note. It's in my wallet. Kinda like a picture, 'cept I don't got a picture of her. Whoever she was."

"Where was that, Artie?"

"Where was what?"

"The orphanage."

"New York. The Sisters of Mercy on the Lower East Side. Bowery, just south of Houston. You know New York?"

"Yeah. I was there for a while, about ten years ago, just after I got out of college."

"College? You went to college?"

"Yeah. Nassau Community on Long Island."

"Wow. Me, I never finished high school. I got in some trouble in New York, juvey, never finished high school. So, you're from Long Island. Your family there?"

"They were."

"Where are they now?"

"My parents are in Florida, a little retirement community near Fort Lauderdale. My sister is in Philly. She's got a family. Two boys and a girl."

"Wow, Snake, you're an *uncle*?!"

"Yeah, I guess."

"Two nephews and a niece. Must be nice."

"I don't know. I've never seen them. Sally's husband doesn't like me coming around."

"Oh. Well, at least you know where they are."

"Yeah."

"Wow, college! What did you major in?"

"Business management."

"So, why ain't you managin' a business?"

"I found other work that paid better."

"Yeah, just like me! How long you been in Vegas?"

"A little over two years. I came out to do some work, and then I got stuck at that table."

"Yeah, the snake eyes. Right. So, you plannin' on stayin' here?"

"Probably. A while, anyway."

"Yeah. Vegas is where the money is, Snake. That's why I'm stickin' around. For a while, anyway. Lots of job opportunities, ya know? Lots of people like Mr. Rios. And lots of idiots like Mr. Big Spender in the trunk! Heh-heh. God, that was dumb! Tryin' to cheat Mr. Rios like that. . . ."

"Yeah. You shouldn't try to cheat Mr. Rios."

"That's for sure! I hear he's handled quite a few guys like Mr. Big Spender. Took out a coupla them myself. Face says he thinks it's more than a dozen now. This desert must be fulla bodies. Yessiree Bob! Here, wanna cigarette?"

"No, thank you, Artie. I don't smoke."

"Yeah, yeah, bad for your health. Lung cancer, emphysema, second-hand whatever, the *ozone* layer, higher *taxes*, the end 'a the world as we know it. Yeah, yeah, yeah. But I love 'em. Mmmm, that's good. Nothin' like a Winston. 'Winston tastes good like a cigarette should.' Remember that, Snake?"

"Yeah."

"Mmmm. Let's see, the turnoff's up here somewhere. Then it's a kinda long drive on the dirt road, straight out into the desert. I'll know the place when I see it. What time is it now, Snake?"

"Um, let me see. . . ."

"Oh, boy, here we go again."

"It's five-ten. Five-*eleven*. Yeah, five-eleven."

"Five-eleven. 'Nother half hour or so, and our business will be over."

"Yeah."

"Yeah."

———————

"Okay, here's the turnoff."

"You sure, Artie?"

"Yeah, this is it for sure. I know where I'm goin'."

"Okay. . . ."

"What, you don't trust me?"

"I trust you, Artie."

"Damn right! This is the road, see. Straight out into the desert. I swear, this desert looks just like the ocean this time of the mornin'. You ever seen the ocean, Snake?"

"Sure."

"Yeah, the Pacific. Nothin' like it, man. I was in L.A. a coupla times, on work for some people, and I used to see this chick who liked the beach. Her old man had one of them beach houses in Malibu. Her and me used to go *swimming* a lot when he was outta town, know what I mean? God, I love the ocean."

"You shouldn't do that, Artie."

"Do what?"

"Mess around with married women."

"Oh, boy, not *that* again! Look, Snake, I hope you don't mind my sayin' this, but you don't seem to be too bright. Even if you *did* go to college. And you're definitely too uptight. *Way* too uptight. You could use a woman yourself, ya know? A little action, and you'd probably relax a little. Don't be so scared of everything. Women like me. I like women. If they want a little action, I always oblige. No big deal. Life's a gamble, ya know?"

"I thought you said you didn't do that."

"Do what?"

"Gamble."

"Well, not at a casino, Snake. I don't *gamble* gamble. But if you think about it, *everything's* a gamble. You pays your money and you takes your chances. Women. Adventure. *Whatever.* I don't wanna be bored, and I don't wanna be boring. You're kinda boring, Snake, if you don't mind my sayin' so. Face and the others, they say you're kind of a goof, you know? Klutzy. That's why everyone calls you Snake. You're the kinda guy who rolls snake eyes. Me, I'm a different story. I got plans."

"And what would they be?"

"Ha! You'll see! A few more jobs for Mr. Rios, another coupla years here in Vegas, and then I'm outta here. I'm goin' to get me a place out on the Coast, near the ocean. Malibu, maybe. I'm gonna retire early, live the easy life. Wine, women, and song. That'll be me."

"Hmm."

"You should have plans, Snake, like me."

"Oh, I've got plans, Artie."

"Yeah? What?"

"I don't like to talk about it."

"You plannin' on strikin' it rich? Winnin' the lottery? Maybe being named *Momser* of the Year? Heh-heh."

"Stop that! I am *not* a *momser!*"

"Yes, you are."

"Am not!"

"Are so! Oh, hell, let's not do *that* again. See that buncha trees up ahead? Those big boulders near the hills? That's the place, that's where we're headed."

"Okay."

"We've only got the one shovel, so I'll do the diggin', Snake. I'm in better shape than you. I can get the job done fast. That okay with you?"

"Sure Artie. You dig, and I'll watch. I'm just a *momser,* anyway."

"Oh, now, don't pout, Snake. For chrissakes! I'm just pullin' your leg. Speakin' of which, we gotta get *him* outta the trunk."

"Yeah."

"Mr. Big Spender. What's his real name, anyway?"

"I don't know, Artie. I didn't ask."

"I wonder who he is. *Was*. You suppose he has a family?"

"How should *I* know? He's just a job, Artie."

"Yeah. Just a job. Now you're bein' smart, Snake. Don't get involved, don't ask too many questions. Just do the job you're paid for and get out. Go on to the next job."

"Yeah."

"You're not such a *momser*, after all."

"Thanks, Artie."

"Still. . . ."

"What, Artie?"

"I just wonder what his name was. . . ."

———

"Is this it?"

"Yeah, Snake. This is the place. We just turn off here . . . yeah, another few yards . . . okay. Here we are. Pop the trunk, okay?"

"Okay."

"Good. Let's get him outta there. Put him down a sec'. Hey, here's his wallet. A hundred and fifty-seven bucks. You want some of it?"

"No, thanks."

"Okay, more for me. Ah! Driver's license. Wallachinsky, Victor. Portland, Oregon. Hmm, Polack. That's a Polack name, right? Wallachinsky? Must be."

"Yes, Artie, he's probably of Polish descent."

"Ha! 'Polish descent'—I like that. 'Polish descent.' Okay, you take his legs. Careful . . . okay, over here, near the tree. Okay, easy . . . easy . . . there. Damn, he's heavy! How much you suppose he weighs?"

"A lot."

"Yeah, I'll have to dig a deep one for this guy, this *gentleman* of *Polish descent*! Hand me the shovel."

"Here."

"Okay, get in and turn the car this way, so the headlights can show me what I'm doin'."

"It'll be dawn soon."

"Well, dawn ain't here yet, is it, Snake? Just give me some light, okay?"

"Okay."

"There—no, a little more to the left . . . a little more—*there*. Stop! Perfect. Now I can see the ground."

"Okay."

"Here, take my jacket. Careful! That's a genuine Gucci, cost me six hundred bucks. Better take this holster, too. Damn, that piece is heavy! Ya never notice that till ya take it off. Just put 'em on the front seat. Okay. Now, you just grab a seat there, on the hood, and watch how fast I can do this."

"Okay."

"Ouch! Damn! Lotta rocks around here. I don't remember all these rocks. . . ."

"So, when were you here before, Artie?"

"Oh, a while ago. Few weeks."

"On a job?"

"Nah. I was—I was with someone. A woman."

"Oh. Why did you bring her all the way out here?"

"Well, heh-heh, we needed a little *privacy*, know what I mean, Snake?"

"Oh. Another married woman."

"Yeah, so what? What if it was?"

"Was it Molly Rios, Artie?"

"What the hell business is it of *yours*?"

"I'm just asking, Artie. Was it Molly Rios?"

"None a' your beeswax!"

"Sorry."

"You know what, Snake? You talk too much."

"Sorry, Artie."

"Talk, talk, talk."

"Sorry."

"And you apologize too much, too. Anyone ever tell you that, Snake?"

"No, Artie. I can't say they have."

"Well, you do. Trust me."

"Sorry."

"See? You just did it again!"

"Sor—um—hmm."

"Just sit there and watch me dig."

"Okay."

———————

"The trouble with you, Snake—dammit! Another rock!—The trouble with you, Snake, is that you ain't got an *attitude*. Know what I mean? You don't walk the walk, talk the talk. Me, I've got *lots* of attitude. I'm all *about* attitude. I tell you, when you're found on a doorstep with a note pinned to your ass, you learn to develop an attitude. Sister Mary Margaret and all them other penguins, not to mention the *kids*. That was one mean buncha kids, Snake. No respect. So you have to teach 'em to respect you. Same with the foster parents, these nicey-nice, squeaky clean do-gooders who want an instant family. They'd come to the Sisters of Mercy every Saturday, whole groups of 'em, and walk around the place, starin' at us. Just checkin' us all out, like we was meat in the supermarket, ya know? And every so often, they'd point at me. '*Him*,' the perky wife would say. '*Isn't he cute*?' And the perfect husband would smile and nod and say, 'Yes, Janice, if that's the one you want.' Like I was a *dog*, or somethin'! And off we'd go, to Brooklyn or Bayside or Larchmont. I spent four months in Larchmont. That was the record. The others never kept me that long. It'd start out all nicey-nice. They'd tell me to call 'em 'Dad' and 'Mom,' and they'd smile at me and show me this stupid room they said was mine, with all these stuffed animals and crap. Matching bedsheets and curtains, with these pictures of sailboats or Superman or fairy tale stuff all over 'em. And baseball bats and gloves, and a football or a basketball. Picture books. Parcheesi boards. *Legos!* What *is* it with those people and *Legos*, huh? And a desk for my homework, and notebooks and pencils and rulers and stuff. And they'd send me to these fancy private schools, with all these candy-ass blond-haired-blue-eyed kids with names like Shane and Blake and Mallory, all smirkin' and pointin' at me and whisperin'. 'That's him, that's the kid from the orphanage.' Those kids just looked down their noses at everyone. So I'd take stuff from them, books and lunch money and stuff. I figured they were all so stupid, they deserved what they got. And the teachers would scream, and the perky mom would be called in, and back I went to Sisters of Mercy. And it would all begin again, and I got bigger and older and harder to sell. After a few years of that, I decided to make it harder for 'em, you know, get rid of 'em before *they* got rid of *me*. It became like a game, ya know? It all ended up with those last ones, Dave and Mary Singer. I guess I shouldn't 'a taken that stupid necklace. That was in—lemme see—Riverdale. Yeah, Riverdale. I was fifteen by then, and I met these really cool kids in the park, and we used to hang, ya know, and they showed me how to boost beer from the deli and cigarettes from the newsstand. And they had drugs—that was cool. Grass and acid and X. X was my favorite, drop a tab and go all night, know what I mean? But we had to pay for it, ya know? So I took that stupid necklace from Mary's dresser. Hell, she had about a hundred necklaces, I didn't think she'd *notice*. And I was sick of ol' Dave and Mary by then. I figured they were about to trade me in for a new model, anyway, and they could take their baseball gloves and their Superman curtains and their Parcheesi boards and their goddamn *Legos* and shove 'em, just put 'em where the sun don't shine. So I waited till this one night, when Dave and Mary were off playin' bridge at their country club, and I took the necklace. This kid named Rex—he was a badass kid, Snake, really a cool guy, didn't take nothin' from nobody!—he took me down to this guy he knew in Hell's Kitchen, and we pawned it. Got four hundred bucks for it! Hell, I didn't know it was real sapphires. You know what that necklace was worth? Twenty-five grand! Twenty-five grand for a bunch of rocks strung together with gold chains. Dave and Mary hit the roof. She screamed the place down, and he called me some word I had to go look up in the dictionary. Ragamuffin. *Ragamuffin!* Can you believe that?! And he brought in the cops and everything. Sister Mary Margaret tried to talk 'em outta pressin' charges, but I ended up in the system, anyway. Boy, that was fun. *Not!* Those guys in there, in Langton Juvenile, I tell you. I learned pretty quick. Don't look at nobody, *ever,* and don't pick up the soap. And the guards were worse. 'Hey, you! Arturo! Pretty boy! Come over here, son, I got somethin' for ya!' That's when they weren't whalin' on us, usin' us as punchin' bags. I kept a low profile, but this one kid, Billy Carson, he was a smartass. Used to call the guards names, you know, racial names. He ended up in the hospital. Twice. The second time, he didn't come back. I heard he lost one of his legs from the damage. And those guards were never even reprimanded. They just kept right on breakin' legs, and everyone else kept right on lookin' the other way. Jeez. I was in Langton till I was eighteen, and then I was supposed to report in every two weeks until I was twenty-one. I didn't stick around for that, nosiree Bob! I looked up Rex, and we did a coupla jobs together, and I took the cash and got outta New York. Came to Vegas. Found a new line of work. And here I am, with a whole new life and lots of *attitude*. Free, white, and twenty-seven. How old are you, Snake?"

"Huh?"

"How old are you?"

"Oh. I'm thirty-two. I'll be thirty-three next month."

"Ha! I'm five years younger than you, Snake, and I bet I've lived a whole lot more than *you* have! I go where I want, do what I want. I don't answer to *nobody*!"

"Yeah? How about Mr. Rios?"

"Oh, well, yeah. Mr. Rios. For *now*, anyway. But not for long. I got plans. Okay, I think this is deep enough. Come over here and help me with Mr. Walla-walla-bing-bang, whatever the hell his name is, the *gentleman* of *Polish descent*."

"Okay."

"Turn the headlights off first. It's gettin' light enough to see now."

"Okay."

———

"All right, you ready for this, Snake? We're gonna carry him over and just drop him in, okay?"

"Okay."

"Take his feet, Snake. No, his *other* feet. That's it. You ain't done this kinda work much, huh?"

"I've done my share, Artie."

"Well, let's just do this. Here, I'll get down in here, and you roll him over to—ouch!"

"Sorry."

"There ya go with the *sorry* again! Okay, there. Now, hand me down the shovel. It's over there by the tree. Go get the shovel, Snake. Well? What're ya waitin' for, Snake? Why're ya just standin' there?"

"The shovel can wait a minute, Artie."

"Whaddaya mean, the shovel can—*Hey!* What's with the gun? What the hell do ya think you're *doin'*, Snake?"

"My job. It's just a job, Artie. Remember?"

"What the hell are you *doing?*"

"Stay where you are! You just stay right there in the hole. I have a message for you, Artie. A message from Mr. Rios."

"What the hell're you talkin' about? *Hey!* Don't point that thing at me!"

"Shut up! You talk too much, Artie. Did anyone ever tell you that?"

"Snake—"

"Mr. Rios wanted me to give you a message, Artie. He said you shouldn't have messed around with his wife."

"*What?!* What the hell're you *talkin'* about?"

"I'm talking about Molly Rios, Artie."

"Snake—"

"Molly Tamalé, the Mexicali Gal."

"Whaddaya mean, me and Molly, Snake? Mr. Rios don't know nothin' about that!"

"No, but *I* do."

"Snake—"

"Even if I *am* just a *momser.*"

"Snake—"

"You shouldn't have gambled like that, Artie."

"Please, Snake—"

"You should have stayed in Riverdale, played with the Legos, called them Dad and Mom, know what I mean?"

"Snake—"

"Then maybe you would have seen the ocean again. Malibu. Whatever. You could have done whatever you wanted. But not now, Artie. It's too late for that now."

"Please, Snake—"

"Oh, and Artie?"

"For chrissakes, Snake—"

"Listen to me, Artie."

"Snake!"

"Are you listening to me, Artie?"

"Snaaake!"

"My name isn't *Snake,* Artie. My name is *Irwin.*"

"Hi, this is Irwin . . . yeah, I'm the one they call Snake. Who's this? . . . Okay, Stan, I'd like to talk to Mr. Rios . . . Not up yet? What time is it there? . . . Eight? Yeah, it's just going on six here. It's five fifty-seven. Fifty-*eight.* . . . Okay, tell Mr. Rios the job is done, as he instructed, and I'm heading back into town now. He'll know what I mean. And tell him I received the payment, and thanks for the bonus. That was really nice of him. Tell him I'm available for any other jobs he might have for me. When will he be back in Vegas? . . . Okay, tell him I'll see him next week, when he gets back. Thanks. Oh, and Stan? Please don't call me Snake anymore, all right? My name is Irwin . . . Thanks . . . Yeah, Stan, you have a nice day, too. 'Bye."

"Good morning . . . Yeah, it's me, Irwin . . . It's just after six. Six-oh-two—oh-*three.* You sound like you're still asleep . . . Oh, yeah? Want some company? . . . Yeah, I just called there. He won't be back till next week . . . Well, I'm on my way back into town right now. I just did some business for him . . . No, I'm alone . . . Artie? How should *I* know where Artie is? I think he said something about getting out of town for a while. Maybe he did that . . . Okay, I'll be there in about half an hour . . . All right, I'll make it twenty minutes . . . Yes, I've got my key. Don't get up, I'll let myself in . . . Oh, yeah? That sounds nice. I can't wait. Then we can have breakfast. I'll see you in twenty minutes, Molly. . . ."

ODDSMAKER

EDWARD WELLEN

Going down, I lifted my indoor shades brow-high to double-check, by the dim light of the elevator car, my final draft of the Dulcimer's morning lines.

The numbers hadn't rearranged themselves since my last look. I still felt uneasy about them, but they were the best I could do with what I had. I stifled a sigh and slid the shades back in place.

I got out at the gaming floor, holding the printout close to my vest out of habit but ready to post at the sports book.

Then I spotted Betty. Betty Lyons, who runs the beauty salon concession and is her own best ad. Betty, who makes my heart beat faster.

To keep from seeing her, I had skipped our daily dawn session at the Dulcimer's fitness center. Now I jammed the printout in my pocket and made myself one with the potted plant bookending a stand of slot machines.

Betty flagged a passing cocktail waitress and spoke over the ambient whirr and buzz. "Sally, have you seen Al Milledge?"

Wearing the uniform smile, Sally glanced past Betty, straight through the space in the greenery, into my shades.

A better-than-even bet: I shook my head.

It paid off with a nice ambiguity. "Sorry, Miss Lyons."

I curved a limber green limb to mime a tip of the hat. Into my mental tickler file went: Tip Sally some spendable green.

Betty nodded ambiguous thanks. Sally went on her smile-lit way. Betty briskly mounted the stairs to the beauty salon on the mezzanine, all the while maintaining her stakeout of the sports book.

"Do you mind?" A woman with a paper cup of quarters elbowed in to arm-wrestle the end slot machine.

"Luck, lady." An ambiguous wish.

Wasted on a mind set on hitting the jackpot at the end of the dream rainbow. She was already deaf to all but her deposited quarter. In her world, I existed only as an impediment. When I gave her elbow room I ceased to exist.

In my world, the problem was to reach the sports book uncaught. Close by, an exit to the parking lot offered itself.

Trouble was, I'd have to step outside the Dulcimer, pick my way through the parked cars, re-enter by another door. I could take the unconditioned furnace blast that would hit me. But the light. . . .

I had blocked just how bad it had been the last time I ventured outside the Dulcimer during daylight hours. So I found myself betting that though my shades were neither UV-proof nor wraparound, if I moved fast enough, I could beat—or at least bear—the light.

The door opened for me. UV hit straight on and raw sunlight edged in. The explosive *dazzle* brought back why I stayed indoors during daylight hours.

After a few unsteady steps, I made for a palm tree. Fake but not a mirage, and cast real shadow.

I never reached that oasis. I bumped into a hurrying figure, scattered in semblance but solid in substance, and my shades jarred off.

A laid-back drawl. "Watch where you're going, friend."

Fractured light flashed, splinters of sunlight pierced. In a zigzag jungle of chrome and glass, headlight-eyes sprang to false life and burned into mine. I froze like a deer, unable to see or stir.

"Sorry." My own voice jump-started me. I bent to feel around for my shades and we bumped again.

"No, Al. I'm sorry. I didn't see it's you. . . . Don't move. . . . Here you go."

He handed me the shades. I put them on, for all the good they did me. I saw after-images of the same scattered semblance of a man. But the laid-back drawl had finally sunk in. "Thanks, Chuck."

Charles Everett Owens, multibillionaire CEO of DBA, the juggernaut conglomerate, oddly without his entourage.

I have two points in the Dulcimer Hotel & Casino, and had met Chuck Owens when he dickered with the board a few years back for controlling interest. But the Nevada Gaming Control Board began a media-prodded look into the Dulcimer's alleged mob ties. Chuck lost interest in any kind of interest. He backed out, cartooned as saying, "Tain't that I need the taint." It surprised me. He could've put himself forward as a white knight and got himself a very sweet deal. And me a nice profit. But he had smiled at my paltry two points at our first meeting; I overcame the temptation to make the suggestion. Not the first time pride has cost me.

Now a clamp on my elbow. "Let me lend you a hand, Al."

The friendly butcher in my home town had a way of remarking on the weather—"Nice day out, ain't it?" or "Seem like it's gonna rain?"—as he made to weigh the meat. That was your cue to look out. To turn your head and look out through the store window, if you were foolish. If you were wise, to keep your eyes on the scale and look out for his thumb.

I couldn't keep an eye on Chuck's friendly hand; I could wonder what was in it for him to spring to my aid. Many a collision is a collusion; the two of us had been in a rush. My time was merely measurement, his was *MONEY*.

"Appreciate it, Chuck. Can't see a thing for the light." My eyelids felt grainy, my eyeballs red hot, and for once I was not too proud.

The vise tightened. "My pleasure, Al."

He had the build to build on, and more than likely a state-of-the-art exercise room and a world-class personal trainer. He surely felt, and showed he felt, like a guy in great shape.

"Thanks, Chuck. I'll be fine once I get back inside."

Back in we went. But he didn't let go.

Just as well. I wasn't fine. Everything was a blinding blur.

"Where we heading, Al?"

I didn't want Betty to see me this way. "The elevator. Penthouse floor."

Before we covered much carpet, Chuck's grip transmitted sudden stiffness and we stopped dead.

A solid but wavery shadow blocked our path and a gravel voice backed it up. "Are you okay, Mr. Milledge?"

I grinned. "I am now. Chuck, meet Doug Page, our chief of

security. A touch too much of the sun, Doug; Mr. Owens is lending me a hand."

"Oh. Sure. Sorry I didn't recognize you, Mr. Owens."

I felt Chuck shrug. "No law says you have to. It's good to see the Dulcimer's security so quick off the mark."

"Thanks, Mr. Owens."

"Say, Doug." My free hand fished the morning-line sheet out of my shirt pocket. "Will you give this to Joanna at the sports book?"

"Glad to, Mr. Milledge."

Chuck started off with me, then stopped, also with me. "Oh, Page. Would you tell the front desk I'll be in Mr. Milledge's suite for the next few minutes? After that, I'll be in my room if there are any calls."

"Sure thing, Mr. Owens."

Chuck steered me to the elevator and pressed the top button. A pair got on with us. On the ride up I caught a whispered "That's Al Milledge" and a whispered-back "Zat so?"

His grip tightened, but he waited for the couple to get off before he spoke. "The price of fame."

"Yeah." I couldn't help needling him. "How soon they forget, though. I didn't hear 'That's Chuck Owens.' "

The smiley voice broadened its cheeks. "That's because you can't see my beat-up outfit and my week's beard. I've been desert-ratting."

"So that's why Doug moved in." Here I'd been thinking of Chuck Owens with the styled hair and the custom tailoring, extremely personable and eminently presentable.

"I must've looked like some loser putting the arm on the great Al Milledge." By the tone, a fat grin shaped Chuck's voice. "Page let me see the bulge of his gun when he braced me. Good man. A suspicious mind in a strong body."

The car made its final stop and we got out.

"Mind if I ask why the desert-ratting?" Just making conversation as I gestured toward my suite.

"Every now and again I need to get away from civilization. Call it rest and recreation. How about you, Al? Aside from your little foray just now, do you ever leave the Dulcimer?"

"Haven't got sick of it yet." I came up against a door. "Here we are."

I got out my card key, felt for the electric lock. On the second swipe I faced the magnetic strip the right way through the slot. Once inside, I turned and held out my hand.

"Thanks, Chuck."

"I'm coming in. To see you safe, and to talk."

"Fine." If he wanted to pick my brains, I wanted to pick his. I pointed to where the wet bar ought to be. "Help yourself while I find the eye ointment in my medicine cabinet."

"Take your time, Al. Mix you anything?"

"Plain soda, thanks." I wanted a clear head while dealing with him.

I guessed he felt the same way. I heard no stirring or shaking while I tended to my eyes.

―――――

After we raised glasses, I beat him to the punch with what had been on my mind. Within the past week, three of the biggest bookies in Las Vegas had gone missing, leaving a big hole in my calculations.

"Chuck, I'm worried about Rinker, O'Dea, and Todman. Have you heard anything?"

"Exactly what I meant to ask you. I'm left dangling too. Laid bets with all three. Got no feedback. Reason I've hopped to Vegas." The drawl drew closer. "When's the last you heard from any of them?"

"Monday night Todman phoned to ask what I knew about Goforit. I drew a blank, so I stalled him; said I'd get back to him in a few minutes. Figured Goforit was the name of a horse. But when I checked the records I couldn't find a Goforit in any stable. Called back to tell him so, but Todman never answered."

"Cops ask you about that?"

"No. I felt it was confidential, so didn't report it, and apparently the cops haven't traced his calls." Bookies and oddsmakers tend to use cutouts to spare tender Fed ears when we might seem to be tendering betting advice.

"I see your point, Al. The―"

Teletype chatter interrupted. Weekend scores coming in. Though I had put gauze pads over my eyes, I brightened. This is when it all comes together, and I could barely rein in my drive to pore over the figures.

Chuck's smile-shaped voice. "The man of action."

I swung my head around for a blind look at the devices that keep me in touch with the sports world. "I guess I do cover a fair bit of action."

"A man of virtual action, I should say. I bet you love the stats better than the players and the teams and the games."

The words were mild but the scorn in his tone stung.

My real world was this room. True, I had an easy life at the Dulcimer. Everything I needed was at hand. But my world was a solipsistic construct, narrowed by an eye condition and a loner inclination, ruled—no, inhabited—by a man unable to share it with the woman he loved. . . .

I heard Chuck making to leave my world. I stood up and put on a grin. "You got me pegged, Chuck. I factor in the pulled groins and the muddy tracks and the shaved points to arrive at the numbers, but the numbers themselves are whole and clean and elegant."

"Keep crunching 'em, Al. See you around. Take it easy."

I stuck my hand out and braced myself for a bonecrusher but he seemed not to have seen it.

After he left, I stood rooted inside the door, unclasped hand still outstretched.

Take it easy, the man had said. Disdainfully.

Did I already take it too easy? Deep down, did I fear to go out there and put myself on the line? Had I walled myself in with a psychosomatic ailment?

I tore free. Found my phone, thought to hell with eavesdroppers, dialed by feel. Reached the unlisted number of Lee Vandemark, a Wall Streeter of some note. Made with the amenities.

Then, "Lee, what's your take on Chuck Owens?"

Vandemark's tone changed as he shifted a quid pro quo in his cheek. "Funny you should call right now, Al. I'm taking a good friend out to Aqueduct in a few minutes. It would be nice if I had a winner to impress her with. Is there a hayburner you like?"

I grimaced. An oddsmaker doesn't pick winners. An oddsmaker sets odds to make events even. Like everyone else, Vandemark misunderstood. He expected me to make like the Delphic oracle.

"Give me a minute, Lee." I visualized my morning line and made my pick.

The fifth at Aqueduct was a 1-1/16 mile race for fillies and mares. The $150,000 purse would draw decent competition. Miss Sugar, a dark chestnut filly in good condition, had shown she could run on sod, was comfortably weighted. Yet most bettors trying to handicap the race would be passing her up. What they would see as a negative was a positive. Her last race had been seven furlongs on dirt against colts and geldings, and she had eaten their dust. Still, she had fought for her head to make more speed. This meant the rider was saving her for her next race. As far as equine speed and endurance go, seven furlongs on dirt equates with 1-1/16 mile on grass. So now, running against her own kind, and with the crowd underrating her, she would win at the best possible price. Price didn't matter to Vandemark; he wanted a winner. But all the public selectors had overlooked Miss Sugar, so that she was an overlay, had a longer price than her real chance of winning. To me, she seemed a shoo-in—unless the saddle slipped after a half mile and the jockey couldn't handle her properly, and unless a thousand other mishaps.

I spoke with assurance but crossed my fingers. "Bet your wad on Miss Sugar in the fifth."

"Meshugge?"

I corrected him. He thanked me. I got him back on track.

"So, Lee, the bottom line on Chuck Owens?"

"Thinking of buying DBA stock? Don't quote me, but I wouldn't. He's spread himself too thin. Built a house of cards. Has to come up with a lot of cash soon or fold his hand."

"Does he own property in the desert around Vegas?"

Thoughtful silence, then, "Owns personally, directly? Not that I know of. But at several removes he controls Goforit."

Goforit. Todman's last talk with me. "What the hell is Goforit?"

"A ghost town." We wound up the amenities. Goforit. A ghost town, not a horse. And Chuck Owens had chosen not to set me straight on that.

————

I asked around, starting with the Dulcimer's concierge.

Goforit turned out to be a gone and almost forgotten straggle of deserted buildings along a lone dusty street in the middle of miles and miles of miles and miles. Goforit stood a half-day's drive north of Las Vegas, on a desert track that ran off a side road west of US 95. Goforit's hopeful founders in 1872 thought they were in California. Goforit, the whole ruined and abandoned shebang, went for chump change a dozen years ago when Caravan Pictures bought the ghost town with the idea of using it as a film location and tourist attraction. But Caravan itself had given up the ghost, become a shell corporation with just the rights to its old films and a few odds and ends like Goforit. And Chuck Owens's DBA had acquired the successor shebang for inflated chump change.

As soon as I could see comfortably, I looked it up on the Internet. In a brief flurry of publicity that I had missed at the time, Caravan had touted its plans for Goforit, though the Web site had faded with Caravan. But the ghost of the Web site was cached, and I found thumbnails of Goforit. The full-size images showed your generic western street: shots of the buildings lining it, from the livery stable at one end to the undertaker at the other, with the saloon and the hotel and the bank in between, and the boothill off to one side.

My doorbell rang. The peephole imaged a distorted Doug Page. I let him in.

"What is it, Doug? No trouble, I hope."

"Just making sure you're okay, Mr. Milledge."

"I'm fine, thanks."

"You look better. Thinking of going out?"

"What makes you ask?"

"The concierge tells me you been inquiring about ghost towns."

"A particular ghost town. Goforit."

"Yeah. He says he told you Goforit is private property, no trespassing, but he has a whole list of other ghost towns around here you're free to visit."

"Not interested in other ghost towns. Goforit or bust."

"Some special reason?"

You can never be sure of a man's price, but so far Doug had a good track record for trustworthiness. I leveled with him. "Just before Todman went missing, he phoned me and mentioned Goforit. Todman's a friend, and I'd like to nose around there, sniff what I can sniff."

Doug let out a heavy breath. "Todman's a friend of mine too." His glabella creased; he pinched his philtrum. "Tell you what; I got time coming, and a new Hummer itching for a workout. If you're game, I'll drive you there and help you look." Again the workout with the space between the eyebrows and the indentation under the nose.

Before I thought, I said, "You're on."

"Great. We can leave in an hour, if that suits you."

I nodded.

He turned, turned back. "Slap on sunscreen and insect repellent, wear Western boots and a Stetson. I'll get spring water and picnic lunches from room service and gas up."

"Fine. By the way, Doug, is Chuck Owens still at the Dulcimer?"

"Yeah. Booked as Bud Kesten. Comped for as long as he wants." He shook his head at himself. "I know the A list; I shoulda made him on sight." He cocked his head. "Thinking of asking for his help?"

Already I regretted mentioning Chuck's name. "On second thought, I better not. His time is too valuable."

While I changed, I caught the Aqueduct results. Miss Sugar had been scratched. Vandemark couldn't fault me for that.

Doug returned as I secured my braided-leather bolo tie with its turquoise-nugget-center Navajo-silver slide. A gift from Betty. Seldom worn because of the "tie" connotation but reassuring now on leaving the Dulcimer.

He looked me over. "All set?"

I nodded, and passed him a Mapquest printout of the way from the Dulcimer's mosaic threshold to the dead heart of Goforit.

He grinned and drew pints of spring water from a pocket of his bush jacket. "Gotta keep ourselves hydrated." He uncapped them barehanded, handed me one, raised his. "One for the road."

I lifted mine and drank.

A throbbing headache knocked me awake. I felt weight on my wrists. I traded inner flashing for a squint at outer glare, and saw shiny handcuffs. I shot up—in my mind. In body, I sat up stiffly. Upon a bunk in a jail cell. At the head of the bunk, touching the wall, my Stetson rested upside down, my wraparound sunglasses folded inside. I put them on.

My cell was one of a pair, with matching glassless barred windows that showed the thickness of the adobe bricks.

In the other cell a bundle of clothes lay on the bunk.

I swung my feet to the floor, balanced myself upright, and stumbled to my window. Endless desert stared pitilessly back; its hot breath blew past. I could put words to its whisper: Thirsty? Too bad.

I turned from the voice of the sand breeze to the ticking of a clock. It hung beside the door in the facing wall. The minute hand quivered at ten to twelve. Nausea hit me. I dry-heaved in the chemical toilet.

The bundle of clothes in the other cell twitched and sat up.

Doug Page.

He rose painfully. A black eye, a sheepish look. He opened his lopsided, puffy mouth as though to speak, but only blood trickled out. He sleeved his lips two-handedly; handcuffed like me.

I eyed him stonily, accusing him with my gaze.

He turned his head away, admitting guilt. He had slipped me knockout drops and delivered me to Chuck Owens.

Bootsteps broke the heavy silence.

Doug stiffened, then backed into the far corner of his cell.

The door opened. I saw the sheriff's tin star before I saw the sheriff's tan face.

Chuck Owens. An outsize revolver weighed down his gunbelt. Another gunbelt and holstered revolver hung over his left shoulder.

I found as I spoke dryly what speaking dryly is. "What role you playing, Chuck? Kidnapper? Holding me for ransom?"

Chuck smiled broadly. "Ransom? A drop in the bucket. A pee in the sea. If you want it by the numbers: You're under arrest. I'll read you your right."

"Supreme Court cutting 'em down to one these days?"

"I'm the Supreme Court." His right hand slapped his holster. "You have the right to outdraw and outshoot me—if you can."

"Trial by gun duel? What for?"

"Same as Page here. Your life." He thrust the spare gunbelt through Doug's bars. "Here, Page. Take your weapon."

Doug shrank farther, trying to be the shadow of himself.

Chuck dropped the spare to the cell floor, made a lightning draw and triggered a thunder shot. I had heard of the new Smith & Wesson's .50-caliber Magnum revolver. Now I had both seen and heard it.

A new hole through the adobe wall let in daylight. The blast had blinded me to the fact that he had nicked Doug's left ear; he could have blown it off.

Doug touched his dripping ear, looked dully at his bloody fingers, wiped them on his bush jacket, shuffled forward as though shackled with leg irons, bent for the gunbelt, tried but failed to get it around and on.

Chuck leaned against the facing wall, arms folded, watching patiently—too patiently, enjoyably—till Doug figured out a way. Doug stretched the gunbelt across his bunk, lay down, brought the ends together over his waist, and buckled up.

A slow, steady creaking outside brought a twisted smile to Doug's face, a mere twitch, as though he had for a flash forgotten his fix.

The creaking continued. Not the swinging of weathered signs or loose-hanging doors in the breeze, but a heavy tread and the agony of put-upon boards. Then one last loud creak, and silence.

Chuck grinned and glanced at the clock. Five minutes to noon. "Showdown time."

He unlocked Doug's cell door.

Doug's wounded mouth withdrew into his last line of defense—tight silence. Without looking my way, he shuffled out, still as though shackled.

I strained to hear beyond the closed door. At noon on the dot, Chuck's voice rang out. "Go for it!"

A full minute passed. An empty full minute. Then one thunderous gunshot. Hard upon its echo, a creepy giggle.

———————

Chuck slid a beaten copper tray into my cell, then leaned back under three o'clock.

I couldn't muffle belly rumble, but damned if I'd rush to grab food and drink. I gave the thick ham on rye, the beaded can of Sprite, and the polished Granny Smith apple a bored glance, waited a few long beats before picking the tray up. Slowly I carried it to the bunk, slowly seated myself, slowly pulled the tab, slowly swished a cold mouthful before slowly swallowing.

Now I could speak without croaking. I nodded at Doug's cell. "Why?"

"Because I can."

"No. The real reason."

"That is the real reason. I need to and want to. And because I can, I do. Business and pleasure. Dual reason, duel method." Chuck smiled boyishly. "You're wondering how I select my— uh—opponents. Never at random. Serially. One thing leads to another. Take Rinker, O'Dea, and Todman. Couldn't let 'em put the squeeze on me for my losses. Gave each his chance to settle accounts. And you were next in line."

"Why me?"

"Because I respect you. You're the likeliest guy in Vegas to figure out what's happening and who's behind it. So you were already my mark when Page interposed himself. Don't weep for him. He jumped at the chance to put the snatch on you. Another twofer; I've offed a double-crosser, forestalled a shake-down."

"He had it coming. But I can do without your respect."

"In a way I'm doing you a favor. You've been playing the game of life with abstractions. Now face up to reality, play with your life."

I put the apple core on the tray beside the empty Sprite can and fat stripped from the ham.

He beckoned for the tray.

Damn. He was too watchful; I had no hope of slicing it through the bars at his Adam's apple.

On his way out, he paused and turned. "Since you're playing under a handicap, I'll give you a rare treat. I'll be back at five and show you around Goforit."

After his footfalls faded away, I tested the window bars. Blistering to the touch. I found a handkerchief in my otherwise empty pockets, padded a hand, tested again. Shakeproof.

The edge of my bolo slide served to flake adobe from the base of the central bar.

At six to five, I knocked off, and brushed and blew the handful of dust outside.

Chuck's face loomed in the window. "Chip away, Al. The bars are set deep, top and bottom."

Small satisfaction that some dust had got on his face.

On our way out through the sheriff's office, Chuck tossed his key ring into a desk drawer.

The open air closed in on me. But this was the shady side of the street, and the Stetson and the sunglasses helped hold daylight at a tolerable level.

Across the street, the Nye County Trust was another adobe building. All the rest were warped and weathered frame unpainted the gray of time. One fresh touch: ugly bright blue bench in front of Jeff's Hardware.

No signs or doors creaked in the hot breeze.

Nobody in the street. No body in the street.

A big rusty spot in the dirt marked the ex. From that point the track of a single wheel bit its way out of town. Chuck seized my left arm and swung me around. "This way, Al."

From the sheriff's office, we clomped along the wooden sidewalk formed by the joined porches of Goforit's establishments. Past the hardware store, the barber shop, the feed store, then down steps to the ground and past the smithy, to the building that marked Goforit's end or beginning: Scanlon's Livery Stable.

Chuck let go to swing the high doors wide. I moved on my own into blessed dimness.

No neighs, no restless hooves, no swishing tails, no horsy smells. And hitching racks along the way had been unused. Goforit was a no-horse town. That didn't surprise me. What surprised me: no horseless carriage, no Hummer.

Chuck had knocked out the stalls to make the stable a hangar.

A Sikorsky helicopter and drums of aviation fuel took most of the space.

I cleared my throat. "You flew Page and me here?"

"That I did, Al."

An oversized mattress filled one corner. A trapeze-like contraption hovered two feet above the mattress.

I pointed. "That where you bed down?"

He laughed. "Hell, no. I rough it at the hotel. That comes next."

A faint clatter grew louder.

Chuck grinned. "C'mon." He stepped back outside and megaphoned through cupped hands to someone up the street. "I'm here with Milledge."

By the time I joined him, my fingertips had picked up oily grit from the drums and smeared it over my cheekbones, under my sunglasses. We passed the smithy and stepped onto the wooden sidewalk.

Down the middle of the street came a beachball of a boy in undershirt and shorts. He pushed a toy wheelbarrow. A toy shovel and a toy cooler rattled in the barrow. He packed a toy gun. But as he came closer, the toy objects grew mansize and the boy became the most man I've seen in the flesh. He'd've busted a carnival weight-guesser's scale. I'd say between seven hundred and eleven hundred pounds. (Some spread, I know, but I'm no weight-guesser.) That explained the oversize mattress in the livery stable. The high and wide doors would be his only fit.

Chuck turned to me. "That's Bud Kesten, Goforit's caretaker. Goes with a ghost town: he's not all here."

Bud had sharp ears and a high, wheezy voice. "Yeah, I ain't all here."

He giggled. "Sometimes I goes up the trail a piece, and sometimes I goes down the trail a piece, to freshen them 'Keep out' signs." He pulled at his undershirt to unforeshorten his tin star. "I'm deppity sheriff."

Chuck stopped us at the hotel. I made out the faded fancy letters of "Posada" over the door. We waited for Bud to come abreast.

"Hose everything down, Bud."

Bud stopped, sweating profusely. He was probably older than the thirty he looked. Fullblown flesh nullified facial wrinkles, but clearly he pondered. He brightened. "Gotcha, sheriff. Don't want flies."

"Good man."

Bud eyed his vast shadow wistfully, as though wishing he could benefit from casting it, then trundled manfully by dry cracked watering troughs and rickety hitching racks on his way to the stable.

Chuck ushered me into the Posada, past the untended reception counter, waved me upstairs ahead of him, and unlocked the first door we came to.

At the sudden chill an ah! escaped me.

He grinned and pointed ceilingward. "If you had come to in the Sikorsky, you'd've seen the solar panels on the roof. Power for air-conditioning, electric lights, refrigerator-freezer in the shed out back that Bud can walk into." He gestured to a desktop computer. "And you'd've seen the satellite dish that links me to DBA and the Web."

On the screen a gopher popped up from a hole here, surveyed the emptiness, disappeared, popped up from a hole elsewhere.

I looked around at the furnishings. Chuck had skimped on nothing but good taste.

When I turned back, the screen saver had given way to the DBA logo. Chuck typed in "Fourtwoone."

"Pretty careless of you, Chuck. I see your password."

"What does that tell you about the odds, Al? It oughta shake you that I don't care."

But he blocked the screen with his body as some numbers scrolled.

They put him in a bad mood, confirming Vandemark's assessment. I winced. Chuck would take it out on me. And did.

"Let's get on with the damn tour." He hustled me out and down.

———

The Last Chance Saloon. Pushing through the batwings triggered the player piano. Ghostly fingers tickled the ivories.

Chuck saw I didn't recognize the tune. "Stephen Foster's 'Voices That Are Gone.'"

"The words are gone too."

"Good point. I'll commission Marlene Dietrich to sing the lyrics."

"She's long gone."

"Don't play smart, Al, and don't play dumb. Money can do anything. I'll have a computer whiz program Dietrich's voice."

"Good for you." I spoke absently, taking in the long bar. The brass spittoon at the foot of it and the bung-starter on the shelf behind it looked good to bean Chuck with but were out of reach. Chairs and tables were at hand. I heaved a heavy sigh and rested my palms on a chair.

Chuck saw but said nothing, even looked away.

I nerved myself to put everything I had behind the swing and found myself hefting hardly anything.

He whirled with a ready fist, then smiled as I gently set the chair down.

"A breakaway." He waved his hand around. "Goes for most furniture in here. Made of yucca wood. Caravan Pictures used them in barroom brawls to clobber stunt men harmlessly."

We cast long shadows as we jaywalked across to the Nye County Trust building.

Inside, behind the high carved-oak railings, a huge iron safe stood against the wall. Chuck put a hand on the dial, then faced me and raised an eyebrow.

I remembered his password. "I'll stick with a winning combination: DBA. Four, two, one."

"I'm gonna miss you, Al."

"In more ways than one, I trust."

He twirled the dial, pulled the safe door wide. "Here's your trust."

I cleared my throat. "Some tourist attraction. An empty safe."

He reached in. I heard the click of a hidden catch. He began to swing the safe away from the wall. He stopped himself, raised a listening hand.

Creaking neared.

He strode to the bank entrance, leaned out. "Bud!"

A wheezy sigh. "Yeah, sheriff?"

"Fetch two cans of Sprite."

Another wheezy sigh. "Yeah, sheriff." Creaking faded. Bud Kesten, deppity sheriff, spectator, gravedigger, and gofer.

Chuck shut the front door and came back. He swung the safe

. all the way and we passed through the opening into the hidden vault.

My skin crawled. Mounted trophy heads. Many more than three. Chuck had a long, hidden history. But my gaze fixed on the missing bookies. Rinker, with his heavy-lidded eyes; O'Dea, with his bandido mustache; Todman, with his frozen grin. Peering out of portholes in a Stygian vessel. I pulled my gaze from the heads and took in the rest of the room.

I played the friendly butcher. I pointed to a strongbox resting on a shelf. "What's in the box?" His cue to shift his look to the box.

"Diamonds for a rainy day." He smiled big at the box.

I edged back, set myself to whirl and leap for the opening.

Without turning his head, he reached out and held me from darting out and sealing him in with his diamonds and his trophies.

"Not so fast, Al. I wanna show you where you go. Right next to Todman. That's your rightful spot, not Page's." He squeezed the nape of my neck. "Now we can head back." Sly stress on "head."

The walk shook to Bud's tread as we left the bank. He'd made good time.

Bud handed us cold cans of Sprite and we cut across toward jail. I fumbled with the tab, nearly let the slick can slip through sweaty palms, nursed the drink super-carefully, all to fall behind and put a giggling Bud between myself and Chuck.

I spoke casually, but tried to get it all in before Chuck could shut me up. "Bud, do you know there's a vault behind the old iron safe? Dial four-two-one, reach in for the catch, and you'll find a box full of diamonds." I speeded up both my words and my feet as Chuck started rounding Bud. "I bet he'll add your head to those in the vault if he catches you even peeking into the bank, so get him fir—"

I barely had time to tighten myself against what I felt coming. It was worth the knockdown blow. Chuck, with his no-loose-ends philosophy, now had to kill Bud as soon as he found a replacement. And Bud, no matter how sluggish his body, now had the frantic thought planted in his mind. I had changed the dynamics of their relationship. I hoped it would change the odds in my favor in my very near future. I looked up from the ground at Chuck and felt like smiling, but my face told me I must look like Doug.

Chuck hauled me up by my bracelets. "Brought it on yourself, Al. You had to try and wake up sleeping dogs."

"See what he thinks of you, Bud? A sleeping dog."

Bud wheezed a halfhearted chuckle and pushed me along.

"Wait." Chuck planted one hand on my chest and slapped me with the other.

My sunglasses flew off. He stared at my smudges.

"How the hell—" He grabbed my joined hands, pried open a fist. My fingertips told him. "The drums in the stable. Gotta hand it to you, Al. You put one over on me."

I couldn't see how it happened; he moved and my sunglasses cracked and ground under his feet.

"Sorry, Al. An accident."

———

As he locked me back in my cell, Chuck bowed like room service. "Your last-meal request, sir?"

I squinted at him, unable to tell if his face matched his words. His concern for form, sane or insane? I answered, sanely or insanely, "A candlelight supper with a lovely woman."

A specific woman. Betty. I could hear her voice: *Al, I need commitment.* And I could see her face when my words would not come.

Chuck brought me back. "Be serious."

"I am serious." I was seeing the light—and the light hurt.

At seven p.m. Chuck slid the last meal into my cell. The room had a ceiling bulb, so the memorial candle burned palely in its glass on the tray. I failed to appreciate the steak dinner and the vintage claret.

———

Full in body, empty in spirit, I waited till Chuck had gone. Then I used the bolo slide to slice a pair of one-eighth-inch slits in the brim of my Stetson, and frayed the edges. With the brim pulled low over my eyes, and the cheekbone smears reducing glare, I would not be shooting blindly . . . if I had time to draw and shoot at all. I hit the hay with that happy thought.

───────

Riding to the rescue, the cavalry raised a drumming thunder and a storm cloud of dust. The commander held up his gloved hand, reined in, and the troop stopped. The thundering ended, the cloud rolled over men and horses. They grew as grainy as the dust, and all vanished.

I sat up, made out nine-thirty, and tried to piece it together. An outside cue had entered my dream and awakened me to the all-too-real Goforit nightmare.

Bootsteps and the outer door creaking open and Chuck's voice ushering people in. "Inside, friend. Step right in, honey. Fear not, your motorcycle's perfectly safe."

The rattle of keys.

The inner door opened. A biker couple. Male: mid-thirties, bandanna'd head, nose ring, shaved hash marks in his eyebrows, steel-studded belt. Female: teenage, cropped hair, belly-button ring, shrinkwrap Levi's. Both dusty and weary and didn't have to be stoned to look spaced-out.

They stopped dead and stared at me while Chuck opened the other cell.

"Enter, folks."

The guy found his voice first. "You're arresting us? What for?"

"Trespassing on private property. Ignoring the warning signs."

"Hold on, Sheriff. I told you we lost our way to Death Valley. We followed a desert track, it got dark, we saw your few lights."

"Step in, make yourselves comfortable. We'll straighten it out tomorrow."

"No room at the Posada?"

"Want another charge? Resisting arrest."

The girl tugged the guy's arm. "Let's get some sleep. I'm dead."

They went in. Chuck locked the cell and left.

The guy looked at me. "What you in for? Spitting on the sidewalk?"

"You won't believe me."

"Sure I will. That hick sheriff is running a tourist trap, collecting phony fines."

"That hick sheriff is Chuck Owens, head of DBA. Goforit is his private game preserve. He stages gun duels and collects human heads."

The bikers locked gazes and busted out laughing.

Chuck came back with two pairs of handcuffs. He beckoned me close, rolled his eyes toward the bikers. "Want your dessert now?"

I glanced at the girl. She grinned at me. I answered Chuck's arched eyebrow. "Thanks, but no thanks."

He shrugged and moved to the other cell.

The guy smiled. "Sheriff, are you really Chuck Owens?"

Chuck smiled back. "That what this touched-in-the-head feller's been telling you?"

"Yeah."

Chuck tossed the handcuffs into the cell. "Pick 'em up and cuff each other."

They stared at him.

He put his hand to his holster.

Now they began to believe me.

━━━━━━━

A restless night. Lots of tinkling in the chemical toilets.

━━━━━━━

Ten to noon. Chuck passed the spare gunbelt through the bars. The bikers huddled and watched. I tuned them out.

A quick learner, I stretched the gunbelt across my bunk, lay down, and buckled up.

I rose. Chuck was leaning beside the clock. I reached two-handedly for my weapon. He didn't stir. I pulled the gun. A double-action Smith & Wesson .38 revolver. Unloaded but cleaned and oiled. I pulled the trigger. The action was smooth, the hammer had its pin, each trigger-pull cocked the hammer, positioned the empty cylinder.

"When do I get the bullets?"

"Where. Outside. Just before the draw. Any more questions?"

I raised linked hands. "How fair is this? Kinda hard to make a fast draw tethered to myself."

Chuck snorted. "Carpe diem: die carping. That's gonna be your epitaph. Listen up, Al. I make the rules. Remember, it's the only game in town."

I nodded. "The odds are with the house—even one built on sand."

"Yeah, yeah. To answer your question, I'll give you the key, then back up twenty paces while you unlock. Now stop stalling."

———

Chuck arranged us in the middle of the street.

The wooden sidewalk shook and creaked as Bud neared the bench in front of Jeff's Hardware. A final ominous creak as he settled himself to watch. The hot desert breath wafted the strong scent of an after-shave lotion our way.

Chuck took a big sniff. "Hey, Bud, wearing that stink for the girl? You'll gas her to death before you crush her."

Bud giggled.

Chuck rattled six bullets in his fist under my nose. "Hand me your gun."

I wrestled the revolver from its holster. "How do I know they're not blanks?"

He uncoiled his fist. "Carping to the end. Pick one."

I had kept my head bowed for brim shade. I stabbed blindly.

He inserted the bullet, aimed at my head, hooked the trigger, grinned, swung the gun a touch, held steady, squeezed off the shot. It burned past my ear.

His voice cut through the ringing. "One shot wasted. Price you pay for carping."

He finished loading the gun, shoved it hard in my holster. My fingers itched to touch the gun butt lightly to feel if Chuck's thrust had made the front sight catch in the leather. But better not hand him an excuse to fire before I was ready.

He handed me the key. "Now I back away twenty paces while you free your hands. Then I say, 'Go for it.' And we draw and fire."

Now seemed Bud's moment, unless he was just as much of a nutcase as Chuck, or unless his gun was just for show, to ease his gun out while Chuck focused on me.

Bud giggled expectantly.

I ducked my head lower, squinted through the fuzzy slits.

Chuck backed away. "One . . . two . . . three. . . ."

The key felt hot from his hand and sweaty from me. I made it skitter in search of the hole.

Bud giggled.

The key slipped my fingers. I went down on one knee, groped to miss it.

Bud continued to giggle. Chuck reached "Twenty" and waited. I counted on Chuck's patience—or enjoyment—and he didn't let me down.

I swiped wider and wider for the elusive key, till my twists brought my locked hands to the gun butt. Then I drew and fired without getting up, taking aim through the slits.

Chuck had his gun out, too late. His figure jerked and I placed two more shots and he fell.

That left two for Bud. Odds were Chuck wouldn't trust Bud with live ammo, especially after the seed I'd planted. But I couldn't take chances. Still on one knee, I twisted to face Bud.

He sat frozen, his jowls hanging, too stunned to go for the equalizer at his equator if he could. He made a sitting target, and I took my time to kneecap him twice. He toppled off the bench with a thunderous thud. It would take his trapeze to pull himself up.

I shoved myself upright and moved with shaky knees. I made sure Chuck was dead, went through his pockets for the key to his Posada suite. Then I checked Bud's gun. Found it empty. He groaned and looked pitiful. I felt no pity. For a beached whale, yes; not for Bud.

After locating and using the key to my handcuffs, I would have fitted them on Bud. No chance, and really no need. He would keep.

I passed through the Posada to the refrigerator-freezer shed out back, found Doug Page's head in the cooler I'd seen in the wheelbarrow, retraced my steps, climbed the stairs, let myself into Chuck's suite, sat down at his computer and instant-messaged Nevada and Federal authorities.

———

At the sheriff's office I got the key ring out of the desk drawer. The bikers heard the jingle and were huddled in the far corner. They stared at me as if seeing a ghost. A welcome ghost.

———

Leaning into the Dulcimer's front desk, Betty spoke to the clerk. "Any news of Al Milledge?"

I tapped her on the shoulder. She whirled.

We gazed hungrily, thirstily. Often words get in the way of what we want to say. Our lips met and spoke for themselves.

THE DOPE SHOW

———

K.j.a. WISHNIA

"You know, you're probably the only guy I know who opens a porno mag and reads the fine print," said Hughie, taking his eyes off the three-girl routine on the runway.

"You gotta hear this," said the big man from Turkey. " 'The photos, words, and illustrations in this magazine are intended for fantasy purposes only. The editors do not suggest or encourage readers to act out fantasies contained herein—' "

"Tell me the sleazebag editor came up with that legal language—"

" 'We encourage safe sex practices and present this magazine as a safe fantasy alternative to dangerous sex practices.' "

"So now it's a public service. Wonderful." Hughie leaned against the bar and lit a cigarette. "I wish I'd have thought of that when Father Dougan caught me with a stack of his old *Playboys*. Jeez, they still cropped off the bush in those days."

Hughie exhaled up at the pin spots defining a smoky shaft of light over the bar, and looked around the place. It was small enough to be comfortable, with only one way in but four ways out, including two fire exits and the stage door, and that made him less comfortable. Too much craziness could take off in too many directions. Still, it was slightly off the beaten path, smoky and anonymous. Perfect. Or almost.

His gaze returned to the twisting trio.

Then the DJ broke into the thumping strip tune, interrupting Hughie's concentration with a voice that belonged in a sports arena: "And now, ladies and gentlemen, for your entertainment pleasure, please give it up for Candee's own vixen with the fixin's, Tracy Tetons!"

Tracy strutted on stage and started shaking those implanted things, just like she did five times a day, Tuesday through Sunday. Mondays off. Hughie watched her using the pole in a way that was functional but mechanical. Oh, it got the job done, all right, but something was missing.

"She's getting better," Hughie said.

Yilmaz either grunted something noncommittal or hocked up a loogie. Hughie couldn't tell which.

"How'd she come up with the name Tracy Tetons?" said Hughie.

"Because Alyssa Alps and Pandora Peaks were taken."

"She could have called herself Plenty O'Cleavage."

"Also taken."

"You're kidding."

Yilmaz shook his head, his iridescent blazer outlining a pair of pumped-up deltoids. "I think she should have called herself Persistence Pays."

"It's lyrical, but it's not ironic."

"It's not in on the joke?"

"It's too bitchy."

"Bitchy sells, too, my friend."

Hughie took a deep drag on his death stick and blew it out through his nose.

Yilmaz said, "I need to get some air."

"Wait a minute, I'll go with you."

Hughie took one more look around the dark interior of the club. His mark hadn't come in yet, but it was a good habit to double-check even a sure thing.

It was one of his few good habits.

They leaned outside and breathed in the clean desert air. The street off Fremont was all quiet, and misty with late afternoon shadows, portending a shower.

"Boy, rain in Vegas," said Hughie. "What are the odds of that?"

"That's not real rain," said Yilmaz, looking up at the sky. "That's a special effect."

――――――

Earl's butt was hurting. Eleven hours in the driver's seat and it was starting to feel as if eyeless robots had spot-welded his can to the truck's cold steel undercarriage as it rolled off the assembly line back in Flint, when they were still hiring. And for what? A long container full of sand. Nothing worth skimming from *this* haul. No compensation at all for a royal pain in the butt gig like this, and to make things worse, there was no one to laugh it off with.

So when he finally saw the great pyramids of dirt rising over the leafless trees and razor wire-topped steel mesh along the narrow, deserted road, he started to expel the hours of pent-up venom, releasing all that nastiness through his hairy nostrils with several deep breaths.

Okay, okay, under control—dump the load, check into the Motel 21 a few miles back, shower, and hit the bars on the edge of town until he found a semicircle of truckers who would understand the trip from hell and help him forget about it.

Earl could practically taste the foam on that first beer when he pulled up and found the steel gate closed and padlocked.

"Aw, fer chrissakes." He honked a few times, long and loud, and sat there idling. Just twenty feet beyond the galvanized gate, two big pickup trucks and a rot-fringed four-door sat in front of a low white building. A six-foot-wide American flag was flapping on a pole as the sky darkened. Huge piles of broken concrete waited to be ground down into lofty ziggurats of rock and further refined into mounds of sand. Earl checked his watch. The dispatcher had told him that the place closed at 4 p.m. on Saturdays and here he was a few minutes early, so where the heck were they?

He waited some more, as the rain started to pit-pat on the

roof of his cab. Soon, tiny rivers of dirty water were running down the windshield. He honked again, three, four times, and sat there waiting.

Finally some bone-thin guy came out of the building and trotted over to the gate, trying to button his after-work shirt, looking just like a scrap of newspaper as the loose white flaps were whipped by the wet wind. Earl threw the truck into gear, but the guy just stood there yelling something. Earl rolled down the window, letting big drops of dirty rain spatter his arm, but he still couldn't hear the guy over the drone of the big diesel engine. So he set it in neutral, opened the door and leaned out into the hard rain and yelled, "What's goin' on, buddy?"

"We're closed!"

"Whadaya mean, you're closed? I've got a delivery here for you!"

"We're closed! Come back Monday!"

"*Monday?* What the heck am I supposed to do till Monday?" But the guy was already running back inside, white shirt flaps flying behind him.

Jesus, if they think I'm going to . . . Earl decided to sit there until whoever was in there wanted to leave for the night. They'd have to open the gate, and then he could at least push his way in and drop the load. He waited while the rain hammered out hard knocks on the metal roof. The office lights stayed off. No one approached any of the vehicles. It got dark.

Two hours after nightfall, Earl cursed the heartless bastards inside the gate and turned the truck around.

He laid out twenty-nine dollars for a room, then went to a roadside diner with a special seating area for truckers only, and sat there under the pale fluorescent lights staring blankly out the window at the dreary sheets of rain bathing his truck with slick reflections of cold blue and green neon. But thin gray burgers speckled with globular coagulations and single-serving slices of apple pie shrink-wrapped in another state were not enough to satisfy his appetite as he sat there wondering what he was going to do for two whole nights in a hot town like this with only seventy bucks in his pocket.

"So what are you saying?" asked Hughie, lighting another cigarette.

"I'm saying that some porn is arousing, but I don't like these spread-fingered pussy shots. They make it look like a gynecology textbook," Yilmaz explained, waving the sulfrous fumes away from his nostrils. "No mystery."

"You mean they're giving porn a bad image?"

"I mean there's a fine line between seductive and repulsive."

"Oh, yeah," said Hughie, nodding. "Like when you got a buzz on, those sixty-inch tits look *fantastic*. But when you examine them under the cold light of reason, they're merely incredible."

"Okay, okay. Maybe because there was so much repression back in my country, you don't appreciate how excessive it seems to me. But you'd think one of these would be enough. So why do guys subscribe to porno mags?"

"Because they're guys."

"Yes, but I mean, why do they keep consuming new images?"

"Obviously, because we can't get enough of the stuff."

"Exactly. You keep coming back for more. Why?"

"You gotta ask why?"

"Yes. Why the need to keep coming back? Most of it's the same old stuff wrapped in a new package."

"Well, let's hear it for new packages," said Hughie, faux-toasting with a glass of sparkling water.

"It's all about consumption, even if it's only paper. Because porn isn't just selling you body parts, it's selling a myth."

"You mean the myth that in any town in the world, there are girls who'll fuck you 'cause they just love to have hot sex with total strangers."

"Yeah, I guess so. There's all this build-up, and then nothing—just emptiness."

"Just like real sex," said Hughie.

"Maybe for you."

"Droppen-zie dead, you freaking Turk." He went back to watching Tracy, who had started using the American flag as a prop. "She sure ain't made of paper."

"And the emptiness creates a new search for fulfillment."

"It's a vicious cycle."

"It's the dope show."

"Tracy's got talent, ya big bouncer," he said, blowing smoke out with each word. Back when she was Sherri Kayne, she had stolen the show in *Vampire Women of Mars*. She had something special, Hughie thought, some kind of—presence. And she hadn't asked for trouble. First that king-of-the-cheapies director pulls her from a crowd of hot-waxed bikini-lined extras and starts making her over into a B-movie up-and-comer. Natch he starts putting the moves on her. Then her friggin' creep-of-a-boyfriend, Jimmy Crowell, aka Jimmy Crowbar, a three-time loser wanted by the LAPD for chopping up a few late model vehicles, gets his nuts in a knot and tries to wrap a tire iron around said director's throat. And now lots of people want to talk to Jimmy C., but only Empire Studios laid down the real money, which is why this PI from East L.A. is hanging around this crummy Vegas strip club waiting to see if Jimmy the ex-boyfriend turns up or not.

"Drink?" offered Yilmaz.

"Too early. I'm working."

"Oh, right."

It was practically bounty hunting. But it wasn't easy to find a guy like Jimmy C., if he wanted to stay hidden. Jimmy used to hang with the West Coast Hog Fuckers and so he had about a hundred ganged-up places to scurry into like a rat up a drainpipe. Yes, Jimmy C. was sure hard to find. But *she* was a whole other story. He found *her* easily enough. She had been pumped full of implants, had a few skin tucks, and changed her name to Tracy Tetons—and was still hot as hell at 43. But she could also hear her biological clock clanging away like a two-ton church bell in her ears.

"You know where Jimmy is?" he had asked her, leaning against the coats in the tiny dressing room.

"Who the hell cares? Men are pigs. Fuck 'em all," she replied, jamming her eyeliner back into the tube.

"A word to the willfully ignorant. If you don't pay attention to what's going on around you, you are in for a lifetime of being screwed. And the people who are doing the screwing would like nothing better than to hear you say, 'Who the hell cares?' Just a warning."

"Everything he ever told me was a lie, okay? So how am I supposed to know where he is? I just hope I never see the freakin' SOB again," she said.

So he'd had no choice, really, but to pay a few subcontractors to spread the word around the ex-boyfriend's most recent hang-outs letting it be known where Sherri, aka Tracy, could be found, then sit back and wait for the schmuck to walk right into his hands. And to stop him before he broke her neck, which he had threatened to do. But then, every guy feels like killing his girl at some point, Hughie thought. The only difference is that this guy might actually *do* it.

"You think he'll show up?" said Yilmaz.

"He'll show up."

"Ain't you confident."

"Only way to be in this town." Hughie turned his eyes back to Tracy's act.

He said, "Now, *that's* what I call wrapping yourself in the flag."

———

Earl looked up at the cloudless neon skies of downtown Vegas and thought that things were definitely looking better. Twenty dollars had effervesced into beer-and-shot combos, and he was just drunk enough to enjoy the feeling, with plenty of room leftover for some more fun. Then some local hick had walked him around and around the blocks promising him some face time with a legal 18-year-old named Crystal or Chrissy, till his mind was going in such circles that the guy pulled the old give-me-the-money-so-I-can-run-around-the-corner-and-get-her scam and he just handed over a twenty and watched the guy go, and immediately felt like a dope for letting himself get taken in like that.

So when another local hick approached him on the sidewalk and asked,

"What's your favorite color?"

He answered, "Screw you blue."

"Okay," said the hick, ignoring the rest and handing him a blue card that said FREE PLAY on it. "You go in here with that and tell them I said you could have a free play."

Earl wandered up to a wooden shed in the gap between two buildings. Some fat guy who looked like a puffy-necked, cigar-smoking toad occupied a stool behind the painted green counter. On the wall in back of him were rows of numbers and an array of photos of smooth, rosy bodies cut from magazines that caused a stirring in his chest, and fire down below. Blemish-free photos of fecund and callipygous women who silently offered themselves to him in an unspoken promise of what he could do later with his winnings.

The old gray toad took a look at Earl's card.

"Free play?" said the toad. "Free play it is," and he had Earl roll six dice at once from a cup. "Hey! Good roll!" He added up the numbers on the dice. "Two, eight, thirteen, sixteen, twenty, twenty-four." He pointed to the number 24 on the green felt square laid across the counter between them. "What's that say?"

Earl looked at the small green print under the number: "Fifty points."

"Fifty points. Remember, one hundred wins. You're half-way there already. You wanna roll again for a dollar?"

"What do I win?"

"A hundred bucks and your choice of one of these fine gifts," the old gray toad said, jerking his thumb toward a flimsy shelf behind him that held some electronic gadgets and other, unlicensed entertainments. One free roll and he was already halfway there. He looked at all those gorgeous females, and their smiles sweetly sang to him, urging him to do it.

He bet a dollar and rolled.

"Hey!" said the toad, counting up the score and pointing to the number on the board. "What's that say?"

"Twenty points," said Earl.

"Great, you've got seventy points. Just a dollar for another roll."

He rolled. Mr. Toad counted up the score. "Hey! Two for one! You get two dollars back. You're doing great! Want to roll again?"

Hell, he was getting closer, and so far it hadn't cost him a dime. He rolled. The old toad counted up the numbers.

"Twenty-eight! What's that say?"

"Bonus!"

"Bonus! The pot doubles to *two* hundred dollars, for a five-dollar bet. Okay? Five dollars."

He rolled.

"Three, five, six, ten, sixteen, twenty-two. What's that say?"

"Fifteen points."

"That's eighty-five points. All you need is fifteen. Five dollar bet?"

The women on the wall told him that if he kept going, they would soon be his.

"Okay."

"One good roll will do it. Two, three, six, eight, eleven, thirteen—sorry, buddy, you lose. No play. Try again?"

He plunked down a five and rolled.

"Four, nine, twelve, seventeen, twenty-three—I don't believe this. What's that say?"

"Twenty-eight."

"Twenty-eight! Bonus! The pot doubles to *four hundred dollars* for a ten-dollar bet. Ten dollars? One good roll will do it. Ten dollars?"

He took up the offer.

"Two, three, seven, thirteen, nineteen, twenty—what's that say?"

"Five points."

"You've got ninety points. One good roll will do it."

He rolled.

"Twenty-eight! I don't believe this! The pot is *eight hundred*, for a twenty-dollar bet."

He rolled. It was a winning roll. But the old toad counted wrong. He knew the numbers. He pulled the old "What's that say?" bit and Earl shifted his eyes to the board for less than a second as the mottled old toad scooped the dice up.

"Three points," said Earl.

"Three points. Ya got a ninety-three. All you need is seven for a twenty-dollar bet."

And suddenly Earl realized that he had dropped fifty dollars already. It happened so quickly. But his pockets were definitely empty. He had no more cash. How could that be? But he was so close! How could that be?

———

"And this," said Yilmaz, pointing to the text.

"What?"

"*Boobalicious*. Is that even a word?"

"Aw, give it a rest already," said Hughie, lighting another cigarette.

"Wish you'd give it a rest," said Yilmaz, waving the smoke away with the tit mag.

"You picked a hell of a profession for a guy who doesn't like the smell of smoke. It's still legal here, isn't it?"

"For now."

"What's that mean?"

"The service staff are talking about getting a ban on smoking in the workplace."

"Get outa here. I thought anything goes in this town."

"It does, but it's also a strong union town."

"How is that possible?"

"Because the big hotels and casinos can't pull up stakes and fuck off to Mexico or Malaysia. That's how."

"Oh. Can I still get that drink?"

"You ready for one?"

"Tracy's last show starts in ten minutes, right?"

"Right."

"I'm ready."

Yilmaz two-finger waved the bartender over.

"Your bosses okay with this?" asked Hughie.

"I'm okay with this."

"Okay, okay. I wanna check out the street again."

———

The place was called *Candee's*, and it offered just what it said in red-and-white neon, like a candy cane that's bad for your teeth. Earl parked his truck curbside and walked up to the entrance. Two big guys in suits looked his truck over, and rolled their eyes at each other as he went inside.

The one who was smoking said, "This just keeps getting better."

But Earl had been suckered twice on his way to the land of enchantment, and he wasn't taking any more detours. He sidled up to a stool at the edge of the runway and straddled it heavily, the cushion deflating with a faint *pffff* as his well-worn trucker's butt settled in for a ten-hour ride. Then he ordered a double bourbon with a beer chaser from the waitress who appeared instantly at his elbow.

Now this was more like it. *Definitely* more like it. Warm, welcoming atmo-sphere. No one looking at his grease-stained jeans. Instant service. His every desire fulfilled. And *her.* She was beautiful. She was marvelous. She gave him everything she had to offer, yet she still seemed to be holding back. The contradiction was excruciating.

"She's the *real* thing," he said, throat dry.

"Huh?" said the guy next to him, bewildered by the suggestion, given the vast anatomical evidence before his eyes.

Earl felt a keen electrical tingling, as if Tracy's pendulous orbs were positively charged particles which repelled each other on exposure to air and gave rise to goosebumps as pristine as the bright mountains of the moon.

He erased the memory that there were no more dollar bills in his pocket by ordering another double shot and beer, then another, then some others, as he stared, dazzled by the glitter, and wooed by the dark, seductive valleys between her perfectly smooth golden globes.

When they asked for money, he drew some loopy dollar signs on a *Candee's* cocktail napkin with a flaky yellow pencil and tried to fill in the numbers, but the napkin kept getting wet and it was hard to draw those screwy fives when the paper kept tearing and he was laughing so hard and by then the bouncers were hauling him off, anyway.

———

Constellations had spun half the night away before Earl dribbled his name on an IOU or something and passed out on a mildewy mattress whose springs rose up like bits of ironwood in a furrow of hard-packed earth.

Now he sat there, rubbing at the grit around his eyes. His eyeballs felt like there was sand in them, somewhere deep inside where he couldn't reach.

He had been dreaming of somebody's white ancestors meeting a group of natives, hands held out in greeting, but they did not speak a word of each other's languages, and the whites ended up slaughtering the redskins with repeating rifles.

He sat there for quite a while, rubbing the images from his mind, not knowing what to do with a truckload of sand and too little money to have the only kind of fun that would get a man through a lonely Sunday in this heartless land. But when he reached into his pockets and found no reassuring crinkle of paper, just the dull clink of a few humble coins, he realized something:

He didn't remember a thing.

About last night, that is.

In fact, the only thing he remembered was that he had another day to kill.

He sat there mumbling, "How am I going to make it to Monday?" And he turned toward the corroding aluminum window frame and looked out at the truck.

For a moment he thought it had been knocked over by the wind, then his vision corrected for hangovers and he realized that the rear gate was open and swinging in the early morning breeze.

He shivered reflexively while peeing, then he pulled on his heavy work boots and got a cool whiff of distant prairie as he stepped over the puddles in the gravel parking lot and approached the creaking metal door.

The sand was missing.

He went back to the diner first, driving his empty rig along the highway under heavy gray clouds that made the wet black asphalt look blacker still, thinking about that desk guy at the motel who didn't know squat. *I'm just the night clerk. I'm just the night clerk.* Jee-zus!

As he pushed the glass door's tubular metal handle, the sharp smell of frying onions bit into his nose hairs and the smoke seemed to leave a layer of grease on his skin.

He fished around in his pockets and came up with a handful of nickels and quarters, blew the lint off the coins, and got himself coffee and two donuts, then a couple of refills on the coffee.

He sat and stared at a sticker on the cash register declaring

UNITED WE STAND in red, white, and blue letters. But the shifts had changed, and nobody remembered having seen a rig with a bone-white cargo container coming through around two in the morning.

He drove slowly back downtown to see if somehow—somehow—he could have possibly lost the load on the way to the motel. But even as he scanned the reddish-brown-encrusted hubcaps and broken bottles lining the edge of the road, he knew this was one of those silly dead ends your mind races into when it can't separate the maybes from the are-you-kiddings because it isn't quite ready to face the reality that it managed to lose track of five tons of mother-loving sand.

Get a grip, dude. Reconstruct. No. What's the word? *Retrace.* Yeah. Retrace your steps. That's it. Because he was sure that his cargo was still there when he had pulled into town. And that was only a few hours ago, really. Well, it was—let me see—twelve, thirteen, *fourteen* hours ago. Shoot. Had it been that long?

———

The music twanged, familiar and comfortable, describing a love gone sour in a collection of metaphors relating to farm equipment with bad traction. The light was smoky and warm, just dim enough to bury the grime in the shadows. God, he felt at home here.

Old Glory's stripes hung horizontally on the wall behind the bar, not stretched too tightly, so the thing kind of sagged in the middle.

"What'll it be, sugar?" The hostess smiled at him from her spot over by the plastic-topped beer taps.

"I was here last night."

"No, you weren't."

"Sure I was."

"You must be thinking of somewhere else."

"You must've been drunk." Others cut in.

"Buddy, we're gonna have to ask you to leave."

Several minutes later he realized he was back in the parking lot.

Thrown out of a bar? Just for asking if they saw his truck? Unless he really *was* in the wrong place.

No, that's crazy. He remembered the flag.

He pulled into a truck stop and let the engine idle, filling the cab with burnt, intestinal smells. No. Was somebody yanking his chain? He figured he'd have noticed a big pile of sand along the road if someone had decided to take it for a joyride and dump it in the middle of an intersection as their idea of a prank.

He had retraced his steps, and they led nowhere. So much for trying to figure this out on his own.

Well, I guess it's time to bring the law into it, he reasoned.

———————

"You're a-telling me that someone stole your *sand*?"

"Well, yeah, okay?"

"Five tons of sand."

"Yeah."

The flag curled around the sheriff's sleeve, the only color on the crisp tan fabric. It caught his eye.

"Let me see your license."

He handed it over.

The sheriff squinted at it.

"Earl Q. Sparer," the sheriff said. "What's the Q for?"

"Cucumber."

"Smart guy, eh?"

"Sorry. It's been a long day."

The sheriff looked at Earl's rig. Dark gray clouds were rolling across his mirrorshades.

"Must've been a long night, too, huh?" he said finally. "There's no sign of sand in the parking lot. You'd think they'd have spilled some."

"Well, I don't figure they stole it off the truck while it was parked here," Earl explained. "They took the truck and dumped the cargo somewheres else."

"And brought the truck back to you, all vacuumed, with the gas tank full? Sure they didn't leave a mint on your pillow at the motel, too?"

"That would explain the sticky stuff I found on the back of my neck this morning."

"You leave it idling?"

"No, sir."

"Then they must've had a key. Any idea how they'd get a key? Anybody in this town got a copy of the keys to your truck, mister?"

Cars whizzed wetly by, indifferent to his puzzlement, patriotic colors stamped on their windows and bumpers.

"Must've been some mighty special kind of sand, I guess."

"Yeah, it was real coarse—"

"Quit wasting my time, ya drunk."

He watched the sheriff go.

This place was smack in the middle of some of the friendliest country on earth, but it was starting to feel like the flat butthole of the universe right now.

He sat inside the truck, put his head down in the crook of his elbow for a second and awoke, stiff and numb, about two hours later. It was getting late.

The neon lights were all ablaze, and he drove around staring at them, his eyes bulging and tongue drooping out like a fish slowly expiring in a bucket. So when he caught a glimpse of the curvy red-and-white letters spelling out the magical name *Candee's*, it seemed like he had rediscovered a lost treasure from his youthful days gone by.

The inside of the club was both new and familiar to him, but when he saw *her* strutting across the boards with the old red, white and blue snapping the air behind her, he knew he had found his way back home.

He accepted the immediate offer of a drink before he remembered that there was nothing but lint in his pockets. Oh well, he thought, placing his elbows on the edge of the glorious runway. He propped his head up with his hands, and stared at the heavens above.

He was feeling fine enough to order another round when four hands dropped from the heavens and gripped his arms in a firm, friendly way.

"Yeah?" he asked.

"You ran up quite a tab here last night," said Yilmaz.

"Oh. Was that here?"

"Sure was," said Yilmaz. The other guy said nothing.

Nobody took their hands off him, either.

"Hey, no hard feelings," said Yilmaz, easing Earl off the stool and leading him over to the bar.

"Yeah, it's Vegas," said Hughie. "Crossroads of the world. We'll work it out. No problem."

"You sure?" asked Earl.

"We can work it out," said Hughie, letting go of Earl's arm.

"And just to show you there's no hard feelings—" Yilmaz laid a huge hand on Earl's shoulder and called the bartender over. "Hey Eddie, bring my friend here whatever he wants."

"Really? No kiddin'?" asked Earl.

"Really."

Behind his back, Yilmaz crossed two fingers and shook them twice, the sign for the bartender to spike the chump's drink with a couple of grams of chloral hydrate.

"Say, you guys are all right," said Earl, turning to watch Tracy grind away. She was getting near the climax of her act. "Ain't she something?"

"She sure is," Hughie assured him.

Yilmaz spoke close to Hughie's ear: "It's slow-acting. It'll take a good half-hour."

"Oh, great. Another half-hour of this B.S.," said Hughie.

"What's your problem? It's the club's money."

"He's a *distraction*."

"We could always hit him with a baseball bat."

"Wood or aluminum?"

"Call me old-fashioned."

"Wood it is, then."

But Earl was oblivious to their words. He was mesmerized. Then as he watched the music of Tracy's perfect hemispheres tracing geometrical arcs and bisecting them on the return swing, something seemingly unrelated clicked in his mind.

Where would you hide a twenty-foot high pile of sand? And suddenly he knew the truth in his heart.

In the refinery.

But just as he was finishing his drink, the double doors swung open, flooding the floor with neon, and out of the corner of his eye he saw a sharp-nosed biker with a thin *vato* mustache come in and stride too quickly toward the runway.

"That's my guy! It's Crowell!" said Hughie, dropping his cigarette on the floor.

Tracy froze in mid-pivot, horrified, but the music kept on pounding as the two big guys jumped on the biker, took him down with a pair of knees in the back, and slammed his face repeatedly into the linoleum floor tiles in near-perfect accompaniment to the slamming beat.

Yilmaz held Jimmy C. down and twisted one of the punk's wrists up so Hughie could slap the handcuffs on it. Tracy was screaming something nasty, Jimmy was flipping like a shark on a hook, and Yilmaz and Hughie had broken out in a sweat trying to get Jimmy's other wrist shackled up. But finally it was all over. Hughie stood up, wiped his brow with a couple of bev naps the waitress handed him, and looked around the room.

"Hey, where's the freaking truck driver?"

He looked outside and saw that the truck was gone.

The dusky wind blew up great puffs of dirt, blocking out the sky in a small region of this wide planet. Then the rain picked up, and that settled the dirt some. Earl parked the truck a little way past the big steel gate, and walked slowly downhill to the refinery, loose chunks of asphalt and broken glass scraping under his thick-soled work boots.

The ground had been excavated, the dirt mined. The soil had fallen away in so many places it was easy for a big guy like him to slip in under the chain link fence. But the grade was steep and loose, and he slipped half-way down the pile of dirt and pebbles, which skittered after him and hopped into his boots.

He carefully slid the rest of the way down the sloping walls of the big sand pit and landed on a reassuringly flat surface of dark granular crystals. Pulverized rock of some kind. Coal or garnet, maybe. He shook the pebbles out of his boots, and kept wandering, searching for a particular kind of sand.

The amber glow of the security lights licked the curved wet surfaces of three metallic storage towers, making them look like three tall church candles standing in a row. The glow turned the treetops orange, too, as if they were about to ignite into flames. Sporadic clumps of dead leaves clung to the branches like tiny pterodactyls, ready to spring.

He was staring up at them when he stepped off the flat granular path and slipped more than a dozen feet down a loose dirt hill, so soft he sank up to his ankles and got dirt in his shoes.

And it rained hard blows.

Damn! So much frustration.

He was so tired of looking. Tired of having to go from here to there, and always having to make repairs, and fill out forms, and wait, and wait to fill out more forms. Tired of always stumbling through the mud.

The rain was softer now.

He thought of Tracy's tender touches.

Yes. It was good to finally sleep in the sand.

———

He went through the power screen six times, until he was as refined as the sand they mixed him with.

DEATH OF A WHALE
IN THE CHURCH OF ELVIS

———

LINDA KERSLAKE

"I'm not marrying your mother."

Amanda Duncan whipped her head away from the window, the full force of her icy glare hitting Ken Marvin in the face. He immediately regretted the words, and began concentrating intently on opening his in-flight packet of peanuts.

"She's been planning a church wedding for me for years," she explained, "and it's just easier to go along with her. Our running off to Vegas is killing her. She had such a fit when I told her, I'm surprised she even agreed to come. And *please*, don't tell her we're sharing a room tonight."

"The mighty Deacon Duncan in Sin City. I'm glad we brought a camera!"

"Ken, stop it! She's afraid your mother will tell everyone back home about this."

Both women attended The Mt. Hope Church of the Redeemed, Faith Through Works Synod, where his mother was choir director and hers served as a deacon. Whenever they met, there was a subtle competition for recognition of good works, or as her father called it, gaudy business.

"Well, my mother will be there too! They're flying in for the ceremony tomorrow, then on to help Habitat for Humanity in Atlanta."

"There, you see? She'll spread the rumor that while she rushed on to house the homeless, Mom stayed to gamble!"

He didn't see, but he pretended that he did. He munched his peanuts, which were as stale as this conversation was getting to be.

They sat in silence, both staring at the clouds zooming by. The trip to Las Vegas had been his idea. When Amanda's dad, George Duncan, promised them twenty-five grand for a wedding present, he said they could use it for whatever they wanted: a wedding, the down payment on a house, or the honeymoon. Amanda ran right out to buy the latest issue of *Bride's Magazine*. Ken, a financial advisor in a tight market, started house hunting. He wasn't about to let this opportunity pass them by.

He found a stately ten-year-old brick house in a posh suburb not far from his work with a lap pool, wine cellar, multi-media room/office, total security system—including the grounds, and a five-stall garage. And best of all, it had an impressive circular driveway leading up to a portico with white pillars.

The house screamed success.

He needed this house.

It had been a hard battle, but here they were on their way to the Bellagio for a short, and hopefully sweet, honeymoon. The only problem was the wedding.

"How about the Justice of the Peace?" he asked. "I hear she's a real character." More silence.

"The Venetian does that incredibly romantic ceremony in a gondola, on the canal," countered Amanda, snuggling up against his arm.

He estimated that would cost at least a couple of grand, and quickly rejected the idea.

"What you two need is a rockin' wedding at the Church of Elvis, like we did." The voice floated back from the seats in front. A blond-tipped crew-cut head popped up to eye level.

"They pick you up in a pink Caddy. Dad would love it, Sis. Who doesn't like the King? 'Love Me Tender'? 'Hawaiian Wedding Song'?" Robby, her brother, and his new wife, Carol Ann, had come along to stand up for them. They had eloped two months ago, causing quite a stir. He'd dropped out of college and so far hadn't found a job, so she was supporting them with her two-year nursing degree, working the night shift in a nursing home. They'd jumped at a chance for a free trip to Vegas.

"Robby wanted that Viva Las Vegas package, the one with Ann-Margret in those crazy hot pants. It was great!" said Carol Ann, pausing from her knitting.

Amanda thought this over, a smile tickling her lips.

"That *would* be fun, and Mother adores Elvis."

Ken sighed and began to relax, winking a thank-you to his future brother-in-law.

———

The plane landed at Las Vegas International, and Ken and Amanda each grabbed their carry-ons. Robby hurried down the aisle while Carol Ann struggled to get their bag from the overhead compartment. Once off the plane, they rushed through the terminal, drawn to the Mecca of adult pleasures like dieters to chocolate, darting between bug-eyed gamblers leaving, joining the flow of fresh hopefuls arriving. Amanda marveled at the slot machines lining the walls.

"Is nothing sacred here?"

"Nothing," answered Robby. "I've even seen machines in the cans." He stopped to check his wallet after being jostled by a tanned man carrying no luggage and wearing shades. "Gives a whole new meaning to the phrase 'nonstop entertainment.'"

They exited the terminal just as a sleek white limousine slid to a stop at the curb. George Duncan lumbered out the rear door, his hulking frame squishing through the opening and expanding to full size just as he enveloped his daughter in a hug.

"Princess!"

"Daddy!"

Ken stared at the limo, hoping it wasn't coming out of his windfall. He'd already agreed to put everyone up for two nights at the Bellagio. Carol Ann found him a great rate on the Internet because it was the slow season, but he didn't want things to get out of hand.

"A limo?" she asked, eyeing her father.

"Nothing's too good for my little girl!" He clapped Ken on the back with his pawlike hand, causing him to lurch forward, then ushered Amanda toward the car. The driver took the bags and stowed them in the trunk. Climbing in, she found her mother, Sylvia, sitting pristinely in a cool aqua shantung silk pantsuit, unwrinkled even in the desert heat. She wore Chanel sunglasses, the new pearlized ones, that obscured her eyes. Amanda smoothed her own rumpled shift, wondering how the salesclerk could have sold it to her as 'the new-carefree-linen' with a straight face.

"Mother, how are you?" asked Amanda as Ken slid in beside her.

"Fine, dear. How was your flight?"

"Fine. Just fine."

Ken nodded to his soon-to-be mother-in-law. He found himself tongue-tied in her presence, awed by her ageless beauty. She was kind to him, and generous to a fault, but she had a cool demeanor that discouraged close contact. He'd never seen her hug anyone, only be hugged by George.

As soon as they were all in, George opened the refrigerator and uncorked a bottle of Dom Perignon. Beads of sweat popped out on Ken's forehead, not entirely from the warm desert air. As if reading his mind, George smacked him on the knee.

"This one is on me, tiger!" The cork popped out, rebounding off the window and landing in Sylvia's lap. She flicked it off, and Amanda reached over and blotted the champagne droplets with a wadded-up Kleenex from her pocket.

Glasses were passed around while Carol Ann raided the snack tray, twisting open a jar of green olives. Everyone except Sylvia and Carol Ann took a glass of champagne. George made a toast to the couple.

"Driver, take the Strip in. We want to see the lights."

As they turned from Tropicana onto the Strip, Ken stared at the realistic skyline of Manhattan displayed at the New York, New York Casino. A screaming group of tourists flashed by, belted into the roller-coaster seats.

The Strip glittered like jewels in the navel of a giant belly dancer, sucking up enough power to run a third world country for days. People milled around in shorts, jeans, and little black dresses that had cost someone a small fortune. You could smell the money on the warm, desert breeze.

Amanda pointed back to the castlelike structure of the Excalibur, but Ken was noting the location of the Denny's up ahead, hoping several meals could be eaten there.

His eyes bolted forward to the Aladdin, and Amanda gasped as the fountains in front of the Bellagio burst into life. Colored lights played against the sprays of water that danced to classical music, throwing a welcome mist on the dazzled onlookers gathered at the water's edge.

They turned down the drive to the Bellagio, and a bell captain rushed forward as the limo stopped.

"This way," he said, ushering them into a private entrance, away from the main one. Their bags were swiftly unloaded and they were shown to a special desk for check in. Ken fumbled through his duffle bag, looking for the Expedia confirmation of their reservations.

"See the treatment you get when they think you've got bucks?" beamed George.

A gush of warm air behind them announced the arrival of another guest. He was dressed in a matte gray silk suit cut to perfection for his formidable frame. Gold glinted from his cuff links and the ring on his right hand. Brushing past them, he moved with the air of someone accustomed to preferential treatment. Startled, they stood aside and gave him a wide berth.

"Natelli? I think you have a suite for me."

Amanda thought she heard a small gasp from her mother. When she turned to look, Sylvia stood with her back to them. She had slipped her sunglasses back on. She was studying an Italian oil painting that Amanda prayed was a copy, because if it wasn't, they could never afford this place.

"He must be one of those high rollers, a big fish," whispered Ken. "I think they call them sharks."

"Whales," corrected Robby.

The man glanced back at them, smiling absently as if that would excuse his behavior. The receptionist pulled his account up on the computer, then reached for a packet with his name neatly printed on the outside. She pressed a buzzer, and a man in a maroon jacket with gold braid quickly appeared from behind a sliding panel.

"Here you go, Mr. Natelli. Glad to have you with us, sir. Your suite is on the sixteenth floor, overlooking Lake Bellagio. Antoine will be your personal valet for the duration of your stay." The young man tipped his head as he was introduced. "If there is anything he can do to make your stay more comfortable, please call him. Anytime, twenty-four/seven." She tried dazzling him with a sparkling smile, but he failed to notice.

As he turned to follow Antoine, he paused, staring at Sylvia.

"Lucky—is that you?" His tanned face erupted in a smile, and his eyes gleamed with hope.

Time froze for a split second while they all tried to reconcile their image of Sylvia with this saucy nickname.

Amanda giggled, then looked at her mother.

"You must be mistaken. My name is not Lucky," she said. George moved protectively to her side.

"Sorry," said Mr. Natelli, "it's just that you look so much like . . ."

"You're wrong," said George.

Natelli looked directly at him, and George stared back. They were like two bull elk getting ready to battle it out in an ancient rutting ritual. Then Natelli glanced around at the others. Backing up one step, he turned and strode down the hall after his valet.

Ken found their confirmation slip and handed it to the woman. She read it then glanced up at him.

"But your reservations are for our budget rooms . . . made online."

"Yes, through Expedia."

"Then you check-in in the main lobby. Straight down the hall, then veer to the left." She handed the paper back to him, dismissing him and returning to her work at the computer.

"What? No Antoine for us?" quipped Robby.

They shouldered their bags and proceeded to the lobby, awed by the Fiore di Como, a garden of glass flowers hanging from the ceiling created by Dale Chihuly. Blooms of every shape and size exploded in glorious color overhead.

They made their way to the desk and registered. After receiv-

ing keycards, everyone but Robby headed to their rooms to unpack. He darted into the casino.

After a quick shower, Amanda decided to call her parents to
see if they would join them for dinner.

"Ah, honey, that's not such a good idea. You kids go have some
fun. We old folks will just rest up for the big day tomorrow."

———

Ken suggested they eat at a nearby casino using a coupon for an
all-you-can-eat buffet he found in a tourist guide. They rousted
Robby from the craps table, interrupting what appeared to be a
whammer of a losing streak, and headed off.

After filling their plates at the buffet, they commandeered a
booth and began unloading their trays. The food proved to be
unremarkable, except for the quantity. But they were hungry,
and ate in silence the first few minutes.

Amanda marveled at the amount Carol Ann was able to eat
and still keep her figure, although she looked a little plumper
than she had in her wedding pictures. She'd have to make sure
she didn't gain weight after she and Ken were married.

"Did you call the chapel yet?" asked Carol Ann.

"No," said Amanda. "I haven't had time. Which one was it
you guys use?"

"The Church of Elvis," announced Robby. "They were awe-
some." He sliced into a rubbery prawn. "Hey, think we can
score some tickets for that heavyweight bout tomorrow afternoon?" he asked Ken.

"I don't know; Tyson's looking pretty hot, and I heard they
were all sold out."

"Dad got tickets," said Amanda, swallowing a tough bite of
prime rib, "but don't tell him I told you. Act surprised. It's your
bachelor party."

The men erupted in a hoot and slapped palms across the table
while Amanda rolled her eyes.

She suggested the ladies get their hair done while the men
were gone, and Carol Ann agreed.

The couples strolled hand-in-hand down the Strip in the direction of the Treasure Island Hotel to catch the evening performance of the swashbuckling pirates doing battle with HRM

Navy. Then they returned to their hotel, stopping to watch the fountains soar over a thousand feet in the air, then cascade down through incandescent lighting.

Ken and Amanda hailed a cab, heading to the Marriage License Bureau. That made one less thing to do tomorrow. Robby and Carol Ann retired to their room.

———

The phone jarred Amanda awake shortly after dawn.

"Yes?"

"Sweetheart, you'd better come to our room."

"Now, Dad?"

"Yes, now! And bring everybody else, too."

She called Carol Ann, who agreed to meet them there after she located Robby, who had returned to the casino last night to recoup his losses and hadn't come back to the room yet.

They all stumbled through the door to her parent's room about the same time, Robby looking exhausted and smelling of smoke, the others just dopey from sleep. George was alone, pacing.

"I ordered up some coffee. Grab a cup and have a seat."

They obliged, sitting in the chairs and on the foot of the bed.

"Dad, where's Mom?" asked Amanda as she started to sip her coffee.

"That's the problem. I don't know!"

Cups halted in mid air.

"You lost Mother?"

"No. Yes! She left sometime during the night. I was asleep."

Amanda glanced around the room again, noticing several tiny bourbon bottles from the honor bar sitting by a bottle of branch water.

"Were you drinking?"

"Not me, honey. Your mom."

"Mother doesn't drink."

"Correction. Your mother doesn't start drinking, because she doesn't stop."

While Amanda tried to make sense of this, he went on. "Your mother has a drinking problem. And a small one with gambling, too."

"Stop it! She does not!" Amanda jumped up and paced in front of the window looking out on the mute fountains. "I've never seen her take so much as one drink."

"That's true. As long as she attends her meetings, she's fine."

"What meetings?"

"She's in AA, the twelve-step program, for drinking and gambling."

"That's impossible! When did she have time for that?" Sylvia was always on her way to work or to the church for some committee meeting.

"Let's just say she doesn't really drive a bookmobile every afternoon."

"I can't believe I never knew about this!"

"She stopped drinking when she found out she was pregnant with you. And then when we got married . . ."

"You mean she was already pregnant when you got married?"

Ken and Robby stifled grins, but Amanda saw and ordered them out of the room.

"Not yet, sweetheart," said George. "We need them to help find her."

Spreading out a map of the Strip, they agreed to start at the closest casino, checking every bar and gambling room until they found her. George would stay in the room by the phone and run command central from there, and he would notify them if she returned. They exchanged cell phone numbers and left.

Amanda headed north to Caesars Palace, covering the west side of the street, and Ken the east, starting at Bally's. Robby and Carol Ann ran south toward the Monte Carlo and Paris Casinos. They rushed in and out of casinos, which were moderately full at that early hour, glancing in every bar and cafe along the way. The temperature was rising faster than a fish fart, and the sun pelted them with withering rays when they weren't inside. By nine o'clock they were wilting from heat and hunger.

As Amanda entered the Mirage, she noticed the high roller from the night before, Mr. Natelli, arguing with a woman on a stool whose back was to her. The woman slumped forward, slopping her drink down her blue pantsuit. As she turned, Amanda realized it was her mother.

"Mom! What are you doing here?"

Sylvia tried to focus, wobbling on the stool, her right hand glued to the pull handle of the slot machine. Her normally coiffed hair hung limp in her eyes, and she'd outlasted her makeup by hours, revealing how much work it took daily to maintain the façade.

"That's okay, I've got her. You can leave now," she said, coolly dismissing the man. She was relieved when he let go of her mother's other arm and walked toward the cage. He spoke with the cashier, signed something and left.

Amanda placed a frantic call to George, who spread the word that Sylvia had been located at the Mirage, compulsively dinging the $500 slot machine, mumbling something about being $45,000 in the hole. They pried her away from the machine as she chugged the last of what was far from her first bourbon and water. George inquired about her debt, but was told the marker had been picked up. He glanced at her diamond ring, relieved to see it glittering from her left hand, knowing it would hardly make bail on that amount.

Between the five of them, they got her through the lobby of the Bellagio, but her feet never touched the ground. While Amanda and Carol Ann helped her into a chilly shower, George had a talk with Ken and Robby.

"I don't know how to tell you boys this, but I can't give you the money I promised you. Not yet. I need it to buy back Sylvia's marker."

Ken glanced at Robby, wondering how much he was getting, and why.

"That's fine, sir," he said, mentally calculating the interest charge on what this weekend would cost him if he had to put it on his Visa.

"Dad, that's not fair!"

"Son, I had no idea your mother was going to have this trouble. With the market down, I'm in a little bit of a cash flow bind. Construction business has slowed down."

"Oh, like you're the only one? I bought that Global.com stock you-know-who recommended." He glared at Ken.

"Hey, I said I was sorry! The projected earnings were good. . . ."

"Save it. Just don't ever expect me to ever listen to . . ."

"Quiet!" admonished George. "The women don't need to hear about this."

Amanda and Sylvia shuffled into the room, Sylvia wrapped tightly in the complimentary white terry robe as if it restrained what little dignity she had left. She could not meet their eyes, not yet. After two cups of coffee, she started coming around.

That was when the tears started, both hers and Amanda's. Carol Ann excused herself and went to their room.

"You kids run on too," encouraged George. "You've got a lot to get ready. This is your big day!" His forced enthusiasm seemed as appropriate as a stripper at a church picnic.

Amanda ran ahead to their room while Ken stayed to talk to Robby. She wanted to throw herself down on the bed and cry her heart out, but there wasn't time. She pulled herself together and called the Church of Elvis. A wedding consultant agreed to come over at noon to arrange the details for the service and collect the payment. When Ken came in, she was rapidly brushing her fluid, blonde hair.

"So, Robby and I were wondering, do you think your dad will still give us the tickets for the fight?"

"You have got to be kidding! Is that all you can think about?"

"Well, he already paid for them, and we have to know by noon."

"That's when the chapel advisor is coming."

"Oh."

"Oh—I won't go to the fight, or Oh—I can't be here?"

Taking a step back, he answered.

"You know so much more about all that crap honey, and you have such good taste . . ."

"Kenneth Luke Marvin, I swear . . ."

"No fair using middle names! My mother does that, and I hate it." He edged toward the door. "Just make sure you get the Elvis in that white rhinestone outfit, the one with the eagles and the cool collar."

"Just give me the checkbook and get out of here!"

"Put it on the Visa."

"What happened to 'If we can't pay cash, we do without'?"

"I'll explain later." He jumped to avoid the flying hairbrush as he slipped out the door.

Amanda's father called, asking her to check in on her mother while he and the boys were at the fight. So much for male leadership in a crisis. When the wedding advisor arrived, she found it very easy to plan things without Ken there to contradict her wishes. She chose the hunky, younger black-clad Elvis for her own reasons, singing "Love Me Tender" and "Teddy Bear," and the reception afterwards would serve mint juleps, fried peanut butter and banana sandwiches, and little White Castle cheeseburgers. No wonder the King died of a coronary.

They would be picked up in the legendary pink Cadillac with chrome-edged fins, driven to the chapel and back, with a complete series of pictures and a video of the ceremony. She and her mother would both get to dance with Elvis. If they wanted flowers, they would have to make those arrangements themselves.

Amanda signed the papers, and handed over the Visa, her first official charge as Mrs. Kenneth Marvin.

With that done, she called Carol Ann and told her to meet her at her mother's room. A rather subdued, pale Sylvia greeted them, and they convinced her to go down to Olives for a late lunch on the terrace overlooking Lake Bellagio.

Next, they walked to the beauty salon and each had their hair done. The girls finished before Sylvia who had decided on shimmering gold highlights to perk her up a bit. They passed the time browsing through shampoos, gels and fingernail polishes. Amanda tried on a black wig, and Carol Ann grabbed a long red one, howling at their image in the mirror.

"There you girls are!" Sylvia had finished her appointment and looked restored to her former polished self. She suggested they each have a hot rock massage, and then insisted on picking up the tab for their beauty enhancements. They returned to their rooms around four o'clock.

Amanda laid down on the bed, relaxed from the massage, her skin glowing and softened from the aroma oils they had used. She planned to just close her eyes for a minute, but awoke when Ken returned at six.

"I thought I was late! I just knew you'd be all ready," he said, ripping his T-shirt over his head and heading for the shower.

She slipped into her pale lavender georgette dress, already regretting the choice as it clung to her skin. After painting her nails and answering the phone three times, she stood at the window watching the last rays of the setting sun extinguish themselves on the Eiffel Tower across the street.

Twilight stalked the day like evil conquering good, culminating in those few brief moments during dawn and dusk when there is still plenty of light, but you can't see anything clearly. A time when God, if He wanted to, could reach down and snatch a soul from this world unnoticed. She felt a shiver run through her.

Ken emerged from the bathroom in a traditional black tuxedo, freshly shaven with his dark hair slicked back. She smiled and walked toward him.

"Now I remember why we're here," she said as she touched a small nick on his left cheek. "A little nervous, are we?"

"Just a little."

He bent to kiss her, and after a few seconds, she pulled away.

"Any more of that and we'll miss our own wedding! Come on. We need to meet the others down in the lobby in five minutes."

"Did my folks call?"

"Yes, they just landed. They'll meet us at the chapel."

When they arrived in the lobby, the other four were already there.

"You look gorgeous, honey!" George told her. "Your mother has something for you."

He stepped aside, and Sylvia held out a miniature rose bouquet, white with tiny lavender violets, for her to carry down the aisle.

"Thanks, Mom. I'd totally forgotten about flowers."

Both women teared up, and the men, fearing another deluge, were relieved when Elvis walked through the revolving glass doors, causing quite a commotion. Dressed in a sleek black shirt with rolled-up cuffs, pleated trousers, and white buckskin shoes, he required a second glance from almost everyone in the lobby, especially the women. He carried a Martin D-28 acoustic guitar slung lazily across his back. Cameras flashed, and he nodded at all the ladies, his mouth curling into a sexy sneer. Heavily pomaded Clairol-black locks shined blue in the overhead lights. He made his way over to the Duncan party.

"You folks havin' a wedding?" he asked in a sultry tone.

"That's us!" said Amanda, feeling her cheeks blush.

"Right this way, ma'am. Your chariot awaits!" He offered

her his arm and they led the group out to the glistening pink Cadillac.

Robby, the last one out, turned to address the onlookers.

"Elvis has left the building." He bowed, and a few women applauded.

George, Sylvia, Carol Ann, and Robby all squished into the back seat, glad for its six-foot width. Amanda slid into the center of the front seat, followed by Ken.

"I thought we had the older, puffy Elvis in the white spiky collar. The one with the cape."

"He wasn't available. Now hush."

The car roared to life with all 325 horses stampeding under the hood. A CD player jerrybuilt through the radio speakers played "Blue Suede Shoes" as they rumbled down the driveway. Once on the street, the Elvis performer crooned along, turning up the volume to attract attention. Sylvia ducked down in the back seat, presumably to save her hairdo. Carol Ann sat on Robby's lap, ignoring his off-key voice as he sang along.

As they pulled into the chapel parking lot, Ken waved to his parents who were leaning against their Ford Focus rental car. His mother, Peggy, was dressed in her navy polyester travel suit, with a thin strand of pearls to dress it up, and his father, Dwight, had on a rumpled camel sports coat. They both looked hot, and stunned.

Led by Elvis, they filed into the small white church, which reminded Amanda of ones she'd seen in Hawaii, the tiny ones built—often in a row along a beach—by the missionaries from competing denominations. She and Ken remained in back, while the others took seats in the front pews. Peggy sat straight-backed across the aisle from a subdued Sylvia, both shooting stiff smiles and sideways glances at the other. Carol Ann sat with her head bowed.

Elvis appeared from behind, looping his arms through Ken and Amanda's.

"Now remember, this is your big day. Don't let anything or anyone ruin it." Amanda smiled, and quit fidgeting with her bouquet. The photographer snapped a picture. "Now I'm gonna go up there and sing 'Love Me Tender,' and when I start the second verse, you two come on down the aisle." They nodded and he sashayed down the aisle, grabbed the microphone and signaled to a mid-aged Ann-Margret off to the side to start the background tape. When she leaned down to press the button, her hot pants hiked up a little too high on her aging thighs. She wore a tight orange sweater stretched over cone-shaped breasts that required Playtex assistance to remain that close to her chin.

His smooth voice sailed out over the small audience, as smooth as Black Velvet, amazingly like the real Elvis's. They all stared as he gyrated slowly through well-rehearsed movements, all introduced years ago by the King. Peggy, whose ears seldom heard anything but organ or piano, tried hard not to enjoy it, but the others seemed to. Amanda was so entranced by his performance Ken had to tug her arm to get her started down the aisle. They were up to the front before anyone even noticed them. Applause broke out for Elvis as he finished.

"Thankyou. Thankyouverymuch," he mumbled, Elvis style. "You're a wonderful audience." He turned and stepped behind a small pulpit, reattaching the mike.

"Dearly Beloved," he began in a somber tone, "we are gathered here to celebrate the union . . . Jumpin' Jehoshaphat!" He stumbled back, knocking a white trellis covered in dusty silk roses into the wall behind it.

George thought it was part of the show and took a picture, but everyone else looked around to see what had startled Elvis. Ann-Margret scurried forward, peeked under the pulpit, then screamed. Everyone rushed forward, seeing a hand with a chunky gold ring dangling between the curtains that covered the hallow space under the pulpit. Elvis pulled them apart, and they found the body of Mr. Natelli, the whale, stuffed inside. With a moan, Sylvia fainted dead away.

Peggy fumbled through her tattered TWA tote bag to find her foldable plastic cup, then rushed out to the drinking fountain for water to revive Sylvia. Elvis left to call the police, and they all returned to their seats. Tears streamed down Amanda's face as Ken tried to console her. Peggy Marvin quietly helped herself to a mint julep from the reception table.

The police arrived, with the coroner in tow. Wally Deaver, a square-jawed detective with the mottled skin that years in the Nevada desert sun will give a blond, led the way. He asked everyone to sit down until he could get their statements.

"You can't honestly think we had anything to do with this," said George.

"Am I to understand that none of you knew the victim?"

Dead silence followed while Sylvia sipped her water, Amanda tried not to look at her mother, and George sweated.

The astute detective said, "Just what I thought." He moved over to the body. The police photographer was leaving, and the coroner had finished examining the body.

"Looks like somebody smacked him on the back of the head with something flat. We bagged a hymnal with a few hairs on it. Then a puncture wound, possibly with an ice pick, to the brain. Entry wound is through the right ear. Death was probably instantaneous, sometime between four and seven. Doubt he even saw it coming. I'll know more when I get him back to the Body Shop."

Wally smiled at the coroner's pet name for the morgue.

"So, where were each of you from four o'clock on?"

"Well, the boys and I were at the fight, and the girls were back at the hotel," said George.

"So the men were together the whole time?"

"Yes."

"Except when you went to the can, Dad," offered Robby.

"And when you went to get more beer," said Ken.

"Well, that left you totally alone and unaccounted for too, didn't it, smart-ass?" Robby shot back.

"Okay, okay," said the detective. "How long was that?"

"I don't know, about ten minutes I think," said George.

"More like twenty-five or thirty," said Ken. "I remember wondering if you'd fallen in."

"There was a long line!"

"Ladies? How about you?"

"I was asleep. In my room," said Amanda, looking almost angelic in her bridal dress.

"Same here," said Sylvia, a tad too quickly.

"I watched a movie," said Carol Ann. "Pay-per-view, the new salsa dancing one. I'm sure the desk will verify it."

"Do you know how expensive those are?" complained Robby.

"I thought Ken was paying for it!" she whispered back.

"Just because you ordered it doesn't mean you stayed to

watch it," commented the detective. He turned to look at Peggy and Dwight next, but Ken intervened.

"The folks just got here in time for the wedding."

After a few questions about the time their flight landed, he made some notes and told them they could all go for now.

"I'll be in touch in the morning. Feel free to enjoy the hospitality of our lovely city a little longer, until I clear you to go."

"But we're due in Atlanta!" shrieked Peggy. "We'll miss the dedication by Jimmy Carter!"

After a brief consideration, he gave them permission to go, providing they left phone numbers where they could be reached.

A somber group rode back to the hotel with Elvis. Even his enthusiastic rendition of "Jailhouse Rock" couldn't bring a smile. They dispersed to their rooms, making no plans to meet for dinner.

A call came from Detective Deaver just before eight o'clock the next morning requesting a meeting at nine. They agreed to meet in Robby's room, and everyone was waiting when Wally arrived. They had ordered a tray of coffee and breakfast rolls, so the detective helped himself to coffee with cream. He split a fat-free bran muffin open and slathered butter on both sides, then sat in a chair by the window with the morning sun behind him so he could see their faces.

"Found something interesting last night when we got the body to the morgue."

They sat up, paying attention to every nuance as he spoke.

"Anybody here sign their notes with an 'L'?"

He scanned the group, his eyes resting on Sylvia. Her face hadn't moved a muscle, partially due to Botox, but also because she wasn't breathing. Sweat began to glisten on her forehead.

"Not for years," she said quietly. "I used to be known as Lucky."

"Did you write the note, 'Meet me at the Church of Elvis at five o'clock.' And sign it 'L'?"

"Most certainly not! I had no desire to see Tony again!"

"So now it's Tony?"

"Officer, my wife . . ."

"Detective."

"Okay, okay, Detective . . . my wife used to know him but she hasn't seen him in years."

"How did you know him?"

"He owned the hotel casino when I danced in the Folies Bergère."

"Mother!" gasped Amanda.

"Cool!" said Robby. "I always said you had great legs!"

"So all this was a secret?"

She glanced at Ken, who was wise enough to keep a straight face.

"Seems like a motive to me."

"I never even spoke to the man!"

"Then can you explain why the security camera at the chapel caught you going in just minutes after Mr. Natelli?" He laid the pictures out on the table in sequence: Elvis coming in, Tony Natelli in, Elvis out, Ann-Margret in, another Elvis in, Elvis out, Sylvia in, Sylvia running out. He held up the last picture for her inspection.

"Oh, all right! I was there, but I just went to see about the flowers! He was dead when I got there!" She collapsed against George's shoulder, crying.

"See here, my wife could no more kill anyone than I could!"

"That brings me to the next bit of evidence, a marker from the Mirage found in the victim's pocket, with your wife's name on it, for forty-five grand. Care to tell me about that?"

Sylvia cried louder.

"I tried to see him, just before noon. Sylvia hit the mother lode of losing streaks last night, and when I went to pay the marker, they said Natelli had covered it."

"Bet that didn't set too well," said Wally as he helped himself to the last croissant, flicking a kiwi slice off the top. He refilled his coffee cup, draining the last of the cream into his cup.

"The jerk wouldn't even discuss it with me, just like before. Said he'd only talk to her."

"What about before?"

George and Sylvia exchanged glances, and she nodded.

"When Syl worked for him years ago, he was obsessed with her. They dated for a while, but when we met, she tried to break it off. He went nuts, sent around some goons to rough me up and run me out of town. The sleaze wouldn't talk to me then either. I just wanted to get her out of her contract. So when I left, she came too. We musta moved four, five times that first year to shake the tail he had on us."

"So what's the problem now?"

"Right after she left, he ran afoul of the Nevada Gambling Commission, some drug-related charges. They yanked his gambling license. He blamed it on her—said he'd lost his lucky charm. He's been trying to find her ever since, his Lady Luck." He squeezed Sylvia's hand and went on. "He's opening a casino in New Jersey next year. Or he was, I should say. I was afraid he'd come after her again, now that he'd seen her. I needed to get that marker paid off and get him out of our lives forever."

"Congratulations. He's gone. Now, who else knew he had the marker?"

"No one. Well, I guess I told the boys about it, at the fight."

Ken and Robby looked worried. The fight arena was a poker chip's throw from the chapel, and their alibis were canceling each other out.

"So, Robby, you knew this old boyfriend of your mother's held a forty-five thousand dollar marker over her? That tick you off, son?"

"Sure, but that was Dad's business. I don't have that kind of money!"

"Or ever would have, if your Dad had to pay the marker instead of giving us each twenty-five grand!" said Ken, realizing too late that also gave him a motive for murder.

The detective whipped his eyes from Ken's face to Robby's and back as they glared at each other.

"I think I'd better take you boys down to the station for a little more questioning. Feel free to consult an attorney, although I'm not officially charging either one of you. Yet."

Carol Ann wrung her hands, and Amanda noticed she wasn't knitting like she usually did when she was nervous. Her knitting bag sat in the closet zipped shut.

"Let me see those pictures again," said Amanda.

Detective Deaver handed her the pictures. She flipped through the sequence until she came to the one of Ann-Margret.

"Mother, where was the body when you walked in?"

"Face down, in front of the pulpit. I thought he'd fainted," she sobbed.

"So whoever killed him stuffed him in the pulpit after you left."

"Why yes, that's right," Sylvia said, hope flickering in her eyes.

Amanda stared intently at the picture again, noting Ann-Margret's tall boots. A perfect hiding place for something long and thin.

"This doesn't look like the older Ann-Margret we had at our ceremony, the one with the pointy bra." She turned to the detective. "Do you still think an ice pick was used to kill him?"

"Something just a little bigger."

"Like a number three knitting needle? Hidden in a boot?"

"That would work," he said. "Who knits?"

All eyes went to Carol Ann.

"Go get your needles," said Amanda. When Carol Ann didn't move, Amanda pulled the bag out of the closet, holding out one badly bent needle and the long red wig from the beauty salon.

"Don't be silly! I can explain. I sat on it! And I didn't even know we weren't going to get the money."

"Yes you did, honey. I told you about the marker when I called from the fight," offered Robby.

"Shut up, you idiot!" she shouted. "We're married, you can't testify against me!"

"You didn't murder him, did you?" asked Robby, looking younger than his years.

"As a nurse, you'd know just where to aim," said Amanda, "and you're used to shifting bodies around."

"Someone had to stand up to him," she hissed at Robby, "and it clearly wasn't you." She stared at him with loathsome eyes. "We needed that money your dad promised! You lost almost that much in the casino last night, and with the baby coming . . ."

"What baby?"

"Ours, you dope. Why else do you think I married you?"

He sank back against the bed pillows, his freckles standing out like black pips on white dice.

The detective had heard enough. He escorted Carol Ann out the door, leaving a stunned family to wonder what to do next.

"I'm ruined!" whispered Sylvia. "Now everyone back home will find out about this."

"They won't hear about it from me," said Ken. He looked at

Amanda. "Well, should we call and see if the chapel is free? We've already paid for it."

"I've been thinking. I don't think I want to start my married life in Sin City after all. I think we should head home, and Mom and I will start planning a nice, small church wedding. How about that, Mom?"

Sylvia reached out and hugged her daughter, smiling for the first time since she'd arrived back in Las Vegas.

NEIGHBORS

JOHN WESSEL

Harry Chase sat in the back of a small casino chapel watching as bikers dressed in wedding casual—black leather, chains optional—exchanged prayers for endless roads, a long happy life together. He was wondering if the Bulls had covered the spread. Another man might have been praying for his own wife back in Lockport, Illinois—another man wouldn't have put five large on the Bulls in a rebuilding year—but Harry knew better than to ask for any favors. He assumed God was a player and had his own action.

It was early evening, Harry's favorite time in Vegas. The chapel was full of dreams, the night was young, anything was possible. He would hit the buffet, eat light—he had another two pounds to lose, he was avoiding dairy—and then head for his favorite roulette table, number six, where Jackie the Beneficent turned the wheel—St. Jackie, goddess of the lucky spin, the perfect bounce.

A group of tourists peeked into the room. He watched them come up the aisle, heads craned, hands full of cameras, guidebooks, postcards. They held a lot of celebrity weddings in here—third-rate sitcom stars, eighties musicians—Harry knew the place as well as the guides, he thought. He'd listened to enough of them give their tired spiel.

This group was Italian, most in their fifties, with dice-shaped nametags from EZ Tours in New York. Harry turned and watched them finding seats, listening to the guide run through the history of the casino and the wedding chapel. She wasn't bad, Harry admitted. As a guide and as a woman. Tall, little granny glasses, a nice figure. Long blond hair, newly cut. She had a cute way of leaning against the pew, using one tan loafer to scratch her calf. Harry wondered if she was local. He'd never seen her before.

One of the men seemed to appreciate her, too. He sat directly in front of her, listening intently. He laughed at her jokes, smiled at her references. Harry knew just enough Italian to follow along. He stared at the man, then examined the others in the group, studied their clothes, their shoes. He watched, and waited for a sign or tell—a sideways glance, a half smile. . . . *I see you, Harry.* . . .

There were three men, but only one of them stood out. The one asking all the questions. He had a scar on one cheek, and a heavy build jammed into a cheap sport jacket. And he seemed to be alone. The other men each had wives.

Or was that a cover too?

Relax, Harry, he thought. It's been ten years. You're a thousand miles from home. Not even your family knows where you are. You covered your tracks like a goddamn Indian.

He needed a drink.

———————

Looking back on it now, Harry saw the events that drove him from his home in Chicago as a series of unfortunate natural disasters. The point guard from Kansas twisting his ankle in the final four, for example . . . the wet track at Arlington that wiped out Harry's trifecta . . . even the wild left hook that floored Harry's boy Eduardo in the second round—a freak thing, really, one in a million, all the papers said so—these things were out of Harry's control, something he explained, repeatedly, during a series of conversations in a west Chicago storefront, where Harry signed a series of forms that took his restaurant, his car, his house, eventually his name. At first it seemed best to apologize, plead, beg. And then it seemed best to run.

He'd heard good things about Canada. So he left one morning the way any commuter might, with no bags, just a brief case, climbed on the 151 bus, transferred at Union Station, took the 10:08 north to Toronto, moved from small town to small town like a circus carny, finally settling in Saskatoon. A year later he moved on to Thunder Bay, then Vancouver Island, Winnipeg, Fairbanks. He bought a new name in Nogales, Arizona, from a man amused to be selling fake paper to a gringo; bought a used Blazer and kept his possessions to what would fit in back. He worked either as a bartender or a short order cook—he'd learned to cook in the army, and there was always a diner or greasy spoon needing a grill man. There was always a local sports book to take his bets.

As for his wife . . . their marriage had been shaky at best. *My fault*, thought Harry, lying in his bed one night in British Columbia, a rented cottage, a diamond-blue lake. Harry still getting used to the silence. No garbage trucks, no sirens. No thumping bass from the floor above. The gambling had made her crazy, drove them apart. *That was all my fault . . .*

For the first year or so he sent her cryptic postcards—*Hong Kong unreal . . . looking forward to the Seven Corners*—relayed through relatives, family friends. She had a collection of small teacups. : . . He bought one or two, wrapped them carefully in bubble wrap and packed them beneath his socks, carted them from city to city. He underlined the local attractions in a Lonely Planet book and drove to each one, taking pictures of waterfalls and scenic overlooks and seeing them less and less through her eyes. One morning—the streets full of snow, Chicago weather—he bought a cloned cell from a street hustler in Montreal and phoned her. He couldn't decide which was sadder, that he had to identify himself to his own wife, or the way she said nothing, then hung up on him. He mailed one more postcard. He left the teacups in a Chinese restaurant.

It's for the best, he thought. This way they'd leave her alone. Someday he'd make it up to her. And the next time he met someone . . . he'd make better choices. Be a better man.

Harry had no illusions about his own fate, though. Someday, someone would find him . . .

"What'll it be tonight, Harry?" Reverend Tim, the ponytailed bartender in the Dealers Lounge, was already reaching for Harry's brand. He was used to seeing Harry about this time every night, used to Harry's vague answers about his day and his past. Everyone in Vegas had baggage, came from somewhere else. He'd worked on Wall Street himself, before receiving the Word and a mail-order ordination.

"Crown Royal?" said Tim. "Single? Or double?"

"What did the Bulls do tonight?"

"Spurs by eleven, Harry. I keep telling you, don't bet against the Spurs."

"I don't like the Spurs," Harry said. "I like the Bulls." He climbed on the barstool carefully, as though getting on a horse. "Better make it a double."

He was on his third drink when the guide came through the lobby, off duty now, her plastic name badge gone. Her name was Anne Turner, he'd caught that much in the chapel. He watched her hesitate before finally taking a seat a few stools down from Harry.

"Bacardi and tonic, please," she said, putting her purse on the counter. He noticed the white skin on her ring finger. Harry's wedding ring was currently in a pawnshop in Reno.

He watched Tim light her cigarette, watched as she crossed her legs, did that thing with the loafer absentmindedly scratching her leg. She looked tired. Harry thought she was near his age, thirty-five or so, a graduate of one of those women's colleges—Smith or Vassar or something—where she'd learned Italian and maybe French as well, thinking she'd use them on leisurely trips to Europe, traveling in much different circumstances than EZ Tours provided—Harry could construct a whole life for her if given enough time; it was a bad habit of his.

He asked if he could buy her a drink.

"I have one, thanks," she said, then looked at him closer, as if studying his accent hanging in the air. "You're from Chicago?"

"Born and raised," he said. "You?"

"Rockford," she said. "Small world, huh."

"A big old goofy world," Harry agreed. It was unusual for him to give out personal information so freely. But there was something disarming about her. "I saw you in the chapel, a little while ago . . ."

"Herding my sheep," she said, stirring her drink. "I shouldn't complain, they're a good group. Better than most of the faculty groups."

"You left out a few of my favorite stories," Harry said. "The one with the midget wedding, for example. Always a crowd pleaser."

"I wasn't so sure how that would translate," she said, smiling—a real smile, too, not the kind she used on her job. It left her face softer, a bit weary. "Academics don't have the best sense of humor."

"So this group . . . they're all professors? From Italy?"

"One or two are from Columbia," she said. "I think it's some sort of exchange program. But everyone's practicing their Italian. You must speak it if you were listening before."

"A little. My family's from there, originally. And my old man slipped into the vernacular whenever he had too much wine." He could smell her perfume now, competing with the smoky air in the casino. "New York's kind of a change from Rockford. . . ."

"Tell me about it."

They talked for a while about New York and Italy, and Chicago, and Rockford.

"I miss it sometimes," she said. "Not the town. My family . . ." Her sister had twin girls. Her father raised dairy cattle. He asked her a few questions; she seemed reluctant to say more. He didn't press her.

"Here's to the great Midwest," Harry said. "Farmers, corn, and soybeans."

"And cows. Don't forget the cows."

"Let's drink to the cows."

It had been a while since he'd done this, talked to a woman who wasn't a dealer or a pit boss. He was slow to notice the way she slipped off her shoes and grew more comfortable around him, slow to catch the signs she was transmitting, letting him buy her a second drink, then a third, not pausing a beat in her story when he moved to the stool next to hers.

"—two weeks in Guadalajara, a week in Paris, I never know where they're gonna send me next. Which makes it sort of fun. I just have to cram for each trip like finals in college. Read the guide books." She shrugged. "Fake the rest."

"How long have you been doing it?"

"Oh, I don't know. Forever."

"Some of the men must give you a hard time. That guy tonight in the blue sport jacket, for example . . . he looks like a handful. He sure doesn't look like a professor."

"Mr. Rossi? He's a sweetheart, really. I think he teaches comparative lit. But his Italian needs some major work." She checked her watch, slipped her shoes back on. "I should get going . . ."

"When does your group leave tomorrow?"

"Nine a.m. We're going to Red Rock Canyon. Lots of cactus, apparently. According to Frommer's."

She was staying in the hotel. "A very tiny room," she said. "A very tiny bed." This was not a sign even Harry could miss.

They were upstairs, kissing, when Harry told her he thought the room would do just fine.

———

Housekeeping woke him at ten, presented him with fresh towels. He'd been dreaming of blue seas and dark mysterious fish, an underwater world glimpsed through the windows of a glass-bottomed boat. He showered and shaved and used the small coffee maker and wondered at his luck in finding Anne. The note she'd left—*if it's Tuesday, this must be Red Rock*—struck the perfect note; no complications implied. He had a vague memory of her slipping from bed, her hair down. He remembered how small she'd looked in the moonlight.

His own job was at the far end of the strip, a small trendy restaurant—New Southwest cooking, served on square metal plates—where he waited tables and sometimes tended bar; his own home was an hour away, a two bedroom apartment in a very untrendy suburb. He'd lived there a year. The walls were still bare. There were lawn chairs in the living room, an old chaise lounge for a couch.

He worked the lunch shift, left at four, brought home a Cobb salad and ate it standing in his kitchen. He reviewed the horses scheduled for tomorrow at Churchill and Arlington Park, phoned in a few bets, mostly offshore books. He took his second shower of the day. What was Anne doing? He pictured her hiking through the Canyon. And what was she wearing? Cute walking shorts maybe. White sneakers. He looked through his wardrobe and tried to remember when he had last shopped for clothes.

There was an outlet mall a few miles from where Harry lived. Sammy's Sportswear promised designer clothes at insanely low prices.

"Just like Versace," the salesman said, when Harry picked up a pair of slacks and found a shirt he liked. "Better, really. Because this you can wash. The dry cleaning eats you alive these days, am I right?" The shoes were half-price. He told the salesman to bag his old clothes.

At seven Harry walked through the casino's main lobby, stopped briefly at the gift shop to buy a paper, saw Anne with her group inside Chow's; she waved at him with her chopsticks. She was surrounded by the three men from her group. The big one in the blue sport jacket sat just to her right. He looked over at Harry, a smile that doubled as a smirk.

He played video poker for an hour or so, just killing time. He talked to Jackie, his favorite roulette girl at table six, but didn't play. There was always a buzz in this place, from the crowd, from the action, it pulled you in, but for some reason tonight Harry felt beyond its grasp.

"Finally," Anne said an hour later, appearing suddenly at his side. Her perfume took him back to last night. "They're going to see the show at the Bellagio. I think they can make it two blocks without me."

"How was the desert?"

"Dry," she said. "Very dry. I need a drink."

He took her away from the Strip, to a place Harry liked with a small trio and good Scotch and they played pool, straight eight ball; she had a nice, soft touch. He introduced her to the owner and the waitresses and then drove her past a few other favorite haunts, local bars mostly but a few artsy spots too, that house where so and so lived, the famous writer, the hot singer, galleries, a sculpture garden mixed with cactus and white sand. I'm acting like a tour guide, he thought. It had been a while since he'd felt like sharing these things with anyone.

"This is nice," she said at one point, sipping a Mai Tai through a straw. He liked her sundress and sandals, her bare legs, the way she changed the radio station without asking. He liked just about everything about her.

It was midnight when they stopped at Molly's, a casino/taco

joint used by locals the way gamblers in other states use lottery machines, a daily quick fix; just three tables and a single-zero wheel, wedged between a Laundromat and take-out Thai. The wheel wasn't smooth like those on the Strip; it made loud clicking noises with each turn, like a car with a flat. They sat on bar stools and watched chips being moved on the layout. Harry explained the rules, a bit of strategy.

"I have to bet something," he said. It felt like his lucky night. Nineteen red was his usual bet but he moved it one over one for the hell of it. In honor of Anne.

"Because we're neighbors," he said to her, smiling. A Rockford girl.

"Aren't the odds rather bad in roulette?" Anne said.

"You did your homework. It depends on the table, how you bet. But yes, you're better off at blackjack, or even slots. I like roulette, though. Watching the bounce. You play this number or that number and the rest is fate."

He was moving chips around now, making inside bets, corner bets, he felt like it was his night. And he kept winning. Nothing big, he didn't want to jinx the feeling by pushing it.

"I could really use your help tomorrow," said Anne. "It's gambling day, for my group."

"Doesn't the casino provide someone?"

"They have a little presentation planned," she said, nodding. "But I don't think they stick around. If you're not busy, maybe you could come over and help me answer questions . . . it would really help."

"Sure." Her leg warm against his.

Slow down, Harry . . .

In the parking lot he had this sudden urge to tell her who he really was. Just confess, get it out there for once. The moment passed. They held hands, kissed leaning against the hood of the car, like teenagers. He felt insanely happy.

"My place is just a few minutes from here," said Harry. "It's nothing fancy, believe me. But if you want, if you feel like it . . . Instead of your hotel."

"That would just be so nice," she said.

The gambling seminar provided by the casino was indeed cursory, enough to make everyone feel comfortable around the tables, without the strategy needed to win anything. There was a slide show with cartoon dice, a short Q & A. Everyone had Styrofoam coffee cups and pastries balanced on their knees. Afterwards, Harry tagged along with Anne from table to table, answering questions, relaying things through her, letting her translate. It reminded him of the postcards he sent to his wife, through his sister-in-law. Most of the group had a basic idea of the games.

They had a late lunch—they were on Vegas time now—and Harry stood in line at the buffet chatting with a lady from Manhattan. It felt nice talking to strangers again and everyone was very nice to Harry.

He was headed to the men's room when he saw Reverend Tim motioning for him from the Dealers Lounge.

"Nice shirt," Tim said, fingering the material. "What is this, silk?"

"Don't start."

"New pants, too. And shoes . . . I'm sure she approved."

"It's that obvious, is it?" Harry said and Tim laughed.

"She seemed real nice, Harry. Good for you. Good for you both." He leaned across the counter. "Reason I wanted to talk . . . there's a guy asking questions. About you."

"Really."

"Big fella," Tim said. "Eye-talian. Wondered if you'd be in. This was last night, maybe two, two-thirty."

"What was his name?"

"Lemme see. Russell? Ross?"

"Rossi."

"That's it," Tim said. "Had a bunch of questions . . . where you lived, how long you've been in Vegas. Hinted he might be a fed . . . you been paying your taxes, Harry?"

"What'd you tell him?"

"Nothing," Tim said. "I mean, you're in the book, he can find you if he wants to talk to you. Right?"

The lights seemed brighter now. Harry walked back to the table, sat down next to Anne. His heart was pounding. The conversation turned to tomorrow's final day and the group's trip to

Hoover Dam. Rossi sat at the back of the room, just like Harry would do.

"I'm bringing my kids the next time," someone said. "They'd do better at the video games than I did today."

"My kids would like the water park," said another. Harry found it hard to concentrate. He laughed when the others laughed, nodded absentmindedly, said yes I see . . . yes, you're right. *Time to go, Harry*. For a second he was back in that room in west Chicago, someone's hands on his throat. He stood to go.

"All this water." It was Rossi, moving his coffee to a closer seat. "Harry, you're the expert on Vegas. Help me out here. Because I find this fascinating. I mean, we're supposed to be in the desert, right? And yet you see nothing but water everywhere . . . the fountains, inside and out, the water sculptures . . . theme parks, with log flume rides." His accent was New York, but it seemed to come and go. Harry realized he'd never really heard him speak Italian.

"They have Lake Mead," said someone. "The Colorado River . . . I don't think water's such a problem."

"We'll learn more about this tomorrow," said Anne. "At the dam."

"Yes, okay," said Rossi. "But even so . . . don't you find it curious? I mean, it's still a desert, isn't it? Water should be like gold around here."

"I think that's the point," Harry said. His voice sounding strange to him, as though his ears were stopped up.

"We're supposed to be impressed by all the wealth? The money? The same reason they build these ridiculously huge buildings?"

"Something like that."

"Maybe you're right," Rossi said. "Unfortunately, it's always someone else's money." He smiled. "Isn't it, Harry?"

"God, what a day," said Anne, taking off one earring and walking to the bathroom. It was only nine p.m., but both of them were tired. The small hotel room seemed like a refuge now to Harry. "The noise level in that casino . . ."

I should just run, he thought. He'd done so before, with much less provocation. How big was Rossi, anyway? Too big to fight, it wasn't Harry's style anyway . . . he must be two-twenty at least. And where was Rossi now, in his hotel room, probably, phoning Chicago. . . . *I've got the bastard.* . . .

He waited until Anne had closed the bathroom door, then unzipped her briefcase.

Andrews, Mazzio, Rossi . . .

The names were written in neat blue script, one to a folder. Rossi's original reservation form was here; it listed a Brooklyn address. *Rossi, Michael.* Harry didn't know New York well enough to tell if it was bogus or not. There was no driver's license or social security number on the form, nothing personal. The rest must be back in the travel agency's office, and he'd have to ask Anne directly for that. He wrote down Rossi's room number. On the nineteenth floor . . . Harry's lucky number.

The toilet flushed; Harry returned the files, zipped the bag. Had she laid it here, on the desk? Or on the chair? He couldn't remember, and she was back in the room before he could decide.

"Do they make the rooms that noisy on purpose, do you think? To distract the gamblers?"

Harry said he didn't know.

She sat on the edge of the bed, examining the heel of one of her shoes. "Damn, I can't believe this is breaking already, these were so expensive—"

"I know a guy can fix that," Harry said. His voice sounded flat. "How'd the rest of the group do? Professor Rossi, for example?"

"You know, I'm not sure. I didn't see him after lunch."

"Have you talked to him at all?"

"No more than the others," she said. "He's kind of an odd duck. Turns out most of the others in the group don't even know him. He's not from the university . . . I'm not sure what he's doing on this tour."

Harry said there must be an explanation for that.

"I suppose. But I'm too tired to worry about it," she said. "Besides, after tomorrow night I'll be back in New York, and Professor Rossi can go his merry way."

Harry woke at three, staring at the ceiling. Drunks laughing in the hallway, the parade of neon outside his window. He listened to Anne's gentle breathing beside him.

Just get up and leave. Now. It didn't make any sense. The

guys back in Chicago weren't exactly known for their subtlety. Hiring someone who could fit in with a group like this . . . why bother? Plus, if he's asking all these questions . . . he must not be sure it's him, not yet. *So why not just pull me aside, put a gun to my head and find out? Why the song and dance?*

Rossi was what, six-two, six-three?

He could see the ball bounce back and forth on the wheel.

———

If it's Sunday this must be Hoover Dam . . . Her note was taped to the bathroom mirror. She'd be back at three. The flight back to New York left at seven. He folded the note, saved it like a kid with a valentine.

He rang Rossi's room, let it ring until the operator came back on and said the party wasn't answering, did Harry wish to leave a message? He called long distance and got the number for Columbia University. There was no Professor Michael Rossi listed.

His landlord Mrs. Loomis was outside his building when he parked the Blazer. She told him Harry's brother had stopped by yesterday, wanted to be admitted to his apartment . . . she wasn't sure she should do that. So she didn't. "I'm hoping I didn't cause a problem," she said. "You know. A family squabble."

"No, you did the right thing," he said. No wonder Rossi left the casino after the buffet lunch. And if he's been here once, he'll be back. . . .

He checked the locks. There were new scratches on the patio door. Or was that his imagination? Harry had a gun, a Luger that he bought from a Navajo at a gun show in Las Cruces. He kept it loaded and wrapped in a Motel Six towel under his bed. Just bringing it out now, checking the bullets—something clicked in his mind.

He decided to pack.

There was a routine to leaving . . . he gave himself over to it, cleaned out the carryout leftovers in the fridge, bagged the sports pages and old racing forms that made up his library, paid the few bills sitting in his shoe box, picked up some dry cleaning, filled the Blazer's gas tank. He bought some fruit and bottled water and a new map of Mexico. He'd never been there. He could stop at Nogales first, say goodbye to Harry Chase. He could be in Santa Cruz by nightfall.

Something was holding him back, though, and he couldn't tell if it was his age, that he was just getting tired of the whole damn thing . . . or something else. Like Anne. How much could he tell Anne anyway? How much did he trust her?

He drove to Fremont Street, a place he rarely visited, lost himself in the crowds of conventioneers and low rollers, sat with the housewives playing nickel slots, barely concentrating. He drank whatever they offered him. Twice he got the note out of his pocket. Twice he started to call Anne on her cell.

Just leave, Harry, go. . . .

———

Boulder City was an hour's drive from Vegas. There were no casinos there so Harry had never seen the point in visiting. He found a row of tour buses; one of them must be Anne's. He asked two different park rangers if they'd seen her group. His description—a very pretty blonde lady with a group of professors, EZ Tours—didn't ring any bells. Harry paid for a tour of his own, and then walked down a long series of steps to a sightseeing platform. The sun was unbelievably bright, bouncing off the white concrete. He bought a lemonade and a candy bar and walked to another platform, waded through another group of tourists. Everyone was in shorts and windbreakers, everyone spoke French, Spanish, Japanese . . . where were the goddamn Italians, thought Harry.

And then he saw them, a small half circle gathered around a female ranger, two flights of steel steps below. There was Anne, one hand shading her face from the sun; Rossi, a few feet behind, watching the way Harry would watch; a man apart. He'd shed his jacket, was dressed in a loud red shirt and white slacks, wire sunglasses, white shoes. He still didn't look like a professor. What was he doing here? Why was he still maintaining the façade?

Harry followed them until they'd finished their tour, heard Anne announce that the bus would leave "in thirty minutes, people, don't be late, okay, please?" It was souvenir time.

He watched Rossi leave with the other two men, then caught

up with Anne outside the gift shop. He loved the smile she gave him.

"What are you doing here?" she said. "Is something wrong?"

"No, but I had to see you—we have to talk, now—it couldn't wait—"

"I'm coming back, you know. To the hotel. Didn't you get my note?"

He hesitated. He'd rehearsed this all the way here but now his mind went blank.

"Let's sit down," he said, pulling her out of sight, to a wooden bench.

"Harry, what's this about?" She lit a cigarette, waved away the smoke. "Sorry, I should quit these—"

"Don't go back to New York, Anne."

"What?"

"Come with me. I'm leaving Vegas . . . I was thinking maybe Mexico but if you'd rather go somewhere else, that would be fine, no problem, maybe Mexico's too rough for you, or too hot, it doesn't matter. . . ." Racing now to explain it, and hating the confusion he saw in her face. And dreading how this would end. *I lied to you, Anne . . . please forgive me . . .*

"We could go to Europe," Harry said. "I always wanted to see Venice . . . or Athens—"

"Harry, don't be silly . . . I can't just leave."

"Why not?"

"Because I *can't.* This is my job. These people are my responsibility." She patted his hand, like a nurse with a patient. "Harry, you *knew* I had to leave today."

"I know but—"

"Come to New York," she said. "Or wait—I can get another tour group for Vegas, they must do them all the time. One or two weeks, after I clear my calendar, they have me going to Orlando and Naples and then I can be back."

He shook his head. "I won't be here in one or two weeks."

"What?"

"Anne, has Rossi ever asked you about me?"

"Professor Rossi? No, why would he? Harry, what did you mean, you won't be here?"

"Are you sure? Think about it. Maybe it was just an aside in a conversation . . . or maybe you overheard him asking someone else in the group about me . . ."

"What does Professor Rossi have to do with this?"

"I'm leaving now, Anne. My bags are in my car." He checked the hallway again; there was still no sign of Rossi. "Come with me. . . . forget the tour group, you've got your purse . . . whatever you need we can pick up later. . . ."

"Harry, I have to get back," she said, as though playtime was over. She kissed him and started to get up and he knew he'd have to tell her everything or lose her forever.

Ten years of his life. It wasn't hard—once he started, everything spilled out. She didn't look at him, just smoked nervously, tapping her foot—he could see her thoughts spinning, trying to decide where to land. Was he nuts? Or for real? And how could she decide this so fast?

"I should have told you before now," he said. "I started to, several times, believe me."

She didn't answer. She was looking past him, for a second he thought Rossi was there and he turned and faced an empty hallway. When she finally spoke her cigarette was finished and her voice was a whisper.

"You left her," she said.

"What?"

"Your wife. *You left her behind. . . .*"

"I had to, Anne. I had no choice." Afraid at first of being called a criminal, a thief, he saw now what she was thinking . . . *You would leave me too, Harry . . .*

"I wouldn't," he said. "I swear."

"But how could I be sure? After what you did? How could I trust you?"

There was no answer for that.

"You really think Rossi works for these men in Chicago?" she said.

He nodded.

"After ten years . . . they'd still come for you? Was it that much money?"

"They'd come if it was a dollar fifty," he said. "A bus token. Anything in my pocket that should be in theirs . . . they'd come." He tried to keep the panic out of his voice. He was frightened right now, but not of Rossi. He was scared of losing her. "I know it's not fair, asking you like this."

"I've only known you three days, Harry."

"I know."

"Three days."

She shook her head.

"I can't say yes or no out here," she said. "In the middle of nowhere. Meet me tonight, back at the hotel. We leave for the airport at six."

"Anne . . ."

"That's the best I can do, Harry. I'm not asking for much. Just a few hours to digest all this. Before I decide."

"So you're thinking about it at least?"

"Yes," she said. "I'm thinking about it."

───────────

He sat in a small lounge near the elevators on nineteen. He read *USA Today*, and when someone walked by he nodded and talked about the weather, just another friendly tourist. When Rossi got off the elevator Harry asked if he'd seen today's paper, and he showed him the gun.

"If you're robbing me, you're going to be very disappointed," Rossi said. His room was just across the hall. "None of those little tricks you showed us in the casino worked very well."

"Open the door," Harry said.

"Is this a joke then?" Rossi said. "One of those practical jokes—is there a camera somewhere?" Still not moving, just that annoying smile—Harry had to shove the gun hard in his back to get him to open the door. He didn't blame him, he wouldn't want to do it either. The hall was much safer.

"Stand over there," Harry said, after patting him down. "By the TV. Put your hands up on the shelf." The room was even smaller than Anne's. The bed had been turned down, with the radio left on low, wrapped mints on the pillow.

"I want to know how much you told them," Harry said. He wished he'd brought some rope. Or stopped at one of the adult boutiques on the Strip, they all sold handcuffs. "Do they know I'm in Las Vegas? And are you the only one here?"

Rossi didn't answer. The wallet was cheap plastic, with the

price tag still tucked in one pocket. There was just a New York driver's license, and cash, two or three hundred in mixed bills. No credit cards.

"Can I sit down now?" Rossi said, and Harry nodded, motioning with the Luger. "We did so much walking today, I'm going to sleep real real good tonight. Hoover Dam is one of the seven wonders of the world, did you know that?"

"Whoever sold you the license should use better ink," said Harry, tossing it back in Rossi's lap. "It's a fake. What's your name?"

Again, no answer. Harry realized he would have to be rough to get anything out of him. It wasn't his style but he was frightened enough to adapt. He'd been worked over a couple of times back in Chicago. He figured he knew the basic steps.

Rossi must have been thinking the same thing.

"The rest of the group's back at the hotel now too, you know," said Rossi. "The airport bus leaves in a few minutes, and if I'm not there someone will come looking for me. Hotel security perhaps, then the Las Vegas police." Calm, reasonable. Still the professor.

"What's your real name?" said Harry.

"It was originally known as Boulder Dam," said Rossi. "And did I mention it's one of the seven wonders of the world?"

He used the side of the Luger. It caught Rossi by surprise. He slid off the chair, landing on his knees, face down, blood dripping from one nostril. "Son-of-a . . ." The curse landed on the carpet. So did Rossi, when Harry's second blow came even harder, and connected with Rossi's cheekbone.

"You do that again," Rossi said but didn't finish the threat, gagging now, sniffing back blood. The New York accent was gone. So was the smile.

"So what's your fucking name?" Harry put the gun to his temple.

"Top desk drawer," said Rossi. "In the Triple A packet."

There was a 9mm Glock guarding the drawer. The real wallet was curved black leather. Another thousand was tucked in the fold; these bills were new, crisp hundreds. The driver's license belonged to a Norman Stone. Norman had a Visa, MasterCard, American Express. Norman was an organ donor. And Norman had a private detective's license, too.

"They're using P.I.s now?" Harry said. "They don't have enough thugs on the payroll?"

There were photos below the packet, six or seven, grainy exposures from a cheap zoom lens. Harry and Anne sitting and talking in the Dealers Lounge, driving in Harry's car. Harry coming out of Anne's room . . .

"What are these for?"

"Take a real wild guess, Harry." He struggled back into the chair. His mouth was bleeding now, too. "Get me a goddamn towel, will you? And some ice—they usually fill the bucket by now—"

"How much have you told them?"

"Christ, Harry, I think you broke my fucking jaw—"

"How much?"

Rossi wiped his hands on the drapes. "The real question here, Harry, is how much has she told you? Because you're doing her, aren't you? Unless you're playing Scrabble in there at night. Or Monopoly. You playing Monopoly with her, Harry?"

"Leave her out of this."

"Little Miss Anne Turner, our fearless leader . . ."

"I said *leave her out of this.*"

"Jesus . . . I get it," said Rossi, a slow grin spreading across his face. "You think I'm here for you, don't you?" He was laughing now. "You crazy fucker. No wonder I couldn't trace you. What'd you do, steal somebody's lunchbox?"

"What are you talking about?"

"Her name's not Anne Turner, Harry. It's Myra Hendricks. And the last guy she played board games with disappeared. As in quote unquote disappeared."

"Bullshit. You've been following me, asking questions about me—"

"Only because you're with her, Harry. Believe me. Before Tuesday I never heard of you in my life."

"I don't believe you."

"And normally, quite honestly . . . I could care less what you believed. But since you're pointing a gun at me . . ." He shrugged. "Like I said, her name's Myra Hendricks. And she's not from New York, not originally . . . she's from downstate Illinois."

"I know where she's from. She told me that."

"Did she also tell you about her husband?"

"She's divorced."

"Well, that's one way of putting it," Rossi said. "Jack Hendricks felt the sudden need to take a midnight stroll eighteen months ago. No one's seen him since. Myra got the money. Or rather, she will get the money, in another month, when they finally declare the husband dead. After that I doubt we'll ever see Myra again."

"That's bullshit."

Another shrug.

"Who's paying you?"

"That's confidential." He paused. "A family member. But everything's public record. Check the papers, knock yourself out."

"I still don't believe it." And most of him didn't. But a part of him couldn't decide . . . the part that had kept him alive these past ten years, the toughened, calloused part . . . that whispered anything was possible, anyone could betray him. And remembered every hesitation of Anne's, every reluctance to answer simple questions.

He stood up, gripped the Luger in his palm. He'd have to hit him harder this time, enough to knock him out, give Harry a head start. . . .

"You thinking of living with her, happy ever after?" Rossi said. "Be my guest. Buy a house in the burbs, raise lots of rug rats.

"But I wouldn't go for any late night strolls if I was you," Rossi said.

———

She was waiting for him in the secluded spot they'd both chosen, sitting on the bench like a schoolgirl waiting for a bus.

"I thought maybe you'd changed your mind," she said. "I packed but I don't really have the clothes for Mexico, maybe we could stop somewhere—"

She stopped, seeing something different on his face. He didn't try to hide it.

"Rossi's name is Norman Stone," he said. "He's working for your father-in-law."

"What?"

"He's on to you, Anne. He told me everything. But I don't care." Driving over here he'd realized, it's better this way. She would understand him better. They would leave Rossi far behind, just start over, both of them, clean and fresh and it would all be okay. "Whatever happened . . . I just don't care."

"Harry, what did he tell you? What are you talking about? Because you're scaring me again. Sit here, with me. Slow down."

"There isn't time—"

"Harry, whatever he told you, it was a lie to get away from you. Don't you see?"

She reached for his arm. Her face blank somehow. He bent down to kiss her.

"Harry . . ." It was Rossi. Stepping out from behind a fence. A different gun in his right hand, military stance . . .

The ball bounced

"Move away from her, Harry," Rossi screamed, "I can't get a clear shot."

The wheel spun

Harry felt the first shot whiz by him.

"Shoot him, Harry," Anne said, clinging to him. "For God's sake, just shoot him, now." Looking into his eyes . . .

She is not who you think she is, Harry . . .

There were shots that sounded like popped balloons. One of them stung Harry's left arm, the one closest to Anne, and she screamed, and turned towards him. She was saying something, over and over, and it took a few seconds for Harry to understand.

"I can't go back with him, Harry. *I can't.*"

He was sitting on the ground, the sun in his face, his chest on fire.

Last bets, everyone . . .

"Harry!"

He tried to talk but there was just a gurgling sound . . .

The wheel slowed . . .

He raised his own gun and emptied it into Rossi.

"Harry . . . my God, Harry, hold on," Anne said. Everything was spinning now. His last sight was of Anne. Crying, holding onto him. He couldn't feel her, though. He couldn't feel anything. There was just her perfume. And the dealer smiling, saying he had won.

And then the wheel finally stopped.

THE END OF THE WORLD
(AS WE KNOW IT)

LISE MCCLENDON

I knew he'd lost a couple thou. He couldn't stop whining about it. I didn't know how my sister put up with his incessant carping: The pool was too cold, the room was too small, I left hair in the sink, the drinks were watered down and weren't delivered fast enough. I knew he'd lose at the tables, and I knew he'd complain about it. But the telegram was the last straw.

Send Lawyers Guns Money Stop
Shit hitting fan Stop
Herb

Couldn't somebody stop Herb? I handed him back his rough draft.

"Cynthia will know what to do," he muttered, folding it into his pocket.

"She'll know you're on your Warren Zevon bender again. She'll just call. She won't send money."

She better the hell not. That would mean I had to stay longer in Vegas. And I was fried. "Look, Herb. Just get on the plane tomorrow and go home. She loves you." Why, I had no idea. She obviously didn't love me, her only brother, because she sent me with her wacky husband for four whole days to Las Vegas. I took a breath. The heat was brutal. I was losing it. "Nobody sends telegrams anymore. If you want to talk to her, just call."

Herb stalked through the big brassy doors of the casino, out into the drive where taxis and limos waited for their sorry clients to quit losing money. Vegas was a beautiful dream when I first arrived, the gorgeous weather, the dry heat flattened out my hair, the blue pools to cool off in, great restaurants, a show or two, some with topless showgirls. Even the beeping and blinking of the casinos had been charged with excitement at first. The endless gambling tables, skimpily clad cocktail waitresses and bars around every corner ready to pour you whatever your heart's desire, had seemed like a wet dream. Not exactly satisfying but good for a few rushes of adrenaline.

That high lasted three days and two-and-a-half nights. Now the cards that refused my mind-meld, the parched, smoky air, the incessant ringing electronic gadgetry, and Herb Monroe, accountant, duffer, and whining machine, had made me change my mind. Not to mention that I, too, had lost a thou.

Where the hell was he going? I followed him outside, worried that in demoralized angst he might walk in front of a car. "Hey, come back here!" He was halfway down the block, walking through those mist machines that cool passersby in cafes along the sidewalk. I caught up with him in front of New York New York.

"Western Union. That's where I'm going," he said firmly, taking long strides south. "She'll help. She knows."

"What does that mean? She knows what?" Cynthia was an accountant too, in the same firm. "She knows what a stubborn ass you can be, Herb."

He kept walking, sweat beading on his forehead. His khakis were loose on his hips, but his new Vegas-bright shirt featuring hula dancers was stuck to his back. He squinted into the sun. "She'll know what to do, Aaron. She knows the particulars." He stopped suddenly. "There it is." He stepped off the curb and barely missed being hit by an SUV the size of Indiana.

"Watch it!" I felt strangely reluctant to plunge across twelve lanes of traffic. He darted and jumped, avoiding carloads of children in minivans, Humvees ready for the next suburban war zone, and the elderly in slow-motion Cadillacs. I let out my breath as he reached the far side. "I'm going back," I hollered.

He trooped across the strip mall parking lot toward the tiny U-Pack-M with the Western Union sign on the window, swinging through the door. If the Morse code floated his boat, that was his problem. Herb was an adult. My stint as babysitter was officially over. My sister had taken me aside at the airport and made me promise to keep an eye on her husband. Yes, she'd paid my ticket, but enough was enough. Besides, I was close to the Bellagio, and I hadn't had the chance to see the famous Picassos.

The hike up to their door was long and hot but punctuated by fountains. Inside it was cool and not as loud as the other casinos, although I'm sure losing money was just as popular here. A quick tour around the lobby and the chi-chi restaurants, a gin and tonic at one of many bars, and a peek at Pablo's cracked view of human beings, and I was ready for a nap. My flight didn't leave until morning, I had already lost more money than I should have, and I had a headache even gin couldn't touch.

Slapping on the sunglasses, I wandered back through the wall of heat to our hotel. Herb would probably try to recoup his losses. He'd been at that since the first night. The room would be quiet, I could pull the drapes and nap. In the elevator a heavily botoxed woman of indeterminate age gave me the eye. I must be getting old because all I wanted was that nap.

Two aspirin and an hour later I was called from a dream reminiscent of a Hunter Thompson orgy by the telephone. Before I woke up all the way I thought Herb had learned to do impressions. But it wasn't Herb, it was a Vegas cop. He told me Herb was in the hospital with a skull fracture or something. They'd found my name on his courtesy charge card. Hit by a car crossing the Boulevard? No, more like a tire iron.

The cop met me in the emergency room in the hospital not far from the Strip. Herb had been bushwhacked coming out of the U-Pack-M by some guys who really did pack 'em. They pistol-whipped him in the parking lot and were run off by a mailing clerk. Herb was unconscious.

"Does he have enemies in Las Vegas?" the cop asked me.

"I don't think so." I tried to think. "Have you called his wife yet?"

They left it up to me. Thanks, guys. Cynthia was in the office in St. Cloud, working late. When I told her Herb had been beat up, she began to cry. That delayed the tongue-lashing she gave me for not protecting him by about five seconds.

"He's a grown man, Cynthia. Why would he need protection?"

She sniffed. "What about the money?"

He hadn't told her. "What money would that be?"

"The money he won. He told me yesterday he won six thousand dollars at blackjack."

"You don't win six thou at blackjack, Cyn. At least I don't, and Herb sure doesn't."

She gave a little moan. "He wouldn't have it on him, Aaron. In your room. Isn't it there?"

Just to get her off the phone I told her I'd look in the room when I got back. I waited a couple hours in the ER for him to wake up, but the nurses finally told me to bag it and come back around nine that evening. I drove the rental car, world's sexiest white Dodge sedan, to the Hard Rock Café for a burger and a beer. It was only seven so I went back to the room for my third shower of the day.

The light on the phone was blinking when I got out of the bathroom. I listened to the message: "Aaron, it's me again. You know the song, 'The end of the world as we know it.'" Cynthia sang the old R.E.M. tune. She had a great voice, one I always associated with her being fourteen and singing for my high school band before Dad found out what she wore. "Well, it is and it isn't—the end of the world. I got the telegram and the money. Thanks for taking care of everything. Can you get him home okay? It's important. Okay, love ya, brother."

Before I could figure that out, the front desk called and told us they were comping our room for the four days. "Because of the—why?"

"For our loyal customers. Just say thank you, Mr. Nelson," the clerk said, laughing. So I did.

I set down the phone and tried to clear my head. Was I still asleep? Did I need another shower? I shivered in the air conditioning. What the hell were Cynthia and Herb up to? I pulled on my jeans and started to search the room. When I was an MP in the army I never had to do searches, but I knew how it went, cushions, drawer bottoms, mattresses. But the room was clean. No money, no telegrams, no answers. Herb's suitcase was standard issue JC Penney with his dashing polyester wardrobe to match.

I tried to call my sister again but got her machine. I told it, "This'll be the end of the world, all right, if you don't tell me what the fuck is going on."

Herb was groggy when I finally found his room in the hospital. The nurse left us alone, said I only had a few minutes. I got to the point.

"What's this about money you wired home?"

He moaned and shut his eyes.

"Herb, who hit you?" He moaned again. "What the hell is this about? Are you in trouble?"

His eyes popped open and he murmured an affirmative. "Casino," he whispered.

"Have you been counting cards or something?"

He gave one last dramatic groan and promptly fell asleep. Even as mad as I was I couldn't shake him awake, not with his bandaged head and IVs going in and out. One side of his face was purple and swollen. I backed out, wondering if the man with the tire iron would give it another go. It seemed unlikely in a hospital. The nurse told me Herb was still in serious condition with a traumatic head injury and I wouldn't be able to take him back to Minnesota for at least a week.

In the lobby of the hotel I plugged quarters into the pay phone instead of the slots. I needed to talk to Cynthia but she wasn't home again. What the hell? It was past midnight there. I left another pissed-off message that wouldn't make her call me but made me feel better.

The hotel's gambling halls were thick with tourists, nicotine-stained fingers checking cards, rubbing felt, massaging temples. Plump ladies flushed with excitement; young kids kicking the slots. I ordered another gin and tonic and watched the mass of humanity go about what had to be one of our stupider pastimes. Had Herb been scamming the casino somehow? He was a terrible gambler, in my humble opinion, although I didn't play with him all the time. I got bored with blackjack and would watch craps for awhile or spin the roulette wheel. When I got back to the table, Herb would have moved around, found a dealer he thought was luckier, and usually told me he was down a few hundred and trying to make it back. Hey, weren't we all.

No, Herb hadn't won a bunch of money gambling. He wasn't a good enough actor to hide that from me. I'd known him since he and my sister started working at the same firm, a couple years after I got out of the service. In my real estate office I sent him clients now and then, and there hadn't been any complaints. Before our divorce my wife and I socialized with Herb and Cynthia a couple times a month, barbecues, movies, dinner. Herb treated my sister pretty well, considering she could be a raging banshee when she got wound up. She used to whale on me when she was a teenager, like when we had to can her from the band. If only she hadn't worn those black leather hot pants.

That REM song she sang me ran over and over in my mind. What did she mean, the end of the world? Was she running away from Minnesota, from her home, with Herb or without Herb, with whatever money he had wired her? And where was that from anyhow? Would she be at Mom's? Doubtful. At her friend Louise's in St. Paul?

Something about her response to Herb's getting thrashed bugged me. Was it the money she was worried about—or Herb? She hadn't offered to come take care of him, even though he was in the hospital. Those of us who loved her realized practical jokes and gruesome Halloween costumes are more her style than maternal instincts. My little sister. She made you want to sigh sometimes.

Instead of sighing I opted for drinking. I couldn't leave on my flight in the morning anyway. It was going to cost me something to get that changed. I hit the payphones again and called the airline, begging for understanding. I must have sounded pathetic because they left the tickets open, to use when Herb recovered.

I tried Cynthia again and this time she answered.

"Baby sister. If you don't explain this to me I'm gonna have to strangle you."

"Aaron." She yawned. "I'm asleep."

"Talk to me. Now. Herb said something about a casino. Is he in trouble? Who beat him up?"

"I don't know." She had a pouty way even in her voice. "He's a grown man. He does what he pleases."

"I don't think it pleased him to get pistol-whipped."

"Mmm. Maybe not. But he went to Vegas. He took the chances."

"What chances?" The gin began to churn in my gut.

"With the casino. Oh, I can't explain it, Aaron."

"What casino? This one, where we're staying?"

"Yes and no. I'm hanging up now."

I looked at the receiver, cursed, and banged it down. Too cheesed off to sleep, I hiked up and down the Strip in the night and the neon, pounding the pavement until the edge wore off and I could sleep.

Slipping the key card into the lock, pushing open the door, the first thing I saw were the polka dot boxers my ex-wife had bought me strewn across the purple carpet. My suitcase lay open, upside down. Herb's suitcase, minus the things I'd taken to the hospital for him, had been jumped on by somebody large, its sides caved in. Drawers hung open, chairs were overturned, a good tossing had by all. And by somebody as pissed off as I'd just been, somebody who hadn't found what they were looking for. Unless it was polka dot boxers.

I spent a few minutes straightening up and put on the deadbolt and chain. Apparently Herb had some money that was either somebody else's or they thought they deserved it. That wouldn't be gambling winnings. But a casino was involved. *This* casino didn't seem upset with us. Why did they comp the room? What had we done to deserve a free room besides lose a few thou? That couldn't be very unusual. Neither of us was a high roller. An idea bubbled up like tonic water. Was Herb a thief? My head hit the pillow with that unhappy thought.

In the late morning I killed my headache with a greasy three-egg breakfast and a swim in the pool. My pale Midwestern skin hadn't seen this much sun since childhood summers at Rainy Lake with the leeches and mosquitoes. These days air conditioning was my summer weather of choice.

But all this avoidance, pretending to be simply on vacation, didn't make me quit cogitating about Herb and Cynthia. Two American kids doing the best that they can, I hummed to myself as I dressed and drove to the hospital again. A little ditty by John Mellencamp that I used to love to play on the guitar. I wondered why I had stopped playing (I knew when—after I married Jeannie) and promised myself for only the five-millionth time that I would start again. It never happened, in the same way that Jeannie and I never worked on our marriage. Sooner or later you forget the fingering.

Herb seemed perky this morning, or at least more alert than yesterday. He said he felt a lot better.

"I think I can leave tomorrow, I'm working on my doctor." He glanced furtively at the door and winced as the pain of the quick movement hit him.

"You don't look so good, old buddy. You better stay flat for a few more days. The nurse said a week would do you good."

"A week!" He wrinkled his nose and lay back on the pillows. "I gotta get out of here."

"Don't worry about it. I fixed the tickets. The hotel comped our room. Things will be okay." *Tell me this is the end of it, big fella.* I squinted at him. He seemed nervous. Maybe it was time for his meds. "Did you talk to Cynthia?"

He nodded. "This morning."

"You gonna tell me what this's about or do I have to pistol-whip you?" I sat on the edge of the bed. He rolled away from me. "Come on, Herb. Somebody tossed our room last night. And beat you up. You have to know what's happening here."

"Did the cops say I knew who it was?"

"How could they? You were out cold. Look at me, bub." He rolled back a little. "What's the deal? You do something bad?"

Jesus, I sounded like I was his dad—and he was two years older than me. I would never take a free trip with a relative again. The strings attached to this one were strangling me. He was silent, twiddling with his hospital gown.

"Who was it, Herb? You said something about the casino yesterday."

"I did? What did I say?"

"I asked if you were in trouble and you said, casino. That's all."

He seemed to relax. I knew how he felt. When I had drugs to get my nose straightened out I told the doctor several embarrassing tales, including how I lost my virginity with a girl who worked at the PX on the base. I even told him her name, something I couldn't remember on a normal day. He regaled me with the stories and slapped my back on my next visit.

"I must have been thinking about all the money I lost. Cynthia was very understanding." He worked up a sympathetic look.

"That's not her story," I said. His eyes cooled. "She says you wired six thousand dollars to her. Is that what you were doing in the U-Pack-M?"

"No. You saw me lose at blackjack. I'm a terrible card player."

"You are. You stink at cards. Always have."

He scowled briefly. "I just sent her the telegram to show her I realized how seriously I'd messed up. And it worked. Thank heavens. I didn't know if I could go home again."

"So you're saying my sister is lying."

"Aaron, knock it off! You misunderstood her. She was just upset because of the, um, the attack."

"Okay." I was more than fed up now. And he'd talked to Cynthia so they could get their stories straight. "So what did these guys look like, the ones who beat you up?"

He closed his eyes. "I'm tired. I need to sleep."

"You want me to send in the cops now? The ones out in the hall?"

His eyes flew open. "Are they waiting for me? To talk?"

"Unless you talk to me." I had no idea where the cops were, but they should have been here torturing him. I stood up to leave.

"No, stay, Aaron. The cops are so—" He gulped.

"Serious? Yes, they don't much like liars."

Time to go home. I'd been out West too long, I was starting to sound like a John Wayne movie. I squinted at Herb's quivering form under the sheets and squelched an urge to say, Pilgrim, I don't cotton to no yellow bellies neither.

But he was my sister's husband. So I sat down on the bed again and waited.

"There were two of them." His eyes darted around the room in classic liar style. "Dark, Italian or Mexican or something. Very nice tans, I remember thinking. Then they brought out the guns and I—I think I fainted. It might have been the heat though. That parking lot was really hot."

"Everything in Vegas is hot in August."

"True. The asphalt was sticky. I remember thinking that as I went down."

"So they didn't talk to you? You just toppled over like a pussy?"

"No, no, they said something about giving them my money. I said I didn't have any, I lost it all on cards. They didn't believe me. Right there in the afternoon sun, a robbery. Can you believe it?"

Actually, no. "Then what happened?"

"They pushed me around a little. I had nothing to give them.

But they seemed to think I did. I pulled my pockets out like this—" he mimicked the motion "—but they just got madder. Then the one with the mustache—"

"Mustache? What did the other one have, a beard?"

"Nothing, I think. I don't remember him so much. The mustache one did the talking." I motioned him to continue. "That guy gets out a gun, a big one. And the other guy gets out his. And I faint."

"Just like that."

"I might have said, please don't kill me or something like that."

"So you don't remember them hitting you over the head."

"Um, no. Not really." He looked up at me. "Will you tell the cops for me? Please, Aaron. You know the police better than I do. I always feel so guilty around cops."

That stopped me. Usually the innocent feel that way. But I supposed the guilty do too, and with more reason. I cruised the stifling streets where a bank thermometer said it was 116 degrees, and ran from car to casino, a.c. to a.c. Pausing for hydration in the bar (tonic water is very medicinal and gin, well, it had to be good for something besides pickling private detectives) I figured Herb's story was half true, if that. The mail clerk had seen two men pistol-whipping him, so that part was probably true. And he possibly did faint at the sight of weapons. He was that sort of a boy scout.

I spied a casino office sign in a far corner of the gambling hall and made my way through the tables to it. As I knocked a young woman, a dealer, came by with her card tray and opened the door with a code on the numbered panel. She paused, looking back at me. I told her I was looking for whoever comps rooms so I could thank them. She pointed me to another office where a receptionist talked on an intercom to someone named Connie.

When she walked out my heart stopped for a second. She looked so much like Jeannie they could have been sisters. But Connie's hair was bleach blonde, very Vegas, and she wore a tight-fitting red suit, something that Jeannie would have called professionally slutty. Which I, like most men, find attractive. She shook my hand and the words came out of my mouth: "Can I buy you a drink to thank you?"

Her laugh was genuine, not fake like her hair. "It's a little early for me, Mr. Nelson."

I looked at my watch. "Have you had lunch?"

Her name was Connie Rossi, her title was Guest Relations Manager, and she knew a good place for lunch where we could talk away from the sounds of gambling. In the elevator I had to keep telling myself to be cool, to slyly get information from her about the room, about Herb. I didn't feel very cool—or sly. In fact, despite the arctic blast of air conditioning, I felt very un-cool. In a hot sort of way. It disturbed me and made me think of my mother, which is very disturbing at such a time. How she used to say, "Eh, so now you thinking with your you-know-what?"

The restaurant was on the top floor of the hotel, very quiet and classy. And expensive. Oh, well, I gulped as we ordered $30 lunches. I was too much of a Midwesterner to ever be a high roller. I felt my coolness return. I ordered us each a glass of Pinot Grigio which Jeannie had liked. When it came I thanked Connie again for the complimentary room.

"Just doing my job," she said. She had pretty blue eyes, even though there were gobs of mascara on them. It felt better finding her faults.

"I don't know if you heard about my brother-in-law's, um, accident." She looked concerned. "He was attacked a couple blocks from here. He's in the hospital with a concussion."

"Oh, dear. I'm so sorry." She patted my hand, which under most circumstances I would have enjoyed. Even this one.

"Yes. It's darn shocking." The sly one works his magic.

"Do you—I'm sorry, Aaron, is it?" I nodded, my slyness evaporating. "Aaron, do you need a few more days? I'm sure we can do that."

"You can? That would be great, thanks. But, well, why exactly are you comping our room? We aren't big gamblers, although God knows we lost a few zillion pesos."

She gave a delicate shrug, smiling mysteriously. "It's best to just say thank you, Aaron."

"I heard that. So—thank you. But with Herb's attack and all I feel like I really should get more information. Did Herb do something for you, for the casino?"

She smiled again. "You should really talk to him about that."

Our lunches came, medium-to-small by Minnesota standards but hearty enough. The wine helped wash down my steak. And give me time to think up a new tack.

"Here's the thing, Connie—may I call you Connie?" I've been waiting all my life to say that to a woman, a sad confession. She gave permission. "I was going to write off this whole trip on my income taxes. But without a hotel bill, it makes it a bit sticky. Herb is an accountant, he'll probably find a way, but I need documentation. Now, I'm not saying I want to pay the bill." I laughed, *har-har*: silly sly fox that I am.

She looked perplexed. I elaborated, spinning. "Let me back up. Are you giving Herb some documentation for this trip? A receipt or something? Because he is in the hospital and I need to get things arranged for him."

"It's an odd request, Aaron. But taxes are of course a big deal. You can't deduct your gambling losses unless you show you've actually been to Las Vegas?"

"Something like that." I ordered her more wine. I had no idea what I was talking about.

After I paid the bill (praise the lord for Comping Connie, the total was $95 plus tip), I followed her back to her office, waiting by the receptionist for her to make a few calls. I'm sure she would have preferred I disappear, but I couldn't take that chance. I called my room to see if I had any messages. There was one, from the hospital.

"This is Aggie Webb, I'm a nurse on Four Central. It's about three-thirty. I thought you should know that Herbert Monroe has checked himself out of the hospital AMA. That is, 'against medical advice.' I hope he's okay but please tell him to be checked by his personal physician as soon as he gets home."

I dialed the hospital. The nurse said the doctor had seen Herb about two and told him he had to stay another two or three days. After the doctor left, Herb got into his clothes and checked himself out, bandaged head and all. She was ticked off about his bullheadedness. I sympathized with her, then promised to get the knucklehead to a doctor at home.

When Connie came back out, I was pacing the small reception area. I stopped and took a breath. She had no documents in her lovely slim hands.

"I've made a few calls." She crossed her arms, showing me

how busy she was. "It took more than a few, really. It's funny." She frowned. "I can't help you with your tax receipts. That would be illegal, you know. But I can tell you that your brother-in-law did some accounting for our CEO. This was his way of saying thank you."

"For the CEO? What's his name?"

"Matthew Birdsong."

"I've heard of him. Wasn't there a big article about him in some magazine?"

"*Forbes*. He's a very bright man. We're very lucky to have him."

She apologized for not being able to tell me more, then shook my hand. Which was nice. As I left I realized that falling for somebody who looks like your ex-wife is as stupid as going on a trip with your brother-in-law. Even when the brother-in-law vanishes into thin air.

Herb never came back to the hotel. I waited for him in the room for four hours, watching golf tournaments and C-SPAN, got hungry, went to a restaurant with a view of the front doors. I ate, I drank, he never came in. I thought maybe I missed him on my trip to the men's room, but he wasn't upstairs. He wasn't in any of the bars. He wasn't playing blackjack. I drove back to the hospital, half-expecting to see him slumped on a curb somewhere. Had the pistol-whippers gotten their greasy hands on him again? Should I call the cops? I didn't want to call my sister and tell her now I'd lost the sorry bastard.

The next morning was as hot and dry and Herb-less as the day before. I went out to the parking lot to report him missing to the cops. But the Dodge—or rather its occupants—had other ideas.

There were two of them, just like Herb's story. One was going through the trunk, he had the spare tire and tool kit on the asphalt. The other one stood in an open passenger door.

"Hey!" I said slyly. "That's my car."

The one under the trunk lid moved quickly, securing my shirt at the collar before I noticed he was close. He had long black hair and a chiseled face. Was I back in a Western again? I managed to squeak out, "Who the hell are you?"

He threw me against the car. "Where's the money?"

"What money?" Isn't that the standard response? This was so

surreal I felt detached, except where my spine was rubbing the fender. "If Herb took some money from you, he didn't tell me about it."

"Where is he?"

"I was just going to report him missing. He's AWOL."

The second man came into my line of sight and spat on me. "White scum." The saliva ran down my cheek. I had plenty of humiliation in the Army, but this was a first. The two men were both bigger than me, the spitter in a ragged flannel shirt with many broken snaps and the big one, the strangler, in a black Sturgis Rally T-shirt. Their types were not unknown to me; lots of Native Americans lived in North Central Minnesota.

I wriggled a bit, making the big one in the T-shirt tighten his grip of my throat. "Hey," I croaked. "I haven't done anything to you, eh? I don't know where he is. Or his money."

The big one looked at the Flannel Shirt, who had braids and a thick neck. They both looked at me. This repeated, as if they were discussing me silently. Finally they let me up. I could hear my words, the way I'd reverted to the old phraseology of the countryside in my panic. I wiped the spit off with my sleeve.

"Wh-where're you guys from?" I rubbed my neck. "Crow Wing?"

The big one went for me again and I dropped my arms. No use struggling. "Just a guess. I live near there." My arms were pinned to Dodge's hot metal. "I like to go up there. It's pretty country. In the—the fall, you know, when the leaves turn."

Rally Shirt squinted at me in close-up. I readied for another lougie. His breath smelled like coffee. I tried to imagine all of us having a cup back home, shooting the breeze at one of the old cafes in the small towns around St. Cloud. I was suddenly very homesick.

"Tell you the truth—if you find Herb, you can beat him to a pulp for me. Break his arms. Be my guest."

The younger one, Flannel Shirt, started to laugh, a chuckle bubbling up from his well-toned chest. Rally Shirt loosened his grip as he caught the laughter, letting me go to wipe tears from his eyes. I stood where I was, smiling like a deer in headlights.

Finally the big one slowed down enough to say, "Get the fuck out of here."

I sidled away, back toward the safety of the hotel. When I was two car lengths away, I turned back. They were still chuckling.

"Say, I was wondering. What did Herb do to you guys? Did he steal some money?"

Flannel Shirt turned. "What the fuck you think?"

"Right. But how?"

"His numbers," the other said. "Juggling the books."

"He's your accountant?"

They looked at me like the stupid white scum I was that day. Stupid and white came easily, the scum was courtesy of them. As they walked away, the big one kicked the side of the Dodge with a very large motorcycle boot, leaving a dent that would cost me plenty.

Back in the room I took another shower and called the cops. I reported Herbert Monroe missing and my rental car burglarized and vandalized. The paperwork took the rest of the day, even though the cops came out to the hotel to see the damage. The car got a lot more attention than Herb. Apparently people disappeared from Las Vegas with a fair regularity.

Sometime in late afternoon I called Cynthia to break the news. No answer, just: "the number you have called has been disconnected or is no longer in service." I stared at the receiver, sitting on the edge of my bed, and listened to the recording six times. Then I hung up and sang my sister's favorite song. End of whose world, sis?

On the plane flying home I asked the stewardess if they had any old issues of *Forbes Magazine* up in first class. Somewhere over Colorado she brought me a stack of ten magazines including three *Forbes*. I'd seen the issue all over Minnesota because the cover featured a native (literally) son. There he was: a handsome Indian man, Matthew Birdsong, wunderkind business whiz who grew up on a reservation in Minnesota, went to college, and came home to help his tribe build one of the first, biggest, and most successful Indian casinos in the U.S.

I skimmed through the rags-to-riches story, or in this case, loincloth-to-loot. Finally, in a discussion of his business practices, I found the link.

"Rumors flew for weeks among employees at the Crow Wing Casino that layoffs were coming. Was business bad? Reports were that machines and tables were busy all day and most of the night. Busloads of gamblers arrived from Chicago and other

Midwestern cities. However, due to financial irregularities the management announced a quarter of employees would be let go and tribal distribution would be substantially reduced this year. Birdsong, now CEO of one of Las Vegas's biggest casino hotels, said the auditors in St. Cloud had found profits to be exaggerated in the last quarter. Calls to Herbert Monroe, chief auditor at White Birch Accounting, were not returned."

Were the Vegas Indians casino employees Herb had helped get fired? Or were they employees of Matthew Birdsong? Had Herb double-crossed the man he was cooking the books for? In the manner of life in general I was never to know exactly.

In November the Securities and Exchange Commission indicted Matthew Birdsong for fraudulent accounting practices, accusing him of skimming money from Crow Wing Casino to pad the accounts in Vegas to drive up the stock of the casino's holding company. To celebrate I went up to Crow Wing one frigid night just after Thanksgiving to lose a few dollars in slot machines, to bet a few at the tables, to drink coffee all night with my kin. About three in the morning I spotted Louise, Cynthia's old St. Paul pal, playing keno. We were both sober, an unfortunate byproduct of Indian gaming.

Louise looked tired, dark circles under her eyes. "What do you hear from Cyn?"

"You kidding? Vanished into thin air."

She shook her head sadly and looked toward the gaming tables, as if there was something else.

"You heard from her, didn't you?"

Louise frowned then smiled then burst out laughing. "You won't believe it, Aaron. I can't tell you where she is, she wouldn't tell me. But guess what she's doing?"

A vision of black leather hot pants popped into my head. She was my little sister. I just knew. "Singing in a band."

The day before Christmas a letter arrived with Canadian stamps. No return address, a Winnipeg cancel mark. Inside were two 500-dollar bills, Canadian. A small note was fixed to the paper clip.

"Rock your world courtesy Matthew Birdsong. Go, bro. The music is calling."

NICKELS AND DIMES

RONNIE KLASKIN

Once upon a time, in the summer of 1973, there were two sisters who went on a car trip with their Mommy and their Daddy, who were both school teachers and thus had the whole summer off. They left from Long Island New York and were driving all the way to Los Angeles, where their Uncle Phil, Aunt Miriam, and their cousins Jon and Karen lived in the Valley. But Uncle Phil, Aunt Miriam, Jon, and Karen are not important to this story, so it's perfectly all right for you to forget their names. Neither is Los Angeles or any of the other places, mostly Holiday Inns right off the Interstate, with game rooms and pools, where they stayed for one night at a time, or the dozens of Stuckey's, where they stopped for bathroom breaks and root beer and an occasional pecan log.

What's important is Las Vegas, with its neon lit Strip, big hotels and glittery casinos. They got a room at one of the moderate-sized and moderate-priced hotels called Dollars Dreaming, which had a big flashing neon one-hundred-dollar bill as a marquee. The room had two queen-sized beds, one shared by the parents, Brenda and Jeff, and the other by the two girls, Laura and Julie. The hotel served a large and cheap buffet breakfast and lunch, and boasted a big outdoor pool. It had a casino, of course, filled with slot machines and all sorts of gaming tables, but the sisters were not allowed in there. They were too young.

Laura, the older sister, was ten, almost eleven. She was a quiet, studious girl who was always reading. She was a good reader and had graduated from reading Nancy Drew books to those by Judy Blume, which weren't mysteries but told of things like menstruation and pimples, things that were of the utmost interest at that time of her life. Then she discovered mysteries by Agatha Christie, of which her mother had an entire collection.

Laura was not sure about what she wanted to be when she grew up. Maybe a teacher, like Mommy and Daddy, so she could have the summers off, as well as Christmas and Easter and a bunch of other holidays. Laura was an extremely practical young person. Or possibly she could be a detective, but she wasn't very sure how you went about that. Or a writer, or movie star. A year before she had considered becoming a ballet dancer, except that she wasn't really very graceful, and more important, Laura had heard her dancing teacher say that ballet dancers had to be skinny, and she liked ice cream and cookies far too much. She was tall and slim then, with straight, dirty blonde hair and a totally flat bosom which she feared would never develop.

Julie, who was just seven, was not at all like Laura. She was small and wiry with short red curls and a spray of freckles across her upturned nose, and was always moving. Kinetic energy, Jeff called it. She wasn't anywhere near as well behaved as Laura. She wasn't a bad kid, but her teachers said she talked too much in class, and she didn't always pay attention or finish her homework, and she didn't get very good marks on her report cards. She had also been known to lie on occasion. But she was popular, with a lot more friends than Laura ever had. She knew all of the dogs and cats in her neighborhood and constantly begged Brenda for a pet, which Brenda said was nagging, and explained that they couldn't get one because Laura had too many allergies.

One of the things that made Laura have itchy eyes and sneeze a lot was cat hair. Julie didn't ever see Laura sneeze when she pet a dog, but Brenda said a definite no to any sort of furry pet. Even hamsters and gerbils, which Julie said could live in a cage in her room, and Brenda could tell Laura never to go in there and steal any of Julie's things anymore.

Another thing that gave Laura allergies was lavender. She had found that out when Grandma Helen had given them each a small bottle of lavender perfume. Grandma Helen always gave them exactly the same thing, hoping that they wouldn't fight over whose present was better.

Laura smelled the perfume and went into a sneezing fit. So

she traded her bottle with Julie for a gold locket that Julie had found lying in the street. At first she told Julie that the locket was just a piece of junk, but after the trade, she said she thought it was real gold. Julie was really angry, and, after that, every time Julie was mad at Laura about something or other, she would put some of the perfume on a piece of tissue and stick it between the pages of the book that Laura was reading. When Laura opened the book she would sneeze for hours. But she never told on Julie because then Brenda would find out about what happened with the locket, and she'd probably be punished and not be allowed to watch her favorite TV programs for a night or two.

───────────

They checked into the hotel a little after three on Thursday, changed right into their bathing suits and took a dip in the pool. Brenda made sure that the girls were well covered with suntan oil because it was very hot and sunny, 109 degrees, even that late in the afternoon, and she didn't want them to get bad sunburns. Both girls had very fair complexions. Julie was the better swimmer, but she also enjoyed splashing Laura, who complained to Brenda, and then Brenda said that twenty minutes in that hot sun was enough for the first day in that awful heat, and it was time to go back to the room and take showers. Julie whined a bit, and Jeff gave her a light tap on the bottom of her two-piece bathing suit.

Laura was disappointed too. The lifeguard at the pool was really cute. Laura was just beginning to notice these things. He wore his blond streaked hair long, almost to the bottom of his ears. Gold hair glistened on his suntanned arms.

"So what?" Julie said when Laura told her she had a crush on the lifeguard. "He's too old for you," Julie said. "He must be more than twenty, and besides, he has a pimple on his chin."

Laura touched her chin and then her forehead. She was just beginning to break out in pimples and had loads of blackheads on her nose. She hoped that Julie wasn't going to tease her and say she was ugly because of it.

"His name is Ken," Julie said.

"How do you know that?" Laura asked.

"It's written on his shirt," Julie said. "And he has a big bulge in his bathing suit, you know where." Julie began to giggle.

"You're not supposed to notice that," Laura said.

"I thought you wanted to be a detective," Julie said. "If you're a detective you've got to notice everything, just like Nancy Drew does."

Julie had inherited Laura's Nancy Drew books, though she never had much patience for reading, but on rainy days when she couldn't play outside, she had read just enough of them to know that girl detectives looked for clues.

"Not that sort of thing," Laura blushed. She had noticed Ken's bulge also, but she wasn't going to let Julie know that.

When they got back to the room, Brenda said, after they all showered, they would go to Circus Circus, and then out for dinner, but that this would have to be an early night. They had traveled over four hundred miles that day and were hot and tired. Besides, they had three more days there, so they'd have plenty of time to spend at the pool.

———

Circus Circus was fun. There were lots of games that the children could play, games like throwing balls into cup-like containers or knocking down pins. If you won, you could get prizes, like stuffed animals, but not any money. Jeff gave them each three dollars to play the games, which cost a quarter apiece.

Julie was the better player and had a good pitching arm. She won two small teddy bears, a light-brown one with a blue ribbon around its neck, and a dark-brown one with a red ribbon and a large stuffed panda.

Laura was disappointed. She didn't win anything. She loved teddy bears and had really wanted to get the light-brown one, but she wasn't nearly as good at games as Julie.

Brenda said she didn't know where they would put them, but since they were traveling in Brenda's big, brown Ford Country Squire station wagon, not Jeff's old Rambler, even though Jeff did most of the driving on this trip, Julie wasn't worried. Julie and Laura could nap in the back, still in their pajamas, every morning, when they left the Holiday Inns at five o'clock so they could get a few hundred miles in and still stop in time for a swim. The back of the wagon was loaded with pillows and blankets, so Julie knew there would be plenty of room for the stuffed animals too. She was so excited about having won the panda that she actually gave Laura the light-brown teddy bear, since Laura was clumsy and never won anything.

Then they watched the acrobats and tightrope walkers. They laughed at the antics of the clowns. Finally they went to dinner at one of the other hotels, where Jeff had made a reservation.

They saw people playing the slot machines while they waited to be seated. Bells rang, lights flashed, and coins poured out of the machines. Nickels, dimes, quarters, half dollars, and large, shiny silver dollars. And this wasn't even in the casinos that didn't allow children. It was on both sides of the line outside the restaurant. There were lots of kids standing on that line, watching the slot machines, but they weren't allowed to play.

Jeff grumbled about having to wait when they already had a reservation. He removed his change from his pocket. He put five quarters in one of the machines and won ten more. Then he put them back in the machine and lost nine of them. The last quarter netted him two more, which he put in his pocket. "For later," he said.

"I thought we agreed to play only nickels and dimes, nothing larger. We need to budget," Brenda said.

"This doesn't count. It's only the loose change that was in my pocket," Jeff said.

"We had an agreement," Brenda said.

"Okay, okay, nickels and dimes. Only nickels and dimes. Or maybe you'd rather go downtown, where they have penny slot machines," Jeff said.

"Let's not be sarcastic," Brenda said.

"Can I play the slot machines?" Julie asked.

"May I, not can I," Brenda said.

"No," Jeff said. "Children are not permitted to play."

"Why not?" Laura asked.

"Because it's gambling and children are not allowed to gamble."

"But Julie gambled when she won the teddy bears and the panda," Laura said.

"That's different," Jeff said. "Teddy bears and pandas are not the same as money."

"I don't understand why it's different," Laura said.

"Because it is," Jeff said.

Finally they were seated at a round table with a red and white checked tablecloth. They had steak and baked potatoes with sour cream instead of butter, and vanilla ice cream on apple pie for dessert.

"Time to go back to the hotel and to bed," Brenda said.

"I'm not sleepy," Julie said.

"We've had a long day," Brenda said, "and we have a lot to do tomorrow."

Julie lay in bed next to her sister. She hated sleeping in the same bed as Laura, who was restless when she slept and sometimes kicked her. She thought that she'd be kept awake all night long, but they both fell quickly into a deep sleep.

The next morning they ate a buffet breakfast in the hotel. Again they had to wait on line. There were lots of slot machines on both sides of the line. It was before breakfast and the grownups were already playing. Some of them were winning money.

Julie wished she was a grownup. She thought she would come back to Las Vegas as soon as she was old enough and then she could gamble all she wanted.

They had orange juice, cut up melons, bacon and sausages, eggs, hash brown potatoes, pancakes, and French toast. Then they went to see some more of the hotels.

There were stands in the street that looked like they might hold newspapers, but instead they had little guides full of advertisements and discount coupons for lots of stuff to see or to buy in the gift shops.

Brenda wanted to do some shopping in the hotel gift shops that used the coupons.

"That's not for me," Jeff said. "I hate shopping. Why don't I go back to the hotel while you girls shop?"

Brenda glowered at him. "Do what you want," she said.

"I'll see you in the room before lunch. Take a cab back. It's too hot to walk," Jeff said.

Laura was kind of glad. Mommy and Daddy had been fighting a lot on this trip. She figured they were getting on each other's nerves. She and Julie were getting on each other's nerves also, but then they usually did, even when they were at home.

She and Julie had saved their allowances for weeks to buy all sorts of stuff on the trip.

The girls bought liquid silver necklaces (they had collected a lot of those discount coupon books) for themselves and for their best friends. Brenda bought presents for just about everyone, for both grandmas and grandpas, all the aunts and uncles and cousins, a dozen of her friends, some of the other teachers in her school, and Peg, their next door neighbor who was watering their plants while they were gone.

———

When he got back to his hotel, Jeff went into the casino. He changed a twenty-dollar bill into twenty silver dollars and went to a dollar slot machine. He had no intention of telling Brenda he played the dollar slot machines. She was probably spending quite a lot more on silly bargain gifts for the entire world than he was in gambling. But she still tried to boss him around about how he spent their money.

He lost the first ten dollars. If I lose the rest, he thought, I'll switch back to dimes. But when he lost the rest, he went back to the cashier and got twenty more silver dollars. He lost the first nineteen.

The twentieth one won a thousand dollars.

Jeff was ecstatic.

Then he thought, I can't even tell Brenda that I gambled silver dollars. She'd have a fit. From now on it would have to be nickels and dimes.

He cashed in the money, which weighed a ton. Then he went to their room and hid the ten hundred-dollar bills in his eight-millimeter camera case.

———

They stood on line waiting to get into the cheap lunch buffet at their hotel. Jeff unwrapped a roll of nickels. He dropped one into one of the slot machines that flanked the line. He pulled the arm. Cherries and watermelons and peaches twirled around and around and then stopped. Jeff put in another nickel. This time five nickels clanked out.

"Oh, please, Daddy," Laura said. "Please let us play the slot machines."

"Please, Daddy. Pretty please," Julie said.

"Just one week's allowance worth," Laura said.

The line moved very slowly.

"It's illegal for children to play the machines," Jeff said.

"Oh, please let us play," Julie and Laura said in unison.

"But we can play them for you," Jeff said.

"Jeff, no," Brenda said.

"Up to one week's allowance," Jeff said. "Not a penny more."

"Oh, Jeff, what in the world are you doing?" Brenda said.

"We'll put the money into the machines for you and anything you win, you get to keep," Jeff said.

"It's not fair. Her allowance is bigger than mine," Julie said.

"Only one week's allowance. Not a penny more," Brenda said. She used that tone of voice that Julie knew there was no arguing with. But at least she had given in to Daddy, and they were going to play the slot machines after all.

"Well, I'm going to play with Daddy," Julie said and was delighted with her small victory when Jeff said okay.

Laura was just as happy having Brenda play her dollar allowance for her. But they lost it right away, and Laura figured that maybe gambling was not such a good idea.

Julie's allowance was only thirty-five cents a week. It really sucked being the younger one, she thought. Laura always got more of everything than she did.

Jeff counted out seven nickels. He put the first one in the machine and pulled the arm.

The fruits went round and round. Bells clanged. Coins clattered.

They won a whole dollar. As much as Laura got for one week's allowance.

By the time it was their turn for lunch, Julie had two dollars and seventy cents in her pocket.

"I want to play more," she said.

"We have to eat," Brenda said.

A thin young man with the name *Charlie* embroidered over his shirt pocket escorted them to their table.

They grabbed plates at the buffet and filled them with salads and baked ziti and macaroni and cheese and chicken and turkey and roast beef and ham.

"Can we get dessert also?" Laura asked, eyeing the cakes, cookies, pies, red, green and yellow Jello molds, and assorted cut fruits on the dessert table.

"After we finish our main course," Brenda said.

Laura ate fast. She didn't know if she could finish all of the food she had piled on her plate, but she really wanted dessert. Especially the chocolate brownies, which were her favorite, and chocolate chip cookies, which were her second favorite, and chocolate cream pie, which was her third favorite.

Julie pushed her food around her plate. "I'm not very hungry," she said.

Her face was flushed. Her eyes were glazed. She appeared to be feverish.

"When are we going back to the slot machines?" she said.

"Not till we finish eating," Brenda said.

"I'm not hungry," Julie said.

Brenda looked at Jeff.

Jeff looked at Julie.

When they finished their main course, Laura asked, "Can we get dessert now?"

Brenda nodded. "Just one dessert each."

Julie had eaten hardly anything. "I don't want any dessert," she said.

"Can I have hers?" Laura asked.

"Just one," Brenda said. "You don't want to get fat."

"I'm not fat," Laura said.

"If you want to be a ballet dancer, you have to stay thin," Brenda said.

"I don't want to be a ballet dancer. I think I'm going to quit ballet lessons," Laura said. She had already quit piano lessons, after two years.

Brenda had a rule about these things. Brenda had a lot of rules. If you started any lessons, you had to stick them out for two years. Laura had gone to ballet lessons for four years already, since she was six, and now she was ready to quit. She'd rather stay in the house and read.

Julie refused to take any lessons. School was bad enough.

"Can I go back to the machines now?" Julie asked.

"Don't you want to keep all of that money?" Brenda asked. "If you play it, you might lose it all."

"I want to go back to the machines," Julie said.

"Then while Laura and I have dessert, you go back to the slots with Julie," Brenda told Jeff.

Jeff nodded.

"Lose it all, no matter how long you have to play," Brenda whispered.

———

Rosa put out another tray of brownies. They seemed to go the fastest of all of the cakes. Rosa was tiny, only five feet tall. She hated being short, because she had always wanted to be a showgirl and wear those beautiful feathered costumes. But even though everyone told her that she had a very pretty face, the only job she managed to get in Las Vegas was working at the dessert table at the buffet. Just her luck. Here were all these delicious cakes and cookies, and she wasn't supposed to eat any of them. Every once in a while she'd filch one and stuff it into her pocket. If she kept up this way, she'd be as fat as her mother and her aunts.

Oh, oh, Rosa thought. Here comes Jerry, the security guard. If he saw her pocketing the oatmeal raisin cookie, he'd report her for sure. He had it in for her ever since she refused to go to bed with him. She told him she was a virgin and intended to remain one till she married.

"Maybe you could marry me," Jerry said.

"No thanks," Rosa said. Not if he was the last man on earth.

He was probably too cheap to go to a prostitute, Rosa thought. That was probably the only kind of woman who would have him. Prostitution was legal here in Las Vegas. Jerry could afford one. He earned a decent wage, unless he gambled it away. Rosa thought that Jerry was crude and unattractive. He was tall and large-boned and always had a scowl on his acne-scarred face. When he did smile, showing crooked teeth, all yellow from chewing tobacco, it gave her the creeps.

A young girl and her mother came up to the buffet table. The girl put a brownie on her plate.

"Just one," the mother said.

"That's not fair," the girl replied. "You let Julie go back to the slots just because she won. And you lost my whole dollar for me, right away. The least you could do is let me have a double dessert."

The mother scowled. Then she smiled. "Well, okay," she said, "But only two. Not more than that."

The girl took one of the chocolate chip cookies and put it on her plate.

The mother just took some honeydew melon and a bit of Jell-O.

Rosa wondered how the girl had lost the dollar. Had the parents let her gamble? That was a really dumb thing to do. Luckily Jerry had not caught them at it. You didn't want to get onto Jerry's bad side.

When the girl and her mother left, Jerry came up to her. "You doing anything special tonight?" he asked.

"Look, I told you before, I'm not interested in going out with you."

"You don't know what you're missing," Jerry said.

Rosa shrugged her shoulders. She didn't want to offend Jerry any more than necessary, but she had to tell him something to get him off her case. She said, "I already got a boyfriend."

"Oh, yeah?"

She should have let it go at that, but she suddenly felt the need to elaborate. "Yeah, Charlie, the guy who works at the entrance to the buffet and brings the people to their tables."

She had never actually dated Charlie. But she wouldn't mind if he asked her out. He reminded her of Frank Sinatra.

"Him. He's skinny, like Sinatra. I don't see what you see in him." Jerry flexed his arm showing overdeveloped muscles.

"Sorry," Rosa said, and then added, just to be safe, "We're engaged."

———

It took fifteen minutes for Jeff to lose Julie's entire two dollars and seventy cents.

Brenda and Jeff were quite relieved.

"Tomorrow we'll go to Hoover Dam," Jeff said when they got to their room. He needed to get away from the slot machines for a while.

They rested for an hour and then Jeff, Brenda, and Laura put on their bathing suits.

"I have a belly ache," Julie said. "I don't want to go swimming."

"You can just sit at the pool," Brenda said.

"I want to take a nap," Julie said. Brenda felt Julie's head. It felt warm. "I'll stay in the room with you then. I'm not leaving you alone," Brenda said. "You might have a slight fever."

She had looked feverish at lunch, Brenda thought.

"You can go swimming," Julie said. "I'm just going to sleep."

"Poor Julie," Brenda said. "You're upset that you lost all that money."

"I'm all right," Julie said. "I just have a belly ache. That's why I didn't eat my lunch."

Brenda picked up her book and lay down on her bed and started to read.

Julie lay down also. A while later she got up. "I have to go to the bathroom," she said.

Brenda didn't respond. The book lay open on her chest. She snored lightly.

On the way to the bathroom, Julie grabbed a handful of change that Jeff had left on his dresser. Six nickels, three dimes and two quarters. She went into the bathroom. She wrapped the money in her handkerchief, the one that had violets embroidered on the corner, so that the coins wouldn't jangle. She flushed the toilet. When she came out of the bathroom, Brenda was still fast asleep. Julie tiptoed to the door of the room. She opened it quietly and slipped out into the hall, closing the door softly behind her. Then she ran to the line that was waiting for the buffet.

———

Two weeks earlier, a child had been kidnapped and murdered. She had been a guest at the Dollars Dreaming Hotel. She was a small thing, not quite six years old, and she had roamed away while she and her three brothers were horsing around at the pool. The brothers were supposed to be keeping an eye on her, but you know how teenage boys can be.

Anyway, they didn't find her body at the hotel, but partially buried in the sand in an undeveloped area, a few blocks off the Strip. The parents had gotten a ransom note to put the jackpot money they had won in the casino, the night before, in a paper bag and leave it at a certain place downtown and not to notify the police.

The parents hadn't told the police about the ransom note until it was too late. They didn't want to anger the kidnapper.

Somehow they got confused. It was their first time in Las Vegas and they didn't know the city. They couldn't manage to find the spot that the kidnappers had specified. A day later, the police found Amy's strangled body.

Charlie had seen her just before she was kidnapped. She wasn't very pretty, from what he recalled. Skinny, with stringy yellow hair and sharp features. Charlie worked at the buffet, seating the customers. He hated working there and hoped one day to wait tables at one of the dinner restaurants. There at least you got tips. And the food was a lot more expensive to begin with.

Ironic, wasn't it? Here he came to Vegas from New Jersey, hoping to be a singer, the next Frank Sinatra, maybe, and now he was aspiring to be what every failed performer hated to be, a waiter.

He had seen the little girl—Amy, he found out her name was, after they discovered her body—hanging around the slot machines where you waited to be seated for the buffet. She was in a bathing suit, one piece, blue with pictures of colored fish. It looked like it was still damp from the pool. She didn't seem to be with any adults. Charlie thought he should have gone up to her and brought her to one of the security guards, right then and there. But then Rosa came up to talk to him and he stopped noticing the little girl.

Charlie felt guilty as Hell. If he had done something sooner, maybe she'd still be alive today. But he hadn't told anyone that he had seen her and now he couldn't. They'd probably fire him, if they knew, or worse, suspect him of the crime.

Today there was another little girl hanging around the machines. At least she wasn't wearing a bathing suit, but navy blue shorts and a pink polo shirt. She was small and cute, with bright red curls. She was feeding nickels into one of the slot machines. Which was illegal.

Charlie stepped away from the buffet table. This time he was going to report the child to security before anything happened.

And then Rosa came over again and informed him that she had told Jerry that she and Charlie were engaged.

Charlie wouldn't have minded if it were true. He was attracted to Rosa and would have liked to ask her out, but he was afraid that he'd be rejected. And, frankly, he was more than a little intimidated by Jerry.

After Rosa left, Charlie noticed that the little girl was gone.

———————

The good-looking lifeguard was not on duty that day so Laura was not upset when Brenda rushed out to the pool and told her that she and Jeff had to go back to the room right away. Laura wondered why Brenda had left Julie alone in the room by herself. She would have been in big trouble if she had done something like that. She was always getting into trouble for things that Julie had done, or not done.

But when they got back to the room, Julie wasn't there.

"I fell asleep and when I woke up she was gone," Brenda said.

Brenda wanted to call the police right away, but Jeff thought they should contact hotel security first.

"I bet she went back to the slot machines," Laura said.

"She had no money," Brenda said.

But then Jeff noticed that all of his change was missing from the top of the dresser.

They rushed out to the slot machines outside of the buffet. Jeff and Brenda ran up to the security guard.

Laura walked over to the skinny man who had seated them at the table. The one with the name *Charlie* on his shirt.

"Maybe you've seen my sister," she said. "She has curly red hair and was wearing blue shorts and a pink shirt. I know pink doesn't go with red hair, but she insisted, and she's a very stubborn little girl."

At first Charlie thought he would say he hadn't seen her. But then he remembered what had happened to Amy and he just couldn't keep it to himself. "She was here," he said. "She was playing the nickel slot machines. I was just about to report her to Jerry, that's the security guard, when I had to take a customer to his table. When I came back, she was gone."

"She must have lost all of her money and left," Laura said. She hoped that was what had happened.

"Maybe she went back to your room," Charlie said.

"I don't think so," Laura said. "We would have passed her in the hall."

"Did your Daddy or Mommy win a lot of money in the casino?" Charlie asked.

"Probably not," Laura said. "Daddy promised Mommy that he would only gamble with nickels and dimes. They're on a budget. I don't think you can win a lot of money with nickels and dimes."

"I think your Mommy and Daddy should call the police, anyway," Charlie said.

Laura started to worry when Charlie said that. If he told her to call the police, he must think that something was really wrong. She wondered if it was like one of the mysteries in the books she had read. A robbery, maybe, or a murder.

Laura decided that she would have to be like Nancy Drew or Miss Marple, even though Miss Marple was very, very old, and that she would be the one to find her sister. Or maybe she'd try to think like Hercule Poirot with his little grey cells, even if he was a man and had a mustache. Much as Julie annoyed her at times, at least Julie had been nice enough to give her one of the teddy bears that she won at Circus Circus. Laura wouldn't want anything bad to happen to her.

But she didn't know how to start. Maybe she should just walk around the hotel and look for Julie.

The security guard was yelling at Brenda and Jeff when Laura went to ask them whether she should go back to the room and see whether Julie had returned.

"You let a minor gamble? Don't you know it's against the law? I should have you both arrested," he screamed. His voice was quite high-pitched for such a large man.

"We can talk about that after you find our daughter," Jeff said. "Right now that's our main priority."

"If anything bad happened to her, I'm going to hold you responsible," the security guard said.

Brenda began to cry. "What do you think could have happened?" she asked.

"Maybe she was kidnapped," said the security guard. His name, Jerry, was embroidered above his pocket, just like Charlie's was.

Brenda cried louder.

"And you don't belong in the lobby in your bathing suits," Jerry added.

"Look, our daughter is missing and all you care about is that we gambled a few coins for her and dress codes," Jeff shouted. "I want you to find her. Right now. Do you hear me?"

All the people waiting on line for the buffet turned to stare at them.

Laura tugged at Jeff's arm. "Charlie says we should call the police," she said.

"Who's Charlie?" Jeff asked.

"That bastard," Jerry said. "First he steals my girl, and now he's trying to do my job for me." He rushed over to Charlie's post and grabbed him by the collar.

"Let him go, Jerry." Ken, the lifeguard, walked up to Jerry and pulled him away.

At first, Laura hadn't recognized Ken because he was wearing clothes. He wore a pair of blue jeans and a red plaid shirt. He looked different than he had when he was half naked. He wasn't as good looking either.

"Call the police," Charlie said. "Maybe your daughter was kidnapped, just like the other girl, Amy, the one who was murdered."

"Shut up," Jerry said. "This is my job, not yours." He tried to punch Charlie, but Ken pinned his arms behind his back.

"Murdered?" Brenda cried louder.

"A girl was murdered?" Jeff said. He glared at Jerry. "When? Where? Why didn't you tell me to call the police right away?" He put his arm around Brenda's shoulder.

Rosa, having heard the commotion, walked from the dessert table, carrying a chocolate cream pie, which she shoved into Jerry's face. "Don't you dare talk to Charlie like that. I love him. We're going to get married. You leave him alone, you creep."

Then Rosa picked up the phone from Charlie's workstation and called the police herself.

Charlie looked at Jeff. "Did you win a lot of money in the casino?" he asked.

Jeff squeezed Brenda's shoulder. He shook his head. "No. Of course not. Why?"

"Because if you did, that may be why your daughter has disappeared. The other girl, Amy, was kidnapped because her father won a jackpot."

"Oh, Jeff. I'm so scared," Brenda said.

Jeff's hands dropped to his side. He couldn't look Brenda in the eyes. He looked sheepish as he muttered, "Well, uh, I did win a thousand dollars. I didn't want to tell you. I thought you'd be mad at me."

"Playing nickels and dimes?" Brenda asked. "A thousand dollars, playing nickels and dimes?"

"Well, no," Jeff said. "I played silver dollars."

Brenda stopped crying. "You bastard," she said. She slapped Jeff across his face. She wiped her eyes with the side of her hand. She sniffled.

Ken reached into his pocket and handed Brenda a handkerchief.

Brenda wiped her nose.

Laura sneezed.

Brenda handed Laura the handkerchief. Laura blew her nose. She sneezed again and again.

The handkerchief smelled of lavender.

Laura looked at the handkerchief. It was small and one corner of it was embroidered with violets. It was Julie's handkerchief.

Laura pointed to Ken. "He's the one. He's the one who kidnapped Julie." She sneezed again. "This is Julie's handkerchief, the one that Grandma Helen gave her, the last time she visited. Mine had pansies on it."

Ken dropped his hold on Jerry. He started to run.

Jerry, his face covered with chocolate cream pie, turned and ran after Ken.

He tackled him, just as the police marched in.

After questioning Ken, the police located Julie tied to a chair in small shed behind the hotel. It wasn't air-conditioned. Julie was all sweaty and had wet her pants. Her hands were tied behind her back and she had a red bandana wrapped around her mouth. When the policeman removed it, she began to sob.

They brought Julie to her parents who were waiting in the lobby. Brenda rushed up to Julie, gathered her in her arms, hugged her, held her close and rocked her. Julie began to cry.

"I'm the one that found out that Ken was the killer," Laura said.

"Who found out, not, that found out," Brenda said.

"Killer? Who did he kill?" Julie asked, and began to cry harder.

"We're going to have to take you down to police headquarters," one of the policemen said. "But you'd all better get dressed first."

Julie snuggled against Brenda's breast.

Jeff patted Laura on the head. "I'm very proud of you," he said.

———

After a long afternoon at police headquarters, they returned to the hotel. The management offered them a free dinner and refused to charge them for their room. The police said they could leave Las Vegas, but that Julie would have to return to testify when Ken went to trial.

Brenda and Jeff decided to leave Las Vegas the next morning, but to continue on their trip to Los Angeles. They wanted to make life for Julie seem as normal as possible. They left Las Vegas early and spent two days at Disneyland before visiting Uncle Phil and Aunt Miriam. Uncle Phil and Aunt Miriam had a dog, a golden retriever named Harley. At first Laura was apprehensive, but when Harley put his head on her lap, she pet his soft fur and her eyes didn't itch and she didn't sneeze. "I don't think I'm allergic to dogs," she said. "Just to cats."

———

Julie ended up returning to Las Vegas, way before she was an adult. She had to testify at Ken's trial. Jeff took time off from his job to be with her. Neither of them had any desire to gamble. When they got home, Julie read all of Laura's hand-me-down Nancy Drew books. And Brenda bought Julie a dog, a female basset hound that they named Lavender.

Ken was sentenced to life imprisonment for killing Amy, and to twenty additional years for kidnapping Julie.

———

Now, while remembering the names of Uncle Phil and Aunt Miriam and the cousins Jon and Karen is not important to the story, I thought you might want to know what happened to the rest of the cast, over the years.

Jerry left his job at the hotel and became chief of security at a house of prostitution. He married a five-foot-eleven, dark-haired prostitute who kind of looked like a much taller version of Rosa and had been a showgirl when she was younger.

Rosa did not marry, or even date, Charlie but ended up marrying one of the cops who had rescued Julie. She had five children a year apart, and ended up fat, just like her mother and her aunts. She started a business baking chocolate cream pies and raisin oatmeal cookies and distributing them to the hotel buffets.

Charlie became a headwaiter at one of the dinner restaurants and married a croupier from one of the casinos. He never did become the next Sinatra or even make it as a singer in one of the smaller hotel lounges.

Laura became a psychiatric social worker. She and Julie and their parents had needed a number of years of therapy after they returned from Las Vegas and Laura had felt helped by it. But she never mentioned to anyone that she always slept with a small brown teddy bear with a blue ribbon around its neck.

Ironically Julie was the one who became a writer. She wrote mysteries. She was never compared to Agatha Christie, though. Her books were very dark and brooding, and bad things always happened to small children. She never returned to Las Vegas, after the trial, and won't go anywhere near a slot machine.

Brenda insisted that Jeff put the one thousand dollars that he won toward the kids' college accounts. After the girls finished college, Brenda and Jeff divorced.

"It was bound to happen," Laura said. "I'm surprised they waited this long."

"I feel kind of guilty, that it was all my fault," Julie said. "I never should have sneaked off and gone to those slot machines by myself."

"It wasn't you. It started before you ever bet anything. It was the thousand dollars that Daddy won," Laura said. "They had an agreement to play only nickels and dimes and he sneaked back to the hotel and broke it. And then he hid the money and didn't even tell Mommy that he had it. And I don't believe, if you hadn't been kidnapped, that he would have told her either. Even when Charlie asked if he had won any money in the casino, he lied. Mommy could never really trust him again. He should have stuck to nickels and dimes."

"Yeah, nickels and dimes," Julie said. "Only nickels and dimes."

EVEN GAMBLERS HAVE TO EAT

RUTH CAVIN

It was a local scandal—the kind exciting enough that the neighborhood women kept making some excuse to run to the grocery store to discuss a new twist of the plot with their friends. First, Aaron Plotkin was leaving Akron and his good job at Topnotch Tire for some deserted place in the West. And why? As he put it, to "change his life for the better."

"What could be so better?" inquired the women of one another. The rest of his life, he could stay at Topnotch Tire—he's their genius, no? Could they make tires without him? Who else can add and subtract like Aaron Plotkin? [The speaker's knowledge of accounting skills was not extensive.] "And in this Depression yet, where college graduates are selling apples on the sidewalk! And what about Molly? She's supposed to go out to the middle of the desert with him? Thank God they aren't already married! It's meshuggah! Crazy!"

The desert wasn't in Molly's future. She flatly refused to go. "Leave Mr. MacReady in the lurch?" Molly felt the weight of her position; she was Vice President MacReady's private secretary. (The women speculated, possibly unfairly, just what that word "private" signified, in this case.) "Give up my own job?" Molly told Aaron scathingly. "Uh-uh! I stay here!"

But Aaron went. Leaving Molly, both parents and six siblings back in Akron, he followed his dream. The gossip chorus would really have sizzled if the women had got wind of that tidbit. Because Aaron's almost lifelong dream was to cook for a living.

The bug had bit him as he watched his mother, who cooked for her brood with love and grumbles. But men didn't cook—not unless they were paid for it, not unless it was their job, not unless they could be called "chefs." Aaron wanted to be a professional chef. Reading in the newspaper about job opportunities in the West, he saw his chance. He'd live simply and work until he had enough saved to open a restaurant. A small one. No fancy stuff. Good home cooking. To start, at least. Later on—who knows?

And that's how it worked out. He got a job. He rented a tiny room in a town called "Las Vegas." A Mexican on his shift said the words meant "The Meadows." Some "meadows" in the middle of the desert!

Aaron missed his family terribly, even Max, his wild younger brother. (Molly hardly at all). But his dream restaurant was taking shape in his mind. Las Vegas would grow from its present size—one church, a few rackety bars and the only store, selling whatever was available, to a place sought by tourists. Meanwhile, he worked, slept and saved.

He had made casual friends with a few of his coworkers, all men. He knew no women—the women in Las Vegas were either married or questionable. The few entertainers arriving with the new hotels, could, of course, have been from another planet as far as Aaron was concerned. And the "ladies of the night"—he found it embarrassing just to walk by the building near his rooming house where they held forth. He did invite Molly to come "just for a visit," but her answer—"Not on your life!"—didn't upset him the way he would have expected. Aaron was much more interested in his kitchen than his bedroom. Much as he'd like to see her, he would have had to step away from his stove and look after her. In spite of a rapidly growing influx of tourists, Las Vegas was still a gritty town. Fistfights were a regular feature of barroom evenings. Visitors and some residents had been knocked out and robbed after midnight on the night streets, and the few respectable women in Vegas never went out unaccompanied after dark. There had been some shootouts, and there was talk of clandestine meetings of the Ku Klux Klan. Vegas kept the sheriff on his toes.

Now, with the horizon bright with the imminent repeal of the gambling ban, bad boys from the East were hurrying into the town. They were bad boys with money and visions of casinos as cornucopias overflowing with the gambling dollars of tourists from Los Angeles and other lucrative settlements as far as the Pacific Coast and—who knows?—the Atlantic Coast as well. But they were hardly making the town respectable; gangsters didn't miraculously turn into gentlemen when they stepped off the train in Nevada.

There were plenty of rumors that some of the men paying visits to the new hotels on the street that had been named the Strip were bootleggers from the East, trying to set up money-making gambling deals. Only half believing it, Aaron stepped carefully when the new people were around.

From the start, Aaron's Eats picked up a customer base. Well, it was the only real restaurant in town.

———

The day before the celebration of "One Year Anniversary of Aaron's Eats," Aaron was up on a ladder hanging crepe paper ribbons above the tables when he heard someone open the street door. A little nervously, he turned and was amazed to see his youngest brother, Max, standing in the middle of the floor.

"Max!" he cried, hastily climbing down from the ladder. "What in God's name are you doing here?" The fervor of his greeting had an undertone of something different. You couldn't help loving Max, but their grandfather had rightly always called him *Der kleine Tyvel*—the little devil—and it was only partly from affection. Max was not always in trouble, but then again, he wasn't always out of it either.

"You'll be glad I came," Max said.

"Of course I'm glad you came."

"I've got a great deal for you."

"Yeah? I can't wait to hear it. But sit down. I've got some cold beer." And he established his brother at one of the oil-cloth covered tables while he went to the kitchen for the bottles.

"Now," Aaron said. "What've you got yourself into now?"

"Into is right," Max told him. "I'm right in there with a really smart bunch of fellows. From the old neighborhood."

"From Akron!" Aaron was dubious.

"Akron, hell. These guys are from a real place—Brooklyn, New York!"

"You were in Brooklyn?"

"Jeez, Ary, don't you read the papers?"

"The only papers we've got don't write about Brooklyn, New York."

"Naw! I met these fellas at home, our own home, Akron. See, you don't even know nothing out here. The tire factory had a big strike. And these guys brought a bunch of people to work in the factories instead of those Bolsheviks, and see, they had to protect them, so they had their guys patrolling the buildings, making sure they were ok, and that the Bolshies didn't do no damage. You should thank me, too. Molly was right there in the middle of it, but they knew that all they had to do is bother her one little bit and they'd have to deal with me!"

"Molly! My God! Are you sure she's all right?"

"I told you. Sure she's all right, with me taking care of her."

"She never told me."

"She's pretty mad at you." Max leaned over until he was right in his brother's face. "Listen, Ary," he said. "Little brother has gotten to know some people who will make you so rich, as soon as Molly hears about it she's on the train to Nevada. So listen good." He favored Aaron with the grin that his family—and a score of young women—found hard to resist.

"What people?" Aaron asked. "Who are they?"

"They're businessmen. They've got piles of money to invest, Ary. And would you believe it? One of them took me out to lunch, and we talked about you. You're in clover!"

"You and this businessman talked about me?"

"About your restaurant. You wait. He's coming out here and he told me he'd be sure to get in touch. His name is Golding, Lucky Golding."

Aaron couldn't guess what Max was talking about, but he felt he didn't need to take it seriously. It was just Maxie being Maxie.

Max, though, kept waiting anxiously for word from the "big businessman" from Brooklyn, New York. But in vain.

Until one evening, after about a month had gone by. Max, who was waiting tables, came running into the kitchen. He grabbed Aaron by the arm, nearly upsetting the stew his brother was stirring, and gasped "He's here! He's out at a table! He's here!"

Aaron sighed, put down his spoon, untied his apron and went out into the public dining room. Going up to the man sitting alone with a highball glass and a cigar, he said, "My brother says you spoke to him in Akron."

The man stood—he was really very small, and very slight, except for a pot belly. He put down his cigar and shook Aaron's hand vigorously. "Golding. Lucky Golding. D'lighted to meetcha. Yeah, sure, I remember the kid. He told me what a great cook you are, and this meal sure proves it. You got a future here. You wait and see. As soon as that law goes out, there are going to be a lot more people coming here to gamble without having to worry that the state is gonna step in and take twice as much of what you win in fines. Listen, I'll give you five to one we'll even get soma these Mormons slipping over from Utah, pretending they're just here to see the mountains. But you and I know different, no?

"Listen; we can't talk business here. Come up to the Golden Gate—that's where I'm stayin'. Gotta suite there. Little place, but wait till my hotel is done. Have dinner with me t'night?"

"My restaurant is open for dinner and I'm the only one cooking."

"Okay, okay. Tomorrow, then. Come when you close. Close early, huh? Gotta talk." He picked up his beer glass and drained it, and went out into the sun.

"Well, he sure means business, doesn't he?" Max asked.

"Maybe, but not with me."

But when the tables had been cleared and set up for the next day and the dishes washed and on the racks drying, Max begged Aaron to "at least talk to the guy, please, Ary."

There was fear in his voice.

"What are you afraid of, little brother?" Aaron asked gently.

Max actually gulped. "He's an important guy, Ary. He—he has ways of getting what he wants."

Aaron sighed. "Well, let's find out what he wants first, OK? Don't worry, Maxele. I'll be careful what I say."

———

Aaron had never been in a hotel dining room. He was impressed by its size, by the huge vases of artificial flowers here and there around the room. He was struck to see that each table had a "tablecloth" actually made of cloth. But when the dinner was set before them, he couldn't help comparing it to how he would have made it. He certainly wouldn't have so disastrously overcooked the lamb shanks, for instance, nor let them swim in such a tasteless, watery sauce. There were never such lumps in his mashed potatoes, and he'd have handed in his apron before he'd serve a pie with so soggy a crust. But of course, he wasn't there to criticize the food.

He took a big breath. "You know, Mr. Golding, when my brother came here—that is, he thought—he hoped you could find some kind of job for him. At your hotel, I mean," he added hurriedly.

Golding nodded. "Sure, sure. The hotel ain't finished, but when it is—sure; don't you worry; we'll find something for him. Always something for a smart young guy to do. Open a new hotel in a new town—there's lots of jobs. Tell him not to worry; we'll get to him." All of which sounded to Aaron what it was—a put-off. Max would be lucky if he ended up a bellboy.

"Here's the deal," said Golding, when they had gotten to coffee and the New York man's cigars. "I'm building this hotel here, see? You know about it; everybody knows about it. It's going to be something—the best architects, the best designers. Costs millions. Wait and see. Knock your eyes out."

Golding waved to a tough-looking man whom Aaron had noticed standing near the window during the whole dinner. The man left the room and returned with glasses and an unopened bottle of bootleg bourbon while Golding was still describing the wonders of his hotel. He opened the bottle and Golding poured two drinks, topped them up with water from the carafe on the table, and handed one to Aaron. Well, Aaron thought, he sure isn't suffering under Prohibition—and later realized that Golding was not only not suffering, Prohibition was making him the millions he had for building hotels.

"Now you know," Golding went on, after drinking half his highball in one long draught. "There's a lot of movement in the state legislature to repeal the ban on gambling in Nevada. Hell, we're in a Depression. The state needs money, and there ain't a better way to get it than to open it up to tourists who come here and want to spend, spend, spend. Now listen to what I've planned."

He leaned over the table. "I got the architect—and believe me, he's the number one architect in the country—maybe the whole world. I got him to put in a whole extra floor. Maybe if somebody wants to have a convention there or a big wedding or something they can use it; it's gonna be finished and all. But really, it's a waiting room." He laughed loudly. "That's what I call it, 'my waiting room.' He leaned so close Aaron could feel his breath. "It's waiting for that law to be repealed, and the next day I'll open a casino that'll make the Frenchies who own Monte Carlo jump into the Mediterranean ocean!"

Aaron started to speak, and Golding held up his hand.

"I know, I know. You wanna know where you come in."

Aaron opened his mouth again, but Golding forestalled him. "Here's where you come in, Plotkin. I want my casino opened the day that bill gets signed. I wanna get ahead of everybody else, but my hotel won't be done yet. That restaurant of yours is just in the right place. I want to fix her up—I'll pay you good, and I'll pay all the expenses. I want it to be whatcha might wanna call my 'Casino in Waiting.' We run the games from there until the hotel is ready and then we move the whole kit and caboodle over. And you don't have to worry," he added. "There ain't nobody in this town—in this state—who wants to discourage building up Las Vegas with gambling. Nobody!"

Aaron thought that was a somewhat extravagant statement, but he saw what Golding was getting at. Legal gambling would draw crowds from the whole West Coast—even the whole country.

However, he wanted nothing to do with gambling. If he could have stopped the rough poker games that his current clientele insisted accompany their laden plates, he would have. He was smart enough to know that it wouldn't be the food but the gambling that was going to bring the crowds in. But they had to eat, didn't they? Tourists from California and Utah (Mormons to the contrary notwithstanding) and then from farther and farther away would want more than the plain meat and potatoes that was all the railroad workers and construction workers were perfectly happy with.

He also was wary of any connection with the "businessman" from Brooklyn or his like. As diplomatically as he could, he turned the offer down.

Nevada's repeal bill went through the legislature, the governor signed it and the antigambling law was history. The town began to change drastically. The Strip became more colorful every week as another entrepreneur entered the race for tourist money. Aside from his worries about Max, Aaron was happy. The restaurant was getting a real reputation; tourists were filling the tables and often waiting in line to get in. He had some steady customers, who swore Aaron's food was the best this side of—wherever they came from. Aaron was so busy he hardly had time to write to Molly, but he sent her brief (and tantalizing) notes, telling her she would really like Las Vegas now. The town was becoming civilized. The restaurant was doing real well, and it was fixed up beautiful; she'd love it. He got a postcard back from Virginia Beach, where she'd gone with her mother and Aaron's oldest sister for a vacation. "Having wonderful time," it said. Period. Well, he didn't wish he was there, either.

In spite of Max's fears (and to tell the truth, Aaron's as well) Lucky Golding didn't seem to resent the turndown. When the hotel was finished and opened with a grand blowout, he hired Max as a bellboy. The job wasn't hard, he was a strong young man. The tips were generous and he got to mingle with—well, carry the bags of, say "Yes, sir," and "Thank you, Madam" to—celebrities he had only read about in the tabloids or seen on the movie screen. Aaron kept at him about not doing anything really dumb, like trying to sell reefers to the guests or giving them tips on how to win at the tables (as if he knew). "You're dealing with dangerous people here," the big brother said. "Golding is pretty low to the ground, but so is a rattlesnake. You may think he's your friend, but he couldn't care a button for you, you're nobody. He'd only notice you if you did something stupid, and then, watch out!" Max would nod solemnly, which hardly made Aaron feel any better.

Golding opened his casino in the hotel, and sent his guests to Aaron's Eats for dinner. That was fine with Aaron. His restaurant had a growing reputation now, little brother had brought him luck, and he was grateful. He was happy to be a citizen of this thriving town.

Of course, there were still street brawls and holdups. When the fifteen-month-old daughter of one of the railroad workers went missing, Aaron, along with the other volunteers, spent two full nights searching for her. They didn't find her. Theories flew through the air and landed in the local newspaper: She had run into the desert and had died of sunstroke. She had fallen down a well. She had been taken for ransom (although no ransom had been demanded). Ugliest of all was the solution put about by a handful of rabble-rousers and directed at the few Jews who lived in Las Vegas and the Jewish tourists now coming in from the West Coast: The medieval canard that Jews kidnapped and killed Christian children in order to drink their blood at secret religious ceremonies was resurrected. "Well of course, you never know" started to be heard in the bars and grocery stores.

The missing child was discovered unharmed; she had wandered off and been picked up by a farmer who was trying to scratch out a living in the countryside beyond the town. She was too young to be able to tell him who she was, and it was several days before he trotted into town on his horse holding the little girl in his arms. By that time rumor had done its work.

———

And then one early morning Aaron arrived at the back door of Aaron's Eats to find every window broken, shards of dishes littering the dining room, and Max, who usually worked at the restaurant on his day off, lying beaten and bloody amidst spilled and scattered food from the now-empty pantry shelves.

Aaron didn't stop to check whether his brother was alive or dead. Max couldn't be dead—he was the little brother. Aaron ran out into the street, waving at the sparse traffic coming down the Strip, howling "Help! Police! My little brother!" A milk truck stopped and the milkman and Aaron picked up Max's limp body—he was still breathing, but painfully—and drove to the town's only hospital.

Max had been badly beaten. He had two broken bones, three missing teeth, and a bad concussion. But the doctor was optimistic. Aaron blamed himself, letting his brother get mixed up with the gangsters from Brooklyn. But why? Why? Because he'd turned Golding down? Why?

He'd damn well find out—and right away. The doctor said he'd call him if there was any change, and he raced on foot to the hotel. There he frightened the desk clerk into giving him Golding's suite number, and when the man stammered it out (and was subsequently nearly fired for doing it) Aaron didn't wait for the elevator; he ran up the stairway to the fourth floor and pounded on Golding's door.

It was opened by one of the grim bodyguards, who was just about to punch him—or possibly shoot him—when Golding appeared, wearing a bathrobe.

"What is it?" he demanded. "What the fuck do you want? Why are you breaking into my room, waking me up—are you crazy?"

"Yes, I'm crazy. Crazy to find my restaurant wrecked and my little brother almost dead on the floor."

Shock showed on Golding's face. "What! What are you talking about?"

"Don't lie to me," Aaron shouted. "I don't care what your apes here do to me, you'll be sorry! That's my little brother you've nearly killed—maybe he is killed!" And he suddenly sank sobbing to the carpet.

Golding turned to his bodyguards. "Do you know what happened?"

They both shook their heads.

"I gotta find out. Maybe it's that Dutch Horburg—maybe he thinks we've got a hand in that restaurant. Keep him quiet until I get some clothes on. But don't hurt him! Understand?" They nodded.

When Golding had gotten the story out of the enraged and terrified Aaron, he seemed to puff up and become not only larger, but taller. "You think I would do that?" he demanded. "You think I'm such a *goniff* that I'd do that to a young boy who made a mistake? What kind of a mistake so terrible could a bellboy make? Steal a shirt maybe? Even say he insulted a guest—you think Golding doesn't have enough guests he couldn't lose one or two? You think I'd do something like that? I ought to get you beat up for that. Sure I'd yell, that's what you do when you're mad. Listen, if somebody cheats me, if somebody rats on me—he'd feel it. But a young kid like your brother can't do Golding no harm even if he tried—you think I'd do something like that? I'm a monster?

"Come on!" he took Aaron roughly by the arm.

"Where?"

"We're gonna go back to your restaurant. Figger out who did that!"

He said something Aaron didn't catch to his bodyguard, and almost dragged Aaron out of the hotel and down the street. When they got to Aaron's Eats, Golding pointed to the front of the building. Covering most of the wall were huge letters, white paint dripping down from them. JEW BABY RAPIRS! they screamed. BABY KANIBLS! KILL JEWISH KANIBLS!

Aaron stared at it numbly. "You think I'd write something like that?" Golding demanded. "You couldn't think I'd write shit like that in a million years."

"Then why?" Aaron asked, his voice full of tears. "Why would they do something like that to my little brother?"

"I'll tell you why," Golding said harshly. "Because you're a Jew, that's why. Because they think if that little girl had been hurt or killed, it's your fault, just because you're a Jew. You and your little brother could have been in Kalamazoo since before she disappeared, and they'd still pick you for it. Look, Aaron, leave this to me. I know how to take care of the shitheads like this."

"But how do you even know who they are?"

Golding's laugh sounded more like a curse, "Listen, Aaron, any good businessman has to keep his eyes open for shits like these. You never know when you need the information.

"You want to go back to the hospital, no? McSorley!" he called out to the gorilla standing by the door. "Get the car!" He turned to Aaron. "McSorley will drive you there. I know you're worried about the kid—what's his name, Milton?"

"Max."

"Okay, so it's Max. You go be with Max."

"But the police . . ."

Golding snorted. "The police! Listen, I wouldn't faint with surprise, one or more of the slime under those white sheets they wear could be cops. Aaron, I keep on top of this stuff. I'm a businessman!" And with this rousing speech, he reached up to pat Aaron reassuringly on the shoulder and gave him a gentle push toward the door.

———

At the hospital, Aaron sat in his brother's room, worrying. Never mind the restaurant. He'd give up the damn restaurant, he'd go back to Akron, he didn't care. Just let Max live. Outside, the town was stirring, with no sign that something terrible had happened.

Some time in the late afternoon an orderly arrived pushing a wheeled stretcher. With a nurse helping, he got Max on the stretcher and went off down the hall—"X-rays," the nurse told Aaron. The bed was still empty when the doctor came in; by that time Aaron had convinced himself that he'd never see his little brother alive again. But the doctor's news was good. Good? Beautiful!

"It will take a while, but he's going to be all right."

"Thank God," breathed Aaron. And when the orderly brought his brother back to the room, Max actually was able to open his eyes and manage a weak smile at Aaron before shutting down again.

Aaron spent the night at his brother's bedside. Some time around five in the morning there was a commotion in the street; shouts, automobiles racing down the Strip. Aaron thought "drunken tourists" and forgot it until he heard the local radio station when he went home to change.

"The mangled body of Jonathan Whately, rumored to be the organizer and head of Las Vegas's clandestine Ku Klux Klan, was found this morning at the edge of town. The police have no information on how he was killed. Several other Las Vegas residents suspected to be Klansmen seem to have left Las Vegas in a body, a welcome departure for all the good citizens of our town concerned."

L'Envoie

Max did recover, after many weeks in the hospital. When he was discharged he moved in with his brother Aaron at Golding's hotel, the Golden Peacock. They were living there rent-free, as befitted the most highly valued member of the hotel staff.

"Listen, it's not for your good, it's for mine," Golding told Aaron. "That jerk I got in the kitchen can't cook for shit. We're gettin' real high-class customers here. They want real high-class food. So I'm makin' you my top chef."

Aaron's dream had come true. He moved his knives to the hotel kitchen without ever setting foot back in Aaron's Eats. An entrepreneur from Los Angeles was delighted to clean up the mess that Max's attackers had left. He transformed the site into a high-end women's clothing and jewelry boutique.

An acquaintance of Golding's taught Max to serve as croupier at the roulette table, and what with that and a changing supply of attractive and more or less unattached young women, he settled in.

Molly married the head of the Production Engineering department at Topnotch Tire, had four children in quick succession, and never did come out to see Las Vegas.

THE MAGIC TOUCH: A PETER PANSY DETECTIVE YARN

A. B. ROBBINS

Howie Tabor had the fastest hands in town. None of the pros on the Vegas Strip, nor any of the street magicians on either coast, could do *up-close* magic like Howie. The only thing that kept Howie from the pro ranks and a career on stage was his speech: Howie made Gomer Pyle sound like Laurence Olivier.

One Sunday afternoon, Howie stuck a single silver dollar into Big Beulah and hit the two-million-dollar jackpot. He now had enough money to buy the upscale tricks and illusions that set the big acts apart, and decided to make a run at a stage career. His idea was to develop a show that would not require him to speak. One murder and a few bizarre events later, I was in Las Vegas at Howie's hire to find out "Whut in the hayell wuz goin' awn."

My shingle reads Peter Pansy ~ Private Eye, and, please, no wisecracks about the name. I used to be one of those by the book, gold-badge guys out of L.A. Robbery/Homicide. Now my beat is what I ever-lovingly refer to as Beverly the Hill.

As is my habit, I was sitting in my office at Numero Uno Rodeo Drive, wearing Gucci loafers, an Armani suit, Lagerfeld shirt, and a gold lamé shoulder holster, in which I keep "Golda," my gold-plated .357 with mother-of-pearl grips. I was laid back, listening to the honeyed tones of Johnny Mathis, sipping on a Perrier, just waiting for who knows who, to come in and ask me to do who knows what, who knows where, when I got a phone call from my friend, Kam. I met Kamal Masik during my stint with Robbery/Homicide when he joined an investigation. He is an ex–Navy seal and real-life tough guy. Kamal, with his history of covert legal violence, is now the leading female impersonator in Las Vegas, yet he still does work he can't talk about for one of those government alphabet agencies. Kam is my closest friend and a sometime work associate. It was he who recommended me to Howie.

I took advantage of the opportunity and drove my XKE, top down, to Vegas. When I pulled off of I-15 at Tropicana Avenue, I called Kam. He said to meet him and Howie at his place. Place my ass. *Palace* was more like it. They were waiting out front as I drove up. Kam, his olive complexion and Mediterranean look enhanced by Las Vegas solar power, looked as if he stepped from the cover of GQ. However, when he spoke, you didn't know if you were going to get a young Anthony Quinn or Jane Russell.

"Peter, Howie. Howie, Peter," Kam said.

"Ah'm pleasured to makin' yer 'quaintance, Mister Pansy," Howie said. "Thissa here's a awful mess we got." He was a good looker, a bit under six feet, muscular, and smart. He just sounded funny.

If you want big tricks built, Vegas was the place to be. If you had an idea, there were geniuses who could make it happen; or, better said, make it appear to happen. Choreography, original music, costuming, staging, everything you needed, just around the corner. Think of the stunts you've seen on TV, the Statue of Liberty, the Empire State Building, elephants, lions, tigers, and bears, oh my . . . all of them made to vanish before your very eyes. The competition is fierce, and industrial espionage, better known to us commoners as stealing, runs rampant. It appeared someone out there didn't want another player on the field and was willing to stop at nothing to accomplish that end. The police literally didn't have a clue. Now it was my turn.

———

"Mister Pansy, I . . ."

"Call me Pete or Peter, please, Howie."

"Pete, whoever done murdered Gerald Tannon was good. I mean, real good at magic, the way it happened and all. The po-leece is looking wrong at it. Mis-die-rec-ted, jes like with sleight-a-hand in a card trick."

"Tell me how it looks to the police."

"Gerald designed a trick for my act that he wuz demonstratin' that night on his compound. There was five of us a-watchin'. As I was told t' do, I cuffed o' Gerald's hands behind his back, and bound his ankles with duct tape. He was standing on a oversized black silk body bag that me and Gabe zipped up over his head. I tied it with a large gold twistie. Gerald's voice came through the bag kind'a muffled like, o' course, but he told us to take the hangman's noose, set it around his neck, then place the looped other end over a hook hangin' from this sixty-foot crane. When finished I was t' step back behind the rail. Then, Leon, his assistant, started the crane's engine, engaged the winch, and hoisted the loaded bodybag to about fifty feet. We all stood there just a'watchin', wonderin' what the gag was goin' to be. Pretty soon the bag starts jerkin' around a little, and we laughed."

"What made you laugh?" I asked. "I would think it was pretty serious."

"Not when you know good and well he was going to escape. Hay-ell, that's what we wuz there for. His escape."

"What happened then?"

"Well sir, the jerking gets real violent then stops, so I turn to Leon: 'Okay, what's goin' on?' Leon shrugs and says, 'I don't know,' says it weren't the way it was supposed to go. I says, 'Well, get his ass *down*!' 'Bout that time my cell phone rings. It was Gerald, laughin'! 'Howie,' he says, 'I'll see you on the Strip later. Quit starin' up at that empty bodybag. I switched places with the dummy up there.' So then Gerald's car starts up in the parking lot, the lights come on, the horn honks twice, and he drives off. Hot damn!, the guy's good. As we wuz leavin', we made some comments about how stupid you feel when you been had. My buddy Karl said it best: Bein' slickered by the master don't change the fact none that you done been slickered."

"Who discovered the body?"

"Leon, Gerald's assistant." Leon had come to work the next morning, started the crane, swung the boom around, lowered the dummy into the prop area behind a small shed, and went about his work in the shop. At about noon he went out back and saw two coyotes "tearin' at the body bag. It must'a been a fright. They wuz gnawin' on Gerald's arm and neck and low-growlin', shakin' their heads from side-to-side trying to tear off flesh. When they heard Leon, they run off, and poor old Leon, he could see Gerald's face gnawed on and his unblinkin' ol' dead eyes." Howie went silent after this telling of events, as if trying to wipe Leon's description from his memory bank.

"What's your take on it, Howie?" I asked.

"The cops said it musta been a recording of Gerald's voice the sonofabitch killer played over my cell phone to draw us away. Shee-it, is what I say. It was Gerald who drove off in his car, I know it. He is, was, that good. Somebody killed his ass and planted him back on the crane. Damn po-leece won't listen."

"The trick was built for you. Do you know how it works?"

"Nope, I never performed it. The secret went out with Gerald. We got to get us a technician to figger it out now."

I sent Howie off to make a few phone calls and try and locate a *trick master*, as he had called it. In the kitchen, Kam and I sat down to a cup of coffee. I asked about the other bizarre events he had mentioned on the phone.

"The first crazy thing," he said, "was one night driving on East Flamingo. Howie stopped for a red light, which then proceeded to cycle through red, yellow, and green. But each light stayed on for only a few seconds. After about twenty cycles, the light went solid green. The minute Howie made it across the intersection, his airbags deployed. He lost control and jumped the curb."

I said, "That's strange all right, but a bit benign."

"Agreed. But a few days later at the Louvre Hotel and Casino, downtown, he gets on an elevator and presses the fourth floor button. The elevator goes all the way to eighteen, the top floor, stopping on all the even-numbered floors. However, the elevator door never opens. On the way down, same scenario, only with the odd-numbered floors, all the way back to one. Then the elevator went to the fourth floor and the door opened."

"Again, rather harmless. Could happen to anybody."

"Now get this, Weird Happening Number Three. Saturday, Howie drives his Ford Explorer to the gym, and when he comes out there are five identical Explorers parked side-by-side in the lot. None of them his. *His* turns up in the Police Compound, after being towed from a No-Parking zone. How about that?" I was beginning to wonder myself. "The police brushed the incidents off as pranks against Howie. They didn't feel they were tied to the murder."

We didn't hear Howie enter the kitchen. He started talking while pouring himself a cup of Joe. "It ain't that mysterious, Pete," he said, "when you hear this. I found a remote-controlled detonator that activated my airbags."

Kam added, "Howie drives East Flamingo almost every night, same time. It was simple to rig the light sequence and set it off when he pulled up to the intersection. So whoever it was, had to be close by."

"Yup, and my office is in the Louvre Hotel," Howie said. "Easy to program the elevator's computer, then ambush me to pull the stunt."

"And I suppose you go to the gym at the same time every Saturday?" I asked.

"Sure do."

"Well, no more regularly scheduled events for a while. Deal?"

"Deal!"

He seemed so grateful for a partner in this mystery. Mischief was mischief, but murder was cold and calculating. "You two seem to feel the murderer is a trick master, what with the pranks going on. But the killer would need no knowledge of the trick to kill and then place the body back on the crane. Couldn't he have been spying on Gerald, and follow him as he drove away from the demonstration?"

"Could," Kam said. "Unless you're wrong, Howie, and the voice you heard on the phone was a recording, or an impersonation. Then someone who knew the trick could have sabotaged it, and it was Gerald up on the crane all along, no dummy in place."

"Damn, it could'a happened either way, sure enough."

"Are you sure it was Gerald's voice, Howie?"

"It sure sounded like him, Pete. But, I dunno, couldn't swear to it. How in the hell do we find out?"

"I start nosing around and earn my keep, that's how. By the way, what happened to the dummy that was supposed to be in the bag?"

Howie and Kam looked at each other sheepishly, as if to say why didn't we think of that. Kam sighed, "That's my Peter," and grinned.

———

I figured the best place to start was at the scene, so I jumped in the Jag and beat it over to Gerald's compound. Leon didn't know who I was. I became a reporter from L.A. "Freelance," I told Leon, handing him my card. "Name's Anthony Nucase. You've probably seen my byline in some of the rag mags."

"What can I do for you, Mister Nucase?"

"I don't think the local press has given this story its due. They're missing the boat not putting the emphasis on your perspective. I'd like to make you an offer for an exclusive."

"I've told all I know. How could an exclusive be made of that?"

"You leave that part to me, son. Did you read the story about then-President Clinton having a lovechild with a blonde Martian? That was my scoop."

Leon agreed to five hundred up front and two thousand upon publication.

"Show me around first, after which we can sit awhile and refresh your memory about what you saw that night."

I was taken for an intimate tour of the lot, and Leon let me in on some of the secret illusions still in the works. "I'm not in Gerald's league, yet," he said, "but I'm gonna get there, you wait and see."

"Do you know how the stunt worked that killed Gerald?"

"I already told the police I didn't."

"That was the police, and there's no sense making a good stunt public, right? But you must have some inkling as to how it was pulled off. Good apprentice like you."

"No sir, I sure don't. Some things Gerald held real close to his vest and didn't let on about at all. He worked all kinds of crazy hours, just so no one would be around while he was testing stuff. That included me too."

I got the feeling he was lying.

It's amazing what you can do with a few innocent words taken out of context. By the time my conversation with Leon was over I had enough info to do a great piece for next week's supermarket edition of *The Inquiring National Globe*. You see, I really did write that piece about Clinton and a blonde Martian, based on fact, and a very innovative interpretation (my own) of the actual statements made (the interviewee's own). Please note that the statements used were all attributable, but not necessarily made on the same day, at the same place, or about the same subject matter, or to the same interviewer. Anthony Nucase was real, sort of, and possessed enough clout to publish any time he wanted. Truth be known his . . . my . . . sister Angelica owns the paper. She also made up my pseudonym. Sis used to call me a nutcase, then Mr. A. Nutcase. Mr. A. Nutcase became Anthony Nucase, my byline.

———

That evening back at Kam's, I said, "What time are you through with your last show?"

"My last stunning appearance is at 2 a.m. Why?"

"Let's take a hard, close look at Gerald's compound, unannounced and unexpected. I believe we can figure out how that stunt worked ourselves, and Howie needs to be there too."

"Meet me in the hotel lounge at 2:15," Kam said. "I'll need a few minutes to freshen up my lipstick."

"Cute," I replied.

"Dazzling, actually," he said, and walked off. He turned dramatically in the doorway. In his best Mae West, he said, "Oh, by the way, some old friends of yours will be there tonight. You might want to come early and have a few dances."

I did! It was a great crowd.

At 2:45 Howie, Kam, and I parked about a mile from our destination and walked in. The three of us were damn near ready for anything. Kam had provided night-vision head gear and ultraviolet search equipment. He had his Glock; I had Golda, my gold-plated .357, and Howie was armed with a brace of throwing knives in a quick-draw rig, the likes of which I had never seen.

After a quick look-around, I asked Howie, "Exactly where was Gerald standing when you zipped him into the body bag?" He looked around to get his bearings. "Someone done moved the crane, but I believe it was right there. So he musta been standin' . . . about there." He walked over to a spot and pointed down. "Yup, there's the crane tracks, and with the boom a'leanin' forward, it had to of been within a few feet of right here."

"How in the hell could you cause something to disappear from this spot?"

"On stage you'd have a trap door," Kam answered. "Out here, well, I guess you *could* have a trap door."

The three of us were a sight, down on all fours, scratching the dirt and examining the ground with ultraviolet, crawling around in an ever-widening radius. Kam hit pay dirt, no pun intended. "Look at this," he said.

It was the outline of a square something, the outline highlighted by two different color sands under the UV, not visible to the naked eye.

"What do we do now, dig?" asked Howie.

Kam, still down on his knees, looked up. "If this is a way in, there's got to be a way out."

"This here place covers 'bout twenty acres, so where do we look fer t'other end?" Howie answered his own question: "Starting where no one could see you when you come out," he offered. "Behind, or inside, one of these structures, in order for Gerald to reach his car unseen while we watched the stunt."

Twenty minutes more of intense searching turned up the entrance, which led down to a tunnel. Another twenty minutes underground, and we discovered twelve more entrances, a labyrinth of tunnels connecting them, and a large (twenty-foot by thirty-foot) workshop, with a twelve-foot ceiling. Lying under the main trapdoor was the dummy, two more intact body bags, and a thirteen-channel remote control, each channel controlling one of the trap doors.

"Damnation!" came from Howie when we sat down at the desk in the underground workshop. "I been comin' here for years, and never had nary a clue this stuff was here."

Viewed together, the dummy, the body bag, and the trapdoor yielded the trick's mechanics, and although we were now aware of the how, they shed no light on whether the murder had taken place on or off the crane. One thing for certain, the murderer knew of this underground labyrinth, and I believed Leon knew more than he was letting on. How much more was anyone's guess.

———————

After a little shut-eye, we went to the Peppermill for breakfast and discussion. I said, "Put the compound under surveillance. That murdering joker is bound to be egotist enough to return."

"Better idea," Kam rebutted. "I take leave from my show for a few days and plant myself in the tunnel system. Besides being present if the creep shows, I can examine what's down there. Whoever it was more than likely left traces of the visit."

"How in the hayell do we figger out if Gerald was up there all the time, or planted after he was dead?"

"That will fall into place when we have all of the pieces," I answered.

"I kin get a bootleg copy of that there po-leece report," Howie said.

"Go for it. And while you're at it, get all the info you can on the deceased: His family, heirs, business dealings, friends, enemies, and the like. And Kam, do as you suggested and visit the labyrinth. If you find something, call. If not, we'll meet at your place in forty-eight hours. Meantime, I've got an article to write."

Murdered Magician Communicates With Apprentice
by Anthony Nucase

"It was as if his voice came to me from inside a
tunnel," Leon Hastings told this reporter. "It
happened after hoisting him up with the crane.
The noose was tied around his neck, I shut off
the engine, and started climbing down from the
cab when I heard it. 'It's as plain as the dirt
beneath your feet,' it said. I also saw
something in the dark over by the office, but I
didn't pay attention to any of it, thought my
mind was just playing tricks. But . . ."

There was enough innuendo in the article to let anyone who
had knowledge of the labyrinth know that I had knowledge of
it too.

I telephoned my sister as soon as the article was finished and
asked for its inclusion in this week's edition, which was due out
on the stands in three days. Knowing full well the magazine
was ready to go to press, but that it could be done, I expected a
playful hard time from Sis and was not disappointed: "Why
certainly, Mister Nutcase, for *you*, anything. Stop the presses
and all that jazz, just like Claudette Colbert and Clark Gable in
whatever movie that was. Well, this is no movie. What makes
you think you can call out of the clear blue and get anything you
want? Just because you're my favorite only brother, is that it?
Well . . . okay! Now, you owe me one. No, make that another
one. Ta-ta for now, Peter darling."

At this point it became a waiting game for me: for Kam to
call, for Howie to get back, and for the article to come out.
Speaking of which, when Howie came back that afternoon, *he*
invited *me* out for dinner and dancing. Quite an incredible
night. Vegas is one hell of a place to wait.

At 10:45 the next morning I was awakened by a call from
Kam. Damn, I never sleep in like that, and I didn't even hear
Howie leave.

"Sounds like I woke you, bro. Whatever did you . . . ?"

"Never mind. What's up?"

"Been reading through a bunch of notes Gerald left behind, a lot of technical magic stuff, a locked box I've been wondering whether to open, and several tricks in varying stages of completion. What do you think?"

"Bring the box and papers, and come on back to the house, we'll figure it from here."

"Right. Oh by the way, Howie called me and told me how precious you looked when he left this morning."

"Prick!"

"Thank you, dear, I'll be home soon."

Kam and Howie showed up at the same time. There wasn't a flicker of the goings-on from last night. It was straight to business, as Howie pitched an envelope onto the coffee table.

"That, mah dear frayends, is the po-leece report. And, Jacob Finegold, Gerald's and my lawyer, done tolt me he's gonna read Gerald's will tommorra. If'n we want ta hear it private-like, be at his office at nine in the mornin'. Plus I got a whole lotta other info, too."

"First let's dust this box I found for prints," Kam said. "I've handled it gingerly, so any prints left should be undisturbed. He placed the metal safe on top of the police report and in short order lifted two sets of prints. He drove them over to another of Howie's friends, who made a special run on them. Neither set was Kam's.

The box was a medium security office type, the kind used mainly for protection from fire. We forced it open with the help of a drill, chisel, and pry bar. In it we found Gerald Tannon's life story. It was in note format, handwritten, and in chronological order: the makings of his autobiography, and possibly the unmaking of his murderer.

The police report, when Howie got it, held nothing special. It stated that the autopsy showed Gerald Tannon had died of asphyxiation from the noose placed around his neck during the execution of a special effects stunt. Approximate time of death matched the timeframe within which the stunt had been performed. The only reason to suspect foul play was the phone call received by Howie Tabor, the caller claiming to be the deceased, and also the deceased's car being driven off while he was hanging from the crane. It also stated that currently there are no suspects.

The additional information Howie gleaned was another matter. Our victim had a first cousin living in Vegas, with whom he had a very vocal and hostile relationship.

"Shee-it, I found out Gerald done everything for that boy when he arrived from back East, 'bout six years ago. Seems the kid, twenty-one-years old at the time—Randy Nimoy's his name—had the showbiz bug real bad. He tried his hand at stand-up, got to where none o' the freebie lounges or funny rooms wouldn't even let him in no more. So he went to Gerald for some magic tricks and illusions, which he got. Hay-ell, Gerald even sent him to a school for magicians. The kid promptly failed the course. Dandy Randy Nimoy was not destined for stardom. He blamed bein' at the bottom of the bucket on his well-heeled, well-connected cousin, who refused to go the extree mile. Dandy Randy is still in showbiz, though. He handles the karaoke nights in a coupla tough dives on Boulder Highway."

"Why don't we each take a handful of Gerald's notes to read as tonight's homework assignment," I suggested. "In the a.m. we'll catch the reading of the will at attorney Finegold's office, then tomorrow evening we can drop in and catch Dandy Randy's Karaoke Show, wherever it happens to be."

"Rita's," Howie added. "T'morra night he's at Rita's. Bad place, that is."

"Bad is best," Kam chimed in. "I think I'll take the night off, wouldn't want to miss anything bad."

Two-thirty that morning Howie knocked on my bedroom door. "Pete, take a lookee here, at this," he said, handing me the notes he had been reading. Several of the paragraphs were flagged with neon stickums. They described Gerald's first foray into showbiz with a partner named Zachary Richter. Zachary, according to the notes, was talented but a slacker, and a bit of a lush. After about two years of trying to pull the act together for a push at the big time Gerald had enough and ended the relationship. Zachary disappeared without a trace, abandoning his wife and two-year-old son. After he vanished, Polly Richter and Gerald had an affair for about a year, then parted ways. Polly remarried, and after some legal wrangling, her new husband adopted her son Leon. The same Leon who had been apprentice and assistant to Gerald. Polly never told her son anything about his real dad. She instilled in Leon a love of all things magic, and on Leon's eighteenth birthday she contacted Gerald and asked if he would employ him. "If he can cut it," was the reply. Leon came to Vegas, tried out for Gerald, and made the cut in spades. The relationship between Polly, Zachary, and Gerald, by agreement, was to be kept secret.

I looked over at Howie, who had sat down next to me on the bed.

"Do you know where Polly Hastings lives now?"

"I believe its somewhere's in Indiana. It shouldn't be too big a problemo to find out."

"Find out, call her, and fly her here, if she'll come. I'm still not too sure about Leon not knowing anything. Too convenient."

"Kin it wait until mornin'?"

"Of course."

"Good. Kin I stay?"

I scratched my head, wrinkled my brow, and said, "Wellll . . . ," as I leaned over and turned off the light.

———————

There were two items in Gerald's Last Will and Testament.

(1) To my cousin Randy Nimoy, I hereby bequeath One Dozen Rubber Chickens and One Dozen Rubber Turds, as an award befitting the biggest Chicken-Shit I know, and I request Attorney Finegold send this press release to the entertainment editor of the Review-Journal:

The late Gerald Tannon, of Magic Sanctum fame, has bequeathed to his cousin Randy Nimoy, "One Dozen Rubber Chickens and One Dozen Rubber Turds, as an award befitting the biggest Chicken-Shit I know." Gerald's estate is being handled by attorney Jacob Finegold, who has been charged with delivery of the aforementioned prize.

(2) There will be a contest held to determine the recipient of my estate. The contestants, who are listed

below, are to design a trick, illusion, or stunt, which costs less than five thousand dollars to produce. They must deliver it to Mister Finegold no later than five o'clock on the thirtieth day after the reading of this will. Mister Finegold, whom I have chosen as executor of my estate, will in turn choose three judges, who must agree unanimously on the winner.

The contestants are:

Abe and The Babe
Dandy Randy Nimoy
(I'm still giving him a chance at the family jewels.)
Leon Hastings
The Cunning Carsons
The Magnificent Millicent Blaire

My estate's value as inventoried in this will, and certified by Noble, Knoble & Nobull, CPA's, is six-million-seven-hundred-fifty-one-thousand dollars and eighteen cents. Go figure!

Finegold looked up over his spectacles and said, "The contestants have been notified and will be here for the official reading at four this afternoon."

I placed a manila envelope containing Gerald's autobiographical notes in front of Finegold. "Sir, what can you tell us about this?"

He took the contents from the envelope. "How did you come by these notes? The last I saw of them, Gerald picked them up here at the office after I had finished reviewing them for possible libel, and was going to place them in his fire safe. Where in the world were they?"

Howie detailed to his attorney the events that led us to the discovery of the labyrinth. Amazing: Howie's speech was actually beginning to sound lyrical to me.

"You know something strange, Mr. Pansy?" Feingold said. "Someone broke into this office two nights before the murder, but nothing is missing, and nothing appeared to have been disturbed. Do you think it could be related?"

"At this juncture I'm inclined to say yes. But *how* is a crapshoot."

We left the office and headed back to Kam's. Howie's mission was to locate Leon's mom. My Southern California tan was fading, so I intended to catch a few morning rays of Vegas sunshine, and Kam had some business at the Federal Building. Tonight we would confront cousin Randy, and tomorrow my article would be on the stands.

Three o'clock, Howie came by with a shit-eatin' grin on his face to say Polly Hastings would arrive in Vegas tomorrow morning. She had asked him not to say anything to Leon because she would very much like to tell the story herself, in person. Good work Howie!

Fifteen-after-five my cell phone rang, it was attorney Finegold. "Mister Pansy, I believe I now know who broke into my office, and what was done."

"What happened?"

"Well . . . before I could read the part about Randy receiving the Chicken-Shit Award, he described to all present the gist of it. Said that he and Gerald had conjured it up as a great publicity stunt, if something were to happen to Gerald."

"Is that not possible?"

"No, it's not. Gerald originally had left everything to Randy, but changed his will over a year ago. Gerald told me he had no contact with his cousin since he made the change. He asked me to handle the document with the utmost secrecy. He even quipped, 'I would love to give my bequeath to Randy before I die. He still thinks he's the beneficiary.' Does that sound like someone who would let on to his prank? I don't think so. No. Randy is trying to save face. Do you think he's the murderer?"

"I couldn't say so with any degree of certainty. Let's just say he's high up on our list of one."

———

Rita's is not the sort of club that comes to mind when you think of Las Vegas. Kam described the décor as *early gauche*. The three of us caused a stir just by showing up well groomed and in clean clothes.

There's an adage that states, "Never carry a gun if you don't intend to use it." We were there to light a fire under Dandy Randy, not to shoot anyone, so we weren't packing. Except for

Howie, who was wearing that quick-draw knife-throwing outfit under his doe-suede bomber jacket.

Randy came from backstage and started the show within a few minutes of our arrival. Not bad, actually. He was a song stylist rather than a singer, and did a bit that had Johnny Carson interviewing Marilyn Monroe and J.F.K. He had lifted the routine word-for-word from one of the Headline acts on the Strip. He spotted Kam and announced over the mike, "Wow folks, guess who's visiting Rita's tonight? It's the screamingest Queen this side of the Strip, Faggot Kam the Female Impersonator, and it looks like she's brought two of her sisters with her. Arnold, why don't you go greet our guests?" Arnold came walking over from the bar. Six-two, maybe 325 pounds, and wearing the most grotesque Hawaiian shirt I had ever seen. All the measurements for this guy were big numbers, except that Arnold's hat size and IQ were the same.

"You the pansy?" Arnold asked Kam, while putting his index finger on Kam's forehead.

"No, I'm the Queen, he's the pansy," Kam answered, while pointing at me and grinning.

"What do you think of my gay, colorful shirt, faggot?"

"That's why all elephants wear gray, Arnold. It makes them look so slender."

Arnold made a move on Kam, and a few of the bigger guys in the crowd started to move toward us. Before the hulk at the next table could get to his feet, Kam had broken Arnold's pointing finger, thrown him to the floor, stomped on his groin, and rendered him immobile. I backhanded the hulk from the next table after he stood up, and broke his nose. Howie jumped up onto our table screaming at the top of his lungs, getting the crowd's attention. While they watched him, and in a blazingly fast move, Howie retrieved a knife from the holster behind his neck, threw it, and scored a bull's-eye on the dartboard hanging some 30-odd feet away. His next throw stuck in the wooden plank floor between the feet of a dude every bit as big as Arnold. The place had become so quiet you could hear the knife vibrating like a tuning fork. Howie looked over the crowd and asked, "Next?"

I leapt up onto the stage and threw Randy down onto the dance floor.

"Don't move, you chickenshit bastard, just listen. I know you know about the labyrinth under the Magic Sanctum, that you've been there and probably committed the murder. I also know you broke into Attorney Finegold's office to sneak a peek at Gerald's will. I can't prove it yet, but as Little Bo Peep is my witness, I will."

Out in the parking lot Kam said, "That was quite a show, Howie. I think they got the point. And Little Bo Peep as your witness? Peter, that was a stroke of brilliance."

"Thanks, just seemed like the thing to say."

Howie looked at Kam and shook his head, "Damnation, I ain't never see'd yer tough-guy side."

"I'm just a powder puff," Kam replied.

"Yeah, fer sure, man. But you gotta be talkin' 'bout gunpowder."

Leon's mother arrived from Terre Haute at 10 the next morning. I picked her up at McCarran International and figured a stop at IHOP would break the ice before going to the house. No dice. Polly Hastings wanted to get right down to it. Polly Hastings is a beautiful, well-tailored, intelligent woman, whose profession as a news anchor on a major TV affiliate in Indiana led her to a straightforward, no-nonsense approach in her personal life as well.

She, Kam, and I sat down in the living room over a snifter of Gran Marnier, and it was she who started the conversation.

"Just how does my son figure into all of this intrigue, gentlemen?"

I answered, "What I find hard to believe, Mrs. Hastings, is that anyone as bright as your son could work as closely as he did with Gerald, for as long as he did, without learning of the existence of the labyrinth beneath the Magic Sanctum." Then I filled her in on everything that had transpired to this point.

"Gentlemen, Leon's dad Zak, Gerry, and I were called 'Two Lads and a Lady' when we first started on the showbiz trail. Gerry was the brains behind the outfit, I was window dressing, and Zak supplied comic relief and chatter while the stunts were happening. He was quite jealous of Gerry's acclaim and top-banana status, and became vocal about his displeasure."

"Describe vocal," Kam said.

"Name-calling in public, yelling for no reason, drunken behavior on stage during the act. Gerry attempted to work around and overcome Zak's imagined misgivings to no avail, and after about two years the act split up. I had left a year earlier to embrace motherhood. I have not seen nor heard from my disgruntled ex-husband since he disappeared over two decades ago. But something Mister Pansy related has given me pause. Zak did a perfect impersonation of Gerry as part of our act. In fact, even off-stage you'd never know if it was Gerry or Zak on the phone or at the door."

"Unt zoe. . . ." Kam spoke in a caricature German accent. "Vot vee now haff iss a phantom zuspect who hass not been zeen in tventy yearz. Veddy interesting."

"Please let me call and meet with my son and fill him in on the past. Then I'll bring him here for you to question. I do not think my boy would lie to me, or to you. And I definitely do not think he is capable of murder."

"No disrespect intended, ma'am, but that's what Al Capone's mother said," quipped Kam.

"I think that would be a terrific next step," I said. "And please call me Pete, and call Mister Laugh-A-Minute over there Kam."

"Call me Polly. May I borrow a telephone and a car?"

———

Kam answered his phone. It was attorney Finegold asking that he come to the office, no explanation given. Kam said sure, and left. I went out and picked up a copy of the paper that contained my article. Howie was there when I got back; he had also picked up the paper. "How in thunderation kin you git away with makin' up shee-it like that?"

"Easy. English is such an incredible language for making *nothing* sound like the obvious."

Twenty after two, Polly and Leon came driving up.

After two hours of questions and answers, and becoming

comfortable with Leon and Polly, I felt assured Leon was innocent. Leon seemed sincere in his grief and guilt. He thought if he had been more attentive he could have prevented the murder. Gerald had taken great pains to keep his secret from the whole world, and as good as Gerald was, why could I not believe he could keep it a secret from his assistant? An assistant who played by the rules, and always did as he was told. A bright guy, Leon: He just had no street smarts. Howie concurred.

My sister Angelica reached me on Kam's house phone.

"Peter darling, someone has called and asked for a way to get in touch with Mister Nucase. He left a cryptic message that he said you would understand . . . 'Tell Mister Nucase someone wants to talk with him about the underworld, and that the word *underworld* should be written in capital letters.' Whatever does that mean?"

"Bingo. Jackpot. Blackjack. We've got a shark on the line. Give him my Nucase cell phone number, and tell him to call at anytime. Oh, and Sis, I owe you big time."

"Haven't I heard this before? Well, good, I'll collect big time. Be careful, you nutcase. Underworld in capital letters doesn't sound like a fun game."

Kam arrived in a new Hummer 2 with a footlocker-sized crate in the back. "This, my fellow Americans," he said, presenting the crate like a prize on *The Price Is Right*, "and what's in here," pointing to his head, "will lead directly to our culprit."

"Hey Pete, I'd be willin' ta bet ya any amount you kin count, and give twenty-to-one odds, that both them there containers he jest pointed to are empty."

"Funny, sonny. You guys help me in with this thing."

It was heavy. When we set it down in the music room, and opened it, Kam started performing again.

"Lady and Gentlepersons, we have before us Dandy Randy Nimoy's entry into the Estate Contest. Does it seem strange to you that it was completed only two days after the reading of the will? Okay, it did to me too. This dandy little stunt was stolen from the labyrinth, and we can prove it. How, you ask?" He reached into his briefcase and pulled out a set of plans. "These plans, for this trick, were taken by me from the labyrinth. The tricks for all of the other plans I found were still down there. Only this trick was missing."

Leon chimed in, "I recognize some of the parts! I ordered them for Mr. Tannon."

"And, Lady and Gentlepersons, as far as the contents of this other empty container. . . ." Kam went on to say that after he realized what he had, he'd gone over to Randy's house. No one was home, so-o-o he did what the police can't, or shouldn't do: He made himself a guest. Inside, he found the notes and drawings that were used to pull the stunts on Howie.

"Where is Randy appearing tonight?" I asked Howie.

"Back at Rita's. This should oughta be fun."

Kam was swaggering, "Let's celebrate first. Dinner on me at Lombardi's."

We agreed to meet at Lombardi's at nine.

———————

The call came through halfway through dessert.

"Meet me at Mount Charleston Lodge in forty-five minutes," the unfamiliar voice said. "Drive out 95, take a left on 156, then drive the loop to 158 and 157. Be alone, no cops, and no ride-alongs. I'll be watching and signal you. I have info on what's going down, Mr. Nucase. If you want it, don't betray me."

"How do we handle this one, Pete? You're not going up there by yourself," Kam said.

"I can handle this creep. Whoever he is, he believes he's dealing with a reporter. So I'm going to finish dessert, take a little mountain drive, and catch me a two-legged varmint. You and Howie go on out to Rita's to check if our caller is Randy."

"Could be a accomplice," Howie added. "It don't have to be Randy hisself. Possible six million dollars, a feller might go lookin' fer some help."

Mount Charleston and the Lodge are right around the corner from Vegas. Mostly locals go there. It's rustic and wooded, and at almost 12,000 feet the peak is above the snow line. In the old days, it was the only source of timbers for the mines in the area. Now it's the Toiyabe National Forest. Beautiful place to catch a murderer.

We were all so busy plotting and planning no one saw Leon leave the table. Damn boy, he had hot-wired my Jag and took off for the rendezvous alone.

"He's got a good fifteen-minute jump on us. Get in," Kam ordered, as he started the engine of his new tricked-out Hummer 2. It was the first time I saw Polly lose her composure.

Fifteen minutes was too big a jump to make up, especially against my XKE, but we were pushing it. Coming around a sharp bend on 158, the only thing that saved us was Kam's extraordinary driving skill. He saw car headlights heading straight for us on our side of the road, and the white stripes veering sharply to the right. He yelled "Damn," and cut the wheel sharply to the left, head-on into the oncoming car. We braced for the crash and nothing happened, other than we heard the tinkle of broken glass. We got out of the car and realized someone had rigged a clever stunt. A large mirror had been propped up across the narrow highway to make it look as if a car was heading straight at us as we rounded the curve. Black roofing paper covered the center stripes and shoulder markers. Additional paper had been painted to show the lane heading straight over the embankment. "How the hell did you figure that?" I asked Kam. He answered, "I saw my own license plate number reversed in the mirror, and went for it."

About fifty feet down we spotted the headlights of my car. Leon had not been so skillful.

"Oh my God, no!" Polly moaned and started over the side.

Howie stopped her, and held her. Kam and I made the climb down.

I cupped my hands and shouted to Polly and Howie, "He's alive, but hurt real bad." The seatbelt and roll bar saved his ass.

Kam told Howie to lower the winch. We rigged a stretcher of sorts using the canvas and struts from the convertible top. Secured it and the unconscious Leon to it with duct tape from the boot of my wrecked car. We made sure his neck and spine were immobilized. Kam on one side, me on the other, we let the winch pull us up as we kept the stretcher and Leon from hitting the rocks.

After getting Leon to the emergency room at Mountain View Hospital, I sent Kam and Howie to roust out Dandy Randy and see what he'd been up to. No more pussyfooting around—hurt the sonofabitch if you have to. Polly and I would do the pacing and keep them apprised of Leon's condition.

Two hours later, Leon was brought out of surgery, with a positive report. Several broken bones, all reset, and in casts. Concussion, severe enough to cause a major headache that would last for days, but no permanent damage. Internal hemorrhaging, in check. He was in critical but stable condition. Sedated though he was, Polly relaxed a little after being let in to see him.

Kam called me first, and I gave him the good news. He gave *me* news as well. He and Howie had snatched Randy from Rita's parking lot, restrained him, and brought him to Kam's. He was not the one on the mountain. There were plenty of witnesses to attest he had performed that night. His story was, Yes, he had pulled those pranks on Howie. But someone, a stranger, told him about the tunnel complex and Gerald's changing of his will. He broke into Finegold's office to check the will for himself, and also visited the labyrinth. He did not kill Gerald. However, after the murder, he took the opportunity of stealing the trick. Randy felt he was set up to be a fall guy. I said he's full of crap, has an accomplice, and did it all. I told Kam to keep him there for me, I would be home as soon as Leon wakes up from his anesthesia.

Polly and I were sitting in Leon's room in the Intensive Care wing, when a man wearing scrubs came in. He pointed a .45 automatic first at Polly, then at me. "Zak," Polly said, "my Lord, what are you doing?"

"Shut the fuck up, slut. You two almost made me kill my son."

"Zak, I . . ."

"I told you to shut the fuck up. You just listen. For years I've been watching you and my son. You never even told him about me. If you had, I would have come back. He didn't know that the shit-for-brains TV producer you married was not his real father. How could you do that?"

"I nev . . ."

"Don't you say one more word or I'll blow your brains out right now. The last straw was you getting Gerald to give him a job. I watched his admiration for Gerald grow. Your *fucking* ex-lover, my *fucking* cheating ex-partner earning the fortune that should have come to *me*, and getting the love and respect from my son that was rightfully mine. So I killed the bastard slowly on his own stinking trick. I . . ."

It was my turn to get in on the act. "You sick bastard, you're going to kill us anyway, so do it now. I don't want to hear any more of your Goddamned pitiful story. You're making me cry."

"You think I won't? You think I won't?" he repeated, his hand trembling.

"I know you will, but you're going to make us listen to more of your shit first. Well, I for one . . . ," I started to say while turning to Polly. As I did, I whipped my .357 magnum from the gold lamé holster under my jacket and put a slug into his forehead, dropping him on the spot.

"Jesus, Pete, how did you know you could do that?"

"The hammer on his .45 wasn't cocked, and with him waving his hands around while spewing his venom, I knew he couldn't cock it and get a shot off before I got him."

———————

Leon didn't win the estate: Abe and the Babe did. But they kept Leon on and gave him a piece of the action. Dandy Randy is still wowing them at Rita's. Kam went back to being the plain old Number One Drag Queen in Vegas. Abe and the Babe, and Leon, designed an act for Howie that, at my insistence, included him talking. I also named his act, *Howie the Hayseed Houdini*. Beside my fee, Howie also replaced my XKE.

And me . . .

As is my habit, I was sitting in my office at Numero Uno Rodeo Drive, wearing Gucci loafers, an Armani suit, Lagerfeld shirt, and a gold lamè shoulder holster, in which I keep "Golda," my gold-plated .357 with mother-of-pearl grips. I was laid-back, listening to the honeyed tones of Johnny Mathis, sipping on a Perrier, just waiting for who knows who to come in and ask me to do who knows what, who knows where, when I got a phone call from my friend, Kam.

Now, that's an End

CATNAPPING

GAY TOLTL KINMAN

When I hit Las Vegas, which wasn't often, I usually headed for the MGM and a certain blackjack table, my heart palpitating over its normal range—not good for a guy at fifty, and a beefy 6'2" one.

This time I strode into the Mirage, my heart in the same condition. A pair of beauties they were, I was told. Blue-eyed, white, with paws as big as dinner plates, the Siberian Tigers held court in their den with all of their admiring subjects on the other side of a thick glass partition.

The male paddled around in his pool, and just like every other male of any species, watched her, the female, sprawled ladylike on a ledge, one leg draped over the edge, asleep.

Perhaps.

Was he waiting for her to wake up so he'd have company? Or an audience? Was she sleeping, or just pretending? Would he wake her up when he couldn't stand to be alone anymore?

Was he any different from me?

Everyone loved those tigers judging by the crowds in front of the glass, and in the shop buying stuffed replicas.

But someone loved them a lot more.

And that's the real reason I was here.

Someone was planning to steal them. I was here to stop him.

"Why" was a question, but not the question. The question was how. If I knew that, my job as a P.I. would be a lot simpler. I liked simple these days, but that wasn't what I was getting.

The other reason I was here was Marge. She's a dental hygienist in Los Angeles, and she was attending a convention at the hotel.

I could tell them right off from the other conventioneers. The jokes. Like what ride in amusement parks do hygienists like most? The molar coaster. How can you not like them?

Oh, yeah, there was a third reason I was here.

My daughter.

Marge said I had to call her this time, arrange to meet her, blah, blah, blah.

Marge knows how to get me to do what she wants. So the call was on the agenda, but first I had to stop a catnapping.

Before I let the management know I was ready to start work, I started. I closed out those beautiful furry bodies and looked around the den. Fake rocks, cavelike on three sides, with a ledge on the left, walkways and a real cave on the right. Above, blue sky. Nothing in between.

Couldn't imagine trying to steal those two. Pussycats they looked like, but I wasn't going in there to find out. Not on your life, or rather mine.

I took out my notepad and jotted down a few things. Can't believe how much I forget things these days. It can only get worse was a thought that didn't thrill me, so I didn't think about it anymore.

Instead, I took a moment to think about the good things in life—Marge, the tigers, and dinner tonight at Tillerman's, where the locals go. A nice Chivas on the rocks in the lounge first, then seated at my favorite table with fresh lobster—and it always was, ironic for a place out here in the desert, but that's Vegas—with a bottle of Raymond Cab.

Enough of that, back to work. I went to the Security Office and met up with Doug Hassenfeld, the Chief. We'd worked LAPD together. I'd done a few cases for him before.

We chatted a bit about life in general, what was it like back in Los Angeles now, how's the wife. He knew mine was dead, the big C, about the time he took the job here. I hadn't introduced him to Marge yet, but I would.

He had another officer, Karen Grafton, and one of the tigers' trainers, Melissa Caldwell, show me everything. I mean everything. Somehow those two pussycats weren't looking so cute anymore, particularly when I learned the amount of poop they produce and what it looks and smells like. Not too surprising that there was a lot of it when I saw what they ate. They ate well. But, again, that's Las Vegas.

They herded the two out while I climbed around the den in borrowed boots. The smell was something I hadn't expected.

Did I think they'd smell of baby powder? Open at the top, the tigers got the desert heat but misting was a constant so it was damp and coolish.

"The tigers were bred in a wildlife park," Melissa told me, "not a jungle, and they never had to hunt for food. They're used to humans now, but that doesn't mean they won't revert to their wild nature in a blue-eyed blink."

I didn't plan to find out. Ever.

They showed me the security system—cameras, sensors, alarms, you name it, top of the line as far as I could tell—Las Vegas again. No way could anyone steal those two.

I shook hands with Melissa and Karen as we were now on a first-name basis. Melissa gave me her card. As soon as I was out of their sight, I jotted down that she talked about them like they were her children. She was maybe in her mid-twenties, Karen about five years older.

I heard my name being called and turned around. Melissa. "I forgot to ask you, Mr. Kendall," she said, "when will the south camera be back in operation?"

I don't think my mouth dropped physically, but it sure did mentally.

"I'm not sure what you mean."

"Your company said they were going to replace the south camera, but it's still not working."

"The south camera? I'll check on that for you." I pulled out her card. "I'll get back to you as soon as I can."

"Okay!" She strode off, her ponytail swinging.

South camera?

I looked around the walls and finally found a camera swiveling to watch the crowds. On the bottom of it was the label, "Kendall Security Agency."

I sat down in the nearest chair.

Coincidence?

I didn't think so.

I thought back to the way Doug had introduced me to them and that I was setting up a security system for a proposed wild animal park. News to me, but I thought that was supposed to be part of my cover.

Neither of them had even blinked.

They thought I was Kendall of Kendall Security Systems.

But I wasn't.

I put that thought aside and thought about what Doug had really hired me for. The attempt was supposed to be made sometime during the July Fourth parade with fireworks, when the hotel's security staff was watching out for pickpockets, room thieves and all the other arts of war that go on in a hotel. Especially a Las Vegas hotel. Doug had hired extra security, but there's only so much that can be done. Doug couldn't change the place into an armed camp. And even that might not work. Not many people knew about the proposed crime. I had learned about it from a guy I caught trying to burglarize one of my clients. Before I handed him over to LAPD, he tried to trade the information for a lighter charge. Told him I'd think about it, got on the horn to Doug and gave him the info. Silence on the other end of the line for a bit. Then he asked me to come over, look around and do what I could do. I went back to my guy in lockup and told him I needed more information. Too sketchy, he could have made it up. I let him think I was on his side, believed him, and that I was doing a little horsetrading with the D.A.'s office on his behalf. But that was all he had. Nada else. He'd given me his whole wad. I wanted to get him out so he could get more information for me. Especially the 'how.' Armed robbery, bail and transient are not used together positively in one legal sentence. So that option was out. I had to go with what I had, hoping he could pick up something else in jail which wasn't an option I expected to be able to take to the bank.

I knew the target and the timing and that was it.

I went back to the den but all I saw was one of the workers hosing down the cement rocks. I knew what he was sluicing off. Then he hopped down into the drained pool and scrub brushed the sides and bottom.

Yuk.

A plan formed in my mind.

I turned away and looked at the small furry tigers in the shop's window. But I could see the guy's reflection. Thin, maybe 5'4", no bulging muscles there. Bet he wasn't thinking warm fuzzy thoughts about the tigers, as I'd bet that Melissa did all the time, no matter what the work involved. Just like any mother.

He glanced up occasionally. Pigeon shit from pigeons flying en masse around the opening. He was probably saying, "Thanks a lot, guys." But he had enough sense not to keep facing up too long.

I made another note. "List / employees / access."

Then I started thinking about the 'why.' Money was up there. Always tops the list of motives. But other reasons came to mind. A collector who wants rare things? A publicity stunt? I went through the other motives like the seven deadly sins, greed, revenge, envy. A sloth was not being stolen here. I gave up. Having met so many nutsoes in my days, most of the time their motives made no sense to me.

Time to rendezvous with my dental hygienist and see if I could get some lunch stuck in my teeth. Maybe she'd cut class and do some flossing. Up in our room.

———

Telephoning, not anything else, was what Marge had in mind. Under her eyes, I called my daughter. Marge stood there while I did it. No pretending I was talking to someone else. Pregnant at sixteen, my daughter had dropped out of school, moved in with the lowlife who'd had a string of petty theft convictions. Maybe that's how he thought he was going to support his new family. At least she didn't marry him. Nor did she have the child. She aborted both the baby and the lowlife. And her family.

I had changed her diapers, stayed up with her when she was sick, helped her take her first steps. Couldn't believe the daughter I raised would do all those things. And at sixteen. When I was her age—Enough of that.

Got bits and pieces of news about her but never from her. She got on a work-study program that the Alhambra Soroptimist Club, a women's club next to Los Angeles that helps young girls, sponsored and she straightened out. Got a full-time job and kept getting promoted until she worked some mucky muck here in Las Vegas. Bought a house. Bought a nice car. Lived well. Worked hard. So I heard.

Guess those are all the things you could say about me. Yeah, I worked a lot. Loved the job, took all the overtime I could get.

That bought us a nice house, nice things. Okay, so I didn't take many vacations with them, but made sure they went someplace nice.

Know her mother was in touch with her through the years, nothing regular but enough to know she was on the straight and narrow. Somehow I was the villain in all this. Can't say I didn't speak my piece in the beginning. Didn't back down too much. Hell, I was a cop, thought like a cop and still do. That's who I am and I can't change.

Couldn't understand what she had done and why, and why she just didn't come home again. We had the money to pay for college. She came to see her mother in the hospital near the end when I wasn't there.

Gotta say I was there a lot. Found out about her visit from the nurse, not from Lois. Then after Lois died . . . well, I'd probably do and say the same thing all over again. So there I was, sweating like a pig, when she came on the line.

Marge had given me some suggestions to get the conversation going. Yeah, I'm real good at those kinds of conversations, just like working the room—not me!

Marge stood there, hands on her hips, making sure we were actually talking.

Talking. I was talking to a stranger, and then suddenly I wasn't. She was my pre-sixteen year old, chatting away, like she'd be home from school soon. I had to get the old handkerchief out. I think I heard Marge laughing when she left.

There'd be three of us for dinner tonight at Tillerman's. She said. She'd call them to make a reservation. She knew the manager at the Mirage, would have them put us in a suite, stuff on the cuff. Had to whoa her down as soon as I got my jaw back up where it should be enough to talk. I told her we were already getting the room free since I was working for the Mirage on a case. I didn't go into details.

After I hung up, I realized she must know other people, might have an insight into why the white tigers might be stolen. Suddenly having dinner with a veritable stranger didn't look too bleak. Old man, I thought, you're always a cop, working, now you're going to pump your own long-lost daughter for information.

The young woman who walked into Tillerman's lounge was my mother. Not that I knew her at twenty-five but I'd seen the wedding pictures. She was so beautiful. No, gorgeous. For a minute my heart stopped, Chivas halfway to my mouth, eyes popping.

The scene played in slow motion on my mental computer, now on overload. Jeannine. No longer a flat-chested, pimply teen-ager. Oh, no. Saw two guys at the table near the doorway stop and stare.

Glad Marge was there with me, otherwise I wouldn't have known what to do.

Hey, give me a murder scene and I can handle that. Hate these family things, emotional things.

Jeannine floated over, the guys behind her watching, wondering when they could make a move on her.

I stuck out my hand, not knowing what the proper etiquette was, but I needn't have worried. Women know the right things to do. And she was a woman. Holy cow, I produced this creature?

She gave me a kiss on the cheek and sat down on the padded bench beside me, her arm through mine for a minute.

We chatted. No, Marge and Jeannine chatted like they'd known each other for years. I just grunted occasionally. In top form for me, socially.

Jeannine went over to talk with the maitre d'. Gave him a bunch of orders I was sure. Bowing and scraping was not quite the word, because he wasn't that kind of a guy. He was the kind of a maitre d' who would give her anything. That's Las Vegas. Anything, anytime.

But he knew her. She came here a lot? The cop in me still observing. Dinner was—the best I've ever had. Raymond Cabernet, yes. But a year not on the winelist, and judging by the other prices, off the Richter scale for my budget. It was liquid velvet. Drinking the wine, I could believe myself a connoisseur. Now I understood the words—complex, flavors, nose.

When the last of the lobster shells disappeared into the sunset, I was a P.I. again.

"The reason I'm in town," I said, and told her what she should know to answer my questions.

"Is that the reason you called me?" Her eyes held a hint of amusement exactly like her mother's. My mother, her mother. She brought the women of my life, who were no longer on this planet, alive. I took a gulp of water. Then I realized from her words, somehow I had missed a cue. I looked at Marge, but she looked as mystified as I felt. Jeannine must have sensed our confusion if she couldn't read the stupid look on my face.

"I thought you were asking me because of the security system at the Mirage."

"Kendall Security Systems," I said slowly, guessing that there was no coincidence.

"I am Kendall Security Systems," she said.

Afterwards Marge assured her that we had no idea. Marge kept looking at me, but I can't fool her, so she knew I was telling the truth about not knowing about the connection. Then I wondered if Doug had thought I was part of Kendall, or if he just hired me for the past jobs because we had worked together. Maybe both.

We got back to my questions. "Why would anyone want to steal them?" I asked her.

Without batting a blonde curly eyelash, she went to the heart of the matter. "The tigers are the Mirage's drawing card. It's what sets them apart from all the other hotels here. Everyone's looking for a shtick. Without it, they are just another hotel. Without the tigers, the Mirage might be in serious financial trouble. They have a way high profit margin and operate on that. If they drop even one percent, they could have a problem. Without the tigers . . ." she let the sentence hang. "I'm guessing, they'll hold the tigers for ransom."

I looked at her face, intelligent, and watched the words form in her mouth. I had two brains. One brain processed the information she gave me. Now the 'why' made sense.

The other brain listened to my mother, pre-me, talking. I shut that part of my brain down.

"So what will they do with the tigers if they get the ransom?"

"They don't need them, can't use them or exhibit them, so they'll probably kill them."

A frozen hand clutched my heart. I gasped. Not on my

watch. No way, José. Don't even think about touching the tigers while I'm responsible for them, I wanted to shout to the world.

"There's an element here in Las Vegas who would do anything to make more money. And there's an element here, Dad, who would help them do it."

Dad.

For a moment I was back being a social oaf. That brain door had sprung open.

I slammed it shut.

Back to work.

"Do you have any names?" I pulled out my notebook.

Doug would probably know them. I wondered if that thought had occurred to him. Since the tip came from out of town, maybe he wasn't looking at locals.

"I had the tour with Melissa and Karen, so I know the basics. Anything else you can tell me about the security system?"

"I've got stuff in there I never even told the Mirage about."

"You're checking employees?" I thought about Doug. Did he know? Was he one of them? I hoped not. But there was a lot of money to be made in Las Vegas, greed eased a lot of consciences.

She laughed. "Would you believe animal abuse complaints?"

Yeah, I would.

"We want to be sure that when we go to the D.A., the complaint's not going to go anywhere. In fact, those two get treated better than our homeless."

———

The tigers were in their den, both lazing around, only a few people and no kids banging on the glass. Everyone at the parade—and the fireworks.

I was crouched in the chute that connected their indoor den and the show one. The iron gate separating me from the tigers was down and pinned in place. No way it was going to be moved. No matter what happened. At the other end of the chute, their path to their indoor lair, was locked on the inside. In essence, I was locked in, but I was the one who could do the unlocking. The smell of the tigers was strong in their chute. Had they marked their territory?

There was another entrance to the den about twenty feet away, a door for maintenance, feeding, and all the people who cared for the tigers.

It came down to the fact that I had to trust someone on the inside to get into the chute. I swore her to secrecy. Tell no one, not even your bedmate. I played on her love for the tigers, her babies. She was momma. If she told, they would die, that's the way I put it to her, no finesse used. She had to be with me one hundred per cent otherwise I could be the tigers' next meal and looking at them blue eye to blue eye made me feel like the main course.

My gut instinct was usually right. Besides that, she was the one with the most to lose in this caper.

Melissa, the human mom. She was the only other person who knew what I was going to do. Not the head of Kendall Security Systems. Not Doug. Not even my bedmate.

I had boots on, a work jumpsuit that Melissa had outfitted me with, and covered with some sort of aroma that tigers weren't interested in and that negated my human smell.

Don't wear any cologne or hairspray, Melissa had warned me, or anything with a fragrance.

Crouched down, my calves whimpering, I wondered how long I could hold out. Stakeouts had never been my long suit. And I couldn't have a cigarette. Fireworks at 9. I was sure that's when they were going to make their move.

Move. There was a movement off to my right.

Herbie. Hose in hand.

He cleaned up at night? With the tigers in the den?

He placed the hose carefully over a concrete crag, then climbed to the top of the concrete mountain. It took me a moment to remember the built-in ladder on the other side.

What was he doing?

Bright light flooded the den.

What the hell!

The tigers got up and padded across the side of the pool toward me. Some signal for them? Daylight? Some sound? Now it was time for them to go into the night den?

They couldn't get through the grate that separated us. The smell of their bodies and their hot breath made me sweat. They were so close. The male and I were looking each other in the eye. Blue to blue.

They weren't cute anymore, not nose to nose, they were jungle animals, man eating tigers. He checked me out, his tongue licking the sides of his mouth.

Their smell drifting toward me on the draft.

I didn't move a muscle except my eyes. I couldn't even close my eyelids.

Sweat was coming out of every pore probably canceling out whatever that stuff was that Melissa had put on me. Bored, the tigers drifted away.

I tried to bring my heart rate down. Herbie was doing something. The light—a helicopter!

Why hadn't I foreseen that?

Cops never look up, that's a known fact. Hide anything above eye level and it's safe.

The tigers gathered around the foot of the ladder. Maybe Herbie wasn't about to descend all the way.

Grappling hooks. Two of them came down. One landed in the pool. The other conked Herbie on the head. He yelped. I saw blood.

Everything was perfectly clear in the light.

The tigers looked interested.

Herbie pulled out a gun.

No!

I scrabbled for the grate and yanked the pin, out along with my forty-five.

A tiger put his paws on the bottom rung.

Herbie shot.

I shot.

Herbie fell.

The tigers investigated.

I stood there shocked.

A heavy net dropped through the opening. I stared at it trying to compute what was going to happen.

Holy shit!

Herbie must have had a tranquilizer gun. They were going to airlift the tigers out after they'd been tranquilized.

Then I had another thought. How was Herbie, a hundred-

pound weakling, going to drag a six-hundred-pound unconscious tiger onto a net that was now dangling in the pool along
with the grappling hook?

I didn't have to wonder long.

The human-size door opened again, and in walked Godzilla.
Not quite but almost. He wore a grey sharkskin suit, tailored for
him. Who had shoulders like that? Bull head, hair slicked back.
This was not a guy I wanted to meet anywhere. He looked at me
and then at the tigers.

"What the fuck is going on? I heard two shots, they'd supposed to be out by now." He thought I was Herbie? Herbie was
out of sight, sprawled in a concrete ditch.

"Shoot them," he said. Did he think I had a tranquilizer gun?

One of the tigers growled. That was enough for me to step
back. A big step.

He had his own gun out and I saw him push off the safety and
aim for the tiger as it took another step forward.

Godzilla backed up.

In the background I heard the fireworks, overhead, the roar
of the helicopter.

Think! Think!

"Wait," I said, "I'll tranquilize them, you get out for a
minute and then we can haul them off. Everything's under
control."

"Shoot 'em now or I will."

"Boss wants them alive." I made a wild guess.

"Fuck it. The chopper can't stay there forever."

The tiger took another step. I thought he was just curious, but
then I wasn't the one it was advancing on. Godzilla must be
sweating. Probably didn't smell too good, or maybe he smelled
really good to the tiger.

Bam!

The human-size door hit the wall and there stood Melissa.

Oh, shit!

"I saw what happened. What's going on? What are you doing
to Rufus and Betty?"

Rufus and Betty?

"Who are you?" The human momma tiger. Even Godzilla
was about to back away from her, then he remembered the tiger.
The lady or the tiger?

"Rufus, back," she said in a commanding voice like she was talking to a puppy.

"You," this to Godzilla, "Put that gun away, he's not going to hurt you."

I glanced from the tiger to Melissa. Who would I believe?

Godzilla looked at her like she'd just dropped from Venus. He was trying to keep the gun on the tiger in front of him and Melissa behind him.

Then she saw me. "What are you doing?" she said to me. "You lied to me. You're the one who's going to steal the tigers."

Godzilla's head was swiveling between us. Good, he thought I was with him.

Or did Melissa really believe I was one of the bad guys?

"Get over there," he told her, gesturing to Rufus.

"Yes, of course, I'm moving slowly, because it's not a good idea to move quickly. Good, Rufus, come to mommy."

She was even with Godzilla now. The tiger moved toward her.

Godzilla was bringing his gun up, aiming at the tiger. I was sure he was about to fire off a round at it.

All of a sudden there was a hiss and Godzilla was screaming. Rufus backed up fast. Melissa was spraying Godzilla like he was a cockroach. I could smell the stuff—Mace.

Rufus didn't like the smell and was moving away.

Betty was taking playful—for a tiger—swats at Herbie who looked like he was moving.

I ran over and kicked Godzilla's gun away as he groveled on the cement.

"Put this on," Melissa shoved a mask at me and put one on herself. "I'm going to get Rufus and Betty out of here. Who's that? Herbie? What's he doing here? This place has more people than the viewing area." Her voice sounded strange through the mask.

"Call an ambulance," I said, my voice sounding weird also. "And Security."

"I am Security," she said, pulling out handcuffs and bending over the writhing Godzilla, "For Kendall Security Systems."

She wrestled with positioning his wrists. "Your daughter says Hi."

MISCAST

MICKI MARZ

"**B**ounced him on his head till his neck broke," Aram said.

"What a stupid sonofabitch," Eugene said.

"Don't worry about it," Aram said.

The overturned bucket on which Aram sat rocked, because the handle ends bent but did not flatten on the floor. He scooted the bucket nearer the wall and leaned his spine against a stud for better balance, then closed his eyes as if to saw some Zs.

Eugene did worry about it. He said, "Bo had better get his ass in gear or *he's* gonna be meat hangin' on the rack hisself one o' these days, go around actin' like that."

"Shuddup, Eugene," Aram said, like a man mumbling in his dreams.

"Shuddup yourself, Armpit."

Jim Daniels walked around the two men and stopped a few feet from the window with the yellow coating bubbled up and cracked. Behind it, a flit of wings became a fast shadow and then was gone. Jim rotated his head to give the chubby one, Eugene, that look that would catch a shirt afire. "You're it, Eugene. You're gonna kill him."

"Not *me!* No way. No *fuckin'* way. I ain't killin' him." He pushed off from a short file cabinet on which he had been perched. "I ain't killed nobody in my whole damn life and I ain't gonna start now."

Jim looked through a peeled portion of the coated window again and said, "Your choice."

And poor Eugene knew right then that if he didn't give in to Jimmy D this time he'd have to the next. That, or Jimmy D would mark him for doom down the road. You were either with Jimmy or ag'in him. Eugene broke out in a cool sweat in the shed that served as an office for the auto salvage yard Jimmy D owned on the edge of Henderson. The thermometer outside read 98 degrees.

It wasn't Bo, the nutcase who bounced the life out of an enemy, that Jim Daniels had it in for. This month, anyway. It was an actor kid from L.A.

Jimmy opened the door of his shed-office and went to check on the new hire he had tasked with moving General Motors cars to a different spot in the yard, to the middle section instead of the end. He wanted the Jap cars at the back of the yard. While he strung a yellow line of plastic tape to demarcate the end of where the ShitZu-Itzi-Sans should go, he cast a gaze at the mesquite stand by the culvert this side of the south razorwire fence. Things there were still where they should be, no man or animal appearing to have worked the ground.

He approved the workman's work so far and went on down the rows, mentally taking inventory. All the while, that actor squirt kept popping up in his mind, for Jim D was a bitter man. He didn't start out that way, but it's what the world made of him, is what he told his latest ex-wife. He even knew he was *obsessing* over that actor dumbo, but he learned a long time ago that he couldn't fight it when something like that came over him, so he might as well make his plans.

Pinhead thought he was such hot steamin' shit. Even that attitude Jimmy would have been able to overlook, if the clown didn't have to go and shit on Jimmy's doorstep. No, the shrimp took something from him, and that was not going to go unpunished. In a softer second, Jim thought maybe he wouldn't kill him. Just mess him up. Yeah, that's the ticket. See how many casting directors would slot him for a show *then*, buddy.

The actor entered his life one late afternoon when he and Aram and Eugene were coming off the water at Lake Mead, at a spot about fifty miles north of Vegas. Jimmy didn't like talking away no prize, but the day had been restful, and at that hour he liked seeing the lake form a blue hole in its center as the ripples at the edges increased. He liked seeing how the reeds turned a deeper green on the underside as a stronger wind laid them over. He enjoyed the ring of mountains turning rose at top and purple at the bottom with the sun's slow going down.

Aram was driving. Eugene started in with his harmonica. Jimmy was cool about it all until the notes called up that picture again of how his wife looked the day she told him their account was dry and so was she, goodbye.

Jimmy was about to knock that bar of metal out of Eugene's hand when Aram called their attention to a pair with their truck high-centered on a boulder. Dumb shits did it while hauling out their boat. Nice boat, too. Okay, thanks, thanks, all around when the rescue job got done. Now get the fuck out o' my territory, dorko.

But Jimmy didn't have that feeling right then. No, it was not until the next afternoon when the emotion formed itself into a thing that could be spoken, when they again returned from the lake with only a couple of stripers, no bluegill, no trout, no catfish. Again they met up with the actor and his woman, this time in Overton, thirteen or so miles from his fishing spot. At first it was just disdain for dumbfuck's manner, his look, his too-happy take on the world. Take *this,* suckah, was the unarticulated feeling in Jimmy then. The three were eating hamburgers in the Red Rooster when they saw the actor again. Mark Mandelkorn was his name. He came in with his twig of a girlfriend and commenced to brag about what a great angler he was. Three sheets to the wind after only a couple of beers, when he starts giving a fishing lesson. Shit.

"Pretend you have a rock in your left armpit," the twerp told everyone. "The rock keeps your arm in the proper position, preventing backlash, for better control of your cast." Dumbfuck Eugene was taking it all in like a girl. Meanwhile, the actor-dork continued to hold forth: "Your bait held in your right hand should be even with the reel, so when you make the pitch the bait won't come down like a stone and hit the fish on the head."

Who'd this L.A. crud think he was? Make it worse, Pauline, the bartender, who was at least a hard 50, posed her body in a way so Jim knew she was flirting with Mr. Ass-a-minute, and that made him sick.

The moron said, "I like your sign, Pauline."

"What sign would that be?" She smiled and walked around to

the jukebox, casting a glance back at the girlfriend, preparing to slip in a coin.

"That one." The actor read from a placard:

There ain't no town drunk here!
We all take turns.

"Oh yeah. I don't hardly see it no more."

"And I'll bet you're about to play my favorite song there, hon, aren't ya?"

"Now what song would that be?"

"My favorite: 'I Been Roped and Thrown by Jesus in the Holy Ghost Corral'? Got that one in there, Pauline?"

But the topper was when the prick and his snatch made to leave. The better part of two hours Jim had been dropping quarters in the slot machine nearest his stool; he could just lean to the side and plunk it. He'd turn back before the spinners even stopped, casual-like, as if winning or losing were the same thing.

Then fuckmouth up and says, "Tiff, go see if you can fix that machine for the man."

One quarter. One quarter, and the machine coughs 4,000 of them out for her. Or flashes the sign, same thing. For him. The actor.

Jimmy D was an unhappy man. He snagged no fish that day, he, a damned good fisherman, and some chump-fag actor walks off with his dough.

———————

Tiffany hadn't drunk anything but soda that evening, so she was at the wheel pulling the boat back to Vegas, where it was rented from a friend for a few days. She said to Mark, "Jeez, honey, I wish you wouldn't get so loaded."

"I wasn't that loaded."

"You are."

"Nah. I could drive."

"And I could walk the moon."

"Well, listen. Are you happy? Are you happy, huh? Girl just

won herself a thousand bucks. A thousand bucks! Man. Is the girl happy, huh? Happy?" He tickled her where her shirt spared the waistband of her jeans. She wagged her head in assent and gave off with a grin that said, "It'll do."

_____

Aram didn't like looking at the pockmarks in Eugene's face on his right side, where they were more volcanic than on the left. Therefore, Aram always chose to drive. Coming away from the Red Rooster, the three were silent. Eugene's harmonica was in the hip pocket that didn't hold the can of Red Devil snuff.

Jimmy stared straight ahead as if on the lookout for wild burros that sometimes cross the road like part of a hill broke off and slid. Now and then, Aram shot a glance Jimmy's way to see if he could detect how bad a mood he had been put into by that girl winning at the juke.

Before turning to Jimmy, Eugene poked Aram with his elbow, winked, and then said, "I got it figgered now, pal. Only reason you didn't get lucky today is your pole's too short." Eugene entertained himself with his own hearty laughs. Jimmy said nothing, though there was a twitch at the back of his jaw. So Eugene grew more thoughtful. This time he said, "That guy going on about how anglin' is an art? I bet you didn't know anglin' is an art, the none of us did, did we? Who-o-ee!"

Jimmy said to the windshield: "I don't need no pussy lessons outta some Jew-boy from L.A."

Eugene replied, "No, we don't need none o' that. Nope," and rode silent.

_____

When Tiffany came back into the hotel room from a workout in the downstairs gym, she found Mark shaving. She said, "Those guys last night? They sure gave me the creeps."

"What for? I didn't see anything wrong with them." She looked sweet, a little bit damp for her effort. Yesterday's outing had toasted Tiffany to a honey shade. Her light-brown hair held wheat-colored stripes, all of it tied up on top of her head now in a dust-mop ponytail.

She frowned and said, "I hope we don't see them again." She made him recall how Pauline followed them outside, saying to no one in particular, "I got to get some cigarettes from my car."

Though it had cooled down a lot, Tiffany still had to wrap a Kleenex around the car door handle to open it. Mark opened his door then, and the two stood letting the heat out, looking off into the distance where the jagged, treeless mountains were a flat rust color coated with milky haze. At the end of the street, heat waves still shimmied. In the other direction, a bunch of cars lined up at the Inside Scoop, the ice cream parlor, even though near dinnertime.

Pauline came up and said, "Just a word of advice." Her skin was of a grayish hue and the pores of her forehead were tiny tattoos. Sunlight fired the fine hairs on her upper lip and the sturdier ones along her jaw. She shaded her eyes and said, "I'd watch my step with Jim Daniels and that bunch."

Mark said, "They seem all right to me. Good guys, matter of fact."

"You're not from around here. But in case you're thinking of staying a few days, just so you know, Moapa Valley police have been looking at Jimmy for a murder about two months ago."

"A murder?" Tiffany said. "That man who helped us out at the lake?"

Pauline said, "I'm saying a stranger got caught out in a flash flood, stranded to the axles. Somebody saw them three helping him out there, too, just like y'all. Next time they saw the fella, turkey buzzards picked him pretty much to pieces. His truck was stripped, and his family said his blackjack winnings was gone. Don't say I didn't warn you."

As Pauline stepped away, Tiffany turned her shoulders as if to watch a passing car and rolled her eyes for Mark's benefit.

"Thanks for the tip," Mark said to the woman. "Take it easy now."

Today, however, Tiffany apparently had second thoughts. She said, "Honey, I know you came up here to fish, but could we *not* go back to the lake, just stay in town and do the slots and shows? I mean, I know gambling you can take or leave, but look what I won last night, and I don't see you complaining. You said you wanted to see those cars. . . ."

"The vintage automobiles, yes."

"What car was it you said you wanted to see?"

"Duesy," he said. "A perfect specimen among the eight hundred cars at the Imperial Palace Hotel. Ever hear someone say 'It's a doozie?' Means something superb, something you wouldn't believe. From *Duesenberg*, one beautiful Roadster made in the late twenties. Howard Hughes and Wayne Newton used to own the one that's in the collection now."

"Somehow I can't see those two together," Tiffany said, teasing.

"Sure, it would seat them and Elvis and his ham sandwiches too."

"So we can stay?"

"How 'bout we compromise. Two days in town, one more on he lake. You first."

"Oh, good," she said. And Mark knew she was thinking naybe he'll change his mind about that last day too.

He said, "So, are you going to win us a million dollars? What would you do with a million dollars, sweetheart?"

Without a pause, she said, "Fix Grandma."

"Fix what?"

"My grandma is the sweetest, gentlest, kindest person in the world. She scrubbed other people's clothes and washed their dishes and took care of their kids when she had four boys of her own to do for. Now she's the one needs care and tending."

"But she's *in* a nursing home, isn't she?" He hadn't been going with Tiffany long. He didn't have that much of a grip on her family.

Tiffany answered, "And she doesn't remember her name."

"Baby, you can't fix that," Mark said. "Even Mrs. Reagan couldn't fix that. A whole president on her hands, and she couldn't fix that."

"It's my money. I'll do what I want," Tiffany said. She went over to the small fridge in the room and pulled out a mocha milk.

Mark was right there behind her when she turned around. He took the bottle from her so he could open it and help her not ruin her nails. "I thought we were a team," he said. "We move as one."

"My money is your money then?" she asked. "My money,

that I win fair and square on the slot machines, you not dropping any coin?"

"If I won, I'd let *you* have half. Come on."

"But you aren't even *going* to win, because you don't really want to play, you want to go be sleeping with the fishies, or whatever."

"Just let me finish shaving, get dressed, we'll go. Hey, you know what? C'mere."

He held out his arms, and she came to him with her fists balled up under her chin, as if in protection or supplication.

Tiffany said, "Know what? If I won a million dollars? I mean, what if? Like, who would've thought I'd even win a thousand? Well, I'd first want to give Grandma something to walk up and down the halls with. A teddy bear."

"Uh, we don't have to win a million dollars for that. Seems manageable, you know, without winning the big one."

"But see, the patients in those hospitals, they're all so bewildered. They don't know where they are but they do know something's not right. The ladies carry empty purses around. That's some comfort to them, a purse. They can still recognize a purse. Some of them have soft toys, but they go missing."

"Go missing."

"Yes, well, maybe staff takes them home to their little kids, who knows? I mean, those people are paid less than minimum wage, so you might expect it. Or maybe five stuffed animals wind up in one room, one of the women thinking they're all hers. Sometimes staff puts the toys up high so the patients won't get them, won't squabble, but can only look at them, not reach them, and that's terrible to me. What if I bought dozens and dozens and kept replacing them? Like each week, boom, here's your twenty new teddy bears. Go give them to the ladies. Dozens of clean, fresh teddy bears."

"Ah, honey . . ."

"You laugh. But see, I've been doing pricing. I'd like to buy some big soft rag dolls, too, that I saw. They stand about three feet high. They sell them at truck stops. I saw one at the truck stop in Jean, when we stopped for gas."

"I thought you were looking at Indian jewelry."

"Mostly these, because I saw them first in Barstow when we

stopped to get something to drink. Guess what? They're only ten dollars, and they're, like, huge. I wrote down the name of the manufacturer. I could call, order up a ton. Or some teddy bears. See, I can get them for six or seven dollars, but they're the bigger ones, the ones that don't sell out at Christmastime or Valentine's Day. You go in and ask the store manager for a discount. He'd as soon sell them to you for six dollars, even if they normally go for fourteen, than bother sending them back or keeping them around gathering dust till summertime. I already asked this one guy, at Albertson's, the manager, and that's what he said."

Beautiful little thing, a little on the too-small size, Mark was thinking while he finished up at the mirror. Win scads of money, he'd feed her cheesecake till the cows came home. He said, "Whatever you want is all right with me, Tiff," and saw that smile come back in her eyes. He turned on the shower, and there she was, in the room with him, unbuttoning her jeans. She challenged him with what he could do with his Duesy. At first he answered like a straight-man: "Drive it down Sunset, Hollywood and Vine. Attract an agent. Next step, I'm a famous actor, just from that one serendipitous event."

"Fool."

"That's why you lub me, idn't it, baby? I am your lubbin' fool."

"Well, serendipitous your Duesy into *this*, fool," she said.

In the lobby of the hotel later, they did stop at a slot machine, and while Tiffany plied her luck once more, Mark obtained and delivered soft-serve ice cream and the news that there was a million-dollar jackpot waiting for her at a number of places around town. "Well," Tiffany said, a light in her eyes, "pick one."

"Let's go to Terribles. With a name like that, it's got to be good. Isn't that what the Smucker's ad used to say?"

"If you say so."

He said, "It's got what they call a progressive Triple-Seven Millionaire Jackpot. It's not on the Strip, though. It's north of town."

"Nah, nah, nah, nah. You stuck me in this rinky-dink hotel on the outskirts already. Henderson? Where in hell is that? I want to go where the action is."

"I thought I just gave you some of that."

"My boots are itchin' to go walkin', baby. I feel it in my bones. I am a winnah tonight!"

Damned if she wasn't.

Damned if the girl didn't have a streak of gold built right into her. Make that not precisely 1 million, but 1.83 million. His baby did it! She broke the bank. She had faith. She was anointed.

Mark told her, at four in the morning after the first hullabaloo celebrations were done with, after the first meeting with the casino bigwigs had vouchsafed the truth of it all, after the phone calls to their loved ones, the sex, the promises, the spoken dreams, the tears and spasms of giggles, Mark told her, "Baby, I know you are not likely to believe this after what happened, but if you could erase what all went down tonight, erase the jackpot, put us back in L.A., in that Tujunga bungalow we found together, both of us slinging dishes and searching for gigs, I would just have to ask you to be my wife. You are the one. I knew it from the start."

"You bullshitter."

"You adorable, perfect, glorious Hepburn, you."

"You only say it 'cause it's true," Tiffany said.

They had taken ten thousand dollars cash and went back to the cheap hotel in Henderson that first night and slept upon it, despite the entreaties of the staff at Terribles to stay in one of the premier suites. Mark and Tiffany promised they'd come back later, although he didn't really know in which splendid hut they would install themselves. Now Mark got up from the bed, went to the closet, and brought out a white teddy bear the size a grandma might be. He said, "Happy Millions, baby. It's only a start."

He couldn't believe it. He told the new guy not to bother beyond the yellow tape. Now there he was, zipping up after taking a leak by the mesquite. "Fred! What the hell you doin' back there?"

Fred was a rugged old ex-trucker, maybe sixty, sixty-five. He walked like he had stickers in his shoes. When he came up to Jimmy D, he said, "Got you a stinker back there," and held his pale blue eyes on him a while before he spit to the side. "I'd cover that up with a load of dirt, I was you, before you lay down more tin."

"Come on back to the office," Jim D said.

There he peeled off a hundred and gave it to Fred and said, "Thanks for your work. I'll give you a ring if I need you some more."

"A pleasure workin' for you, Mr. Daniels."

The air conditioner louvers were aimed right down on Jimmy when he called Aram. "Get Bo to call me, pronto."

"He ain't on my dance card, Jimmy. I don't know where to—"

"Raghead, get Bo to call me to-fuckin'-day, or you'll be eatin' your own balls for breakfast, dig? *Dig?*"

Noon, Ron Bodella called. "I know I owe ya," he told Jim.

"Listen and listen to me carefully," Jim said. "Your product is stinking. You did a piss-poor job in covering it up, Shit-for-brains."

"I put lye on it. That shouldn'ta—"

"Did I tell you to listen? Did I?"

The line was silent.

"Your assignment, asshole, is to get you two skunks. I don't care how, I don't care where, I don't want questions, I don't want explanations, I don't want delays. I want two skunks. Dead or alive. You put them out on that heap . . . no. Back up. I'm going to dump a load of scrap there, but I want them skunks out by the trees like they been pests and I had to kill 'em. I want them there by tonight. That's it. Over and out."

He hung up the phone, loosened his shirt, rose from his desk and stood right in front of the blowing airstream and said, "Shit for brains. All of 'em. Shit for brains." But then his eyes took on the smile his lips barely formed.

Tiffany cruised the penthouse suite. "How can people live like this?" she asked Mark.

"They do, all over the world. Not just for a day, not just for a night."

"Where does all the money come from?"

"Only the Shadow knows."

She lay down on the king-sized bed and said, "I mean really."

"I don't know, doll. It's there, right under us poor slobs' faces, but it's invisible to us. You don't really see what's so far above your station you can't imagine."

"I keep seeing all the *poor* people in the newscasts. Flood victims. Starving Africans. Neglected kids." She lay on the bed in her white sundress with the lavender swirls. Spread around her were sheaves of green, like brittle leaves from an exotic tree. The teddy bear sat in a white wicker chair on a cushion of deep-green velvet and gazed out at the horizon thick with yellow smog.

Mark said, "It's time for me to go, hon. I can get in maybe five hours on the water, then I'm done."

"Go. Go," she said. "Bring back a mermaid, if you like. I'm napping, and if this is only a dream I'll soon find out."

He walked over and kissed her warmly on the lips, and said, "What good's a mermaid to me when I've got the whole enchilada?"

"Animal," she murmured, and shut her eyes. Then she opened them as he was going out the door, and added, "Mark? You're not going out there by yourself, are you? You said Tommy would go along?"

"Sure. Then he can take his boat back when we're done, drop me off here, or, shoot, guess what? I got a rich girlfriend. I bet she'd pay for a cab."

———

Jimmy couldn't fuckin' believe it. Again. There they were! That actor shit. That twat shit! On the friggin' *front page*!

The headline again. He stared at it. The caption. The photo itself. It was them, that pair from the lake. She, in a white dress with leetle-bitty strings holding it up. Snip, snip, take it down, but there'd be nothin' under it. The guy, MarkMouth, holding up one corner of a giant check that had *1.83 Million* written on it. What the holy fuck was this? Somebody playin' tricks on him? He tasted something in his mouth like after the dry heaves, like years ago when he was still a drinker and he puked a dozen times with nothing finally coming up but the taste. He felt the inside of his nose prickle. He thought, for a moment, he would cry.

Out of the corner of his eye, he saw a frumpy woman in a cop uniform and a man he recognized as the Moapa County Sheriff sitting at a table two away from his in the restaurant. What the hell? The sheriff raised a finger at him, as in greeting, and nodded. Then he rose and came over to Jimmy's table.

"Howdy."

"Howdy back."

"I'm Sheriff Thompson."

"I seen you around the Lake."

"You wouldn't happen to know anything about a fella named Dean Aspey, would you? Fella got killed over there around Red Rock? You probably read about it in the papers." He put a finger on the newspaper laying on the table.

"What are you talkin' about, Sheriff? I wouldn't know anything about that. Why would you come and talk to me about it?" He met the eyes of the frumpy cop with a name tag that read just JONES.

"Well," the sheriff said, "this fella mighta been the same fella you and your friends mighta helped out on the roadside, according to someone who seemed to know."

"I don't mean to sound rude, sir, but why don't you go back out to that someone and ask some more questions, because I surely do not know to which you refer, and I am just taking me a break here. I run a busy business, and I don't have a lot of time for chit-chat."

"Thank you, Mr. Daniels. I may just be calling on you again sometime." The sheriff turned, but then he eased back and said, "I b'lieve I read in the papuhs your bidness was sufferin' some, didn't I? You file for bankruptcy protection, sumpin' like that?"

"Sheriff," Jim Daniels said, "I'm sure you don't discuss your personal finances in public. Why would you think that I would be so inclined? Have a nice day." He gave Jones a look, dumber than a stump she appeared to be, probably Polish or Russian by the look of her, who took a common name. He rummaged in his pocket for his roll of bills while setting his eyes back on that blasted photo with the two grinning punkin-heads and the fat casino cats beside. Dolts, them two, who never earned an honest buck in their lives.

———

It wasn't the blood on the walls that set investigators back on their heels. Red-patterned walls they'd seen before. It wasn't even the blood on the money. The money, well, you have to admit it, the money was more eye-catching than the mayhem, given the circumstance. Guessing, one could say there might have been a couple hundred grand on the bed. Piles of it. Pillows of it. In the center there was about a yard of blood-soaked bills, but so what? Throw the notes in the washer: Good as new.

No, it was something else that sent chills down the spine. A teddy bear. A big, happy-faced, cuddly, white, blood-soaked teddy bear, lying off to the side, dead as can be.

———

"You were supposed to find him, that's *all*," Jimmy said.

"We did find him. Jeez!"

"Don't you jeez me!"

"Jimmy," Eugene said, "we went to the casino like you said. We knock on the door to their room. She recognized me. Took her a sec, but she recognized me. She opens the door, says, 'Something happen to Mark?' "

"Not *yet*, we're thinkin'," Aram said.

"*You* don't think. You do not think," Jimmy said.

"Sorry."

"You killed her. Right there in the effing casino, you kill her."

"No we didn't," Eugene said.

Jim Daniels looked at him stupidly. Eugene had red all over his shirt, and some on his pants, the biggest portion soaked onto his torso, only partially hidden by his black windbreaker. It was night, and they were outside the office-shed, the light from inside cutting a shaft to where they stood, and the moon, almost a full moon, thrusting its brightness across the geometric patterns of the junkyard and over the features of the men so that the two looked like shades of themselves. "And that is . . . what?" Jimmy asked, pointing to Eugene's chest. "Paint bullets?"

"She fought like a sonofabitch," Aram said. He had scratches on his face dragging down to his collar bone. A black blob was coming out his nose.

"Wipe your nose. Jesus," Jimmy said.

Aram wiped it on his sleeve, looked at it, wiped again. "She punched me. I smacked her hard, but she got in a good punch before that. It was all I could do not to shove my fist down her throat."

Eugene stepped up to Jimmy, his hands hooked in his rear pockets, fear and amazement in his voice. "Jimmy, she took out Bo. Big Bo. She took him out, swear to God."

"What are you telling me?"

Now he heard it: thumping, banging, the sounds like anchors hitting rock under water. Only they were coming from the bed of the truck.

"You got him in there too?"

"Who? Bo? No, I told you," Eugene said. "She—" He stopped himself. Jimmy could tell he didn't want to say it, whatever it was. Eugene stepped backwards so he could utter it. "She broke away from us. Bo come in. I know you didn't tell us to use him, but we figured we needed the three of us if we was going to handle the two of *them* in a crowded place. Don't get mad, Jimmy. It shoulda worked. We just didn't figure on her being all that."

Aram was shaking his head in agreement, an imploring look in his eyes, one that Jimmy had not seen before. He said, "Here's how it went down. She jumps on the bed, starts throwing money around, saying, 'Here, here, take it, just take it and get outta here!' Bo rushes her. She jumps off, takes this thing off a table, I don't know what it was, and whams the shit out of him. He's bald, you know, it cracks him on the skull and he spurts like a fountain. Goes down on his knees in the middle of the bed. I mean, there is money all over the place, and he's a-wailin'. I thought the next-door neighbors would come in. I say shut the fuck up, don't be a fuggin' baby. She up and whams him again, on the fingers covering his head, his ear, man, his eyebrow. It about shook me up. Like a goddamned Tasmanian devil. Bo's a big guy, and he was whinin' like a puppy dog."

"Where is he?"

"Bo?"

"The Easter Bunny, you fuck." Jim looked back and forth at them. If it wasn't so serious, he'd laugh. Like teenagers caught during their first burgle, their minds racing to see which lie would be believed.

At last Aram said, "Bo went off the balcony. Down to the parkin' lot. He thought the door was the door—the way out, I mean. He couldn't see, with what she did to him. He ran right into Eugene here. Pepper in her eyes is not too good for her, way I see it. She's got to be hurt before it's over, know what I mean? It's only right."

Inside the office, Jimmy took a spare shirt off the hook behind the door and threw it at Eugene. He pointed a finger at Aram and said, "You. Sit. Cool your heels. Shut your mouth."

"I know you want to know, and we didn't tell you yet," Eugene said as he was delicately removing his shirt to put in the paper bag Jimmy set out. He was using a tone of voice to curry favor with the angry man before him, while Jimmy looked at him with a portion of made-up hatred in his eyes. Eugene said, "The guy wasn't there. She, that spitfahr, she did the whole thing herself. We don't know where that actor guy is. Honest Injun. We did, we'd have him by the ears, and you know that, Jimmy, you do."

———

Mark got drunk again that night. Only a little drunk, though. It felt good. He could release from his former—*former,* Mom— money woes in Hollywood, as well as the tensions of having hours ago become the kept man of a very rich woman. His friend took him to his house and fed him caffeine, and they reminisced about the New York days when Tommy himself had aspirations for the screen. Now Tommy ran a software company producing modules to support military satellite systems, and he confessed that he was gay, and was so happy now that he had what seemed to be an endless string of beauties in this glamorous town. He waved ta-ta to Mark at the Puerto de Moros Hotel and Casino, and zoomed off in his Porsche, and Mark looked after him with some little sadness, this man the same man he knew before his confession and yet not the same.

When Mark tried to go to the penthouse, the elevator was blocked. When he gave up trying and inquired and got an answer, he felt the blood leave his face and his knees give ever so slightly as if some invisible hand had playfully karate-chopped him there.

———————

Sheriff Thompson spoke to Mark by phone, but the Las Vegas police spoke to him in person for nigh onto two hours. Only because one of the officers let slip Sheriff Thompson's name and suspicions was Mark able to reach out to him at all. At two o'clock in the morning, though.

The sheriff said he would meet with Mark first thing tomorrow. Say nine o'clock for sure; he'd meet Mark at the casino. Mark liked the man's tone, his cooperation. But what Mark liked most of all was that the man did not hold back the way some officers—at least in the movies—do. The sheriff, in his quiet, sleep-drugged voice, named a suspect; no, a whole party, after Mark related the encounters he'd had with anyone since arriving in Nevada. Then Mark said, his mouth as dry as alkali, "My girlfriend is missing, Sheriff." You'd think that news would rouse the sheriff further. All the sheriff advised, however, was that he had full confidence that city police would be surveiling the business owned by Jim Daniels if he was in the least under suspicion, and that most abductees, if that was what she was, especially now with her new-found fortunes, were brought home safe and sound.

———————

Blessed be the light. The light be damned! Too much light! Light, it seemed, as bright as stage lights almost.

Vegas, The City That Never Sleeps, had a military surplus store that stayed open round the clock. It carried, in front, all kinds of dollar items, the army/navy gear attended to by customers mostly in the daytime, the dollar items purchased by the ragtags at night. But Mark glommed onto a camo coverall for sixteen bucks and camo face paint and an MP's baton. He also came away with a U.S. Army Ranger knife, serrated, evil-looking, satisfying in a way an actor who was only acting could never know.

His heart tore when he thought of Tiffany and anyone touching her, hurting her, doing damage to that perfect, sweet, precious heart. He would beg, if he could, any supernal power to *not* let it be so, if only he believed, but it was himself he had to look to, and he would not be conquered, no.

Now, stationed in the auto-salvage yard, he was Rambo. He was Schwarzenegger. He was Fairbanks and Ty Power and Quinn. Cagney and little-Mafioso Edward G. Robinson; and the leanest, meanest, unforgiving monster short of the Werewolf of London. Bob Swagger, the guy in the Stephen Hunter books: Yes, he was Swagger, the man of deadly control.

He was under the witness of moonlight, and he would take them down!

———

Peering into the cracks of the coated office windows, he saw that Jim and the two flunkies weren't there. A smell about the shed that he couldn't name set him to more animal stealth than even before.

He heard voices, tuned to them. Moving toward them, he wondered how he himself would not be heard, boots cracking the surface of the dry earth.

A pile of yellow tape was coiled by a rod used for a stake at the left. To the right of the picture, which could have had a frame, sat a bulldozer, inert, gleaming dully in the moonlight. The three men were about the same height, but Mark could identify by heft the one on the eastern end as Eugene, and then Aram by his monotone. "It'll fit two," Aram said.

A beat, then Jim D said, "May have to fit more than that."

"Pee-yew, it stanks," Eugene said. "That's nasty, I mean nasty."

Mark detested the air, the air he breathed the same as those beings did, whether it was putrid or not, but the stench made it all the more pernicious, generating the first turn of fear he'd felt so far.

The men started on their way back. Aram said to Jimmy, "One thing. I want you to know I's the one who clocked her. Cowboy here was staring off the balcony like a pure idiot. You think you could have yanked Bo back, dummy, by looking over like that?" Now to Jim again: "She'd have shoved him over too, I swear, if I was not on my toes."

"Congratu-fuckin'-lations, Twinkle Toes," Jimmy said. "You're both fuckups, so quit shootin' your faces."

"Hm," Aram said, halting in his stride. "She quit makin' noise. Wonder why."

Eugene said, "I can hear her now."

Mark, hunched down by a Toyota SUV with its top half-sheared off, knew they meant Tiffany, even with so little to go on. She was alive, then!

Jimmy said, "Get her out."

They were so close now. Mark wanted them *now*!

Eugene, on the end of the row of men closest to Mark, went down by the force of the MP baton against his collar bone. *Crack!* He screamed in agony, collapsed, rolled, and appeared to be paralyzed, still moaning.

The two others scattered, Jim running down the aisle for the office. Aram hustled behind a car, but he couldn't escape Mark's sight. "Who the hell is it?" Aram yelled.

Mark closed on him and felt the wind of a thrown object blow by. The rat scampered. Again, the rat called out: "It's you. Come get me, cocksuckah! See what you're made of." He dared to move out from the shadows, up against a wimp actor who had got lucky once. He moved on him with a bar of some kind, some detritus with length and weight, and it did catch Mark's baton and send it flying. Aram swung again. Mark dodged, ran two cars down the aisle, ripped an antenna off its rusted base, yanked on it to see if it would extend. Two inches. Two inches more was what he had, and two inches more is what he used. As Aram swung the next time, the moonlight showed a softened pleasure in Aram's face as if the deed was done, the act was closed, the curtain down. But illusion is what the game is about, asshole, is what Mark felt as he whipped the antenna across his assailant's face. "Ya!" Aram exclaimed, and dropped the rod or post or whatever it was that clamored noisily over the hood of a car.

Mark whipped again and again, yet Aram managed to rise and run, swearing death threats and torture unimaginable upon Mark when the time would come.

Now Mark heard the sounds from afar, the "ummmming" and the clunking, and knew it was Tiffany, bound or buried or both, somewhere. His adrenaline kicked into even higher gear to pursue his prey: Aram, slipping again into the shadows as he zigzagged through the yard. A spotlight from atop the office pinned Mark, blinding him before he could turn away. He ducked behind a car carcass, blinking residual blots away.

Then all was quiet, and Mark realized he'd lost his foe. Worse, Mark had dropped—when?—the stainless-steel antenna whip. He still had the Ranger. His hearing was tuned to what had to be its finest. Every whisper of wind, every far-off passage of a wheeled object, the creak in the power lines as they rocked in the breeze, was claimed. Aram could not take him by surprise. The knife he held was at the ready, out of its holster, gripped sideways for slashing, as he had seen it done in the action films.

———

"Oo-oo-oo-oo." Jimmy D spoke quietly in her ear. "Hop along, Little Miss Hopalong Cassidy. Or shuffle, if you please. Hurry! Hurry, or it will be worse for your Markie boy."

———

That, too, Mark heard, though not distinctly. But he knew that Jimmy had moved her. She was up. Moving. Life!

Jimmy had to be taking her to the shed because there was no other structure around. He'd get to her. Think Swagger. Swagger would not go off half-cocked, expose himself. Take out Aram first. Aram on a Stick: take-out. Jesus, he was getting looney and he knew it.

Up popped the head, as if on cue. Checking. Aram didn't see Mark. Didn't mark the Mark.

A wheel-cover leaning against a Caddy caught Mark's eye. He dashed for it. Aram would hear the thumping feet. Mark couldn't help that. All the better. When his opponent rounded a pickup, Mark was ready. Three minor belts earned in Tae Kwan Do while in acting school is all Mark had, but hey, he'd always been a good student and a hardy kid. He didn't even see Aram's head. It was the shoulders he saw reflected in the windshield of a vehicle, but that was all he needed. He used the hubcap as a heavyweight Frisbee as Aram lurched into the space. The hubcap struck him hard on the temple, and he went down. Straight down; no motion in the mound.

———

Funny how you can have all this going on, Mark thought, and balance so many images in your mind. I see the cops who aren't here to help me but should be. I see the boat, the way it cut through the sun's reflection on the surface water. I see myself, decked out in camo gear, and I am *proud*! Proud to be a Marine, or what the devil it is they say. Man, where's a casting maven when you need one?

———

"You're thinking I'm a rotten guy," Jimmy D told his captive. "I know you do. But, dear, I am a misunderstood guy. Really. Don't believe?" He started laughing. "Neither do I!"

"But see? Am I hurting you? No. I'm letting you sit, like a person, not a bag. Now, I can't unbind your feet because I heard what a hellion you are. I can't unbind your wrists, 'cause, well . . . you know."

The single overhead light inside was off. The spotlight he had turned on Mark only for that one moment was out. Now it was only his role to wait. Wait for The Mark to come. "Daddy, are we there yet?" he said, grinning.

———

Mark took his time. Ten minutes. Fifteen. He'd peeked inside. Black, of course. But Mark had played a blind man once. He'd learned about echolation, cramming for the part, and he knew he could enter, go anywhere, without sight, and *know* without seeing; *feel*, on his face the things which surrounded him.

When Mark turned the door handle and opened the door, he heard Tiffany going "Mmm-mmm," in warning. He said, "Shhhhh."

Jimmy D, the Evil One, said nothing, nothing at all. Mark held up a car mat with a waist, the shape of a man. Jim Daniels let go a round. *Blam!* God, it was loud! Tiffany screamed behind her tape.

Blam! Blam!

Instantly Mark moved in, knowing that Jimmy D would himself be sight-impaired from the flare where the cylinder shot out a circle of flame upon firing.

Mark wrist-flicked the Ranger into Jim D where he stood prepared to fire again. The gun barrel pointed at the floor, the shoulders sagged, and the whole weight of the man collapsed, the knife deep in his chest by the heart. The eyes, when Mark stood over him, shone like eggwhites without a yolk to surround.

Parts, anyone? It took a couple of months for the noise of the incident to settle enough so that Mark's agent—and Tiffany's—could sort through the offers and select the best ones. There were parts, all right. There were promises. There were contracts now, signed.

Tiffany could take them or leave them, she said. But she took them. Mark had his hands full too, but he shifted the obligations handily to spare the time for the wedding plans. No helicopters, gentlemen, please. But you can take as many pix of his replica-kit Dusey as you want, boys.

LIGHTNING RIDER

RICK MOFINA

Jessie Scout tightened her grip on the wheel of the armored car when she spotted her crew members, Gask and Perez, emerging from the casino lobby. Their canvas bags were now empty of cash. Another delivery done.

Relax, she told herself.

Her utility belt and the holster cradling her Glock gave a leathery squeak as she ran a perimeter check of the mirrors around their truck. All clear. *Wait.* A stranger was getting way too close to her.

"Bobby? Hey Bob, check this out, buddy!" A man laughed.

Scout picked them up, distorted on the driver's side convex mirror. A couple of all-night rollers. White guys. Forties. Midwesterners. Mid-management. Suburban. Wife and kids back home. Skip the buffet, Skippy. Bloody Marys for breakfast. Riding higher than the morning desert sun. *Don't come near the truck. Don't you dare.*

"Hey Bob. Get this." The first one is reaching into his pocket.

Scout's right hand brushed the butt of her Glock. Her two crew members were still far off on her right side. They can't see the guy or the flash of metal in his hand. He's *too* close.

"What's the pay off if I play a dollar here? Ha-ha."

He starts to fiddle with a gunport. Jerk. Scout spanks the horn. He recoils, his reddening face contorting in anger aimed up at her as he passes by the front of the truck, hands up, palms open.

"What's a matter? Can't you take a joke?"

Scout eyeballs him hard and cold from behind her dark glasses.

He's mesmerized. She's a young goddess. Tanned, high cheekbones. Chestnut hair, long and braided. Her face betrays nothing. He concedes he is out of his league. No fun here. The rollers walk away.

She heard keys jingle, then the tap of metal on the steel passenger door. It was Gask and Perez, their faces moist, their shirts darkened with sweat under their armpits. "C'mon, Scout, we're cookin' here," Gask shouted over the idling motor, air conditioner, and the truck's sound-absorbing armor.

Scout unlocked the doors from the inside. Gask heaved himself into the passenger seat. Perez sprung up the step of the side delivery door, into the rear with the money. Both men locked their doors as Jessie eased the truck down the casino's driveway and onto Las Vegas Boulevard.

"What's the problem, you hittin' the horn, Scout?" Gask studied his clipboard, then shouted through the sliding viewer window of the steel security wall separating the cab and the rear of the truck. "Next drop is ATMs, Perez. Got it?"

"Got it."

"I asked you, what's the problem, Scout?"

"No problem."

"I think you still don't know what you're doing, do you?"

Scout didn't answer. Gask's face hardened.

"I swear to God, I don't know why they hire you people."

Scout said nothing.

"My last week on the job and this is what you give me?"

"I said it was no problem."

"You sure? You seem a little tense today. Is it a woman thing?"

Scout rolled her eyes. What a pig. "A tourist was touching the truck. I scolded him. He backed off. No problem."

"Fine. Put it in the log. Time. Place. Description. Incident. I'm retiring with a spotless record. Got it. Christ, you got a brain in there?"

"I know the procedure."

"As long as you're sure," he grunted. "Call in the drop."

Scout grabbed the radio handset and said: "Ten sixty-five."

"Go sixty-five," the radio responded.

"Six clear."

"Ten four, sixty-five."

Gask shifted in his seat. "Damn gun, digging into me." He removed his uniform cap and dragged the back of his hairy forearm over his forehead. "You got the AC on full, Scout? You got it up full?"

"Full."

"You sure you know how to operate that thing. Might be complicated for someone like you."

Scout concentrated on the road. Gask had been her crew chief since she was hired as a driver for U.S. Forged Armored Inc., four months ago. Today was his first day back from a vacation and he was bursting to tell her and Perez about it that morning at the terminal while downing his ritual breakfast of chocolate glazed donuts. They were finishing up coffee, ready to head out on deliveries.

"Know where I went, Scout?" he'd asked.

As if she cared.

"Aryanfest," he sucked on his teeth, working them over with a toothpick. "Up north, near your old reserve. Pretty country. Lots of *white*. On the mountaintops. We burned a cross," Gask smiled. "Once I punch out of this job, I'm going to buy me a lake cabin near the border."

Scout and Perez looked at each other, saying nothing. Gask did not keep his beliefs secret. Experience taught them to avoid trigger topics like Martin Luther King, the pope, Waco, Ruby Ridge, Oklahoma City, or civil rights. Scout could deal with his insults but despised the way Gask treated Perez, who had three years with the company.

Gil Perez was a quiet, soft-spoken father of two little girls. He was loyal, honest. Hard working. Dreamed of starting his own car wash business, but one day he made the mistake of telling Gask, who'd spit on his dream every chance he could.

"Ain't gonna happen for you, Refried. You just don't have what it takes. Trust me. I know you, your abilities. It exceeds the reach of your people. Scout's too. In both cases, your folks generally lack the *motivation*, the *dedication*, the drive of red-blooded Americans like me to succeed. You'd best invest all your energy in your job here and maybe one day, if you're real lucky, which I doubt, but maybe one day, you'll have your own crew like me."

Like you?

Scout shuddered at the notion of anyone making themselves in the image of Elmer Gask, Forged's most senior guard and legendary asshole. According to the dinosaurs who knew Gask's story, Elmer was Mississippi white trash, whose family moved in the night to avoid debts. Gask's granddaddy was a Grand Dragon who oversaw the firebombing of churches before he died of complications arising from syphilis. Gask was a former bull with the Nevada State prison system, fired for severely beating a black con.

Then he was hired at U.S. Forged where he earned mythic status. Over his twenty-two years on the job, Gask safely moved up to twenty million dollars daily among the casinos and banks of Las Vegas without a single dollar loss. Not a cent. There had been attempts. Three men had died in botched hits on Gask's watch. Two drifters from Minnesota in '88 when they jumped him and his partner making a two million dollar drop at the Nugget. In 1983, Gask shot dead a 24-year-old Brit named Fitz-something, who was AWOL and wired on LSD when he tried to run off with two bags of newly minted one-hundred-dollar bills outside Caesar's Palace.

No one had, or would, win against Gask. He was the money mover king of Las Vegas. He kept the casinos lubricated, kept things humming. In this town, where every move was a gamble, Gask had the edge and he enlightened every newcomer that his greatness was the reason U.S. Forged entrusted him with the heaviest deliveries and rookie staff. He knew the business and its vulnerabilities, how to inventory a casino during a drop. How to scan faces and sense trouble like a county sheriff's bloodhound. Gask had no family. No wife. No kids. He was the job. U.S. Forged profited by his intense dedication and bigoted intimidation. All packaged in a six-foot-two-inch, two-hundred-thirty-pound button-straining frame.

The cost: $33,500 per annum. With a $22,000 retirement bonus coming his way for his twenty-two 'loss-free' years of service.

Moving north along the Strip, they stopped for a red light near the Hacienda. Gask scanned his clipboard. "We gotta load six ATMs at the next drop. Best use the dolly, Refried."

Perez's face appeared at the viewer window.

"Don't call me Refried, Elmer, please."

Gask's eyebrows ascended. "Why's that?"

"Because I don't like it."

"You don't like it?" Gask watched the casinos roll by.

"Call me Gil, or Perez, please."

"Or what? You gonna complain to the ACLU?" Gask bit hard on his toothpick. "You forget who you're talking to?"

"I'm just making a respectful request."

Gask sucked on his teeth. The muscles of his lower jaw pulsated.

"Well, well, well," he said as they passed the mammoth Excalibur with its fairytale turrets. "Here I am in 1993, crew chief of *'Gil, please don't call me Refried Perez and Pocahontas.'* Ain't America the land of equal opportunity. This is what I get for my last week on the job? Attitude from the two of you." Gask shook his head. "And I get this shit-hole truck today, a heavy day. Still no transmitter. How many times have I told Rat to fix the goddammed transmitter in this one? Today I get the bottom of the heap."

Gask had deliberately not mentioned that Scout had alerted him to the fact they were skedded to have this truck weeks ago. He couldn't stomach anyone telling him anything, let alone a woman. Even worse, a Native American woman. He ignored her. The truck they had was a far cry from the war wagons they usually used. Today they had the company's ten-year-old armor-plated Econoline van. The back up. Each crew used it for one shift every second week while the new trucks were serviced. But Scout thought it best not to debate facts. Let him rant.

"Nothing better happen today on my goddamn watch, right Scout?"

She didn't answer.

He looked at her. "What's with you?"

"Nothing."

"Nothing? I don't think so."

Gask sensed something wasn't right. He was sniffing at something, Something about her was eating at him, something he couldn't quite figure. She was as indifferent as she was on every shift. Maybe it was because he'd been away a week? He kept staring.

"Aren't you embarrassed riding in this tin can today, Scout?"

"I'm embarrassed riding with you today, yes."

Scout knew what Gask was thinking, that she was playing with him and he liked it. She was a challenge to him, an enigma. He knew virtually nothing about her. She said little and rarely smiled. But she knew men like Gask. Knew what they wanted. They told her with their eyes. She knew Gask enjoyed looking at her. Especially now. His eyes had lit on her uniform where a button had come undone, offering a glimpse of her ample breast. Firm and dark, bouncing in her bra until she caught him staring and, without a hint of shame, buttoned her shirt. Gask sucked on his teeth.

"You got a boyfriend, Scout?"

"I don't need one."

"Maybe you don't know what you need."

She said nothing and gazed beyond the glitz of the Strip west to the Spring Mountains, searching for answers. The meaning of her life. Jessica Mary Scout. Born in Browning, Montana. Her mother, Angela Scout, was Blackfoot. Her father was German, a philosophy student on exchange at MSU. He was conducting field research on Native American mysticism at the reserve when he met Angela. He was going to marry her and take her to Berlin. The day Jessie was born he borrowed a truck and was driving to the hospital. He swerved to miss a rabbit, the truck rolled. He was killed. Jessie's mother was never the same. Her heart was broken, and she had buried a piece of it with the man she loved.

Jessie had grown up accepting that her life had brought death.

One of the old women called it the black wind, the bringer of misfortune. And when Jessie was ten, the old woman told her that it would never leave her until the Lightning Rider came for her.

"Grandmother, how will I know him?"

"You will see with your eyes and know in your heart, child."

Until that time, the black wind would always be with her. Whispering. Laughing. Jessie began seeing it. Straw in a black wind. Hearing it in a crow's cry. Felt its presence. She was its harbinger. This was her destiny. Did the mountains know, she wondered, for they reached back to her home.

Jessie had lived most of her life in Browning with her mother. She missed her. Ached for her sad sweet smile, her fragrance, her gentle hands, the way she filled their house with the aroma of bannock. She missed her voice. Was it out there in the mountains? She listened for it, but heard nothing. Jessie yearned at this moment to be with her mother. To ask her.

Would it always be true, what the old woman said? Don't think about it. But the black wind was kicking up, making her remember other times.

Several years after her father's death, Jessie's mother had a second child. A baby girl she'd named Olivia. The father was an alcoholic trucker Angela had met at a bar in Shelby. When Angela was in the hospital having Olivia, the trucker raped Jessie. After he finished, he threatened to kill them all if she told. Jessie was eleven. She didn't tell. Then one winter day, they got word his rig had crashed near Standoff. He was dead. Angela locked herself away to mourn him as the cold winds blew down from the Bitteroot mountains.

As the armored car passed the Stardust, Jessie tried to drive the memories back. It was futile. Even now, a world away in Las Vegas. Please Olivia. Please . . . the wind . . . the black wind was there . . . scattering the snow. Blinding. Biting. The black wind was pushing her, punching her. Jessie was walking as fast as she could. The wind was stealing her breath. Snow melted in her eyes, blurring her vision. Faster. Walk faster. Holding her baby sister to her chest. Olivia naked against her skin. Feeling her tiny warmth. *Growing colder.* Wrapped in her shirt, worn coat, old blankets. Icy wind jabbing at Olivia through the holes. The halo of the car's lights. Snow crunching under its tires as it crept beside her. Warmth spilling from it when the window dropped. "Where you going, there?" asked the Montana Highway Patrol officer. Jessie's face was numb. "My sister's sick." The car squeaked to a halt. The door opened. "You got a baby under there! Let me see. Jesus! Get in. I'll take you to the hospital in Cut Bank!" He was a young cop. Concern on his face. The rhythm of the wipers. He said things into his radio. The smell of his cologne. Her skin thawing, tingling and itching. Olivia is blue. Her eyes are wide open. She does not move. She does not breathe. The black wind is blowing, and the siren was screaming and screaming.

The armored car passed the Mirage. Jessie liked the way it caught the sun. She shrugged Gask off. People like Gask didn't intimidate her. She feared no one. For the knowledge she possessed could not be measured by the twenty-six years of her life, a life steeped in pain, a life broiling with cosmic forces and ancient truths. Her heart had traveled to regions few could conjure in dreams. It was reflected in her photo ID card clipped to her chest. Her pretty face was a mystery. A glint of arrogance in her eyes that squinted slightly to offer a smile. Or was it a sneer, one that revealed to people like Gask a hard fact they couldn't bear: They were insignificant. Jessie's face was a manifestation of righteous contempt for every injustice that had befallen her. It held a vengeful calm. Because she had purchased secrets. Paid in full with her tears. Her blood. Her life. She had come to Las Vegas, a city of risk, not to gamble.

But to collect.

They had come to the next delivery. The armored car exited Las Vegas Boulevard for the casino's driveway. Gask initialed his clipboard. "Ready back there, Re—Gil?"

"Ready."

"OK, Scout. We got a lot of ATMs here. Going to be thirty minutes inside then we got four more big loads. You know the drill. Drop us at the back and pick us up out front. Main entrance. Think your half-breed brain can manage that?"

She was silent, maneuvering the truck through the casino's parking lot.

"You hear what I said, Scout?" Gask looked at her.

"I know my job." She stopped the truck neatly at the casino's rear entrance, looked at Gask then radioed their arrival to Forged's dispatcher. Gask's jaw twitched. He spat out his toothpick and leaned toward her.

"Before this day is done, Scout, you and me are going to have a talk about your goddammed attitude." Gask's breath smelled of coffee and the celebratory retirement whiskey he mixed with it. "Maybe you fail to realize how close you are to having your Pocahontas ass kicked back to the reserve where you'll be reading numbers off ping pong balls to old squaws with no teeth."

Jessie looked at Gask calmly and said nothing.

Gask stared back hard and cold for a long time, then said: "Let's go, Refried."

Gask and Perez got out. Perez quickly loaded the dolly with delivery bags containing nearly a million dollars in unmarked bills while Gask scanned the area. The casino's security cameras recorded their work while rollers and families slowed to watch, making the old joke about their jackpots having arrived. They wheeled the cash into the casino, Gask glancing at the rear of the truck as Jessie headed for the main entrance.

A black wind was kicking up.

———

Half an hour after they'd finished loading the last ATM in the casino, Gask savored the air conditioning and decided to take a leak before he and Perez started for the main entrance to meet Scout.

"You're taking part in Las Vegas history, Gil, did you know that?" Gask said at the urinal while relieving himself.

Perez was bent over a sink, running cold water over his face. "No."

"When I punch out at the end of the week, I'll be leaving with a spotless loss sheet, one nobody in this town can touch."

"Didn't Roger Maddison retire from Titan Federal, a few months back? He put in twenty-seven years without a loss."

"No. I don't think so."

"It was in the newsletter. Your record would be second to his. Third actually. Pike Radeaux at Titan packed it in last year. Twenty-five loss-free years."

"No. You're wrong."

"I've still got the newsletter somewhere. I'll show you."

"That newsletter's bullshit," Gask flushed. "What the hell do you know, Refried? Let's go. Jesus. Why do I waste my breath on you?"

The wheels of the empty dolly cart sank in the lobby's carpet as Perez pushed it to the main entrance. Amid the eternal clanking of the slots, Gask strained in vain to locate the familiar colors of the Forged armored car through the glass doors. No truck. No Scout.

"That damned squaw better have an explanation!" Gask's fingers clasped his radio, knowing the instant he called for Scout on the air, a fuck-up attributed to him was exposed fleet-wide.

He held off.

"Perez, quick. Check the back. Maybe she had a breakdown. I'll search the front lot. Meet me back here. Hurry."

Gask shivered as the sun worked on him, his keys chiming as he trotted. No trace of the truck out front.

Perez returned, breathless. "She's gone, Elmer," he doubled over gasping. "Maybe it was the last drop? Those guys touching the truck?"

Gask's stomach tightened. Four days from retirement. Twenty-two years. His twenty-two thousand dollar bonus was melting here in a casino parking lot because of that stupid goddammed squaw.

"Better call it in, right, Elmer?"

Gask couldn't believe he was being screwed like this. Why?

"Elmer, she could have been taken hostage. Jesus! Call it in!"

Gask scanned the lot, willing the truck to appear. Goddammit. It was a hit. Had to be. On his goddamn watch. His twenty-two grand.

"Elmer! Call it in!" Perez's hand shook as he ran the back of it across his dried lips. "They could kill Jessie!"

Gask put his walkie-talkie to his mouth. "Sixty-five. Sixty-five. This is three. Radio check?"

"Elmer." Gask was wasting time covering his ass.

"Sixty-five. Sixty-five. This is three. Radio check?"

Nothing.

"Dispatch to three. Is there a problem?"

Perez watched him.

Gask swallowed hard. "There's been a hit."

"Say again three?"

"A hit. We can't raise our driver."

U.S. Forged Amored Inc., immediately activated its loss incident procedure, alerting a Las Vegas 911 dispatcher then Len Dawson, Forged's manager for Las Vegas. He notified Wade Smith, his supervisor at headquarters in Kansas City. Smith warned Dawson he would "have somebody's head on a stick if we lost points." Dawson drove to the scene calculating a multimillion-dollar loss with a severe detrimental impact on the company's insurance rates. Maybe the casino could be nailed for partial liability? Dawson cursed the fact Gask's crew had the truck with no electronic location finder. Scout's well-being did not enter his mind as he monitored Forged's attempts to reach her through the truck's radio and cellular phone.

Unit 1065 was not responding.

Las Vegas Metropolitan Police launched a bulletin across Clark County and the Valley. The Las Vegas FBI and Nevada Highway Patrol were alerted. Within two minutes, four marked Metro units arrived at the casino, followed later by an unmarked sedan and detectives Todd Braddick and Chester King from the LVMP robbery detail. Before they could enter the lobby, a crew from Channel Three and Ray Davis, the *Review Journal*'s crime senior reporter, approached them.

"Chester, you got a second?" Davis opened his notebook. "We hear it's an armored car heist with big numbers?"

King smiled. He was six feet six inches tall, a gentle giant whose confidence came from twelve years as a robbery detective. His partner was another story. Braddick had less than two years as a detective, yet he was a brash cock-of-the-walk. Handsome. Single. His laser-sharp eye for detail was earning him a reputation as fast as his switchblade tongue. He exhausted King. They tried unsuccessfully to blow by the reporters.

Davis said: "We heard three to four million, that right, Chester?" King wouldn't take the bait. Then Seleena Ann Ramone from Channel Three thrust her microphone toward him: "Have you found the driver, yet?"

Braddick shook his head. "Give us a break, Hon."

"Hon?"

"Folks, please," King spread his hands apart. "We just got here. You know more than we do. We'll get back to you. Thanks."

Inside, the detectives were directed to an office behind the main registration desk. Half a dozen people watched as Forged's manager was going at it with Theo Fontaine, the casino's security boss.

". . . this is on you, not the casino," Fontaine said.

"Just answer me. Did you, or did you not, seal the perimeter of your facility once my people reported the theft?" Dawson said.

"Your people never breathed a word to us. It was Metro who called us, sir. Don't be putting this on us."

"Excuse us, gentlemen," Braddick said. "Metro Robbery. Braddick and King. We'd like to interview the armored car crew, please. My guess is that is you two?" He pointed at Gask and Perez. They nodded.

"Theo, could you pull all your recorded security video for us," King said.

"Already on it, Chester."

King nodded to Gask. "Sir, could you come with me. Detective Braddick will interview your partner. Theo, we're going to need separate offices."

"No problem," he led them away.

"Detective," Dawson said. "I'd like a word with my staff first, if I may? I'd like to go over the log and drop sheets."

"And you are . . . ?" King said.

"Len Dawson. Manager of Forged's operations here."

"Mr. Dawson, once we're finished, they're all yours."

———

Fontaine led Braddick and Perez to a small meeting room. Plush carpet. Floor to ceiling one-way glass overlooking the outdoor pool. Big mahogany table. Thick leather chairs. Dark paneled walls. Gil Perez puffed his cheeks and exhaled as Braddick took his name and particulars, then asked:

"How much was in the truck when it vanished, Gil?"

"Three million seven hundred thousand. Unmarked nonsequential."

"You sure about the number?"

"I'm the money man, the counter."

"OK, tell me about the driver, Jessica Scout."

"Jessie, was—is a good person. She always defended me in front of Elmer. He's our crew chief."

"You needing defending?"

"He called us names. Called me Refried. Called Jessie squaw, Pocahontas. She's an American Indian. She stood up to Elmer. He's good at his job. Never had a successful hit on his watch. Retires this week after twenty-two years. He's a very tough boss."

"Gil, what was Jessie's demeanor today?"

"Same as any other day. She was quiet. Alone in her thoughts, she was a very quiet woman. What if she's dead? What if she's been killed?"

"Gil, we don't have any evidence of anything. We're only one hour into this. Do you remember anything unusual today?"

"Two guys."

"What about them?" Braddick wrote carefully.

"At the drop before this one. Here, I wrote it on my drop sheet," Perez handed it to Braddick, explaining. "Jessie said two rollers got too close to the truck. She sounded the horn to make them back off."

"Maybe a distraction for something else?"

"You think so? What if they killed her, there was three point seven million left in the load. I was the money man today."

"Yes, you said. And she was scheduled to drive?"

"Yes."

"And the truck without the finder? You knew about that to-day?"

"Yes. Each crew is scheduled in advance to take it."

"*In advance?*" Braddick continued writing. "How long has Jessie been with the company?"

"Four, nearly five months."

"And you? How long?"

"Three years."

"What do you know about Jessie? You two socialize after work?"

"No. She's shy, quiet."

"Any money problems? Debts? Drugs? Gambling? She living beyond her pay?"

Perez shook his head.

"You know what she does after work? Who her friends are?"

"Like I said, she's very quiet."

"So you really don't know her at all, do you Gil?"

"I—I guess, I, man, I worked with Jessie four months."

"Gil, tell me why you said she was so quiet."

"I figure, by the little she told me, she'd had a sad life."

"How?"

"She started to tell me once how bad things always follow her."

"What bad things?"

"Death."

"Death?"

"Detective Braddick, what if she's dead already?"

———

A few doors away, in a dim office, Elmer Gask fished out a stick of gum and a fresh toothpick from his chest pocket, crossed his arms, leaned back hard in his chair and watched King.

"She was a bitch to me all morning, is all I can attest to her 'demeanor.' " Gask's toothpick moved rhythmically with his chewing.

"What do you think happened?"

The toothpick froze as the gum chewing stopped.

"I'll tell you what happened." Gask's eyes widened with cold rage. "I just lost a twenty-two thousand–dollar bonus because of that stupid squaw."

King waited for an explanation.

"I retire at the end of the week. You clock out with a loss-free sheet, you get a grand for every year."

"That's a tragedy. What do you think happened?"

"If I knew that, we'd recover our load," Gask resumed chewing. "She wasn't careful. I told her to be cautious after the incident with the two jerks at the previous drop."

"The two guys who approached the truck?"

"I told her to log it, to call it in to dispatch when we were in here servicing the ATMs."

"Did she?"

"I doubt it."

"What about her past, her personal and career history?"

"Squaw or half breed from some welfare-eating reserve in Montana, or some end of the world state like that. Supposed to have done a good job at security for some faggy antique dealer in New York. If you ask me, she was an equal opportunity hire. Right gender, right race, right useless."

"You don't think she was qualified?"

"I don't hire 'em, Chester."

"What kind of driver was she?"

"Substandard."

"What about her past, any debts, habits, anybody leaning on her?"

"I wouldn't know anything about that shit."

"Tell me about today, what sort of day was it?"

"Routine, we were just making our drops."

"What about the truck? It had no finder?"

"That was her job as driver to deal with that. I told her to get that finder fixed. She ignored me."

"Aren't you her supervisor?"

Gask gave some thought to how he should answer.

"Yes and I supervised her to see the finder was fixed. I was intending to write her up for not following through."

"I see. What do you know about Jessica Scout, her circles?"

"Not a goddamned thing. She never spoke to me. I told you, she was an ice bitch who acted like she was better than everyone."

"Tell me about Gil Perez?"

"He's kind of a shifty beaner."

"That right?"

"Always talking about his dream of going away and starting his own car wash business. Only thing holding him back was lack of cash."

"That so?"

"That's so."

"And what about you, Elmer, what do you talk about?"

"Football and America."

"What about America?"

"She's fucked up real good."

"What really happened to the money?"

"Jessica Scout got herself jammed. Thought she knew it all. Let her guard down, now she's gone."

"That prospect doesn't exactly bring tears to your eyes."

Gask shifted his toothpick to the opposite side of his mouth then leaned to King. "Her stupidity cost me twenty-two grand."

"But you break even."

"How's that, Chester?"

"Scout may have paid with her life."

———

Later, Braddick and King compared notes at a quiet table at the casino's nearest bar, which serviced a keno lounge.

Braddick started. "My guy fears she is dead."

"Mine hopes she is," King said before his pager went off. He read the caller's number. "Looks like the feds." He squinted, tilting the pager for better light. "Yup. FBI's offering to help. I'll call."

"Three point seven. What do you make, Chester? Inside? Outside?"

"All of the above."

———————

Joe Two Knives's dark glasses reflected the sun, cloudless sky and warehouses of a light industrial section of Las Vegas.

What if something went wrong? He watched the garage one hundred yards away. He did not want to be near it in case something went wrong. Nothing appeared suspicious. Everything had gone smoothly. Every detail of preparation had come off cleanly.

He checked his watch then the cell phone on the seat beside him. His hands were sweating inside the two pairs of surgical gloves he wore. The car's air conditioner kept him cool. He kept himself calm. He had been through this before. Twenty-five years ago. *No one will die this time.* But what if she didn't make it? What would he do? He didn't know. It was the one event he did not plan for.

His phone trilled.

"Yes," he said.

"ETA seven to ten."

"Thank you."

Two Knives drove along a back service alley, stopping at the rear of the garage which bore a small painted sign: AAA Armored Repair. It was a rectangular cinder block building. One story. The garage had three auto bays each with an electronic door in the front and rear. He unlocked the building, parked his car in one of the bays then closed the rear electronic door. The garage was clean and empty. It had a small office and a bathroom. He went to a worktable, switched on a scanner, listening as Las Vegas police dispatches echoed clearly.

A horn sounded two quick beeps in front of the building.

Two Knives hit a switch, the door rose, a motor revved, and a U.S. Forged armor-plated Ford van edged inside, the electronic door closing behind it. Jessica Scout stepped out and studied her watch.

"Nineteen minutes since I left."

He tossed Scout two pairs of rubber gloves. "Every second counts. You know what to do."

Scout unlocked the truck's side door, entered, then slid three canvas bags to him. All together, they weighed about forty pounds, he figured, carrying them to the work table. The cash was wrapped in blue plastic, three packages of one hundreds, fifties, and twenties. They covered the table with the bundles, laying each one flat.

"Three million, seven hundred thousand," she said. "Unmarked."

He then took a metal detector wand and slowly passed it over the cash several times. No transmitters. He took one bundle, pulled up his pants leg and rubbed it against his moist skin. Then he took an ultraviolet lamp and illuminated his leg. Nothing. No chemicals. He carefully packed the bundles into white plastic medical containers, with lids cautioning:

DANGER DO NOT OPEN
MEDICAL WASTE
CONTAMINATED CADAVER TISSUE

He sealed the containers, placed them into three small, black suitcases, then loaded them into the car's rear seat. Then he grabbed a utility knife, a roll of silver duct tape, and a small box. His eyes met Scout's. "Ready?"

She nodded and climbed into the back of the truck. He taped her ankles together, then her knees, then her wrists, avoiding the rubber gloves, then her mouth. Again he looked in her eyes and stroked her hair.

She was prepared. Scout rolled onto her stomach.

Two Knives pulled her Glock from her holster. Examined it. He removed the safety, chambered a round, placed the muzzle against Scout's back, laying it nearly flat while pressing it slightly into the fleshy part of her hip. The bullet would graze her. His finger slid around the trigger. Two Knives saw Scout's pretty half-turned face, blinking in anticipation.

Just enough to bleed, he instructed himself.

She nodded.

He fired the gun. Scout lurched, grunting. A small tear, edges blackened with powder appeared on her uniform. Blood soaked the wound. He examined it. A small charred gash. Her skin was ragged and torn. He cut the tape from Scout's mouth and wrists, making sure some blood was on the remnants. The used tape with her blood, hair and fibers from her uniform would be left in the truck.

"Ok?"

"It burns a little, but I'm fine."

"I'll patch it up."

Two Knives opened the first aid kit. Scout removed her shirt. She jerked when he dabbed iodine in her wound, more so than when she was shot. He dressed her wound.

"We're almost through. Stand up."

Scout undid her utility belt, letting it drop to the floor. Two Knives dropped the Glock in the truck. Scout undid her pants, handing them to him. He ripped them near the zipper.

"We're coming up on half an hour," he said, scooping up the knife, tape and kit, dropping them in the trash as he rushed to the small office. Scout, now stripped down to her bra and panties, gathered her hair as she hurried to the garage's washroom.

In the office, Two Knives changed into new, pressed slacks, pin-striped shirt, Gucci shoes, and a conservative jacket. He combed his neatly trimmed silver hair, then slipped on a pair of wire-rimmed glasses.

Taped to the bottom of the desk was a brown envelope with several passports, driver's licenses, credit cards, cash. He tucked it into his breast pocket. Then he gathered everything from the worktable and tossed it in the trash, except the radio scanner. That went in the car. He left a window down so he could still hear it. He opened the trunk. A wheelchair was folded inside. Next, he inventoried the entire garage, nothing was left. Nothing. He closed the doors of the Forged truck then unfurled a white nylon sheet that he cast over the van, pulling it down at spots where it was uneven. He checked the printed note he had taped earlier to the window of the front door.

Closed Indefinitely Due to Death in Family.

"Ready," said the old woman who'd stepped from the washroom. She was wearing a light-knit knee-length sweater over a flower print caftan, flat-soled shoes. An emerald scarf hid her neck, her gray hair reached to her shoulders, framing her face, which was sallow and frowning under large, dark glasses. She was wearing rubber gloves and clutching her brown purse. She was hunched as if she were ill or enduring pain as she walked to the car's front passenger seat.

Two Knives grabbed the trash from the washroom, then tied three large garbage bags from the garage and tossed them in the car's trunk. He hit the switch for the electronic door, drove the car outside, stopping to close the garage door before they drove off down the rear alley.

Several blocks away, he stopped to drop the trash bags in a warehouse dumpster. He knew the schedule. This dumpster would be emptied the next morning.

They were well along Interstate 15 southbound, which paralleled the Strip, by the time their portable scanner crackled with the first dispatch of an armored car heist at a casino on Las Vegas Boulevard.

"So far, so good," he said, tossing the scanner out the window as they neared the Exec Air Terminal at McCarran.

Scout said nothing. She was looking west to the mountains.

The clerk at Desert Airstream Services moved from behind her counter to greet the old woman in the wheelchair and her physician.

"Dr. Hegel. Everything's ready. That's a pretty scarf, Mrs. Duggan," the clerk said after summoning the ground crew. They assisted Hegel getting his patient, Heather Duggan, comfortably aboard her chartered jet, for her one-way flight to Orange County.

Duggan, a reclusive casino heiress, had a terminal condition, her doctor had explained a few weeks earlier. It was her wish to die in California where she was born. Hegel had arranged the trip, paying cash in advance. He'd included large gratuities for respecting the eccentric woman's privacy.

The fresh-cut roses in the jet were a nice touch, Two Knives thought as the small Cessna Citation shot over the Spring Mountains, about ninety minutes after Scout had driven off with $3.7 million in unmarked cash.

That evening after dinner in the restaurant of the Ramada in Santa Ana, Two Knives told Scout that he wanted to do something he'd dreamed of doing all his life and they drove to Newport Beach where they watched the sun set on the ocean.

"I never really knew you Jessie," he said as they walked near the surf. "I was angry at Angela for being with a white man. I'd thought, how could my sister betray her people, her blood. I was consumed with anger. I'd lost my way in the world and ended up in a cell."

Gulls cried above them.

"I never meant for that man, the armored car guard, to die like that in San Diego. It was a terrible mistake. A terrible thing and I paid for it with twenty-five years of my life." The sun painted the creases of his sad, weary face with gold as he searched the horizon. "I did a lot of thinking in those twenty-five years, thinking how I could set things right."

"My mother was angry that I'd written to you in prison. She said you were no good, Joe."

"She has a right to her opinion of me. Especially now. I heard she has less than three months with her illness."

Scout nodded.

"Jessie, your letters kept me alive during my darkest times. Gave me a reason to want to make up for deserting my own blood when they needed me."

"You're the only one who knows the truth about all the things that happened when I was young."

"It hurt me more than you'll ever know, to read of your pain. I knew in my heart you did nothing to deserve it. I believe you were owed a life, and that I could help you get it."

Scout took her uncle's hand and squeezed it.

"Remember, you must never call your mother, or see her. Once the FBI puts everything together, they'll watch. If you're going to survive you must let her spend her last days thinking you are dead. It's better this way. You'll see her in the next world."

Scout brushed a tear from her cheek.

As if reading her mind, he said: "Not even a letter, Jessie."

She nodded. They'd gone over every detail.

"This looks like a good spot." He stopped, pulled a hotel towel from his bag and began to undress. Jessie was surprised. He was wearing swimming trunks. "I've always dreamed of swimming in the ocean," he said.

At fifty-four, he had the firm muscular body of a man thirty years younger, a dividend of keeping in shape during his time in Folsom. Scout noticed a small tattoo over his shoulder that looked like a storm over mountains.

"What's this mean?"

"Ah, that," he said. "I got it from an old chief I met on C-Yard the second year I was inside," he said. "Funny. I wanted an eagle. But he was very insistent that I have this one."

"What is it, what does it mean?"

"He said it was for the entity who delivers calm after the storm. Pretty cool, don't you think?"

Jessie nodded.

"The old man called it, The Lightning Rider."

Two Knives walked into the ocean, leaving Scout standing alone on the beach brushing her tears, feeling the warmth of the fading sun.

GRIEVING LAS VEGAS

JEREMIAH HEALY

Ed Krause lay on his back, staring up at the night sky, his sports jacket surprisingly comfortable as a pillow beneath his head. The desert air in mid-May was still warm, considering how long the sun'd been down. And the stars so bright—Jesus, you could almost understand why they called it the Milky Way, account of out here, away from any city lights, more white star showed than black background.

At least until Ed turned his head to the east, toward Las Vegas, which glittered on the horizon, like a cut jewel somebody kept turning under a lamp.

Jewel?

Ed coughed, not quite a laugh. Better you stuck with carrying diamonds and jade. But no, this new deal had sounded too good to pass up, especially the final destination and the cash you'd have for enjoying it. From that first day, at Felix . . .

———

. . . Wasserman's house. In San Francisco, on one of those crazy fucking hill streets near Fisherman's Wharf that had to be terraced and handrailed before even an ex-paratrooper like Ed Krause could climb up it.

Felix Wasserman was an importer, which is how Ed had met him in the first place, seven—no, more like eight—years ago. Just after Ed had mustered out of the Army and was nosing around for something to do with his life. A buddy from the airborne put him onto being a courier, which at first sounded like the most boring duty Ed could imagine, worse even than KP in the Mess Hall or standing Guard Mount outside some Godforsaken barracks in the pits of a Southern fort.

Until the buddy also told him how much money could be made for carrying the right kind of stuff. And being able to stop somebody from taking it away from you.

After climbing thirty-five fucking steps, Ed found himself outside Wasserman's house. Or townhouse, maybe, since it shared both its side walls with other structures, what Ed thought was maybe earthquake protection, since he'd seen signs down on more normal streets for stores that were temporarily closed for "seismic retrofitting." Wasserman had his front garden looking like a Caribbean jungle, and Ed had to duck under flowers in every shade of red that grew tall as trees before he could ring the guy's bell.

His doorbell, that is, seeing as how Ed Krause was what he liked to call in San Fran' a "confirmed heterosexual."

Wasserman himself answered, turned out in a silk shirt that looked as though his flower trees out front had been spun into cloth for it. Pleated slacks and soft leather loafers that probably cost—in one of the tonier "shoppes" off Union Square—as much as Ed's first car.

"Felix, how you doing?"

"Marvelously, Edward," said Wasserman, elegantly waving him inside. "Simply marvelously."

Give him this: The guy didn't seem to age much. In fact, Wasserman didn't look to Ed any older than he had that day when Ed—working for a legitimate, bonded courier service then—first laid eyes on him. It was after maybe the third or fourth above-board job he'd carried for the gay blade that Wasserman had felt him out—conversationally—on maybe carrying something else for his "import" business. At a commission of ten percent against the value of the parcel involved.

Now Ed just followed the guy up the stairs to a second-floor room with the kind of three-sided window that let you look out over the red-flower trees across to the facing houses and up or down the slope of the hill at other people's front gardens. Only, while there were two easy chairs and a table in the window area, Wasserman never had Ed sit there during business.

Too conspicuous.

Another elegant wave of the hand, this time toward the wet bar set back against one wall. "Drink?"

"Jim and Coke, you got them."

"Edward," Wasserman seeming almost hurt in both voice and expression, "knowing you were coming to see me, of course I stocked Mr. Beam and your mixer."

Ed took his usual seat on one couch while his host first made the simple bourbon and cola cocktail, then fussed over some kind of glass-sided machine with arching tubes that always looked to Ed like a life-support system for wine bottles. Coming away holding a normal glass with brown liquid in it and another like a kid's clear balloon with some kind of red—is this guy predictable or what, colorwise?—Wasserman handed Ed his drink before settling into the opposing couch, a stuffed accordion envelope on the redwood—see?—coffee table between them.

"Edward, to our continued, and mutual, good fortune."

Clinking with the guy, Ed took a slug of his drink, just what the doctor ordered for that forced march up the screwy, terraced street. Wasserman rolled his wine around in the balloon glass about twelve times before sniffing it, then barely wetting his lips with the actual grape juice. Ed wondered sometimes if the wine was that good, or if the dapper gay guy just didn't want to get too smashed too quick.

"So, Felix," gesturing toward the big envelope, "what've we got this time?"

Wasserman smiled, and for the first time, Ed wondered if maybe the guy had gone for a face-lift, account of his ears came forward a little. But after putting down the wine glass, Felix used an index finger to just nudge the package an inch toward his guest. "Open it and see."

Ed took a second slug of the Jim and Coke, then set his glass down, too. Sliding the elastic off the bottom of the envelope and lifting the flap, he saw stacks of hundred-dollar bills, probably fifty to the pack.

Ed resisted the urge to whistle through his bottom teeth. "Total?"

"One-quarter million."

Since they both knew Ed would have to count it out in Wasserman's presence over a second drink, the courier just put the big envelope back on the table, three packs of cash sliding casually over the open flap and onto the redwood.

Ed said, "For?"

A sigh and a frown, as Wasserman delicately retrieved his glass by its stem and settled back into his couch. "I expect you're aware—if only in a general way—of the rather distressing state of the economy?"

"I remember hearing something about it, yeah."

A small smile, not enough to make the ears hunch. "Ah, Edward, both dry and droll. My compliments." Wasserman's lips went back to neutral. "My rather well-heeled clientele hasn't been consuming quite as conspicuously these last few seasons, feeling that fine jewels, no matter the rarity nor brilliance, can't quite replace cash as hedges against the uncertain miasma within which we find ourselves floundering."

Ed just sipped his drink this time, kind of getting off on the way Wasserman made up sentences more elaborate than his garden out front.

"However, the landlord still expects his rent for my shop, and the bank its mortgage payments for my home. And so I've shifted my sights a bit, importwise."

"Meaning?"

Wasserman took an almost normal person's belt of his wine. "Heroin."

Ed would have bet cocaine. "Let me guess. I take the package of money from here to there, and pick up the powder."

"Precisely. Which, of course, would do me no good, since fine Cabernet," swirling the wine in his glass now, "constitutes my only source of substance abuse. Fortunately, though, I have a business contact in the Lake Tahoe area who will gladly buy said powder from you, as my representative, at . . . twice the price."

Ed did the math. "You're saying my cut of this will be ten percent of five hundred thousand?"

"Precisely so. From Tahoe you'll transport the remainder of the cash involved to Las Vegas."

Christ, even a bonus. Growing up in Cleveland, Ed'd always had an itch to sample the glitzy life, but in all his time in San Fran', he'd never been to Vegas. He'd heard everything there—thanks to the casino action—was bigger and better: spectacular tits and ass on the showgirls, classy singers and magicians, even lion tamers. Not like the trendy shit that passed for culture in the "City by the Bay."

In fact, Ed had also seen—three times, at cineplex prices—that Nick Cage movie, *Leaving Las Vegas*. Got the guy an Oscar, and he fucking well deserved it. I mean, who'd ever believe that anybody'd want to check out of the genuine "City That Never Sleeps"?

Felix allowed himself another couple drops of his wine. "When you reach Las Vegas itself, a friend of mine will—shall we say, hand-wash—the actual bills for his own fee of a mere five percent, after which you shall bring the balance back here to me."

Ed thought about it. A little complicated for his taste, given the number of stops and exchanges. But fifty thousand for what would be maybe three, four days tops of driving? And he didn't give a shit whether his share was laundered or not, since Ed would be passing it in far smaller amounts than Wasserman probably had to pay his creditors.

"Felix, with all this running around, I'm gonna need a cover story, and an advance against expenses."

Now a pursing of the lips. "How much?"

"That'll depend on where I'm picking up the powder to begin with."

Another sigh, but more—what the fuck was the word? Oh, yeah: wistful. "Edward, I actually envy you that, even though the Cabernet varietal, in my humble opinion, doesn't really thrive there. You'll make your first exchange in Healdsburg. Or just outside it."

Ed had noticed the town's name on maps, maybe two hours up U.S. 101 from the Golden Gate, in one of the many parts of the state called "wine country."

He said, "Three thousand, then, upfront, given the cover story I'm thinking about."

"Which is?"

"Bringing a chick along, camouflage for flitting around all these vacation spots like a butterfly."

"A woman." The deepest frown of all from Felix Wasserman. "That I don't envy you, Edward."

"Let me get this straight," said Brandi Willette, trying to size up whether this guy who never plunged for more than three well-drinks at a sitting—but did tip her twenty percent every time he settled a tab—was on the level. "You want to take me—all expenses paid—with you on this whirlwind trip over the next four days?"

A nod from his side of the pub's bar, the guy wearing an honest-to-God, old-fashioned sports jacket. "Maybe even longer, we like it in Vegas enough."

Brandi had been there only once, on the cheap with a girl-friend, splitting every bill down the middle. The girlfriend turned out to be a drag, but Brandi loved the gambling, believing firmly that if she could just sense her luck changing, she'd make a fortune, even from the slot machines. The kind of money that'd let her get out from behind a smelly, tacky bar, listening to offers from guys like this . . . uh, this. . . . "It's 'Eddie,' right?"

"No. Just 'Ed,' like you're 'Brandi' with an 'I'."

She shook her head, then had to blow one of the permed blond curls out of her face. "Okay, Ed. We go together, same room, same bed, but if I don't feel like doing the nasty, we just share the sheets, not stain them?"

"That's the deal."

Brandi gave it a beat. Then, "So, how come you're asking me?"

The guy seemed to squirm a little on his pub stool, which sort of surprised her, since Ed had struck Brandi as the ultra-macho type. Probably six-one, one-ninety, with a military hair-cut and big, strong-looking hands. Her pre-dick-tion: A fuck buddy who'd come up skimpy on the foreplay but be a pile-driver during the car chase.

"Well?" she said, wondering if maybe the guy was a little slow in the head.

"It's part of a business transaction."

"What kind of 'transaction'?"

"Just some documents. I exchange what this person gives me for what that person gives me, then I do the same thing a couple more times."

"What, these 'persons' don't trust Federal Express?"

"They trust me more."

"And why is that?" asked Brandi.

"It's confidential."

"Confidential." The curl spilled down over her eye again, and Brandi blew it back away. "You're a spy?"

"No."

"Private eye?"

"No."

Given the guy's limited active vocabulary, Brandi didn't waste her breath on "lawyer," but she did cock her head in a way that she knew guys dug, kind of a "persuade me" angle, like Sarah Jessica Parker did on *Sex and the City*. "So, we're gonna be sleeping together, in the same room, and you can't even share why you're picking me?"

"All right." More squirming. "It's because we don't know each other very well."

Huh, that was sure the truth. On the other hand, Brandi fig-ured she could always just fuck the guy senseless, then while he snored away, search through his stuff, find out what was really going on.

And Vegas would put Brandi one step closer to making her fortune. To attending catered dinner parties at swank homes in-stead of nuking some frozen muck in the microwave before spending the night surfing the cable channels.

"Okay, Honey," said Brandi, "I want to see your driver's license, and then I'm gonna call three of my girlfriends—who you don't know at all—to tell them I'm going on this grand tour."

Ed seemed to mull that over. "All right."

"And one other thing."

"What?"

Brandi leaned across the pub's bar, used her forearms to push her breasts a smidge higher against her tank-top, give him a little more reason to be nice to her. "You ever eaten at Masa's?"

———

As the slipstream from a passing trailer-truck tried to knock the little Mustang convertible onto the shoulder of U.S. 101, Ed Krause heard Brandi say from the passenger's seat, "I think it's another two exits from here."

He glanced over at the chick, her pouty face buried in a road map from the rent-a-car company, and began to question his own judgment. Not that Brandi with a fucking "I" wasn't the right type. Just to the "maybe not" side of slutty, with only one nose-stud and six earrings as body piercings, a small tattoo on the left shoulder that looked professional, not homemade. Decent boobs and legs, too, but overall not so smart or good-looking he thought she'd turn down his offer of a free trip.

Or his offer to help her through the night.

But "eating" at Masa's on Bush Street the night before turned out to be at the bar, since they didn't have reservations. Actually, Ed kind of counted his blessings on that one, because the very chi-chi, black-and-chrome restaurant didn't exactly price out as reasonable. He had to admit, though, he'd tried stuff off the "tastings" menu that the bartender suggested, and it was the best fucking food he'd ever eaten. Ed even had wine, served in Felix-like balloons, and Ed could tell that Brandi was impressed by the way he rolled the grape juice around the inside of his glass before sniffing and sipping it.

Not, however, impressed enough to take him to her place or vice-versa to his, for a little "tour preview." No, Brandi begged off, saying she needed to pack something more than the tote bag she'd carried from the pub to the restaurant—"It's Nine West, Honey, and only forty-nine-ninety-nine, but the real reason I bought it is how the last three numbers on the price tag all lined up the same, like it was gonna bring me luck?"

Thinking, Vegas at the end will make all this shit worth my while, Ed just picked her up the next morning outside Macy's on Geary Street, thinking too that once he got her hammered on a wine tour and fucked her senseless back in their room, he could always go through the chick's stuff, get a last name and address off her driver's license.

In case you ever want to . . . visit her later.

And Brandi was good enough at navigating, Ed could keep his eyes on the rear and side mirrors, make sure nobody stayed with them as he first did fifty-five for a while, then sixty, then a little over before dropping back down to fifty-five. It was a beautiful day, and frankly the slower speed with the top down was a lot more enjoyable than just putting the pedal to the metal.

There were a bunch of exits for Healdsburg, but give the chick credit: She picked the right one for the Inn on the Plaza. As they were shown to their rooms by a pert brunette younger than Brandi, Ed could tell his cover story was watching him to see if he was watching their guide. But all he did was listen to the brunette tell the story of the "bed-and-breakfast," how it had so many skylights because it used to be a "surgery," which Ed took to be where doctors operated before there were hospitals, much less electricity to let them see what they were cutting.

The room was pretty spectacular, even by Ed's images of the Las Vegas glitz to come. For now he could see high ceilings and a king-sized brass bed, a big tiled bathroom and Jacuzzi for two.

If all went according to plan.

Just as Ed was about to tip the brunette and get her out of there, he heard Brandi behind him gush, "Oh, God, he's so cute!"

Which is when Ed noticed the chick grabbing a teddy bear off one of the many throw pillows at the head of the bed and hugging it between her boobs.

Right on cue, the brunette said, "They're even for sale, at our desk downstairs."

As Brandi squealed with delight, Ed Krause hoped that the tab for their dinner the night before wouldn't be an omen for the

stuffed animal and everything else on the trip to Vegas, even if
Felix Wasserman was fronting expenses.

———————

"I still," said Brandi Willette, around a hiccup she thought she
stifled pretty well, "don't understand why we couldn't stop at
that last winery?"

Driving them, top down, along the nice country lane, Ed—
not "Eddie"—seemed to put a little edge on his voice. "Same
reason we didn't stop at the other two—of seven, I'm counting
right—you wanted to hit: I couldn't see the car from the tasting
room."

Brandi swallowed a second hiccup. "Five wineries in one afternoon isn't really enough, I don't think." Then she got an
idea. "Is that the same reason you brought your briefcase from
the car to the room and then back again?"

"Yes," the edge still there.

The idea turned into a brainstorm. "And how come we have
to put the roof and windows up at every stop," she gestured at
the beautiful day around them like she'd seen a stage actress do
once, "even though there's not a cloud in the sky?"

"That's right." Ed pointed toward the glove compartment. "A
little yellow button inside pops the trunk, and I don't want
somebody giving it a shot."

"Couldn't—" Brandi tried to stifle yet another hiccup, but it
was just not to be denied, "—Oh, excuse me, Honey. Couldn't
'somebody' take a knife to the roof, or break one of the windows, or jimmy open one of the doors, and then pop the trunk?"

"They could," Ed's voice getting a little nicer, so when he
slid his right hand over and onto her left thigh, Brandi didn't
brush it away like she had on the drive up from the city. "But
they're not likely to try it when I can see the car, and anyway
that'd give me time to get out there and stop them."

Brandi didn't ask Ed how he would stop them, because she'd
kind of accidentally stumbled into him at the fourth winery—
or maybe the fifth?—and felt something really hard over his
right hip.

A gun.

Which, to tell the truth, excited Brandi more than scared her. She figured when he pitched the trip to her back in the pub that something was maybe a little dangerous about the guy, with his overall aura and "confidential transaction."

And besides, Brandi thought—closing her eyes and letting her head just loll against the back-rest, living the moment with the breeze in her hair and the sun on her face and the birds singing around her—what girl doesn't like something . . . hard now and then?

———————

"I still don't see why I can't come in with you?"

Ed Krause just looked at her, sitting in the passenger's seat of the Mustang. He'd left the top down for fresh air, but put Brandi in the shade of a big tree in the circular driveway of a large stucco house with orange roof tiles. Let her kind of doze off some of the incredible amount of wine she'd put away, maybe—please, Christ?—even lose the hiccups doing it.

Of course, despite all the "I still don't understand this" and "I still don't see that" bullshit from her, there was no reason to make the chick mad, just as she was letting his nondriving hand, and then his lips, start to soften her up for later, in that brass bed.

Or better, the Jacuzzi.

"Like I told you," he said to Brandi, nice as he could. "This is the business part."

She nodded. Sort of. "The confidential part."

Con-fuh-denture-pah. Ed shook it off with, "Yeah. Just sit tight, enjoy the afternoon, and I'll be back in a few minutes."

Brandi seemed to buy it, slumping deeper into the seat with a sappy grin on her face, so he kissed her once and quickly, slipping his tongue in just enough to know she wouldn't fight more of the same back in their room. Then Ed opened the trunk, took out the briefcase Felix Wasserman had given him to hold the money, and went up to the front entrance, painted the same orange as the roof tiles.

The door swung inward before he could knock or ring, an Asian guy standing there, but more like an owner than a servant. Ed shouldn't have been surprised, since he knew Wasserman dealt with a lot of Chinese guys on the imports, only Ed also thought his gay blade could have prepared him for this by providing more than just a first name.

"Edward?"

"Yeah, though 'Ed' is fine. You're Tommy?"

"The same. Please, come in, though I take it your friend is more comfortable outside?"

"Let's just say I'm more comfortable that way."

A wise smile. "I see."

The guy led Ed into a first-floor living room done up all-Spanish with heavy, dark woods, bullfighting capes and swords, and funny lamps. The guy took one patterned chair and motioned Ed toward its mate.

The courier looked around before sitting down, feeling on his right hip the heft of the Smith & Wesson Combat Masterpiece with its four-inch, extra-heavy barrel—for pistol-whipping, in case he had to discourage some jerk who didn't require actual shooting. "No security?"

Another wise smile. "None evident, shall we say?"

Ed nodded, kind of liking the guy's—what, subtlety maybe? "Any reason not to get down to business?"

"As you wish, especially since I don't wish to keep you from your friend."

Tommy clapped his hands twice, and two more Asian guys appeared from around a corner. One carried a briefcase the same make and model as the one Ed had, the other a submachine gun so exotic that even the ex-paratrooper didn't recognize it.

Letting his stomach settle a minute, Ed took his time saying, "And if you clapped just once?"

"Then, regrettably, you'd be dead, and your friend soon thereafter."

Ed trusted himself only to nod this time. They exchanged briefcases—both unlocked, as usual—Ed looking into the one he was given. "Felix told me I didn't have to test the stuff."

"If you did," said Tommy, "he wouldn't be doing business with my family in the first place."

"Good enough." Ed glanced at the guy with the exotic piece. "Okay for me to leave?"

"Of course," said Tommy, standing, "Enjoy your visit to our valleys."

"My friend already has," Ed rising and feeling he could turn his back on these guys as he walked to the door.

———

"Oh, God," said Brandi Willette, nursing the worst hangover she could remember and afraid to look over the side of the car, because the road just fell away down the steep, piney slope. "I think my ears are popping again."

"The change in altitude," said Ed from behind the wheel. "And that bottle from the last winery you brought back to the room probably isn't helping any."

"Please," Brandi holding her left hand out in a "stop" sign while her right palm went from the teddy bear in her lap to cover her closed eyes. "Don't remind me about last night, all right?"

"Oh, I don't know. I think we both liked what happened next."

Well, you can't disagree with the guy on that one, at least the parts of it you remember.

Which were: Coming back to the room around five-thirty, after hitting the last row of wineries with names like Clos du Bois, Chateau Souverain, and Sausal. Feeling free as could be from all the great stuff she'd tasted, and, although Brandi was still hiccuping, ready for anything. Including letting Ed slip her clothes off, the guy more gentle than she could have hoped. After a quick shower together, him touching her just about everywhere, them getting into the Jacuzzi—the guy must have had it filling up while he was stripping her in the bedroom and soaping her in the stall. And then getting a real good look at that snake he had down there, the head on it big as a cobra's. And Brandi telling him to get in first, sit down, before lowering herself onto his soldier-at-attention. She stayed balanced by resting her palms on his shoulders, her nipples just skimming the surface of the sudsy water as she rocked up and down and back and forth—him laughing, because she still had the hiccups—until she came so violently and thoroughly it was like one long shudder that wasn't a hiccup at all. In fact, took them away.

And then him lifting her up, not even bothering to dry themselves off, and onto the soft mattress of the brass bed—her new teddy bear watching—for another, and another, and. . . .

"Hey," from the driver's side, "you're gonna puke, hold on till I can pull over."

"Yeah, yeah," said Brandi, hoping she'd have better luck controlling her gag reflex than she did with the hiccups.

"Okay," said Ed Krause, nudging the chick on her bicep with his fist, "we're here."

He watched Brandi's head try to find its full and upright position in the passenger's seat. After three hours of complaining about everything under the sun, she'd finally fallen asleep—or passed out—a good ten miles from Tahoe City, and therefore she'd missed some of the best fucking scenery Ed had ever driven through. Snow-capped, purple mountains, sprawling vistas down to pine-green valleys. The whole nine yards of America the Beautiful.

And now Lake Tahoe itself.

Brandi said, "I'm cold."

"Like I tried to tell you before, it's the altitude. Walk slow, too, or you'll start to feel sick." Stick in the knife? Sure. "Again."

The chick raised her hand like she had before, reminding him of a school crossing guard, but she managed to get her side door open.

After checking into the Sunnyside Lodge, Ed got them and their luggage to the suite, which had a little balcony off the living room and overlooking the waterfront, more mountains with snowy peaks kind of encircling the lake from high above. Brandi shuffled into the bedroom and flopped face down on the comforter, not even bothering to kick off her shoes. Ed heard snoring before he could secure his briefcase with the heroin behind the couch in the living room, pissed that the key fucking Tommy gave him for the handle lock didn't fucking work, so all Ed could do was click the catch shut.

Leaving the chick to sleep it off, he went back downstairs and did a walkaround, first outside, then in. Big old lodge, dark-log construction, security doors you'd need a computerized room key to open. A moose's head was mounted on a wooden plaque over one fireplace, a bear's over another, a buffalo's over a third.

Ed liked the place. Rugged, with the taxidermy adding just a hint about the history of killing the lodge had seen.

But no pool, and when he asked at the lobby desk, the nice college-looking girl told him it was way too cold to swim in even the lake, because it never got warmer than sixty-eight degrees, "like, ever."

When Ed got back to the room, Brandi was still snoring. But checking how he'd wedged his briefcase behind the bureau, it had turned a few degrees. Ed tilted the briefcase back to its original angle, then stomped his foot a couple of times, harder on the third one.

Brandi's voice trickled out of the bedroom. "What the hell are you doing out there?"

The briefcase never budged. "Testing the floorboards. Be sure they can take us rocking that mattress."

A different tone of voice with, "Wouldn't we be better off doing your testing . . . in here?"

And that's when Ed Krause knew in his bones that Brandi Willette—given how shitty she must still be feeling—had snuck a peek into his unlockable briefcase, just as he'd gone through her "lucky" totebag the night before at the Inn on the Plaza in Healdsburg.

"Honey," said Brandi Willette, in the best seductive/hurt tone she knew, "I still don't understand why I can't come in there with you."

"Keep your voice down."

She watched Ed shut the driver's side door, even almost slam it, in the yard he'd pulled into, a big Swiss-chalet style house on the lakeside in front of them.

Ed turned back to her. "It's like the last time."

"Confidential?"

He glanced into the next yard. "I said, keep your voice down. And stay put."

"All right, all right," Brandi flicking her hand like she couldn't give a damn.

Only she did. After seeing all that "snow" in his briefcase back at the lodge, Brandi could care less about the real thing on the mountaintops and melting in the shaded clumps still on the ground under trees that must block the sun. As they drove, many of the houses—like the one next door to the chalet—looked like something out of that ancient *Bonanza* TV show with Michael Landon that Brandi caught on the cable sometimes, a program she figured he must have done even before that old show *Little House on the Prairie,* account of how much younger he looked as a son/cowboy instead of a father/farmer.

But the snow in the briefcase? Heroin or cocaine, had to be. Which meant big-time bucks, and maybe an opportunity for her luck really to change, even just riding with Ed.

Or figuring out a way to hijack him. After all, the three friends Brandi called from the pub in the city would go to the police only if *she* didn't make it back.

Brandi watched Ed move slowly through the yard and toward the chalet. There'd been a wooden privacy fence between it and the road that wound around the lake. On each side of the fence's gate were these totem poles, like Brandi remembered from a Discovery Channel thing on Eskimos—or whatever they were called when they lived more in the deep woods and not so much on icebergs.

And, sure enough, there were three guys doing landscaping in the next yard who could have been Eskimos themselves. Short, blocky guys, with square, copper-colored faces. The oldest of them seemed to be bossing the other two, one gathering up broken limbs and throwing them onto a brushpile, the other sweeping the driveway of huge pine cones from even huger trees looming overhead. Probably getting the neighbor's place ready for the season.

Brandi noticed Ed giving the three Eskimos the eye as he reached the stoop of the chalet. Then the guy knocked and disappeared inside.

Brandi couldn't believe how cold it could be in mid-May nor how her breathing still wasn't back to normal from banging Ed and then just walking downstairs in the lodge and over to the Mustang. In fact, about the only other thing Brandi did notice was how, about five minutes after Ed entered the chalet, the oldest Eskimo in the next yard came strolling toward her side of the car, smiling and taking a piece of paper—no, an envelope?—out of a bulging pocket in his jacket.

And right then, Brandi Willette, even without knowing what was going to happen next, could feel her luck changing, and visions of what that would mean in Vegas—and beyond—began slam-dancing in her head.

———

Natalya, a fat-to-bursting fortysomething who looked like no drug pusher Ed Krause had ever encountered, settled the two of them into over-stuffed chairs that suited her like Felix's red flowers back in San Fran' suited him, only different.

She said, "Tell me, do you prefer 'Edward,' 'Ed' . . . ?"

"Just 'Ed,' thanks."

Natalya smiled. Not a bad face, you suck a hundred pounds off the rest of her, let the cheekbones show. She seemed to arrange their seating so he could enjoy the dynamite view of the lake through a wall of windows. Ed was pretty sure the chalet had been designed to be appreciated from the water, not the road.

But the view turned out to be less "enjoyable" and more distracting, as some fucking moron in a scuba wetsuit went waterskiing past, and Ed automatically glanced at all the interior doorways he could see.

The fat lady turned her head toward the skier, then turned back, smiling some more. "There's a rather famous school that teaches that between here and your lodge, though I've always felt it a bit too frosty and . . . strenuous to be diverting."

As soon as he'd entered the room, Ed had seen the sample case on the tiled floor next to the chair Natalya had picked for herself. He'd rather it be at least the same size as his briefcase, but then the two-fifty in hundreds had barely fit in its twin on the way to Healdsburg, and this would be twice as much, maybe some of it in smaller denominations to boot.

Natalya said, "May I offer you refreshment?"

"No, thanks. I gotta be going soon."

"As you wish," the fat lady sighing, as though if he'd said "yes," maybe she could break some kind of weight-watching rule of her own by joining him. "I will be needing to test your product."

A switch from Tommy in wine country. "And I'll be needing to count yours."

"Let us begin, then."

"Before we do," said Ed, leaning forward conversationally but also to free up his right hand to move more fluidly for the revolver under his sports jacket and over his right hip, "any security I should know about, so nobody accidentally gets hurt?"

"Security?" A laugh, the woman's chins and throat wobbling. "No, Tahoe City is a very safe place, Ed."

"Not even those guys next door?"

" 'Those guys?' "

"Mexicans maybe, doing yard work."

"Oh," a bigger laugh, shoulders and breasts into it now. "Hardly. And they're Mayans, Ed. They drift up here from the Yucatan to do simple labor—like opening up the houses after the winter's beaten down the foliage? My neighbor's a retired professor of archaeology, and the one who first got them to do landscaping for a lot of us along the lake. In fact, that figurine on the table and the stone statue near the fireplace are both gifts from him." Natalya paused. "I'd have said it was too frigid up here for them, frankly," the fat broad stating something Ed had been thinking from the moment he saw them, "but my neighbor tells me our gorgeous topography reminds them in some ways of their native land."

Ed thought that still didn't ring right: Most people he knew who ever traveled far from home went from colder weather to warmer, not the other way around.

On the other hand, what do you know about Mexicans, period, much less "Mayans" in particular?

Then Natalya opened her hands like a priest doing a blessing. "Shall we?"

Ed brought his briefcase over to her, and he took her sample case back to his chair, accidentally scraping the bottom of the case against the tiles, the thing was that heavy.

"This is supposed to be the best restaurant in town."

Brandi Willette heard Ed's comment, but she waited till the waitress at Wolfdale's—who looked like one of the retro-hippies back in the city—took their drink orders and left them before glancing around the old room with exposed ceiling beams and a drop-dead-gorgeous view of the lake, kind of facing down its long side from the middle of its short one. "It better be the best, all the time you spent back there."

Ed just shrugged and read the menu.

Brandi didn't want to push how long it took him inside the chalet, but she did notice he was carrying a different bag coming back to the convertible. The guy wants to keep things "confidential," that's fine. But it didn't take a genius to figure that if what Ed brought in there was drugs, what he brought out was money. Lots of it. And, given the size of the case, lots more than he used in Healdsburg to buy the shit with.

Then Brandi thought about the oldest Eskimo, and what he'd given her while she was waiting for Ed, what was now nestled in her lucky totebag. Plus what that gave her to think about from her side. For her luck, even her fortune, which was a nice fucking change of pace.

The dinner at Wolfdale's turned out to be maybe the best food Brandi had ever eaten in her life—medallions of veal, asparagus, some kind of tricked-out potatoes. And a merlot that made even a lot of the great wines she'd tasted the day before seem weak. A perfect experience.

Just like the catered dinner parties you'll be going to soon.

But, just as they were finishing dessert, Ed said, "How about we take a drive, see the lake by night?"

Remembering the mountains closer to the wine country they'd already gone up and down with her hangover that morning, Brandi said, "I'd rather see our bed by night."

"We can do that, too. Afterwards."

Well, what could a girl say to that? A guy who'd rather drive than get laid, there was just no precedent for dealing with such a situation.

———

"Ohmigod, ohmigod," said Brandi Willette in a tone that made Ed Krause think of the word *shriek*.

"What's the matter?" him taking the Mustang through its

paces on the ribbon of road—lit only by the moon—switchbacking up one of the mountains on the southwest end of the lake.

"What's the matter?" came out as more what Ed would call a "squeal." The chick pointed over the passenger's side of the car without looking down. "There's no fucking guardrail here!"

"Highway Department probably thinks it wouldn't help. Either you'd go through it and down, or bounce off it and into a head-on with somebody coming the other way."

"Don't even say that."

Another couple of miles—Brandi now groaning, even shaking—and Ed saw his lights pick up the "SCENIC VISTA" sign that fat Natalya had told him about back at her chalet, after she recommended Wolfdale's for dinner. "Let's give you a break."

He pulled into the otherwise deserted parking area, which seemed, even at night, like just a man-made platform jutting out from the side—nearly the top—of the mountain. They'd passed a few other viewing points—not to mention the entire Nevada town of South Lake Tahoe, but when Brandi had said, "Why don't we stop here for a while, try our luck?" Ed had glanced around at the penny-ante casinos with Harrah's, Trump's and a bunch of other evocative names on them, chintzy motels sprinkled among them, and replied, "Nah, I want to wait for the real thing. In Vegas."

As Ed now came to a stop in one of the vista's parking spaces, Brandi finally opened her eyes. "It's dark out. What're we gonna be able to see?"

He opened his door, came around to hers. "A fat broad told me a story about a guy, said nobody should miss it."

Ed could tell the only reason the chick'd leave the car would be to feel her feet on solid ground again, and that was fine. She got out of the Mustang, leaving her lucky fucking totebag on the floor between her feet, and Ed took her hand, guiding her over to the edge of the vista's platform.

"I don't want to go any closer."

"You have to, to appreciate the story I'm gonna tell you."

"Honey, please. I'll do you every which way but loose back in the room—"

"—the suite—"

"—whatever, but please don't. . . ."

"Hey, there it is."

Ed had his hands on the sides of her shoulders now, marching her in front of him, teach her a lesson about going through his briefcase. She was arching over, pushing her butt into his groin, the grinding sensation of their little "dance" making him hard.

"Honey, please. . . ."

"See? Right there, through the tree branches?" Brandi's butt was writhing, like a wet cat trying to get free of the drying towel. "The moon's lighting it up like noontime."

"It's a . . . all I see is this island—ohmigod, way down there?"

"This fat broad told me that back in the old days—eighteen-hundreds we're talking—there was a caretaker for the house that's on the mainland, back under the trees."

"I don't—"

"Seems this caretaker stayed all winter," said Ed, "but he liked the island more, and his booze the best. Fact is, he'd row all the way from here to where we're staying in Tahoe City—miles and miles through the cold, though the lake doesn't freeze over like you might expect—to hit a saloon, then he'd row all the way back."

"Honey, let's go, huh?"

"But this caretaker, he fell in love with that island, so he built his own tomb on it. For when he died, to be buried there."

"Why are you—"

"Only thing is, the poor old coot was rowing back from town one night with too much of a load on, and he went over into the water. They found his boat, but not him. Not ever. And so he's at the bottom of the lake someplace, and his tomb's just falling apart, empty, down there on that pretty little island."

"Honey, this is too weird for—"

Ed dropped his hands from her shoulders to her biceps, and then lifted her off the ground—swinging her legs straight out—and sat her down, hard, on the ledge overlooking the drop-off.

Brandi lifted her face to the sky and screamed like a baby.

Ed said, "I invited you along on this trip—a complete free-bie—and I didn't move on you 'til you let me know you were ready for it."

"Yes, yes," the tears streaming down her cheeks from eyes clenched shut.

"And I don't expect you to help me at all in what I'm doing, just be half the cover story of the nice couple on a vacation."

"Anything, Honey, I will."

"But if I ever . . ." Ed thrust his pelvis forward, into her butt, like Brandi was giving him a lap-dance and he was pounding her doggy-style. She screamed till her voice broke, then began just sobbing and gasping for breath. "Ever . . ." he banged her harder, nearly over the edge but for him holding her upper arms, Brandi now just choking on her own breaths, ". . . think you're double-crossing me, you're gonna join that fucking caretaker down there, deep at the bottom of the fucking lake. Or worse."

"Don't . . . Please, don't . . ."

Ed pulled Brandi with an "I" back off the ledge, almost having to carry her toward the car. He would have done her on the rear seat, too, finish the lesson, but he could smell what she'd already done to herself, and so Ed Krause wanted her back in their suite and cleaned up first.

———

Standing under the showerhead, the water so hot she almost couldn't bear it, Brandi Willette thought, Girl, nobody does that to you and gets away with it. Nobody.

Fuck Ed, the goddamned homicidal maniac, hanging you over the fucking edge of that fucking cliff. Literally fuck him as soon as you dry off, keep Dickhead happy and his fucking mind off killing you, but really fuck him good tomorrow, just like the Eskimo's note said, just before telling you to tear it up.

Fuck Ed with the other thing that gardener gave you, too.

And, for the first time in hours, Brandi actually smiled, even if only to herself. Feeling the luck changing, guiding her toward the fortune she'd always felt she deserved.

———

About two hundred miles into the drive that next afternoon, the scenery now pretty much scrub desert on the eastern side of the California mountains, Ed Krause noticed that Brandi wasn't all that interested in small talk anymore.

Hey, count your blessings, he thought, glancing again to the rearview mirror, not such good viewing with the convertible's top up, but necessary against the withering heat outside: At least today the chick's not complaining every two minutes.

No, their time at the moonlit vista over Lake Tahoe seemed to have had the right effect on little Brandi. Or so Ed would have thought, from the way she romped him in bed after her shower back at the lodge. Good thing he'd taken the trouble, though, while she was still in the bathroom, to go through her stuff a second—shit!

Checking the rearview, like always, Ed saw the same vehicle again. Making three times in the same day, even after stopping the Mustang for lunch and once more for gas.

A dark Chevy Suburban, or some other fucking station-wagon-on-steroids, coming around the last turn behind their Mustang along one of the narrow state roads in Nevada that linked together like a poorly designed necklace from Reno to Las Vegas. Between the sun's glare and the Suburban's tinted windshield, though, Ed couldn't make out the driver, much less how many others were in the thing.

"What's the matter?" said Brandi.

Ed thought about how to play it, both with the Suburban and her. "Don't turn around, but we've got somebody tailing us."

Predictably, the stupid bitch started to turn her head, so he reached over and squeezed her thigh like he wanted to break the bones underneath.

"Owwww! That hurt!"

"It was supposed to. I told you, don't turn around. Right now, they've got no reason to think I've spotted them, and I don't want to give them one."

"You didn't have to hurt me for that."

Ed just shook his head, not trusting his voice right then.

"So," said Brandi, "what are we going to do?"

Different tone now, kind of "We're still a team, right?"

He glanced again in his rearview, the Suburban dropping back a little. "Try to lose them."

Ed nailed the accelerator, Brandi making a moaning noise, kind of like when they'd started again in bed back at the lodge the night before. But the Mustang at least didn't give him any trouble, the V-8 he'd insisted on at the rent-a-car agency coming into its own.

Maybe five minutes later, Brandi said, "Aren't you, like, worried about the police or anything?"

"Lesser of two evils," said Ed, noticing nobody behind them now. Problem was, based on his study of the map that morning before heading out from Tahoe City, there were only so many roads you could take to get to Vegas, so the tail could probably find him, and he didn't have the firepower onboard to stage an effective ambush.

At least not until he found a perfect spot, and after dark.

Brandi piped up now with, "Are they gone?"

Ed tried to remember whether he'd ever said "they" in talking about the tail, decided he had. "For now."

"So," the tone growing a little more impatient, "what are we gonna do?"

"Stay ahead of them. At least for a while."

"How long a while?"

"Until sunset."

"Uh-unh, no way, Honey."

"What the fuck do you mean, no way?"

"I gotta pee."

"So, do it in your clothes, like you did last night."

"That's not funny."

Jesus Christ. "Okay. Around this next bend, then."

"No. I want a real bathroom, not . . ." Brandi with a fucking "T" waving her hand ". . . some spot behind a bush in the desert where a snake could get me."

"The desert, or your clothes. You decide how you want to feel, the next hundred miles to Vegas."

"God, I hate you, you know that?"

Checking the rearview again, Ed was beginning to get that impression, yeah.

———

Brandi Willette, who'd looked forward so much to enjoying this trip to Vegas, now found she'd run out of tissues.

God, she thought, shaking herself dry as best she could before pulling up her panties. I can't wait for this to be over.

Straightening from behind the bush, she looked over to the convertible. Dickhead was slouched in the driver's seat, head back, eyes closed, still wearing that ugly sports jacket to "hide" his gun.

Well, girl, look on the bright side: He doesn't suspect a thing, and that'll make it all the sweeter, once it happens.

"No," said Brandi, out loud but softly as she picked her way back to the car. "When it happens."

———

Having slowed to fifty-five about twenty minutes before—just after he put the top down to enjoy the clear, crisp night air of the desert—Ed Krause kept one eye on the rearview and the other on the highway in front of him, figuring he didn't have to worry about Brandi trying anything until they came to a stop.

She said, "Is it dark enough yet?"

Right on cue. "Dark enough for what?"

Brandi blew out a breath in the passenger seat next to him, like he noticed she did a lot of times—even during sex—to get the hair out of her face.

Why wouldn't you just get a different 'do, the hair thing bothered you so much?

Brandi said, "Dark . . . enough . . . for whatever you're planning?"

Another thing Ed didn't like about the little bitch: the way she kept hitting her words hard—even just parts of words, like he was some kind of idiot who couldn't get her points otherwise.

Shaking his head, Ed checked the odometer. Thirty miles from Vegas, give or take, its lights just blushing on the horizon. "Yeah, it's dark enough for that."

The Suburban had appeared and disappeared a couple times over the prior two hours, not taking advantage of at least three desolate spots where it could have roared up from behind, tried to force him off the road. Which made Ed pretty sure they were waiting for him to make the first move.

Or, like Brandi, the first "stop."

"Okay," Ed abruptly pulling off the road and onto the sandy shoulder. "Here."

"Honey?"

Ed turned to her. Brandi was leveling a nickel-finish semiautomatic at him in her right hand, a Raven .25 caliber he'd seen only once before.

———

Brandi Willette had thought long and hard about how to phrase it to him—even rehearsed some, with the teddy bear as Ed—but decided in the end that less was more. And so she was kind of disappointed that Dickhead didn't look shocked when she said just the one word, and he saw what Brandi had in her hand.

But that was okay. The asshole thought he was so smart, and so macho, and now Ed finds himself trapped and beaten by a girl, one whose luck had finally changed.

"Just what the fuck do you think you're doing?" he said.

Funny, Dickhead didn't sound scared, either, like Brandi also expected. "I'm taking the money. Honey."

Now it seemed like Ed almost laughed, even though she'd worked on that line, too. Make it kind of poignant, even.

"Brandi, Brandi, after all we've meant to each other?"

Okay, now she really didn't get it. "You're going to open the trunk and take out the case with all the money. Then you're going to leave it with me and just drive off."

Brandi saw Dickhead's eyes go to the rearview mirror again, and she thought she caught just a flash of headlights behind them along with the sudden silence of an engine turning off, though Brandi didn't dare look away from Ed, what with that big gun over his right hip.

No problem, though. Her luck was both changing and holding, just like it would in Vegas, when she hit the slots and the tables, or even the—

Dickhead said, "Your friends are here."

That stopped Brandi. "My . . . friends?"

"When we got back to the room at the lodge, after our little talk about the Tahoe caretaker? While you were in the shower, I went through your totebag there and found that gun. I'd done the same thing at the Inn back in Healdsburg, and it wasn't there then. So, I figure the only time you were out of my sight long enough to come up with a piece was when I was inside the chalet, and those Mayans were working in the yard next door."

Mayans? "I thought they were Eskimos?"

Now Ed did laugh, hard. "No, you stupid fucking bitch. The fat broad in the chalet—Natalya—told me they were her neighbor's crew, but I'm guessing they were hers instead, and one of them passed you that gun."

Oh, yeah? "Well, smart guy, that wasn't all he passed me."

"Some kind of instructions, too, right? Like, wait till the courier stops, at night, near Vegas?"

Brandi was beginning to think she hadn't torn up the note in the envelope, though she clearly remembered doing it. Then Brandi let her luck speak for her. "You're the one who's stupid, Honey, you know that? The Eskimo or whatever told me you'd never think to look for the little thingy he put under your bumper."

No laughing now. Just a squint, the eyes going left-right-left.

Good. Finally, Brandi gets her man. The way it hurts him.

Your luck has changed for sure, girl.

Dickhead said, "A homing device, probably based on GPS."

Brandi got the first part, at least. "So they could keep track of us, they lost sight of the car."

"Christ, you dense little shit. Don't you understand the deal yet?"

"The deal is that I get ten percent of all the money in the trunk. Because I'm making it easier for them to take it from you."

"No, Brandi." A tired breath. "The deal is that as soon as they see me get out of this vehicle, they're going to charge up here, kill both of us, and take a hundred percent of the money."

"No, that's not what the note said." Brandi kind of used the gun for emphasis. "What it said was, if you don't get out of this car now, I'm supposed to shoot you."

Ed's chin dipped toward his chest. "Good trick, seeing as how I unloaded your little purse piece there."

As Brandi Willette couldn't help looking down at her gun, she felt Dickhead's hand strike like a rattlesnake at her throat, clamping on so tight and yanking her toward him so hard, she barely could register the silver thing—like a Pez dispenser?— in the fingers of his other—

"Christ!" Ed Krause yelled, as Brandi's head exploded next to his, the round carrying enough punch to spiderweb the windshield after it came out her right temple, leaving an exit wound like a rotten peach, blood and brains spattered over the dashboard and that fucking teddy bear. Ed ducked as a second round shattered the driver's portion of the windshield, a sound like somebody whistling through water trailing after the impact.

Ed shoved Brandi's rag-doll corpse against the passenger door, then yanked the floorshift back to DRIVE and took off. A second later, he thought the Mustang might be in the clear based on acceleration alone when he first heard and then felt the blowout of his right rear tire, the convertible wanting to pivot on that wheel rim, send him off the pavement.

Ed wrestled with the steering, finally getting it under some control, and whipped right, over to the shoulder and beyond it. He pictured the three Mayans from the yard next-door to Natalya's chalet, and he hoped he'd put the Mustang's engine block between him and any likely fields of fire from their vehicle. Ed also hoped they didn't have much weaponry beyond the sniper rifle but knew he was probably wrong on that score, the way they'd handled everything else.

And, after their killing Brandi, there was no bargaining with them, no chance of "Take the money and let me live, or I'll nail at least one of you right here."

Nobody leaves a body *and* a witness behind.

Ed grabbed the little Raven .25 from the floor mat, slapped the magazine back into the butt of its handle, and slid the semiautomatic into the left-side pocket of his sports jacket. Then he slipped out the driver's door, waiting for the Mayans to make their move. They took long enough before starting the Suburban's engine, he was pretty sure one of them did the same thing he'd done: dropped out of their vehicle and into the desert, to flank him while the others rolled slowly toward him.

Just like Ed learned in Small Unit Tactics, back in the airborne. And just like the big land yacht was doing now.

Down on his hands and knees, Ed scuttled like a crab across the desert floor, away from the Mustang. And the money, but it was his only chance: Outflank the flanker, and come around behind all of them.

Ed went into the desert fifty or sixty meters at a diagonal to the road, angling slightly toward the direction he'd driven from. Figuring that was far enough, given the superiority of numbers and firepower the Mayans would think they had over him, Ed assumed the prone position to wait.

Listening to the desert sounds. Trying to pick up anything that didn't move like a snake. Or a lizard, even a tarantula.

Or whatever the fuck else there'd be in this kind of desert.

And he did hear some slithering sounds, then a scratching sound, like maybe a mouse's foot would make on wood, then a little squeak that Ed figured was curtains for that particular rodent.

But now, footfalls. Halfway between him and the road, moving parallel to it. Jogging, the guy moving with confidence toward the Mustang.

Ed rose to a sprinter's start, waiting for the Suburban to draw even with him. Then he used the noise of the receding vehicle to cover his own.

The running Mayan stayed on a line with the big vehicle's rear doors. Smart: That way, its headlights wouldn't silhouette him for a shooter still at the Mustang.

Bad luck, though, too: That relative positioning did pinpoint the guy—a pistol of some kind held muzzle up—just right for the angle Ed had from behind.

Closing fast on an interception course, Ed was all over the Mayan—Christ, no more than five-four, max?—before the little guy could have heard him. Ed used the extra-heavy barrel of the Combat Masterpiece to pistol-whip the Mayan across the back of his head, pitching him forward onto the sand with a "whump" sound from his body but nothing from his mouth.

Then Ed planted his left foot on the Mayan's spine, and—with his free hand—hooked under the little guy's chin and snapped his neck.

Scooping up the Mayan's pistol—another semiautomatic, maybe a nine-millimeter but not enough light on it to be sure—Ed put it in his jacket's right side-pocket, kind of balancing off Brandi's Raven .25 in the other. Then he started to run, trying to match the pace of the Mayan he'd just killed.

Thinking: one down, two to go.

The Suburban was now enough ahead of him, he could see it

clearly approaching his Mustang. When the driver nailed the gas and kicked in his high-beams, the third Mayan began shooting two-handed from the rear seat, Ed closing his eyes against the blaze from the muzzles, so as not to ruin his night vision. He heard both magazines empty into and around the convertible as they passed—some richochets, some thumps, depending on what the rounds hit. Then, hanging a U-ey, the Suburban came back hard. Ed was already prone again, eyes turned away from the headlights, but his ears picked up the sound of the third Mayan emptying another two magazines into the Mustang from the opposite direction.

Christ, a good thing you left the car. And picked off their flanker, who'd otherwise be standing over you right now, capping three rounds through your skull.

Ed turned again toward the Suburban. It hung another U-ey, this time moving back toward the Mustang real slow and weaving a little, let its high beams maybe pick up a dead or wounded courier against the convertible or somewhere near it.

Fuck this.

Ed got into another crouch, then sprang forward, letting Brandi's .25 fill his left hand, since he couldn't waste time fiddling with the maybe-on, maybe-off safety from the first Mayan's semi. He matched that dead guy's pace again as best he could, let the two Mayans exiting the Suburban—one at the driver's side, of course, the other at the passenger rear door— think their pal was joining up. Until they were clear of the vehicle and fixated on the Mustang, each just forward of the Suburban's front grille, using its high beams to blind anybody left alive to shoot back at them.

After drawing a deep breath and releasing it slowly, Ed emptied both of his weapons into those two Mayans, being careful not to hit their vehicle.

His new transportation, after all.

Ed's targets spazzed out like puppets as his slugs hit them, Ed himself now pulling from his jacket pocket the first guy's semi, to close and finish the fuckers. Then he caught the flash of another muzzle from the rear-passenger's window of the Suburban and simultaneously the impact of two, three rounds spinning him around and down, hard.

Shit: A fourth fucking Mayan?

Hoping the semi did have its safety off, Ed squeezed the trigger, putting five shots into the rear door. Hearing a scream, he decided to save the remaining slugs, in case the guy was playing possum. But Ed started feeling dizzy, too, knew he was losing too much blood to wait any longer. Levering up on his elbows—Christ, like somebody's hit you in the chest with a battering ram, tough even to breathe shallow—Ed staggered toward the Suburban, keeping the semi as level as he could. Getting there seemed to take an hour, but when he inhaled as much air as his lungs would hold, he yanked open that rear door, and saw the top half of fat Natalya ooze more than flop onto the pavement, another semiautomatic clattering on the asphalt like it was the tile floor in her chalet.

Fucking bitch didn't trust her Mayans after all.

Then Ed walked around to the front of the Suburban, let its high-beams spotlight his shirt under the sports jacket. He said, "Shit," and, a moment later, the same once more. After that, he didn't see much else to say.

So Ed inched out of the jacket as best he could, found a soft, level spot on the desert floor, and rolled the jacket into sort of a pillow, rest a little easier.

Ed Krause opened his eyes, realized he didn't know how long he'd been out, still just lying there on the desert floor. He was starting to feel cold, which he didn't remember from before. And while some of the stars above him seemed to have changed position, there was no sign yet of dawn to the east.

Just the glorious, heavenly effect from the lights of Vegas.

Ed shifted his head on the sports-jacket pillow as best he could, to be able to stare at those lights, the promise of real money and seeing a place he'd always wanted to visit. Last two times he'd coughed, though, blood came up, so right now he wouldn't bet on even seeing morning.

You're gonna bleed out in this fucking desert, you might as well stay focused on the prize, huh? Shows . . . lions . . . showgirls . . . magic acts . . . tigers . . . casinos.

The Vegas lights started to go funny against Ed's eyes, so he closed them.

Help the imagination, you know?

Slick cars like Maseratis, Ferraris, Rolls-fucking-Royces. Cruising the Strip, just like they did in the movies he'd seen. All the filet mignon and trimmings you could eat, all the Jim and Coke you could drink. Call-girls that'd make Brandi with an "I" look like fucking Spam.

Action of all kinds, nonstop. The genuine "City That Never Sleeps."

Only you're never gonna see it now.

Vegas, Las Vegas. Grieving . . .

ABOUT THE AUTHORS

JAMES SWAIN is a native of New York, and went to college at New York University, where he studied with Ralph Ellison and Anatole Broyard. His first job out of college was as a magazine editor. Swain moved to Florida in 1982. For the next twenty years, he ran a successful advertising business. During that time, he continued to write, and published three books of non-fiction about magic, as well as a novel. In 2001, Swain began publishing a series of books about retired policeman Tony Valentine, who captures people who cheat casinos. Swain is considered one of the world's foremost authorities on casino scams and swindles.

S. J. ROZAN is the author of eight novels in the Lydia Chin/Bill Smith series, and of the standalone *Absent Friends*. Her work has won the Edgar, Shamus, Anthony, Macavity, and Nero awards for Best Novel and the Edgar Award for Best Short Story. She is a former Mystery Writers of America National Board member, a current Sisters in Crime National Board member, and President of the Private Eye Writers of America. She lives in lower Manhattan.

The New York Times found the work of Edgar Award–winning author WENDY HORNSBY to be "refreshing, real, and raunchy." Published internationally, and in many languages, she has written seven mystery novels and a collection of short stories, *Nine Sons and Other Mysteries*. A native of the western United States, she holds graduate degrees in Ancient and Medieval History and is a professor of history at Long Beach City College.

MICHAEL COLLINS writes the Dan Fortune detective series that began in 1967 with *Act of Fear*. The most recent Fortune book is *Fortune's World*, published by Crippen & Landru, 2000. A collection of non-Fortune stories, *Spies and Thieves, Cops and Killers, Etc.*, was published in 2002 by Five Star Publishing.

His awards include an MWA Edgar and two other nominations; three Shamus nominations; the PWA Lifetime Achievement Award; and the Marlowe Lifetime Achievement Award from MWA SoCal. He has published another twenty-four detective novels under the pen names Mark Sadler, John Crowe, William Arden, and Carl Dekker, and three nonmystery novels under his real name: Dennis Lynds.

Currently living in London, T. P. KEATING has found that the glitz of Vegas is visible the world over. If only the Vegas weather could be exported too! This story is dedicated to his wife, Marielle. She is his sympathetic reader and sole authority on what constitutes a killer pair of heels.

J. MADISON DAVIS has published seven novels, six nonfiction books, and over thirty short stories. He has been nominated for the Best First Novel Edgar and twice for the Best Novel Oklahoma Book award. He is a former president of IACW North America, and a professor of professional writing at the Gaylord College of Journalism and Mass Communication at the University of Oklahoma. His latest novel, *Dead Line*, is an original *Law and Order* story. His novel *The Van Gogh Conspiracy* is scheduled for publication in the summer of 2005.

SUE PIKE lives and writes in Ottawa, Canada. Her stories have appeared in *Ellery Queen's Mystery Magazine, Storyteller*, and several collections of short crime fiction, including *Cold Blood V, Bloody Words*, and all five Ladies' Killing Circle anthologies. She is the coeditor of *Bone Dance*, a collection of musical mysteries published by RendezVous Press, 2003. "Widow's Weeds" from *Cottage Country Killers* won the Crime Writers of Canada Arthur Ellis Award for Best Short Story of 1997.

JOAN RICHTER, a former New Yorker who now lives in Washington, D.C., got her start in mystery fiction in a creative writing class taught by Ellery Queen's legendary first editor, Frederic Dannay. She spent two years in Kenya with the Peace Corps, was a stringer for the *New York Times* metropolitan section, and worked for American Express, where she was a delegate to the United Nations' World Tourism Organization. She has traveled extensively throughout Europe, Asia, and Africa, and continues to explore the world. Her fiction often draws upon her experiences with foreign cultures.

LIBBY FISCHER HELLMANN writes the Chicago-based series featuring video producer and single mom Ellie Foreman. *An Eye for Murder* debuted in 2002 and was nominated for an Anthony Award. *A Picture of Guilt* was released in 2003; *An Image of Death* in 2004. All three were simultaneously published by Poisoned Pen Press (in hardcover) and Berkley Prime Crime (mass market). Her short stories have appeared in American and British magazines. When not writing fiction, Libby produces industrial videos and trains individuals to be better speakers. She lives in the Chicago suburbs with her family and a beagle, shamelessly named Shiloh.

TOM SAVAGE is the author of four bestselling suspense novels: *Precipice, Valentine, The Inheritance*, and *Scavenger. Valentine* was filmed by Warner Bros., and the others have been optioned for filming. He has served on the National Board of Mystery Writers of America, and he is a member of IACW. Raised in St. Thomas, Virgin Islands, he now lives in New York City, where he works at Murder Ink, the world's oldest mystery bookstore. "Rolling the Bones" is his second published short story: the first, "One of Us," is in the MWA anthology, *Blood on Their Hands,* edited by Lawrence Block.

EDWARD WELLEN is a man of many talents who has had fiction published in almost every genre imaginable. His short stories have appeared in *Universe, Imagination, Infinity,* and numerous other science fiction and mystery magazines starting in the 1950s. His best known work, the comic "Galactic Origins" series, was a highlight in *Galaxy,* which between 1952 and 1962 published all nine of his pseudofactual examinations of the roots of future law, etiquette, medicine, philosophy, and other social doctrines. He is also no stranger to crime and mystery stories, having appeared in anthologies such as *The New Adventures of Sherlock Holmes*, *Sci-Fi Private Eye*, and *Murder Is My Business*. He is also the author of *Hijack*, a satirical novel of organized crime and space travel. Recently his short mystery fiction was collected in the anthology *Perps*.

K. j. a. WISHNIA broke into publishing when his self-published novel, *23 Shades of Black,* was nominated for the Edgar and the Anthony Awards. He has written four other novels featuring Ecuadorian-American female sleuth, Filomena Buscarsela, including *Red House,* which was a *Washington Post Book World* "Rave" Book of the Year in 2002, and *Blood Lake,* the latest entry in what the *Minneapolis Star-Tribune* called "one of the most distinctive series in mystery fiction." By day, he is an English professor, teaching writing and a notoriously amusing crime fiction course at Suffolk Community College on Long Island.

LINDA KERSLAKE is from the Northwest, where she manages a medical practice and moonlights as office help at the local police department. Her short stories have appeared in *Mystery Times* and *Death Dance,* another IACW anthology edited by Trevanian. She is a member of Mystery Writers of America, Sisters in Crime, and the International Association of Crime Writers. She has finished her first novel and continues to write short stories.

JOHN WESSEL is the author of the Harding series—*This Far, No Further; Pretty Ballerina; Kiss It Goodbye.* He lives outside Chicago.

LISE MCCLENDON is the author of two mystery series, the Alix Thorssen series (*Blue Wolf,* etc.) set in Jackson Hole, and the Dorie Lennox series (*Sweet and Lowdown*) set in WW2-era Kansas City. She lives in Billings, Montana, with her family. She is a former board member of International Association of Crime Writers and currently on the national board of Mystery Writers of America.

RONNIE KLASKIN has had a number of stories published, some in *Ellery Queen's Mystery Magazine,* and *Whittle Communications, Special Report,* among others, the most recent of which was in the anthology, *A Hot and Sultry Night for Crime,* edited by Jeffrey Deaver. She has won prizes for her short stories and poems. She has a MFA in fiction writing from Vermont College.

RUTH CAVIN was born in the very middle of the terrible 1918 flu epidemic, but recent events find her with Thomas Dunne Books at St. Martin's Press for the past sixteen years. While she has published many mystery novels under the company's Minotaur imprint, her output surprises some agents by being quite a bit more varied. Before taking her first editorial nine-to-five job, she was the author of several published books—none of them mysteries, all of them now long out of print. She lives in a suburb of New York and commutes daily to St. Martin's offices in Manhattan's historic Flatiron Building.

Brooklyn-born A. B. "ROBBIE" ROBBINS joined the Marines at seventeen, where he started on the road to his black belt in judo and brown belt in karate. He became a professional ballroom dancer at the age of twenty-one. During his career he garnered a national championship and status as a master performer, coach, and choreographer. Robbie is an outstanding chef and has written a cookbook, *The Convenience Market Gourmet*. Other writing credits include a feature-length screenplay, religious lyrics set to classical music, and a short story published in *Magnolias and Mayhem*. He is at work on a mystery novel called *Dancing in the Darkness,* plus a short story collection based on the character in this anthology. He plays classical and flamenco guitar, has owned a nightclub/restaurant in the New Orleans area, a judo/karate dojo in the Dallas/Fort Worth metroplex, and health clubs in California, Washington, and Texas. He loves sailing, and his idol is Leonardo da Vinci.

DR. GAY TOLTL KINMAN has eight award nominations for her mysteries. She was the 2003 Edgars Chair for Best Children's Mystery, and a presenter of the award; is a scholar for the Center for the Book, Library of Congress/UCLA "Women of Mystery" Program; and coordinates Workshops for Writers at Cal State, San Bernardino. She has published over one hundred and fifty articles and several mystery short stories; had a play produced; coedited a cookbook, *Desserticide II: AKA Just Desserts and Deathly Advice;* and has a recipe in *A Second Helping of Murder*. Anthology mysteries include "Miss Parker and the Cutter Sanborn Tables" in *A Deadly Dozen: Tales of Murder from Los Angeles* (Agatha nominee) and "Neither Tarnished nor Afraid" in *Murder on Sunset Boulevard*. Her gothic novel, *Castle Reiner,* is set in California in 1899. Five children's mysteries featuring Alison Leigh Powers, Super Sleuth, were published by Amber Quill Press.

Sharing initials with Mickey Mouse, Mighty Mouse, Marilyn Monroe, Mitch Miller, and flying candy disks, MICKI MARZ writes stories beneath a two-hundred–year-old, moss-feathered oak tree in southeastern Louisiana. Micki, published under two other names, says trying on new identities suits a felonious mind. When not writing or teaching the occasional writing class, Micki edits abstruse technical documents about how to blow up things and clean up afterward. Fiction work in progress is a tale featuring a child runaway during Depression times, with, of course, a mystery attached to his exploits.

RICK MOFINA'S suspense novel, *Blood of Others*, the 2003 Arthur Ellis Award Winner for Best Novel, is a book from his acclaimed crime fiction series featuring reporter Tom Reed and detective Walt Sydowski. Series titles include *If Angels Fall, Cold Fear, No Way Back,* and *Be Mine*. Mofina is a former journalist who has reported from the Persian Gulf, Africa, and the Caribbean. His true-crime articles have appeared in *The New York Times, Reader's Digest,* and *Penthouse*. Please visit him at www.rickmofina.com.

JEREMIAH HEALY is a graduate of Rutgers College and Harvard Law School. He is the creator of two mystery series, the John Francis Cuddy private-investigator novels under his own name, and the Mairead O'Clare legal-thriller novels under his pseudonym of Terry Devane. The most recent O'Clare novel, *A Stain upon the Robe*, deals with the Boston priest/rape scandal, and it was recently optioned for feature film. A past president of the Private Eye Writers of America, Jerry just finished a four-year term as president of the International Association of Crime Writers, a thousand-member organization with branches in twenty-two countries spread over four continents.